Awakenings

RESTORATION
BOOK ONE

Awakenings

Faith King & Laura Josephsen

OAKTARA

WATERFORD, VIRGINIA

Awakenings

Published in the U.S. by:
OakTara Publishers
P.O. Box 8
Waterford, VA 20197

Visit OakTara at
www.oaktara.com

Cover design by Kay Chin Bishop, www.kaybishop.carbonmade.com
Cover images © iStockphoto.com/warrior woman, Boris Yakov; Alaskan
sea otter, Katherine Welles

ISBN: 978-1-60290-243-5

Awakenings is a work of fiction. References to real people, events,
establishments, organizations, or locales are intended only to provide a
sense of authenticity and are used fictitiously. All other characters,
incidents, and dialogue are drawn from the author's imagination.

⌘ ⌘ ⌘

For
"The Clique"
at the Jedi Council boards on TheForce.net.

Although the years have seen us all go various ways,
we were once brought together by the love of two great things:
writing and *Star Wars.* Without you guys,
I would never have finished writing anything,
and so from the beginning this book has been for all of you.
—*F.K.*

For
My mother, Cheryl Zipfel,

who has shown me through my life what love really means.
Thank you for not only letting me dream,
but for dreaming right along with me.
I love you, Mom.
—*L.J.*

Acknowledgments

Faith wishes to thank:

My heavenly Father, the first and greatest author of all, for the gifts you've given me in music and in writing, and the many opportunities you've given me to dedicate them back to you.

My parents, for putting up with my computer excesses. I know it may sometimes seem I spend my whole life on my laptop, so without your longsuffering tolerance, this book might not have been written in such a welcoming environment. Also, thanks for humoring me when I needed to ramble about the story on those rare occasions when Laura was unavailable.

And Laura, for your ceaseless, patient, gentle, enthusiastic persistence. You keep me motivated, dedicated, and enthused. Thank you for all your patience and friendship, and most of all, thank you for that day you asked if I'd be interested in writing a story with you. Little did I know in that moment what a precious gift of adventure and friendship that God was giving me.

Laura wishes to thank:

My Creator, whose love and imagination is so much greater than anything I could ever begin to comprehend, for all of the gifts you've given me and allowed me to share.

My husband, Ryke, for having so much understanding and support, and for being my sounding board, editor, and best friend. Thank you for your patience in the numerous phone calls and emails and visits as Faith and I worked this story out from two different states. I love you so much.

My children, for being so patient and loving. You mean the world to me!

My parents, John and Cheryl Zipfel, for teaching me the foundation of my faith. You couldn't have given me any greater gift.

Amber Hyde, for encouragement, company, and cream soda. Thank you for being such an amazing friend, and for all of our crazy adventures (even, or maybe especially, the lard cookies!).

And, of course, Faith. I can't even begin to express what a joy it has been to write this book with you—and write it again, and again, and again, until we were both sick to death of rereading scenes and could quote half of it from memory. You're an awesome friend and a fabulous writer. You inspired me to reach for new levels in my writing, and more importantly, in my walk of faith.

The authors wish to thank:

Our fabulous test readers, editors, and fact-checkers through various drafts: Ruth Bandfield, Sharon Banks, Timbre Cierpke, Emily Deckenback, Kathleen Dorsey, Maggie Fung, Laura Hedin, Amber Hyde, Anna Jetton, Kate Johnston, Brenda Josephsen, Mark Josephsen, Ryke Josephsen, Steven Josephsen, Tirzah Julius, Darlene King, Lenny King, Matt King, Sydney Maltese, Shanna McDonald, Janine Mills, Ryan Stevenson, Rachel Williams, Ruth Zipfel, Cheryl Zipfel, and Zachary Zipfel.

The Clique (you know who you are), without whom we never would have begun this adventure.

Jeff Nesbit and Ramona Tucker at OakTara, for offering us this opportunity. It is an honor to work with you.

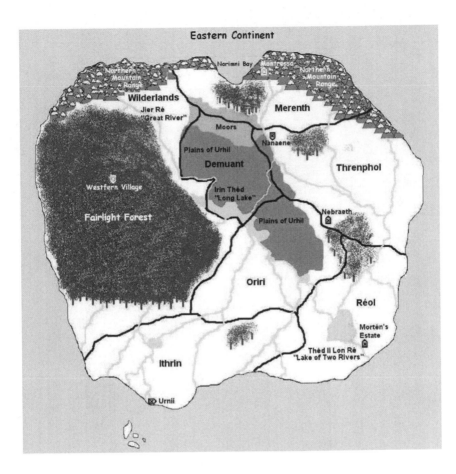

Prologue

Lornesse was unaccustomed to this kind of darkness. At home, safely tucked behind well-guarded walls each night, there were no reasons for the evening shadows to frighten her. But now she found herself in quite another kind of night, one utterly alien to her comfortable upbringing. This was the least of the reasons her advisors had used when they had urged her not to come. In truth, she could hardly blame them; it was their duty to caution and guide her. In the end, though, even they had conceded there was nothing else to be done.

The streets were very quiet, and she wondered if they always were at this hour. Most of the windows were shuttered tightly closed, a meager ward against the chilly autumn wind blowing in from the south. Occasionally, she recognized the faint pulse of light coming between the cracks of the shutters that bespoke a candle still flickering behind. Not everyone in the city was asleep. As she progressed further into the poorer sections, she saw increasing signs of poverty—shanties in disrepair, vicious, underfed dogs wandering freely on every street, and huddled, shivering human figures. She pulled her cloak more closely around her face, wishing she'd had the foresight to bring something plainer. She very much wished to avoid attention.

Strictly speaking, the responsibility for the poor of Nimal did not rest with Lornesse Myron, but with the city's governor. Lornesse was a speaker. It was a position highly revered and respected to be sure, but her duties fell far outside the bureaucratic arena. Still, her father had always tried to make some of the city's concerns his own. He pointed out that Nimal had come into existence almost entirely because of House Leviathan. Therefore, despite not being its official rulers, the city's welfare should also be their concern.

When she was young, Lornesse had suspected her father's passion for charity was a means to stave off boredom. It had seemed to her that, unlike the other eleven speaker families, House Leviathan was distanced from the beast it represented. Her father's ventures to speak with the great sea creatures had been so rare during her childhood that she could count them on one hand. Years often passed between visits, and Lornesse had felt, growing up, that there was really little need for House Leviathan at all, despite her father's assurances to the contrary. Now she knew he had been right.

The wind gusted again, cold, but as ever smelling of salt. Nimal was an isolated city, set on an island many leagues from the mainland, and ever burgeoned by breezes from the sea. Lornesse shivered and hastened her steps, as much from the urgency of her errand as from a desire to escape the cold. At least it was not raining, as it was wont to do on any given night this time of year.

Drawing her fine cloak more tightly about her, her fingers brushed its clasp, an heirloom from her father, and so much more. It was a beautiful piece of craftsmanship, made of heavy, polished pewter, and shaped as a twisted leviathan with two small, perfect diamonds for eyes. It was a symbol of all she had inherited from him—a keen sense of honor and charity, the leadership of an ancient and wealthy household, and the legacy of a speaker, complete with all the gifts and duties that role implied.

It would be difficult to fill her father's shoes, both as a speaker and a philanthropist. As a very young child, Lornesse had cared little about either role. Certainly she had prepared for the possibility, almost from the moment she had taken her first step, but in truth, it had come as something of a surprise when the relic had chosen her upon her father's death. The power of speaker was passed down from generation to generation within the twelve families, and while there was nothing saying it *couldn't* pass to a second or third-born child, most people had expected it to pass to her older brother Kurin. He had certainly seemed to better fit the role. Still, there was no contending the Master's decision, although many of the people had been skeptical thus far of her abilities. She was going to have to work hard to prove herself worthy.

The moon, at least, was very bright, helping her to find her way among the haphazard lanes and alleys. The directions she'd been given were extremely detailed, and both she and Phenni had memorized every last one of them. They'd even traced portions of them together earlier that afternoon to help Lornesse get a sense of bearing in the dark. They had only dared go so far, though, because Lornesse was reluctant to alienate the kidnappers in any way. For the moment, they held all the power in this matter, and if they read any of her actions as being uncooperative, there might not be another ransom offer for months—or maybe ever.

It was now four days since her younger sister Emmaine had disappeared. The Governor's forces had been out searching for her without end since that time, and Lornesse had barely gotten three hours of sleep all together. It seemed heartless to do any normal day-to-day activity. She was desperate to take some action on her sister's behalf. She had managed to send a message to Kurin, who had been attending the university on the mainland, but she had yet to hear a reply. In the meantime, all search efforts had proven fruitless, and they'd had no sign or word of Emmaine until that morning.

The letter had arrived as did all others directed to Lornesse. She'd been sitting at breakfast, making an attempt at a semblance of normal life, but her eggs remained untouched. As for the letters, it was only for the fact that they might contain a ransom that Lornesse even bothered opening them.

The parchment was very plain and coarse—the least expensive that could generally be found. The handwriting was strong and precise, and the language correct, indicating that whoever had written it had some degree of education. It said that if the family wished to see Emmaine alive and safe again, Lornesse must meet with the kidnappers at the appointed location, alone, and they would discuss a ransom.

Phenni had been highly against Lornesse leaving home tonight, the most insistent of any of her advisors. He said it was too coincidental—the timing of the kidnapping, the insistence that Lornesse be alone.

"If anyone were to have some design against you, my lady, he could not pick a better time to act upon it. You are new to your powers, you haven't your father's experience, and—" He left off, pressing his lips together.

"And I have no guardian," she had finished for him.

"You should have departed immediately," he'd said quietly, tightening his fingers around the edge of the tabletop where they'd been studying maps of the city. He was standing at a stoop, leaning forward slightly, his hands on either side of him. "You should have left for

Fairlight right after your awakening. You should have accompanied—"

"How many times have I told you?" she'd snapped. "It wasn't a good time. The city was just recovering from that huge storm, and then we had the outbreak of red fever to get through—"

"Lornesse, I know it seems like a small matter to you, but I cannot stress how critically you need your guardian."

"For magic, right?" she'd pointed out. "For protection? I'm not saying it isn't important, Phenni. Far from it, but really—I have a little magic of my own now. For Emmaine's sake, I am going to this rendezvous, and that's my final word on the subject. I'll get a guardian at the speaker's summit next month, and then you can sleep easier."

She had to admit, however, as she stepped around a rather deep puddle in the middle of a dim alley, that Phenni was absolutely right. This whole affair would have been considerably less unpredictable if she'd had the benefit of a guardian's wisdom. For as long as the speakers had existed, the fairies had been assigned as their protection. Her father's guardian, Mothberry, had been a cranky little thing, and he and Lornesse had never really gotten along. Perhaps that was the reason she had put off acquiring a guardian of her own. Nevertheless, Moth had been clever and extremely loyal to her father, and she found herself wishing she'd had his advice on this matter. Were he here, he might have accompanied her despite their mutual friction. He'd always been very fond of Emmaine.

But Moth had departed for his home in Fairlight Forest with the Grand Magi who had come to perform the rite of awakening on Lornesse. By all rights, she should have accompanied them, and now she sincerely regretted her decision to delay the journey. Still, she wished Phenni would not keep reminding her so frequently of her folly. There was nothing to be done about past mistakes here and now.

She cast her gaze about, searching for the next landmark that would guide her further to her destination. She was getting closer. Looking up, she spied it—a scratched, faded tavern sign creaking in the chilly breeze. Muffled sounds of ribald leisure-making came from within, and weak torchlight filtered out between the building's clapboards. Lornesse swallowed a little, tightening her hand on her cloak and adding a spring of confidence to her step as she continued into the alley past the tavern.

She had not gone three steps within when her path was blocked by the swift shadow of a man, a couple of inches taller than her. A strong hand darted out and grasped her upper arm, causing her to gasp in fright. Then the figure whipped her around, bending her right arm painfully behind her back with one hand and placing his other around her throat.

"Now, listen here, lass," said a strong voice, surprisingly less gruff than she had been imagining, considering the grim surroundings. "I don't know where you're going in such a terrible hurry, but if you want to get there alive, I suggest you hand over whatever coin you've got underneath that fine cape. And don't bother trying to say you have none. I'm not a fool."

"I wouldn't doubt it, sir," Lornesse replied, standing very still, and feeling unexpectedly calm. Maybe she'd feel more afraid when it was over. She did have money with her—probably more than her assailant ever dreamed. She'd brought a small fortune in gold and diamonds, hoping she might be able to appease the kidnappers on the spot if she found them, but she was not about to yield either the valuables or the information to this ruffian. "I would suggest, however, for your own good, that you release me unharmed."

He laughed. "Says what army?" he taunted softly in her ear, his breath sour. Of course, she hadn't really expected him to take her seriously. Certainly if she'd been in his position, *she* wouldn't have taken her seriously, but she felt honor-bound to warn him nonetheless.

Without another word, Lornesse reached up with her free arm and seized the sinewy wrist clutching her neck. She clenched her small hand with relatively little effort, and the feeling of small bones crushing beneath her fingers was grimly satisfying.

The man cried out in horrified pain and released her, whereupon she spun around, seized his neck in turn with her right hand, and lifted him three inches off the ground. It was a good thing he wasn't much taller than she was, or she'd not have managed reaching up that high. Her free hand she clamped over his screaming mouth. "Now *you* listen here," she hissed quietly, "I am on *very* important business tonight, and do not wish to be bothered. Do you understand?"

He nodded, and she released her hand from his mouth. "Leviathan," he whispered hoarsely. His good hand was cradling his broken wrist, and his feet were dangling limply. Although he was a thick and solid man, Lornesse could have been lifting fresh bread dough for all she noticed.

She regarded him a moment before slowly nodding. "You said you weren't a fool; I suppose you were telling the truth." She lowered him until his toes touched the ground but tightened her fingers around his throat warningly. She could feel him try to swallow beneath them. Fumbling with her left hand into her dress pocket, she managed to retrieve two or three rather hefty gold coins and slipped them into his belt pouch. "I must continue alone, or I would have you arrested for attempted robbery," she continued, narrowing her eyes at him. "As it is, I'll speak of this incident to no one else, and there's for your silence. If you betray my presence or impede me in any way, I assure that you will regret it. Don't think I won't remember your face. Are we agreed?"

He nodded slowly, and when she released him, he gave a brisk turn and headed back to the safety of the street, not bothering even to glance back at her. Lornesse watched him a moment more, her brow furrowed with worry. She really had no way of knowing whether or not he would honor his promise. It would be best not to linger.

Through the alley beyond the tavern sign, past a green door in a brick wall.

As part of her mind concentrated on finding the correct landmarks, another was mulling in unease over what had just transpired. It still felt odd, having these newfound powers. The strength of the leviathan was her gift, and through the bond she shared with them she could feel it—simple, steady, and forcefully strong. Her father had often said that, of the twelve brethren, the leviathans were the foundation and the bedrock. She'd never been more grateful for it, but the raw power in her hands still left her feeling small and uncertain. After all, the unnatural brute strength was hard enough to believe in a man, much less a small, frail-looking woman like herself.

When she'd first come into her inheritance, she'd tested her gift by hefting great sacks full of bricks out in the practice yard where her father's guard worked on their swordplay and other skills. She also found she could swing maces and heft swords built for men almost three times her size. She had yet to find a limit to how strong she was. It was the only comfort that Phenni and the others had taken in allowing her to come on this nighttime escapade.

Down a flight of stairs to a footpath along the canal. Follow the canal to the second stone bridge and cross it.

She had not inherited the strength of the leviathans directly upon her father's death. It was not until she had been awakened by the visiting member of the fairies' Grand Magi council that she had come into the full scope of her abilities. First, she had sensed the presence of her eleven fellow speakers, most of whom she had met at one time or another, including Namoné of the eagles, Rhian of the icthus, Emeris of the dragonflies, and her neighbor across the sea, Rastin of House Dolphin, a close friend and confidant. All seemed as vague impressions in her mind, for the most part unheeded, but whenever something important happened to one speaker, all the others immediately sensed the change.

More important than this, though, was the ability to sense the leviathans. Lornesse loved them—much more than she'd ever believed possible, and in a way that was most difficult to express. From the instant of her awakening, she'd felt their presence rushing in like a wave of colorless sight and voiceless sound. She'd gone out to sea the next day, instinctively knowing they would be waiting for her. The size of the sloop she had sailed on paled in comparison to the sight of the great sea serpent that surrounded it when she directed the boat to be stopped. The creature's skin was thick and hard, like gray stone encrusted with smoky crystals. Its voice, when it spoke, had rumbled so deeply that the planks beneath her feet had trembled, and the water had rippled for spans around them. The sailors had gulped and shuffled, some muttering prayers of protection. They stayed well distant from her as she conversed with the beast.

"Welcome, daughter of Edain. I am Sedviruus. You are strange to us."

"I am nonetheless of my fathers," she replied. "I will serve you as the Master has ordained."

"Yes, the Master is wise. I sense your honor."

They spoke for a considerable span of time, and Sedviruus told her of many wondrous things—caves beneath the sea no human eyes would ever behold, stretches of perfect sand and water never touched by sunlight, hidden colors and worlds and treasures—places of peace and serenity, quiet, timeless, protected from the folly of the world that Lornesse knew.

"Tell me, Sedviruus, why is it your kind visits us so rarely?" she asked at last. Now that the mantle of speaker had fallen to her, she dared to voice the question she had pondered since childhood.

"It is the charge of my kind," he said, "to guard and oversee this great hidden dominion of which I have spoken. The leviathans are long in years and slow to change. It is not our intention to neglect the speakers, yet it may seem as if we do, for our sense of time is not as yours. But I come to warn you, Lornesse, daughter of Myron. Change is coming."

"What sort of change?"

"The foundations of the earth are shifting. Soon the water and land will shake and split. Your city will sink into the sea, and the house of your fathers will rest with the ones it fought so long to protect."

It had been a warm day, but Lornesse had shivered. "An earthquake? When?"

"Soon."

He had not been able to tell her more. Lornesse pushed back a burden of worry. This secret she had not shared with anyone, though she must do so soon. The trouble with leviathans was that they could have a very different sense of "soon" than a human. It might very well be years before the earthquake, yet it was a gamble she didn't want to make. It was a matter of some delicacy, though, and she'd been pondering best how to handle it. The city would have to be evacuated, but how could she convince the people? She wasn't sure they would believe her. It had been known for the leviathan to predict disaster before, but an earthquake that could submerge all of Nimal? It would certainly feed the flames of her critics' fire.

But it was still her duty. Lornesse clenched her jaw, steeling her resolve along with it. There was nothing to be done at this moment, but she promised herself that as soon as Emmaine was safely restored, she would advise Phenni of what Sedviruus had told her. They would begin to make plans for what to do. For now, she needed to focus on the problem at hand.

Her journey's end found her at a ramshackle doorway on the opposite side of the canal. Three large scratches were embedded in the door's frame, just as her instructions had said there would be. She paused, her hand hovering over the latch, afraid of what she might find within. Sounds from the street behind made her turn, and she saw two darkly clad figures step out of the shadows, blocking any means of retreat.

Lornesse swallowed. Perhaps Phenni had been right, after all. Perhaps she should have found a way to obtain a guardian before she came here. Power she had, but she was not invincible. At this juncture, however, she didn't have much of a choice. Bracing what little courage she possessed, Lornesse pushed the latch and ducked into the dismal room beyond it.

The flame of a single, steady candle sent faint pulses of light into most of the room, but the corners remained shrouded in shadow. Lornesse straightened herself, pulling her hood back from her face, and waited.

"So you have come, after all," said a quiet voice. "I must confess, I thought perhaps you wouldn't."

"I have come. What is it you want?" Lornesse replied. She hoped they wouldn't waste time with taunting games. "I have money."

The man—whoever he was—did not reply for a moment. At last he spoke. "Compared to power, wealth is merely an afterthought. You of all people ought to have learned that."

Lornesse shivered. There was something so disturbingly *calm* in the man's voice. She would have expected that speaking of power and wealth in such a cold way should have made the man sound mad, but he spoke as though he were merely commenting that it had rained that morning. "Where is my sister?" she asked.

"She is well and safe; do not worry."

"Do not mock me, sir. Were she well and safe, I would not be here." Lornesse had pinpointed the corner of the room where he was sitting, and she turned to face it fully. "If it's humility you seek on my part, you have it. I am at your mercy. Will you please let me know how I might reclaim my sister unharmed?"

"You are so rigid, Lornesse," he said thoughtfully. "The people of Nimal underestimate you." She heard a shuffling sound, a wooden chair being scraped against earth, and saw movement as the man arose.

"Who are you?" she whispered fiercely.

He took a step into the candlelight. He was shorter than she'd expected, his features unremarkable but for piercing green eyes. "Since you asked so politely," he said with an odd little smile, "my name is Maehdron Vittes."

A firm footfall behind her prompted Lornesse to glance back. There was another man emerging from the shadows—one who looked much more as she had imagined a typical villain than Vittes. He leered at her with greedy eyes and tried to seize her forcefully by the arms. With little more than a grunt, she shrugged him off, slamming him back against the wall by the door. The thug made another lunge for her before he was stopped.

"Don't bother," called Vittes coolly, holding out a commanding hand to stop the man. "I already told you, you won't be able to hold her. But she won't be going anywhere soon. She's here of her own volition, aren't you, Lady Myron?"

"Where is Emmaine?" Lornesse snarled, brushing her hair out of her eyes as she regained her footing.

Vittes jerked his head at his accomplice. "Bring the girl," he ordered. The brute crossed the room and disappeared through the far doorway, and Vittes turned back to Lornesse. "Very well, my lady. No more skirting the shore." He leaned casually against the wall, beneath the room's only window, and crossed his arms. "What I want is your power. A speaker's power. It's the greatest to be had in this world, and I don't see why you should have it and I should not."

Despite the gravity of her current circumstances, Lornesse emitted a short, disbelieving laugh. "I'm afraid I can't help you there. You can't *choose* to have a speaker's power. You must be a descendent of the twelve families. A *direct* descendent. Everyone knows that."

Vittes seemed amused. "Do they?" he asked quietly.

The door opened again, drawing Lornesse's attention away from Vittes's perplexing question. The thug re-entered the room, this time dragging behind him a small, filthy figure that caused Lornesse's stomach to jolt with sickening fear. It was Emmaine, but the sight was not encouraging. She was disheveled and ragged, with dark circles under her eyes and a large bruise on her face. Lornesse gasped, unable to find words.

"Lornesse!" Emmaine cried upon seeing her. She reached out a pleading hand, and Lornesse instinctively moved to help her, but Vittes's thug was too quick for her. He had a knife pressed to Emmaine's throat before Lornesse could take two steps.

"Don't move, my Lady Myron," warned Vittes, now standing up straighter and observing the scene with casual interest. "Or she will die, I promise you."

Lornesse could feel her courage dwindling. "I won't move," she promised. "But I still don't know why you've brought me here." She could feel her voice quaver. "I can pay you, whatever I'm able. My whole family's fortune, if you want it," she added desperately.

Vittes sighed. "Have you been listening to nothing I say? If riches had been my sole object, Lady Myron, I would not have requested *you* here. Any underling would have sufficed. I thought I had made my wishes abundantly clear."

Lornesse bit her lip to keep from crying. He *was* mad. What he asked was impossible. "And I told you," she repeated, "only a descendent of the twelve families can be a speaker! And even if you were, you couldn't have the power unless the relic chose you, and that will not happen until I am dead." As soon as the words left her mouth, a chill spread over her body. Did he think—?

"Why?" he demanded. From the ground beside him, Emmaine made a small, pleading sound from her throat, and he held up a warning hand before turning back to Lornesse. "Why should I bother with being chosen? From what I've been led to believe, the awakening will succeed regardless."

Sickened, Lornesse glared at him. "The choosing is a testament of the Master's will. It is the means by which *he* appoints his speakers," she said defiantly, holding her head very straight. "It is not your place to challenge it."

He clapped his hands once, laughing triumphantly. "Ah, yes. The Master. No one's ever challenged any of the precepts before, have they? We've always just assumed they were exactly as we've been told by those bothersome little fairies, but you know as well as I that even some of the fairies questioned the mandates. Surely you are not blind to the dissent among your precious little guardian race. Or does the word *shvri* mean nothing to you?"

A little thrill of anguish ran through Lornesse. She had, of course, heard of the group of fairies who had broken away from their kindred and betrayed their own precepts, but she failed to see what they had to do with her situation.

"I admit it has been to my advantage," Vittes continued. "The fairies have always lorded over humans with their magic and their supposed knowledge of the Master's ways. They think themselves superior to us, and we're just supposed to take their word for it?" He smiled in satisfaction. "I highly doubt the Master even exists."

Tears sprang into her eyes. First he had kidnapped and harmed Emmaine, and then he had taunted and insulted Lornesse. Now he was attacking the very core of her faith. And Emmaine still had a knife at her throat. For the first time all night, Lornesse felt completely helpless.

"You asked what it is I want?" Vittes finally said. He snapped his fingers, and two more men came through the door. One held a sword, the other a small crossbow. "I'm afraid, my lady, what I want will require your departure from this world."

Before Lornesse had a chance to even breathe, Vittes nodded at his henchman, and the crossbow fired. She fell to her knees in shock, hitting the dirt floor with a painful slam, and then crumpled to her side, the short, stiff arrow protruding from her ribs.

There were three things Lornesse was aware of as she died. Emmaine's screams, loud in her ears, the shock from her fellow speakers through their bond, and far beneath the tide, Sedviruus's unmistakable surprise. His last impressions filled her mind.

"Change is coming, Lornesse of Myron. But this change was unexpected."

1

The village of Westfern was in the deepest heart of Fairlight Forest. Here, the trees grew tallest and the streams flowed deepest, the coolest and the most secret. The summer was past, and the forest was making its preparations for its long, cold sleep. The last of the stubborn leaves were losing their battle with the wind, one at a time breaking free and fluttering lazily down to the chilly forest floor.

Flute tried not to let them distract her.

This spell was one of the hardest she had ever done. She was nervous; her whole class was watching breathlessly and Elder Hawthorne seemed ready to jump in with his usual bossy criticism at any moment. He wanted them to make a ball out of the water of the stream, which was difficult because it involved combining elements of water and air magic. The water didn't hold together well if it was stagnant. She needed to make it move, the way the air moved when the wind blew. If the water was nudged into motion in just the right way, the sphere would practically hold itself together.

She was deep in concentration, her eyes narrowed, trying to resist the urge to use her hands. Magic had nothing to do with gestures, but for some reason every fairy sprout had the instinct to try to use them. Flute wanted to impress her instructors. If she was still using her hands with *water* spells then they would never, ever let her proceed to the advanced magic of earth and fire.

Flute prayed silently that she wouldn't have one of her famous clumsy disasters. She could practically hear all of her elders in her head, reminding her that this wouldn't be a problem if she simply kept calm and held onto her concentration. She narrowed her eyes, and the slowly shifting mass of water wavered slightly, almost rejoining the brown stream beneath it. Berating herself, Flute tried to regain her focus. She had a tendency to let her excitement get the best of her.

Flute was always being scolded for her daydreams. Since before she could remember, she had been fascinated by the old stories her elders told her about the great speakers. She had especially loved hearing about the speakers' mighty guardians—fairies who'd had adventures, performed powerful, untold magic, even seen the world outside Fairlight Forest!

Flute's best friend, Jesper, closest to her in age of all the other sprouts in the nursery, told her that if she wanted to be a renowned fairy some day, she should pay more attention to her magic lessons. She knew that Jesper was right, but try as she might, her imagination always wandered back—back to a time nearly nine-hundred years lost, when speakers had existed, and when fairies, humans, and the brethren had all lived in harmony.

There were no guardians anymore. The best Flute could hope for was to become a Grand Magi, but Grand Magi today hardly even left their own villages! The elders were equally boring. Sometimes it seemed to Flute that their only remaining purpose these days was to scold her from dawn till dusk:

"Fluttermouse, you eat more winterberries than you bring back home!"

"Fluttermouse, you would try the patience of a leviathan!"

"Guardians always ate their *chinosa seeds when they were sprouts."*

"And if Taley tried flying through a tree, would you do that too?"

Out of the corner of her eye, Flute caught a glimpse of Elder Hawthorne's face. He was watching her handiwork with a speculative expression. "Remember how much water lives in the sky, Fluttermouse," he advised. "Use it to strengthen your connection."

Flute took a careful sigh, trying yet again to collect her focus. She could do this. Closing her eyes, she called to the water inside her and to the water in the air as Elder Hawthorne had recommended. Then she called to the water she'd taken from the stream and tried to show it how it was not so different from the air around, how it could move in this new place as it had moved over the ground below for so long.

She could feel when it started working. The water was misshapen, but it was beginning to tighten into a pleasant shape—wobbly, but starting to be recognizable as to what she intended it to be. She smiled. She was doing it!

Without warning, something happened. A strange flare of magic, like a cold shiver on a hot summer's day, rippled through her insides. It was completely different from anything Flute had ever felt before—magic she knew she was a long way from understanding. She gasped, promptly releasing her water spell and drenching her classmates in a cold shower.

"Oh, no!" Flute whispered under her breath, a twinge of desperate panic overcoming her as she thought of what a setback this would prove in her studies. She looked down at Elder Hawthorne and the other sprouts, who were all sputtering and shaking themselves free of the cold water. She darted down to Elder Hawthorne. "I'm so sorry, Elder!" she said excitedly. "I don't know what happened! I felt something. It was—"

To her extreme surprise, he didn't seem to care. In a heartbeat she knew she wasn't going to get in trouble. "It's all right, Fluttermouse," he said distractedly. He looked to the east, and she followed his gaze. Instinctively, she knew he was right to look that way. Looking around, she saw all the other sprouts were looking east as well. "I felt it, too," he said.

"What does it mean?" she asked fearfully.

"I don't know."

Over the next few days there was much whispering and speculating between the young fairies in the nursery. Flute and her friends were berated by Elder Wisteria several times for keeping the littler sprouts awake when they all should have been sleeping.

Finally, the council of Grand Magi convened in Westfern, as it was the center of all the fairy villages, and their own Grand Magi Asheford was the greatest and most powerful of the Magi in the forest. Many other visitors came to Westfern, too. Flute was kept busy helping watch the very youngest sprouts that had been brought from all the other nurseries. This had been frustrating, but it did not prevent her from hovering around the council's great meeting tree as much as possible, hoping for some hint of what was being discussed within.

The council consulted the few old scrolls that remained, preciously guarded and preserved for centuries, and debated long into the night for many days, until even Flute grew weary of waiting. At long last, however, they were ready to discuss the results of their deliberations.

"Most of us are of the opinion," Magi Asheford said, "that somewhere in eastern Réol, a new speaker has been chosen."

There was a uniform gasp from the fairy kindred that had gathered

3

in the meeting circle, followed by the low hum of whispers and murmurs. Flute was so excited at these words that her wings snapped open and she jolted several inches in the air, poking Jesper painfully in the side of his face with her elbow. But as usual, her friend was patient and understanding. He simply rolled his eyes and grabbed her by the tunic, tugging her back to sit beside him.

"How do you know?" asked a stranger from another village.

"A speaker?"

"What's Réol?" Flute whispered to Jesper.

"It must be a place, if it has an east," Jesper pointed out knowingly.

"There hasn't been a speaker for almost a millennium!" Elder Heath said. "How can you be sure the surge was a choosing?"

"We can't," said Magi Marinavae wearily. "But it only makes sense."

They proceeded to explain that, according to memory and the old scrolls, a choosing was just about the only thing that could be felt by every fairy, everywhere. The fact that they had sensed the focus of the magical surge in a specific place was another clue.

After that, it was very hard for Flute to keep up with what happened. Fairy sprouts still in the nursery weren't usually told what their elders were doing in important matters, no matter how desperately they wished to know. Asheford and several elders departed Fairlight Forest, journeying to the place called Réol. Flute settled in to wait for their return. Her thoughts were never far from the travelers, and her imagination was more alive than ever with possibility.

The emissaries were gone for a long time, and when they finally returned, all the sprouts could tell that something was wrong. They did not bring a speaker, as Flute had hoped, but they did bring a relic—a ring with a blue stone that was the ancient token of the House Otter.

Once again, the elders cloistered themselves away. Instead of excited, though, they were all worried and grave. Distracted and agitated, they dismissed Flute's questions and those of her friends. By the end of the fourth day, she was so angry about being forced to teach the littlest sprouts new chores that she inadvertently made all her charges disappear in a burst of uncontrolled magic. Fortunately, all the little ones had been safely discovered in the nursery at Autumnleaf, the next village west, but this lack of control had earned Flute two days of weaving baskets with old Henna, her least favorite task of any. And she was forbidden to use

4

magic for a week.

It wasn't fair, she thought, furiously poking the thick, knotted rope of grasses in and out of the basket frame. If she was old enough to care for her small fellow sprouts, why wasn't she old enough to know what was happening about the speaker? And she hadn't *meant* to make the little ones disappear. She loved them as much as anybody else; it had been an accident!

"Flute!"

Startled from her self-pity, Flute looked up to see Whisper, Boisen, and Taley, the three oldest after her and Jesper, flying quickly across old Henna's nest, their eyes wide. She looked over at Henna, who had drifted off to sleep, slumped over her own basket. Flute wondered how long she'd been out. She wasn't usually very talkative, even when she was awake, which was part of the reason Flute found this punishment so horribly boring.

Henna sniffed loudly in her sleep but did not wake. Flute turned to her friends and put a finger over her lips, urging them to be quiet. Taley nodded.

"What's wrong?" Flute asked, forgetting her chore and leaning close to them.

"It's Magi Asheford," said Boisen.

"What about him?"

"He's gone!" Taley said.

"Gone?" Flute asked, confused. "Why? Where would he go?"

"No one knows! He ran away!"

"He took the *relic*, Flute!" Little Whisper's brilliant blue eyes were wide, and sparked with silver flashes, betraying her shock and fear. "That's what I heard Elder Heath tell Elder Osprey."

Flute's own eyes grew larger, and she stared at her young friend in shock. "The relic?" she repeated, appalled.

"It's true." At the sound of another voice, the four sprouts turned to see Jesper, also entering Henna's nest, albeit a bit more cautiously than the other three.

"How do you know, Jesper?" Flute asked urgently as he drew nearer.

"At least I think it's true," he amended, looking grave. "I went to the place where they were keeping the relic. The only thing I found was Elder Hawthorne, and he was very angry. He chased me away."

"The relic," Flute breathed again. The precious otter relic.

"Poprinay said Asheford was a traitor," added Boisen, two seasons older than Whisper. He seemed puzzled. "I thought he was a Grand Magi. What's traitor, Flute?"

Flute frowned. She remembered hearing the word before, but only to describe one other kind of person. "I think it means," she said seriously, "that he's a shvri."

All the young ones gasped. "Magi Asheford was a *shvri!?*" Taley asked in shock.

"Maybe he wasn't before, but he is now," said Jesper slowly. "Only someone as horrible as a shvri would do something like steal a relic from the fairies."

"But Magi Asheford has always been a very wise leader of the Grand Magi, and of Westfern village," Flute said, confused. "It doesn't make sense."

"Fluttermouse!"

All the sprouts turned around. Elder Hawthorne stood at the entrance of the nest now, and he had that look on his face —the look that was always bad news for Flute. "Jesper, you know better," he said, looking at Flute's friend severely.

"Please, Elder," Flute said boldly. "Is it true that Magi Asheford took the relic?"

"You don't need to—"

"Please," she interrupted him urgently, something that would undoubtedly earn her more punishment, but at this point she figured it didn't really matter. "Elder, all we want to know is what happened. Just tell us. Please?"

"Please?" echoed the three younger ones. Jesper seemed stuck trying to decide whether to look respectful, apologetic, or hopeful.

Hawthorne sighed heavily. "You three," he said, waving a hand at Whisper, Taley, and Boisen. "Go to the nursery. Wisteria is looking for you. She is very worried. Go!"

Crestfallen, the sprouts turned and flew dejectedly away. Hawthorne looked thoughtfully at Elder Henna for a moment, then turned to Flute and Jesper. "You two, come with me."

Flute and Jesper followed cautiously, both wondering what sort of new trouble they'd landed themselves in. Hawthorne led them away from the village, to the edge of the stream, where the long, low willow trees made green curtains around the deep, dark pool where the big fish liked to hide in the summer. The winter had come and gone since they had first felt the choosing. Now the new green of spring was pushing out of the tree buds.

"I suppose," Elder Hawthorne said at last as they settled down beside the water, "that you might as well hear the whole truth, rather than try to build stories from scraps of conversation and frighten the younger sprouts."

Flute stayed very still and quiet. She was afraid that if she talked, Elder Hawthorne would forget himself and go back to *not* talking about things.

"Magi Asheford and the others," he began, "myself included, went to Réol. We found the human the relic had chosen. His name was Darius Mortén."

"How did they find him?" Flute asked.

"What do you remember of your history lessons about the speakers?"

Jesper looked at Flute expectantly, and she was proud to answer. Nobody remembered speaker history better than Flute. "The speakers were all descendent of one of the twelve great families," she said. "Upon being chosen, the human was given the ability to see fairies. This was the proof the Master provided to let the fairies know who had been chosen."

Hawthorne nodded. "And so it was with Mortén. He knew when we came."

"So Magi Asheford awakened him, yes?"

Another nod. "Asheford was the one who had studied the awakening the most."

"It is the most powerful magic any fairy can perform," Jesper said knowingly.

"That's right. Magi Asheford was unconscious for two days after it was finished."

"And this Mortén became the Otter Speaker?" Flute asked. "But where is he? Why did you bring back the relic and not Mortén?"

This time Hawthorne shook his head, and he was sad. "Sprouts," he said, "something has happened that I do not understand. It was not the otter relic to which Asheford awakened Mortén. It was that of House Leviathan. He was able to show us, when we asked, that he had indeed descended from that great line—from the last of the daughters of Myron who escaped both the persecution of Maehdron Vittes and the earthquake of Nimal."

"The leviathan *and* otter relics?" Flute repeated, awed.

"He had them both," Hawthorne said.

"How?"

"I do not know." He looked at them both seriously. "Fluttermouse, Jesper," he said, "you are both growing up, but you are still sprouts. You must understand why we have been trying to protect you from all of this. The only reason I have decided to tell you is that I do not yet wish the littlest ones to know anything is wrong."

"What *is* wrong?" Flute insisted. "Why did Magi Asheford go away?"

"Because Mortén was not what he appeared to be," Hawthorne said, his voice fierce. Flute blanched a little, looking over at Jesper worriedly. Elder Hawthorne was very upset about something, but he didn't seem angry with the sprouts. He stopped and collected himself a moment before he continued. "Mortén was very careful before he was awakened, but afterward we began to realize he was not a person who should ever have been given the honor of being a speaker."

"How did you know?"

"Many things. Attributes of his personality which he found increasingly difficult to conceal. Small cruelties to those who served him. Insatiable, selfish ambition. Suffice to say he is a very undeserving human, but as you know, an awakening cannot be undone. It lasts as long as its recipient lives. We abandoned Mortén, but Asheford first managed to steal the otter relic from him."

"So Mortén is still alive?" Flute asked.

"Yes."

"I don't understand," she persisted. "Speakers are supposed to be good and kind people, faithful servants of the Master. If Mortén passed the tests of the choosing, how could he possibly be unworthy?"

"That is something your elders do not understand."

"But why is Asheford gone?" Jesper asked.

"The revelation of Mortén's true character has made us cautious, and for good reason." Now Elder Hawthorne seemed more himself, which meant perpetually annoyed. "Most of the Grand Magi feel we should be very careful with the otter relic. Guard it, keep it safe here in Fairlight

Forest until we understand better what went wrong with Mortén. Asheford does not agree. He believes our best hope of correcting this wrong is to take the relic out among the humans and hope it will choose someone who could work against Mortén. The rest of us believe this hope to be foolhardy and irresponsible. Asheford's plan was voted down by the Grand Magi council.

"This morning, Asheford stole the relic and disappeared. He has forsaken his privileges as a Grand Magi and a leader of our people. He cares more for his own pride than what is best for the fairies. He must never return."

⌘ ⌘ ⌘

The street fair came to the city of Nebraeth once a year. It was a time that the children in the local orphanage looked forward to, and none more so than Xari. She loved watching the brightly-colored acrobats perform mind-boggling feats, and hearing bards sing tales of history long past. Most of all, she loved watching the sword-fighters execute flawless routines. She was entranced by the way they moved and the way the swords flashed through the air like an intricate dance.

When the fair was in town, she almost didn't notice that the other children went away and left her by herself, or that none of them seemed to like her. She could almost ignore the whispers and rumors that surrounded her.

"I heard that when she grows up, the Westerlons are going to come back for her and burn down the orphanage!"

"I heard they left her because they wanted her to finish their work for them!"

"How can you sleep in the same room as her? Aren't you afraid she'll do something to you in your sleep?"

"Westerlons killed my parents."

She could almost, for one day, be normal.

The one time Xari had approached Madam Grenni, the matron who ran the orphanage, and confessed that most of the other children avoided her, Madam Grenni had sighed and looked at her. "You're a Westerlon, Xari." That was all she would say, as if those simple words would explain everything.

They did not explain everything, but the longer Xari was at the orphanage, the more she learned. The Westerlons were fierce warriors from the Western Continent across the sea, and they had staged a ferocious attack on the Eastern Continent not too long ago. They had swept through Xari's home country of Threnphol and had even managed to get over the border into Réol before they were forced back. The Easterlings were still recovering from the war.

One day, Xari overheard the cook telling the milkmaid that Xari was most certainly spawned from one of the invading warriors during that time. "Evil creatures that the Westerlons were! Most likely one of them forced himself on some poor maiden, and there's the result. She's at least half-Westerlon; just look at that face. It's no wonder her mother left her on the orphanage doorstep. It's a good thing for Xari that Madam Grenni has such a kind heart."

Xari had spent an hour that evening looking into the cracked mirror in the hallway outside her room. She didn't understand what made her face so horrible. She was small for her age; she had heard that the Westerlons were short, but that didn't make them any less fierce. Her face was thin, with slanted brown eyes framed by high cheekbones. Her skin was slightly darker than most of the other children's, and her straight black hair was hacked off at her shoulders. Madam Grenni didn't let any of the girls grow their hair long. She said she wasn't going to deal with more lice and fleas than was necessary.

Even then, at such a young age, Xari had realized the unfairness of it all. What did it matter what she looked like? If her father had been a vicious savage, did it mean that she was, too? Why did everyone judge her by who her parents had been, especially in a place such as this? The more she thought about it, the angrier she became. Was it so much to ask for a friend? For someone to love her? She didn't think so.

As time passed, Xari began to lash out at the people around her. She often found herself in trouble with Madam Grenni for causing disturbances throughout the orphanage. *"If you don't get your temper under control, you're going to find more trouble than even you know what to do with!"* the matron told her, time and again. She was constantly putting Xari on discipline, which meant extra chores. Xari didn't care. At least it kept her busy. At least it kept her from thinking about how lonely she was.

Xari had almost not been allowed to go to the fair this year, because she had hit Nara during dinner the week before. Madam Grenni had threatened to keep her in her room the whole time the fair was in town, even though Xari had explained that Nara had called her a funny looking savage. She finally agreed that if Xari was good the whole week, she could attend the fair. It had been very, very hard to not yell at the other children, and to keep from kicking Navir when he called her a bad name, but she had done it.

Every ounce of self-control she had exerted was made worth the effort when she was taken to the city square with the other orphans and released to sightsee for the day. Not even the cloudy skies could dissipate Xari's happiness.

"Don't leave the square!" Madam Grenni said sternly, passing out a few coppers to each of the children. As she pressed them into Xari's hand, she gave her an extra hard look. *"Behave,* Xari."

Xari nodded eagerly and carefully tucked her coppers into her pocket. This was the only time she ever got money, and she wasn't about to lose it. She would probably buy some hard candy from the street vendors later, which would be a treat to last for several days.

Most people were so busy that they didn't pay attention to her, and even when they did, she ignored their stares and whispers. She made her way through the crowds to the sword-fighters, pressing to the front of the throng. They had already started one of their routines. Two men were facing each other, their hands moving in a blur as their swords clashed and clanged.

Time was lost as she stood watching them. It wasn't until someone knocked painfully into her side that she moved her eyes.

"Like the sword fighting, barbarian?" Navir was leering at her. At thirteen, he was four years older than Xari, and much larger. He was with Lillia, who liked her just as little as Navir. "I bet you'd like to learn how to do it. Then you could cut us all up in our sleep."

Xari's mouth tightened, and she thrust out her jaw defiantly. "Leave me alone."

"You must be joking, Navir," Lillia said scornfully. "No one would be crazy enough to give Xari a sword, let alone teach her to use one."

Xari turned her eyes back on the show in front of her, an angry buzz in her ears. She couldn't do anything to them, or she would get in trouble and be sent back to the orphanage. She wouldn't let them ruin this one special time for her.

Navir grabbed Xari's dress from behind and lifted her a few inches off of the ground. "Got any money left, barbarian?" He gave her a hard shake, and Xari heard the jangle of the coins in her pocket.

Xari screamed in fury and swung her foot backward. She felt her heel connect with Navir's ribs, and he promptly dropped her. She landed hard on her side and glared up at Navir and Lillia from the ground.

Navir grinned at her and waved three coppers in front of her face. "Thanks for the money."

With horror and rage, Xari realized that, somehow, her coins were missing out of her pocket. "Those are mine!" she yelled, hurtling to her feet and throwing herself at the older boy. "Give them back!"

If Lillia hadn't been there, Xari thought she might have stood a chance. As it was, she knew she managed to do some damage before Navir finally threw her off. Without fully realizing it, their scuffle had moved backwards. She didn't know what a disturbance they had caused until she heard the dead silence of the crowd and looked up to see that she had bumped into one of the sword-fighters.

Ten minutes later, it was all over. Madam Grenni arrived in a fury, grabbing both Xari and Navir (Lillia had somehow managed to disappear) and dragging them forcefully back to the orphanage. Xari was locked in her room, and when Madam Grenni finally came in, her face was white and pinched with anger. Xari opened her mouth to speak, but Madam Grenni held up a hand. "What you did today was inexcusable."

"But Navir—"

"You punched him. And kicked him. And he has several nasty—"

"He made fun of me and took my money!"

"Then you should have come and found me, and I could have taken care of it!"

"I—"

"I don't want to hear it, Xari! You and Navir upset an entire show at the fair today! Someone—yourself included—could have been seriously injured by those sword-fighters. I don't know what to do to get you to stop this disruptive behavior. Until you can prove you can exhibit some sort of self-control, you will not be attending the fair again—not this year, or any year in the future. I don't care if it takes until your sixteenth birthday when you're of age to walk out of here."

Giving her another fuming look, Madam Grenni turned and shut the door behind her. As if punctuating her punishment, the gray skies opened and poured out their heavy rain. While some of the rich homes in the city of Nebraeth had glass windows that had been brought up on the southern caravans, the orphanage was not one of them. Here, only cheap strips of thick paper separated the small rooms within from the elements. The one in Xari's room wasn't holding up very well, as water quickly poured through it and formed a puddle on the floor.

Xari sat numbly on her bed, her arms wrapped around her knees, listening as the other children began returning from the fair, escaping the downpour. Slamming doors were followed by joyful shrieks and giggles.

None of the girls who roomed with Xari came in. They probably knew she was in trouble, but nobody cared. They didn't want anything to do with her, and now Xari didn't even have the fair to look forward to anymore. Everything had been taken from her. Madam Grenni was going to keep her locked up forever, because how was she going to keep from losing her temper if everyone was mean to her?

She watched the puddle of rainwater slowly become a stream that trickled through the girls' room. If she was such trouble to have around, why was she staying? Nobody would ever want her. She had been living in this place for nine long years, and she was tired of it. She was tired of being teased, ignored, bullied. Why should she put up with it anymore?

She should just run away. That would solve everybody's problems, wouldn't it? Madam Grenni wouldn't be angry and disappointed all the time, the other orphans would be able to have fun by themselves, and Xari would be free from it all. Madam Grenni probably wouldn't even bother to send the local lawmen out looking for her. It wouldn't matter if a tiny half-Westerlon girl vanished. She could escape over the border to Oriri, and cross Oriri into Fairlight Forest. The forest was said to be a magical and dangerous place, but Xari was sure that anything had to be better than this. She didn't care if it was dangerous. Maybe if she had magic in her life, she wouldn't be so miserable.

That was how Xari found herself leaving the orphanage late that night, carrying nothing but an extra dress and a parcel of food stolen from the kitchen. It had stopped raining, but there were mud puddles everywhere. The bottom of her skirt was soaked and dirty within minutes. She didn't stop to wonder how she was going to find her way into Oriri, let alone how she would survive on her own. Fairlight Forest couldn't really be *that* far away, could it? It was west; she knew that much.

As it turned out, she didn't need to worry about trying to find the magic in Fairlight. The magic found her first.

Very few people were out as she trudged through Nebraeth; the fair was closed for the day. Those few who were out were headed for the local taverns, and they were easy to avoid. No one noticed her slipping through the shadows. Once she was out of Nebraeth, she stopped and looked back at the city that had been her home. *Ha!* she thought in exhilaration. *I did it! I left, and I'm never going back!* She struck out down the road toward the west.

She had only been walking for a few minutes when something fell out of the sky and hit her on the head. Startled, Xari looked up, but didn't see anything except a half-moon peering through thick, gray clouds. Rubbing the crown of her head with a scowl, she bent down and scooped the offending object out of the mud. It was a silver ring. A smooth, round blue stone sat in the middle of the ring, and imprinted upon the stone was an otter. As soon as her fingers touched it, a strange, tingling sensation washed over Xari, from her scalp all the way down to her toes. She shivered and closed her fist around the object.

It was at that moment that she realized a tiny little creature was buzzing before her face. *Fairy,* her mind told her in wonder, as she recalled tales she had heard through the years. He was a perfect little person, with wings and dark hair that, upon closer inspection, she saw was actually feathers. His face was miniscule, but he was so close to Xari's nose that she could make out his expression. He looked rather baffled.

"You can see me?" the fairy asked in a tiny voice.

Xari opened her mouth, a bit surprised he was actually talking. "Um—"

"I'll take that as a yes." He studied her for a long moment. "Well. Well, how very interesting." He flew backwards in the air, away from Xari's nose. "The ring was not supposed to go to you," he said, half to himself.

Xari crossed her arms, the ring still clutched in one fist. "Well, you shouldn't have dropped it on my head!" she told him, as if it was perfectly normal to have a conversation with a fairy in the middle of the night.

"I didn't intend to drop it on your head, you silly sprout!"

Sprout? I'm not a vegetable! Xari thought indignantly. "Well, I don't care if it was an accident. You can't have it back." She knew it was rude—it wasn't her ring, after all—but something in her wouldn't let her release it. In the brief minute she had held it, it had become part of her.

The fairy made a sound very much like the cook did when she caught one of the children sneaking food out of the kitchen. "Are all human sprouts so precocious?"

Xari made a face. "What's pre...shockis?"

The fairy sighed in exasperation. "I don't want it back. It isn't mine. Don't you understand? I didn't drop it. You were chosen to have it, and it pulled away from me."

"What do you mean?" Xari asked.

The fairy groaned and pulled at his feathers. "It's no use." He zoomed around her head several times and finally stopped decidedly. "Well, you'll have to do. I must admit I wasn't expecting a human so young, but the Master has chosen you, and he must have a reason for it. All that's left is the awakening, which I can do. However, I was under the impression that human children did not go wandering the streets by themselves so late at night. Where are your parents?"

Xari's brows snapped together in a frown. Was she ever going to get away from that? Did it *always* come back to her parents? "I don't know," she huffed. "I never knew them. I'm an *orphan.*" The word was as bitter on her tongue as always. "What's awakening?"

"Hmm...I'm not sure if that will make things easier or more difficult. What is your name?" he asked, without bothering to answer her question.

That annoyed Xari—Madam Grenni had done that all the time. Not answered her questions. Pursing her lips, Xari retorted, "You tell me your name first."

The fairy appraised her. "You do have spirit. That's good. You may call me Ashe." Muttering, so Xari almost couldn't hear, he said, "We're going to be spending a lot of time together." And louder, "Hold still! I have to bind us so I can keep track of you; you have no idea the dangers you could face."

"I *am* holding still," Xari said haughtily. "And you still didn't tell me what awakening is. And what is a 'bind'? What dangers?"

To her surprise, the fairy chuckled softly. "Precocious," he repeated, shaking his feathered head. "An awakening will make you a speaker." Before Xari could ask for clarification, *something,* some kind of invisible force, struck her, and she stumbled backward, tripping and landing on her bottom in the mud.

"Now look what you did!" she said angrily. "It's bad enough that the *bottom* of my skirt was wet and cold and muddy!"

"There are worse things, sprout, trust me. Now, what is your name?"

Xari stared at him obstinately for a minute, and then relented. "Xari. What did you just do to me?"

"I cast a binding spell," Ashe said.

"What's a binding spell?"

"It is a spell that ties me to you," he said with exaggerated patience. "It ensures that I cannot lose you, and that I can protect you."

Xari pursed her lips. "I don't want you to protect me. I can look out for myself."

"Oh, yes," Ashe replied sarcastically. "I'm sure you can. A young sprout of your age is perfectly capable of caring for herself."

"I ran away from the orphanage," Xari said, glaring at him fiercely. "And I won't go back."

Ashe considered her carefully. "We can discuss our options. For now, you had better come with me. You have a lot of learning to do."

2

Eight years later

Some called it the Misty City. Considering how often its streets were veiled in milky curtains of fog, the name was not without merit. Its rightful name, however, was Montressa—city of wind and sky, boldly carved out of the peaks of the mountain upon which it stood.

On the highest pinnacle was Par Auspré, the ancestral home of Montressa's ruling family. The edifice was magnificent, heavily favoring towers and balconies and crowned with thin, golden spires upon which the city's brightly-colored banners were always flying. Upon occasion, violent winds had been known to tear the banners from their moorings and carry them away, but this happened rarely. It was said that a traveler who came upon a lost banner of Montressa was favored by the paré with good fortune.

The remainder of the city fell away below Par Auspré in layers of tight, winding streets and tall, narrow houses. Long ago, when men had been more inclined to respect the purity of nature's landscape, the city's builders had striven to conform to the mountain rather than subdue it. Primary city junctures had been built on the largest ledges. Many of the most grand and ancient noble estates had portions that extended into the mountainside itself, giving their masters larger holdings without compromising the limited space available on the surface. Meandering pathways, tunnels, and staircases connected the various portions of the city.

There were no stables in Montressa. Many of its residents had never even seen a horse unless they ventured to the foot of the mountains to their sister-city, Valedyne. There, any traveler on pilgrimage to the Misty City was forced to abandon his mount and proceed on foot, for the road became simply too treacherous. Light-footed mules could make it about halfway up, but before long, even they were forced to turn back. This degree of inaccessibility was a marvel to passing strangers. Who would build a city atop a mountain all but impossible to reach? What purpose did it serve? Whom did it even benefit?

Those that expressed such sentiment had never seen the eyries.

Honeycombed throughout the surrounding peaks—great nests sometimes big enough to hold a small hut, tucked in cliffs and large crevices all over the mountains' faces—the eyries were the pride of Montressa. The greatest cloister could be found in the city itself, just below Par Auspré on a ridge where the strongest drafts in all of the mountains blasted up from the canyon below. In the eyries dwelt the eagles of Montressa and their famous Windriders. Couriers, hunters, sentinels—the Windriders served many purposes. It was because of the Windriders that Montressa was one of the most important cities in Merenth, and, consequently, why High Lord and Lady Kavela were so greatly regarded as its masters.

Anathriel Lelaine, handmaiden to Lady Rillandra Kavela, was pleased to have secured duties that allowed her to venture out of doors. The sky was a clear and perfect blue, the early spring air fresh and crisp, and she breathed deeply, grateful that winter was behind them for another year. Winter was harsh and lonely in Montressa. The Windriders were the only ones able to clear the snowbound passes, and sometimes it was so cold that even they could not make the journey.

Spring was a time for festivals. The Freedom Feast was held first, in honor of the opening of the passes. A few weeks later, when the flowering shrubs were in the height of brilliant bloom—the time when the eaglets began to hatch—the city celebrated the Festival of Winds.

For many weeks, the Windriders had been testing and training a new batch of hopefuls. The duties and status of a Windrider were held in high honor, but it was a difficult and dangerous job, and not just anyone was accepted into their ranks. The next day's ceremony, when the new riders would be named, would culminate the hopes of many, and leave others with sorest disappointment.

This year something else of note was to take place. It was common knowledge that after nearly three decades of service, Captain Brennen intended to retire from the Windriders. There was much debate over who would be chosen to replace him, but Anathriel was satisfied that she knew the answer.

"Anathriel, slow down!" Her companion, Taryn val Argon, the newest and youngest of Lady Rillandra's ladies, scurried to catch up behind her. "Your legs are longer than mine."

Biting back a sigh of impatience, Anathriel slowed her pace slightly, but not the purpose in her step.

"How often have you been to the eyries?" the girl asked when she'd caught up. She was always asking questions.

"Often."

"I've never been. Is it frightening to be so near them? The eagles, I mean."

Anathriel had been afraid of the eagles too at first, but was not about to confess this to Taryn. "No," she said firmly. "There is no cause for worry. The Windriders have them exceptionally well-trained."

Taryn gave a small sigh. "I know I should probably be used to them, having grown up here, but I've only ever seen them flying from far away. They're so big!"

It was true. The people of Montressa had, perhaps, become accustomed to the sheer size of the great eagles—so great, in fact, that most trees could not even support them, which was one of the reasons the birds were most comfortable dwelling in the mountain passes. Anathriel's father had told her that in places far enough away from Merenth, people refused to believe such creatures even existed.

"You'll become accustomed, Taryn," Anathriel said. She wished the girl would stop prattling. Anathriel had wanted to come on this errand alone, for reasons that had little to do with the errand itself, but Lady Rillandra wished the older girls to take turns teaching the younger, by example, various aspects of their expected duties. At twenty-two years of age, and still unmarried, Anathriel was one of the oldest.

She was very well aware of the whispers and snide comments that were made about it. Anathriel Lelaine, the proud and brilliant merchant's daughter, was unable to secure a husband. Some said it was because of her humble origins, some said her vanity. Very few bothered to think Anathriel might have purposefully avoided marriage. She had actually had several suitors that she might have done well by, but long ago she'd decided upon the man she wanted.

She reached into her pocket as she walked, fingering two special items inside it that she had brought with her on this outing. They were gifts—gifts intended for one very special Windrider. Her confidence faltered a little, but she kicked it back up resolutely. She'd hinted at her regard for Immen Corper once or twice in the past, and had always been met with a polite and friendly response. Her gesture today would be next door to outright declaration. She was reasonably sure she would not be denied.

Reasonably.

It was not a long journey from Par Auspré to the eyries. The palace was situated on the uppermost pinnacle of the mountain, and the journey to the great hall of eagles required only descending to the second-highest summit, which commanded a view of the vast peaks to the north of the city. The eyries were, however, considerably larger than Par Auspré. The main building was tall, but twice as wide—the largest construction in the city, with an expansive corridor running clean through its length, giving the eagles plenty of room to land.

Descending the last set of stone stairs, Anathriel and Taryn walked straight through the vast southern doorway on one end of this corridor. Immediately Anathriel wrinkled her nose in disgust. She'd always hated the way this place smelled. It was worse in the wintertime, when the perches and stalls went the longest without airing, but there was always a faint smell of droppings and carrion and greasy feathers. She was relieved it was such a fine day, so that the doors were wide open, allowing bright sunshine and fresh air to combat the unpleasantness into submission.

It sounded odd in here, as well. The vastness of the building made sounds and voices sound fragmented and detached, with an overriding echoic quality. This haziness was often pierced by squawking screams of the eagles, and right now, it was almost overwhelmed by the far more insistent sound of their screeching young.

While Taryn gaped, open-mouthed, at her side, Anathriel cast her eyes quickly up and down the two rows of nests, one on either side of the corridor. She was looking for two men. One was the purpose of her errand; the other was the reason she had wanted to come. Just now, she saw neither.

"Anathriel!"

A young man about her own age, dressed in Windrider daywear, was heading towards her, smiling. She smiled in return. "Regen!" she called back. "I can't believe you're indoors on a day like today."

Regen Feldstone only grinned as he trotted up towards her side. She offered her hand when he reached her, and he took it unhesitatingly, kissing it with all the grace one would expect given his pedigree. "If you'd visit me more often, Anathriel, perhaps you'd know I've been named assistant honor guard of nesting this season."

"What a privilege, Regen, congratulations," she said with a sincere smile. Every spring a select contingent of Windriders was chosen to act as honor guard to the young eaglets.

"Yes," he said. "A privilege." He cast a longing glance at the patch of blue sky visible through the far door at the corridor's end. "A privilege that keeps me conveniently grounded." He sighed.

Like many of Montressa's young noble sons, Regen Feldstone had chosen to spend the prime of his youth as a Windrider. It was a traditional practice; many of the noble families felt their sons should understand the origins of their city's success. However, nobody ever expected an heir to make a career as a Windrider, something Anathriel secretly suspected that Regen resented. He would be coming into his inheritance soon, and would likely be a Windrider for only one or two seasons more.

"So what brings you out to us this fine day, Miss Lelaine?" Regen went on, swiftly recovering from all signs of regret.

"Lady Rillandra wishes me to deliver a message to Captain Brennen," she replied. Noticing Taryn standing patiently at her elbow, she shook her head, adding, "I'm sorry, Regen. I trust you remember Taryn val Argon?"

Regen feigned surprise. "Surely you jest, Anathriel. Taryn Argon is no doubt still playing with dolls in her mother's bower, not this handsome young lady all grown up." He threw a wink toward Anathriel before turning his most rakish smile on the younger girl. Anathriel rolled her eyes.

Taryn held up her chin, hands on hips. "Oh, stop it, Lord Regen. I know you recognize me," she said, her nose in the air. "Besides, I am uncommonly tall for my age."

"So I see. Well, welcome to the eyries, Miss Argon," he said, taking her hand to kiss it as he had done Anathriel's.

With the introductions satisfied, Anathriel took Regen's arm in her own, smiling coyly, and began leading him down the rows. Taryn followed a few feet behind, her attention once again captivated by the novelty of her surroundings.

"What is your errand with the Captain?" Regen asked.

"The other ladies and I have finished the sashes of rank for the new Windriders," Anathriel said. "Her Ladyship wishes Captain Brennen to call upon her this evening to choose which he would assign to tomorrow's honorees."

"And she needed to send you?" Something in Regen's tone caused Anathriel to look at him sharply. There was a hint of mischief in his eyes. He leaned down next to her ear. "I know what you're about, Miss Lelaine. Half the court is abuzz with speculation that you've cast your eyes upon our future captain."

"He is to be the captain, then?" Anathriel blurted eagerly, before she realized her mistake.

"Ha!" Regen exclaimed, grinning again. "Now the secret's out, isn't it, my scheming friend? You've given away your heart at last."

Anathriel's cheeks flamed, and she tossed her head proudly. "Just you be quiet about it, Regen, or I might have to twist your ears off," she said in a low voice, glancing around to make sure no one would overhear them. "I wouldn't say I've given away my heart just yet. I've only settled upon my intentions."

"You mean what most people call ambition?" he asked, raising an eyebrow. Then he shook his head, smiling. "Your secret is safe with me—for however long it remains a secret, at least. And to answer your question, most of us suspect that yes, he will be the next captain. I don't know absolutely, though."

Anathriel would have liked to continue this vein of conversation further, but Regen now seemed keen to steer her away from it. "Captain Brennen is in his office, working on last-minute preparations of his own. If you wish, I could convey your message for you."

"No, thank you, Regen, I think Lady Rillandra would prefer if I—" Anathriel paused as new activity at the end of the corridor claimed her attention. An indistinguishable cry had come up from the end of the corridor, and the men who had been working there were clearing a broad area by the end of the far door.

"Incoming," Regen said knowingly.

"Thank you, Regen," said Anathriel wryly. She rather thought she could have figured that out on her own. They paused in their walk, and a moment later Taryn stepped up beside them to watch the new arrival.

Despite the unpleasant smells and sounds of the eyries, it was still a thrilling sight when, with a speed almost blinding, a great eagle swooped gracefully into the corridor and sailed halfway down its length before cleanly landing on the great perch at its center. Anathriel gave a satisfied smile upon seeing it, for if there was any eagle she knew on sight, it was this one.

Her name was Zephyr. She was easily distinguishable, for although she was by no means the largest of her kind, she had a peculiar silver coloring that was very rare. More importantly, though, she was Immen Corper's mount, which explained Anathriel's interest.

"Are you sure you don't want me to deliver your message to Captain Brennen myself?" Regen said quietly into her ear, his voice full of teasing.

Anathriel sucked in her breath. "Yes, Regen, that would be lovely, thank you," she said distractedly. After a moment's inspiration, she added, "Actually—" She turned to Taryn. "Taryn, please accompany Lord Feldstone to the offices and deliver Lady Rillandra's message to Captain Brennen. It would be good practice for you, I think."

Taryn merely gazed at her curiously. "Yes, Anathriel," she replied.

Regen detached himself from Anathriel's hold and offered his arm instead to Taryn. "My lady?" he prompted, smiling broadly.

Taryn giggled and accepted it.

Then Regen looked back at Anathriel. "Behave yourself," he chided, giving her a small wink.

Anathriel didn't bother watching the pair retreat. Her attention was now fully captivated by the sight of the tall, handsome young man who had just dismounted from Zephyr's back and was now standing by the great bird's head, scratching the area around her beak and whispering something to her with a smile.

Since the day he'd come to the eyries as a hopeful initiate, Immen Corper had been the rising star of the Windrider ranks. He had an uncanny talent with the great birds, able to soothe even the most riley of them with a few quiet words. He was talented, serious, steady, and extremely good-looking, with brilliant blue eyes, unruly light brown hair, and fine hands. In Anathriel's opinion, he was the perfect catch, and she was determined to have him.

Her father had been a bit disgruntled when Anathriel had first told him of her intentions. After all, the whole reason they had fought so hard to get her into court was the hope of a noble marriage. With an astonishing gift for trade, Ricco Lelaine had traveled the world and acquired a fortune, settling at last in Montressa to marry Anathriel's mother. Desiring a title worthy to match his wealth, Ricco had seen to it that Anathriel was given a place as one of Lady Rillandra's maidens. Anathriel had come to court at twelve years of age, the youngest in living memory.

Anathriel's father had long harbored hopes that she would be able to use her talents to secure a husband from among the aristocracy, and she had not opposed. She had the necessary wealth and education, and she knew she was very pretty too. Her plans had shifted, however, when she'd met Immen.

Even though he wasn't nobility, Anathriel had pointed out to her father that Immen's status among the Windriders put him nearly on par with some of the noble houses from a political standpoint. If his career was successful enough, he might even procure a title of his own, and Anathriel had skills that could only help advance him in that respect. She recognized Immen Corper's potential, and it hadn't taken long for her father to realize it, as well. She had always been able to persuade her father to whatever end she wished.

Anathriel squared her shoulders and began walking resolutely towards Immen, knowing she looked her best. She'd worked meticulously on her appearance that morning before coming. Her fair hair had been combed out and left to hang loose and long down her back, clean and glistening, scented like flowers. Her gown was snug and flattering, in a shade of spring green that complimented the color of her eyes. All her arsenal of smiles was on hand, ready to be employed at a moment's notice, whichever was called for.

He did not notice her until she was almost upon him, for he was turned away from her, still speaking quietly to Zephyr. Anathriel had to confess she felt a little nervous, not only because of the bold step she was about to make, but also because this close, she was keenly aware of the sharpness of the eagle's beak and talons. She swallowed a little. Fortunately, Zephyr was not an animal reputed to have a temper.

When Immen finally noticed her, his face flashed with momentary surprise. No doubt he was wondering why he had not detected her approach. This was good, for she had been doing her best to make her footsteps light and delicate. She'd worn her best slippers, which would require some considerable care to restore after their encounter with the dirty eyrie floors, but now that was the furthest thing from her mind.

Anathriel offered her most beautiful smile, the one that had enraptured many a young man over the years. "Good morning, Immen."

If she expected some earth-shattering reaction on his part, she was a little disappointed. He merely nodded politely, one hand still stroking the feathers on Zephyr's face. "Good morning, Miss Lelaine."

"Did you enjoy your ride?" she asked brightly, hoping the question didn't sound as superficial as it felt coming off her lips.

"Very much. It is a beautiful morning," he replied, glancing back at the way he'd come with admiration. "I'm eager for the summer."

"Are you looking forward to tomorrow's festivities?" she prodded.

"I suppose I am. There are several fine young men among the initiates. They will make strong riders."

"And no doubt with you as their new captain," Anathriel added, giving him her adoring smile, "they'll do even better."

This comment at last brought a reaction beyond mere politeness. He smiled slightly, and made an expression close to a blush, but not quite. "You flatter me, Miss Lelaine. But please don't presume such a thing yet."

"Would you like to be captain?" Anathriel asked him, suddenly curious. It struck her that she had no idea if it was what he even wanted.

He cocked his head, considering. "Yes and no. I'm afraid that being captain would prevent me from riding as often as I should like, and that I would regret. And yet—" he added, almost hesitantly, "I have a few ideas. I suppose I'd like to see how I'd do. The responsibility would be an honor." He paused after saying this last and then gazed at her with a mildly confused expression. "Was there something you wanted, Miss Lelaine?"

Anathriel blushed prettily. "Please," she said in her softest, humblest voice, "call me Anathriel. I—" She stopped, and took a breath, her nervousness suddenly very real and overwhelming. She reached into her pocket, pulling out the first of the items she'd brought with her and taking a hesitant step closer to him. "I made this for you," she said with a shy smile, unfolding it and handing it to him.

He took it curiously, then offered his first genuine smile upon inspecting it more closely. "It's Zephyr," he said, pleased.

Stitched on the cloth, in perfect detail, was a scene of a silver eagle soaring among the golden mountain peaks under a late sun. Anathriel had invested all of her needlework skills into the piece, spending much of her free time watching the eagles fly in and out of the eyries from the grand balcony at Par Auspré so she could perfectly capture the majesty of Immen's beautiful mount.

"It looks so much like her," he added, gazing back at Anathriel with admiration.

Hope swelled inside her. Some said the way to a man's heart was through his stomach, but the way to Immen Corper's was surely through his beloved Zephyr.

"This is fine work, Anathriel. Thank you."

Anathriel began to breathe easier. Now he was warming up to her. It was time to do what she'd come here determined to do. She retrieved the second item from her pocket—a long ribbon of dark blue satin, richly embroidered with climbing vines and flowers. "I wonder, Immen," she said, again making sure she portrayed the proper combination of shyness and delicacy, "if you would wish to wear this favor tomorrow in the ceremonies?" She held out the ribbon to him, her eyes shining hopefully.

Almost instantly, all the expectation that had been building inside her crashed down like a mountain avalanche. His surprised expression and the fact that he made no move to take the ribbon from her hand told her all too well that her offer would prove in vain.

He paused a long moment before replying. "Again, my lady, I'm flattered," he said carefully, averting his eyes from the ribbon uncomfortably, "but I should tell you that I already have a favor to wear."

Anathriel blinked, taken aback. Another favor? From whom? Was there someone else he loved? She knew of no one in court, unless it was someone uncannily good at keeping a secret, but no one was better than her at unearthing secrets. Could it be a commoner, perhaps? Instant anger and envy flared inside her, and she could only hope her indignation was not showing on her features. A commoner? How could he accept favors from some *nobody* when Anathriel had so often hinted at her own hopes to him?

The disappointment was three times more bitter than she'd ever imagined, but she was not so far gone that she would lose her composure in front of the man. "Well," she finally said, a little brusquely, "thank you, all the same, Immen." With a quick curtsey, she turned heel to flee.

"Anathriel, wait!" he called, and she turned back around with sudden hope. "Do you," he began awkwardly, "do you want this back?" He held out the embroidery still nestled in his palm, dashing all visions of repentance from Anathriel's imagination.

She was almost tempted to take it back, just out of spite. But it was clear he was genuinely fond of the work, for reasons that had everything to do with the subject and nothing to do with the giver. Taking it back would have been a little satisfying to her wounded pride. However, she'd invested a good deal of her time in that piece, and it was a shame to let it go to waste. She had no use for it herself, and if she took it back, she would probably throw it away—a painful reminder of her rejection.

"No," she said, a little sadly. "You can keep it." Then she really did walk away, before he could say another word.

Instead of easing and fading, Anathriel's disappointment only festered and soured as the afternoon progressed into evening. She had held back angry tears the whole way home, a chattering Taryn on her heels, going on and on about how much she had enjoyed the trip to the eyries, and about how very kind Captain Brennen was, and how very handsome Lord Feldstone was. Anathriel let her chatter away, unchecked, her mind too consumed with what had happened.

She threw the offending ribbon off the grand balcony as soon as she arrived back, and spent the rest of the day snapping at all the younger handmaidens for the slightest things.

⌘ ⌘ ⌘

Xari stood up to her ankles in the ocean, relishing the feel of the warm water lapping over her toes. The sky was mostly clear, with only a few wispy clouds drifting along on a light breeze. This part of the beach was secluded, nestled between two cliffs. Lovers occasionally found their way to this spot; two, in fact, had been here when Xari arrived earlier, but one look at her, and they had scuttled off elsewhere.

Despite being at least a hand shorter than anyone else around, Xari knew that people were often wary of her appearance. Her hair, which she had grown down past her waist, was kept in dozens of braids, and her right eyebrow was pierced, both in the style of the Westerlons. She had learned much of the Westerlons in the past years and was no longer afraid to look like one. She usually didn't wear dresses as a proper young lady should—she found breeches much more practical for the work she had to do. Here in Ithrin, strangers weren't scared of her, but they were oftentimes cautious. They had only dealt with the occasional Westerlon warrior and didn't have the fear that the people of Threnphol and Réol did.

Xari had moved to Ithrin, the southernmost country of the Eastern Continent, five years earlier, and had settled at one of the marine harbors. It bordered not only the sea, but one of the large rivers flowing through the country, thereby making it the perfect place for the Otter Speaker to settle, as both sea and river otters populated the area. She had a special affinity and connection to the lovable beings, but they were not the only reason she loved the ocean. The otters were not the only sea-dwellers with whom she could speak.

Grinning, Xari spied what she was looking for and plunged into the water, not caring that her breeches and sleeveless tunic soaked through. She swam deftly out toward a lone rock a short way out of the bay. Xari still had several hours until high tide rose and hid the great stone.

Asheford, her constant companion and confidant, trailed over her head as she swam. When she reached the rock, she clambered onto it, drenched from head to toe, flinging wet braids out of her face. Moments later, a white bottlenose poked out of the water, followed by the long, sleek form of a dolphin. He playfully flung water on her with his nose.

"I don't know why you bother, Diegan," she told him with half a laugh. "I'm soaked already." She leaned back on propped arms and closed her eyes, welcoming the warm sun on her face. "How fares the ocean this week?"

"It fares much the same as it did last week," Diegan replied. "However, I have one thing I'm sure you will find of particular interest. Word passed from the dolphin kin near the coast of Réol. A leviathan has been spotted."

Xari's eyes snapped open. "A leviathan?" she repeated.

Ashe, who had been lazily drifting several feet above the water, wings buzzing, came to attention but avoided interrupting the conversation.

"My kin from Réol's waters said the leviathan was in front of a ship far out on the ocean. They were able to get close enough to hear that someone was speaking to it. Mortén, obviously."

"Obviously," Xari muttered. Mortén was the speaker for the leviathans, which meant he had the ability to perceive where they were, and to mentally alert them of his presence. Xari had the same ability with the otters, but it was useless with any other brethren. It was one of the things that made Mortén being Leviathan Speaker so frustrating. The great sea serpents lived so deep in the ocean, and surfaced so rarely, that Xari had never been able to speak with them, but Mortén would have had little trouble contacting them because of his bond. "Did the dolphins hear what he was saying?"

"Only bits, I'm afraid. You know we cannot speak with the leviathans without a speaker to translate, or we would warn them of Mortén."

"I know, Diegan," Xari sighed. "I hope none of your kindred were seen by Mortén." She had long since persuaded the dolphins to her side. As such, Mortén had held little mercy or patience for their race.

"I do not think so," Diegan assured her. "They were careful. There is something else, though," he continued. "My kin followed the leviathan as best they could once Mortén had finished speaking with it. They think they may have an idea where it lives. However, it was much deeper than they could go."

That news was good because Xari might have a starting point on where to search for the leviathans, and bad because it wasn't as if she could go underwater to tell them that she wanted to talk to them.

Xari spent a while longer talking with Diegan, hearing other tidbits of information that he had gathered from around the sea. Finally, she bade him farewell and made her way out of the water. She glanced up at the position of the sun as she pulled on the sandals she had left on the beach.

"It's getting late," she told Ashe. "I promised Burin I'd put in extra hours at the forge this morning. He's trying to finish that sword for the captain of the guard at Lord Duryen's estate. I'll tell you about Diegan's news on the way."

Xari quickly made her way to the outskirts of town, winding past several homes, until she reached Burin's forge, set apart from both the local residences and the bustle of the town, filling in Ashe as they went.

"Mortén's not in Réol anymore, though. He started heading north several days ago; I've been monitoring, because I guessed he'd be heading that way soon," Xari admitted as she headed around the forge to enter the living quarters through the back entrance.

Ashe kept pace beside her head. "On his way to Montressa, no doubt," he said.

"Exactly," Xari confirmed. Once inside her room, she stripped off her soggy clothing, setting it in a pile of other clothes that needed washing. Then she yanked on a pair of soot-stained breeches and a tunic. "I don't know why he bothers. The eagles know inherently that he's not to be trusted, yet he persists in visiting." She tied her braids out of her face.

"Mortén has his own plans, Xari. I'm sure he has some reason for traveling to Montressa."

"Oh, I know he has his own plans," Xari said, leaving her room to walk down the hallway and into the forge. "I only wish I knew what they were."

The temperature change as Xari stepped into the forge was drastic; she broke out in sweat almost immediately. The smell of coal and hot metal permeated the air, a scent that would bother some, but one that was exceedingly comforting and familiar to Xari. Ashe flew up to land on one of the rafters, watching her from his high perch.

Xari snatched an apron hanging from a nail on the wall and threw it on. "Burin?"

"Here!" Burin's head popped up from the other side of the furnace. His dark, shaggy hair was pushed back with a dirty, sweat-soaked red band, and his dark face glistened in the heat. He had a pair of tongs in his hand. "Would you get the mold ready?"

"Which one?" Xari asked, crossing to a cupboard in the corner.

"On the far left," he directed, not turning around. "I set it out last night."

Xari located the mold and carried it over, setting it on the worktable near Burin while she waited on him.

"So," Burin said, keeping a close eye on metal he was heating, "what news in the ocean this morning?"

Burin Oth'ilin was the other reason Xari had chosen to come to this particular Ithraine fishing village. Originally from the Southern Continent, as was evidenced by his dark skin and hair, Burin was one of the only swordmasters in the country, and one of the best in the Eastern Continent. He had chosen a humble life, making swords in a forge in the prosperous harbor town of Urnii.

Xari had approached him five years earlier, requesting that he take her as an apprentice. She often thought about what it must have been like to have a twelve-year-old girl asking a renowned swordmaster to teach her his craft. For whatever reason, he had agreed, in exchange that she help in his forge, and he had given her room and board in the living quarters adjoining it.

Burin's diligence and honor had taught Xari much in the five years she had lived there. Under his tutelage, she had learned a lot about herself. She had learned to embrace who she was, to stand assured in who the Master had created her to be. Burin had told her that the Westerlons were not all evil, as she had been taught.

"People can be very quick to judge, Xari, and you have the opportunity to take your heritage and show them that not all Westerlons are what they think."

Though Ashe had already told Xari much of the Master, it had been Burin who had convinced her of his unfailing love. Burin helped her see that the Master did not care who her parents were or where she came from, but accepted her as she was—with all of her faults, her temper, and her Westerlon heritage. Of course, this understanding only came because Burin himself had displayed the same kindness that he assured her the Master possessed. He had established within her a faith and hope that she had never before experienced. He was also the only living soul that knew about Xari and Ashe's occupations as a speaker and guardian. When she first came to him, she hadn't told him anything of it, but eventually, she came to love and trust him enough to divulge to him her secret.

Now she briefed him about the leviathan sighting. "It's so frustrating. The rest of the world sees Mortén as a respectable lord in Réol. I can't tell people how much he—" She shook her head, unable to articulate exactly how horrible Mortén was. "No one would take my word over his without proof."

"And what does Ashe think about this?" Burin asked.

"Ashe thinks exactly the same thing Xari does," Ashe said mildly. He was in the habit of staying visible while in the forge so Burin could see and hear him, and now Burin glanced up at the rafter where he was seated. "The leviathans are both incredibly powerful and intelligent. They're ancient...longer-lived than even the fairies. They are not easily fooled, but we have no guarantees as to what they believe about Mortén."

"Frustrating." Xari repeated her earlier sentiment.

Burin smiled over at her. "The Master has a plan for this, Xari. We might not be able to see the path, but that doesn't mean there isn't one."

"I know. I don't doubt that his hand is in my life. I only wish that sometimes the path was laid with big road signs. Like the time I tried to make contact with the dragons, remember?"

"It didn't go so well," Burin grunted knowingly, stirring the coals of the forge and reaching for the bellows.

"Yes, and a nice sign would have been very helpful. You know, something like: *Warning: Dragons Will Try to Eat You. Do Not Approach!* It would make life so much simpler sometimes."

Burin laughed. "Yes, but then you would miss out on the joyous surprises life brings."

"Yes, Burin, because getting my head bitten off would have been joyous for everybody, wouldn't it?"

Still chuckling, Burin gave the bellows a pump. "Come on, youngling. Let's get this hilt on, and then we can have some lunch."

3

On a wide precipice that afforded a good view of the eyries' northern gate, Anathriel stood with her fellow handmaidens, watching an artful display in the distance. This was the first of the many events and ceremonies that would be taking place today. It was called a wind pageant—a display of skill and precision wherein the Windriders guided their mounts over, under, and past one another in graceful formations. The eagles of Montressa were noted for their intelligence, but it took a Windrider of considerable skill and patience to convince an eagle to go where he willed.

Anathriel's eyes followed Zephyr's silver wingspan, so easily discernable from the others, so compliant with Immen's every wish. She could barely see Immen, a small figure in red and gray on Zephyr's back. She was much too far away to spy any trinket he might be wearing, but she fully intended to find one on him by the end of the day. Perhaps she would recognize it and know who had given it to him.

Zephyr drew her wings in tightly to her body and made a swift, diving swoop straight down, just in time to miss Eulaie, Regen's large golden mount, who breezed across Zephyr's wake. There was an audible gasp from the spectators, not only on the precipice where Anathriel stood with the rest of the court, but from other parts of the city below them, where most of the citizens were also crowded to watch. After diving nearly three hundred feet, Zephyr snapped her wings open, catching a warm spring thermal, and slowly glided up towards the pinnacle again, but away from it, farther north.

Three more eagles, including Eulaie, followed Zephyr in such rapid succession that Anathriel found herself wondering how they'd gotten into position so quickly. The four eagles soared together in a line, their broad backs to the crowd, flying farther from the mountain. At last, with perfectly timed precision, they peeled off in pairs to the left and right and wheeled back around the way they'd come. Meanwhile, the group of eagles that had remained near the precipice was performing similar aerial acrobatics.

The wind pageant had always been Anathriel's favorite part of the Festival of Winds. She deeply appreciated beauty in many forms, and even now her fingers were itching for her viol and bow, to play something grand and lyrical to match the power of the wings beneath her. She could see patterns in the performance. Zephyr and Immen were the central leader of every maneuver, from which every other Windrider took his cue, and they did it so subtly she doubted it would be apparent to many. Immen was already a great leader.

Her enjoyment of the wind pageant was the first pure moment of pleasure she'd had since Immen's rejection the previous day, yet even that embarrassing event had lost some of its sting. It had occurred to her that, quite possibly, Immen had *wished* to accept her, but had been honor-bound to keep his word to this other girl, whoever she was. Anathriel chose to ignore her inner doubts about this theory; if she wanted to marry Immen Corper, she would have to fight for him, and no possibility could be ignored.

With that in mind, she was quick to catch Lady Rillandra just after the pageant ended. Under pretense of going to visit her father, Anathriel obtained her mistress's permission to take the afternoon off.

"But I do expect you back in plenty of time for the remaining festivities," the Lady called to her retreating back. "The entire court is looking forward to your performance this evening."

Anathriel waved a polite acknowledgement before she turned and headed up a small flight of stairs that would take her back into the building. She hadn't been exactly lying to Lady Rillandra—Anathriel had never approved of outright lying—but she had not, of course, revealed her true intentions for requesting time away. It shouldn't be too difficult to manage a short visit to her father, once she'd accomplished her more pressing errand.

She made her way quickly through the familiar corridors of Par Auspré, her home of the last ten years. This wing housed the public rooms—banquet halls, a ballroom, and formal sitting parlors. In the western and southern wings were the living quarters for the High Lord's family and attendants. In the north were the apartments of state, where diplomacy was conducted, and where important guests stayed when they came. The latter occurred rarely. Not many of Merenth's other High families were willing to make the arduous trek up the mountain.

The bottom-most level of the eastern wing was the most direct route to the eyries—the same route Anathriel and Taryn had taken the previous day. This was a functional design, for the Windriders often brought Lord Kavela important news from other parts of the province, which could then be brought to him as quickly as possible. Anathriel knew that many of the Windriders would still be milling about after the pageant, so she waited by the doors for a few moments, carefully watching the southern gate of the eyries to see how many of them were leaving for the fair in the city streets below. She didn't want too many people to see her standing here, although she also had to consider time constraints. She couldn't wait all day. Finally, when she estimated that about half or more of the Windriders had departed, including Regen, she dared to head into the eyries themselves.

Through careful observation over her last few scattered visits, Anathriel had learned exactly which nest was Zephyr's. It was located third from the far end, on the western side, and she quickened her pace to reach it now. When she arrived there, however, she was surprised to find the nest empty of any sign of eagle or rider. Instead, sitting cross-legged in Zephyr's nest, was a strange boy.

His head was bent over something in his lap. Upon closer inspection, Anathriel recognized it as some kind of Windrider gear, but crumpled up the way it was, she would have been hard-pressed to say which part, exactly. With deft motions, he was pushing and pulling a thick, bright needle and brown chord through the sturdy leather.

"Who are you?" she blurted, almost unthinking.

The boy looked up at her, at first surprised, but at the expression on her face, he narrowed his eyes. He paused a moment, then said, "I'm Zeth," before lowering his eyes again.

"Where's Immen?" she demanded.

This time, he did not bother to look up. "He's with Captain Brennen."

"Where's Zephyr?" she asked next.

He gave a very patient sigh. "Out flying," he said deliberately, still not looking up. His attention was focused on his work.

A little annoyed by his cool attitude, Anathriel frowned and studied him more closely. He had thick, dark hair and brooding eyes, and an expression that seemed a little bit hard and sarcastic. She guessed him to be around thirteen or fourteen. Then she noticed something else, a tattoo around his right wrist that looked like a chain made of small, narrow links.

A term-slave.

"And what are *you* doing here?" she demanded loudly.

This time he did look up, clearly frustrated. His gaze followed hers to where she was still staring accusingly at the brand, but if he thought anything of it, he didn't say. Instead, he looked back at her. "I am *trying* to fix this bridle, if it isn't painfully obvious," he said, speaking to her as if she were five years old.

Anathriel glared at him. "I would appreciate it if you would be a little more polite. My name is—"

"I know who you are," he said smoothly. He held her gaze for a moment, conveying to Anathriel a disdain such as she'd never seen. Her cheeks flamed.

"Does your master know you're here, *slave?*"

That struck a nerve. The boy inhaled deeply, glaring at her harder than ever. Then he closed his eyes and gave her an overly saccharine smile. "Yes, my lady. He does. Immen Corper of the Windriders sent us a message this morning, saying he had an ornamental bridle that needed reinforcement before tonight's ceremony, and could we please send someone to fix it? Seeing as how my master wished to enjoy the festivities, he sent me. Therefore, I am here obeying the orders of my master, who holds some authority over me, which, I might point out, is a claim *you* cannot make, my lady. So if you would be so kind as to leave me to it?"

Anathriel was so angry after this diatribe that for nearly ten seconds she couldn't think of a single thing to say. She was just building up a nice, scathing retort when the boy spoke up again. He was once more consumed with his stitching. "Incidentally, if you were looking for Immen, he just walked out the southern gate."

Anathriel forgot her retort altogether. She spun around and saw that the boy had been speaking truthfully—Immen was striding purposefully away from the eyries in the opposite direction.

"Blast," she muttered.

Behind her, the boy chuckled. She glared back at him, and he said, "Go on. Catch him, if you can. Flatter him, dote on him, do what you will. It won't do any good. He'll never be interested in a girl like you."

Anathriel pursed her lips and narrowed her eyes. "I won't forget this," she warned, then walked away altogether.

Her anger did not subside in the slightest, no matter how quickly she tried to bleed it off. The strange slave-boy's words seemed to echo inside her head over and over. *A girl like me? What in the world could he mean by that? What does it matter what some insignificant slave thinks, anyway?*

She never lost sight of Immen, but she never could quite seem to catch him, either. Every time she got close, she would get stuck in a crowd of festival-goers, stopping to watch some tumbler or street musician, or standing in a long line to try the first of this year's grilled trout brought up from Valedyne. She almost lost sight of him altogether, but managed to spy his retreating figure slipping down a side street. She pushed her way almost rudely through the crowd at that point, feeling a little ridiculous, even for her standards. She was already hot and sweaty—her dress was multi-layered and not an advisable choice for heavy exercise—and if she didn't find him soon, she wouldn't have time to visit her father *and* make it back to Par Auspré for the rest of the ceremonies.

When she reached the small street he'd disappeared into, so narrow that the buildings overhead nearly touched one another, she traipsed immediately down a set of stairs to emerge into a small but neat, pleasantly lit courtyard surrounded by narrow houses. The courtyard was mostly empty, and the only people there seemed to be eager festival-goers heading for other parts of the city. And Immen.

She breathed a sigh of relief at seeing him. He was standing at the far end of the courtyard by the front door of one of the houses. Anathriel paused and held back in the shadow of the narrow alley through which she'd come.

A moment later, the door opened wide, revealing a very pretty young girl at least several years younger than Anathriel, wearing a plain, dark green dress with a brightly colored pinafore. She smiled when she saw Immen and greeted him warmly with words Anathriel was too far away to hear. When she stepped out of the door, she closed it firmly behind her. On her arm was a small day bag.

Immen put a hand on the girl's shoulder, stopping her just before she stepped down onto the cobblestones. He smiled and said something to her with a pleased expression. At his words, the girl shrieked loudly and joyfully and jumped up, throwing her arms around his neck. Laughing, he caught her and held her close, rocking her slightly from side to side.

Anathriel swallowed and took a couple of steps back, further into the shadows. She had seen enough. This must be her, the girl of whom he'd spoken. Anathriel leaned back against the wall dejectedly, wiping sudden tears from her eyes. He really did favor someone else—a commoner with a boring green dress and garish pinafore. No matter that the girl was pretty and seemingly pleasant.

Through watery vision, Anathriel chanced another glance at the pair in time to see the girl tying a long silk kerchief around Immen's upper arm with a satisfied expression. The two were conversing in a bright and amicable manner.

He'll never be interested in a girl like you, echoed the slave boy's words again.

With a heavy sniffle, Anathriel wrenched her gaze away and squared her shoulders. She needed to get moving, in case Immen and the pretty girl headed back this way. How embarrassing it would be to be caught by him just now.

When Anathriel reached her father's house, she was relieved to find him not at home. This wasn't surprising, really. She'd never before visited him during the Festival of Winds; why would he wait around for her? Instead, she helped herself to a quick sponge bath, cleaning off some of the grime from her walk and brushing her hair. This gave her adequate time to compose herself before heading back to the pinnacle.

That evening, Immen Corper was named the new captain of Montressa's Windriders. Anathriel was not surprised, but neither was she as jubilant as she might otherwise have been. She felt strangely numb and sober. Her smiles and conversation that evening were forced, a pretense she was only able to maintain through years of practice. The only thing genuine was her viol performance. Into her music she poured a good deal of her disappointment and frustration. Perhaps this wasn't quite in character to match a celebration, but most people seemed to enjoy her playing anyway.

As she finally lay in bed after the wearying day, Anathriel had time to ponder her odd mood. What puzzled her most was that, although she felt terrible, she strangely didn't feel *angry* with Immen. The bitterness of rejection—not once, but twice manifested—had done nothing to diminish her admiration for him. If the rude slave in the eyries had been correct, and Anathriel wasn't the kind of girl Immen Corper was interested in, then she'd just have to find out what kind of girl that was and why she didn't match up. Then maybe she could think of a way to capture his attention.

Thinking back on the warm expression he'd been giving the pretty girl, though, even Anathriel knew she didn't have much of a chance.

⌘ ⌘ ⌘

Sparring had long ago become a daily ritual for Burin and Xari. They trained in the large practice room at the back of the house. Xari cherished the time spent in this room, where she had learned so many lessons, and trained both her body and her mind.

Front flip, land firmly, overhead slash.

Xari's two curved blades clashed against Burin's. She had long ago learned to fight with one sword, but six months ago, Burin had informed her they were going to train with two. It was considerably more difficult, but if she mastered double-sword fighting, she would have the advantage against a foe with only one blade. They alternated between using straight blades and curved ones, which meant two completely different fighting styles, but Xari preferred using the curved swords. She learned a combination of skills, like how to use curved swords and straight swords against an opponent holding the opposite.

Grinning fiercely, Burin shoved his blades down, swinging them around toward Xari. His large arms, accustomed to wielding hammers and pounding metal into swords, bulged with muscle. Xari's own arms were well-muscled from her work in the forge, but she was too petite to ever have arms like Burin's. One of his swords came at Xari's head, the other at her midsection.

Jump back, sidestep, twist in, scissor cut.

Burin's two blades came up, blocking the scissor cut. He twisted his swords, breaking Xari's attack. "Come on, Xari! You're not even trying!" His teasing expression matched the tone of his words.

Xari gritted her teeth, moving in again. *Swing around, underhand thrust—*

"Xari!"

Startled by Asheford's sudden exclamation, Xari overshot, one blade going wide. She tried to correct her mistake and overbalanced, wobbling on one foot. Burin slapped her lower back with the flat of a sword, and she fell forward. She held her swords to the sides and turned her fall into a roll. Then she sprang back to her feet, eyes locked on Burin. "What is it, Ashe?" she asked through clenched teeth.

"You're not going to believe this." Something in Ashe's voice made Xari's heart skip a beat, and she spared him a brief glance. He hovered anxiously in the air by the door. In the instant she turned her eyes away, Burin struck. Xari hissed in pain, glancing down at the tiny cut on her left forearm.

"Xari! You're not paying attention! That's the quickest way to lose your arm in a fight," Burin lectured. He took a step back, dropping his swords to his side. "We'll stop now, as it seems Ashe has something to say. You did well, but remember to always keep your guard up, regardless of distractions."

Xari bowed to him, and he bowed in return. Going to the edge of the room, he grabbed a cloth to wipe the blood off of his sword. Xari focused her attention on Ashe. "What is it?" Burin returned to her side with another piece of cloth, which he deftly wrapped around her injured arm.

"I almost couldn't believe it. It's remarkable," Ashe said. "I simply cannot believe that it is coincidence."

Xari rolled her eyes. "Well? Are you going to tell me what it is or are you going to jabber nonsense?" She had been with Ashe long enough to know that he could go on about something without ever explaining what it was. It wasn't because he tried to be confusing, but because he honestly didn't realize he had not yet made his point.

"Oh, yes, yes. Xari—" Ashe paused significantly. "I felt another choosing. Somewhere, a relic has been found."

Xari gaped, and even Burin looked startled. "Really?" Xari finally managed. "Where?"

"In Montressa," Ashe said with excitement. Then he was quick to add, "I believe. Far, far to the north, in any case."

"Montressa?" Xari repeated disbelievingly. One thought flashed instantly to mind. "But Mortén is headed for Montressa."

That could spell trouble in so many ways. She didn't like the idea of him being anywhere near someone who could potentially be a speaker. Of course, without fairy aid, there was really no reason to expect Mortén would know anything about the choosing.

"That is a concern," Ashe agreed. "More pressing, though, is the fact that my kindred will also have sensed it. They will certainly send someone in search of the chosen one."

It was Burin who said, "And they might not awaken him."

"Or her," Xari said pointedly.

"Not if they feel the same way as they did about the otter relic," Ashe agreed. "I believe there may be at least one known descendent of the twelve Houses in Montressa, but there were many descendents to track, and many were lost or forgotten over time. I'm afraid I cannot recall all the names. My people, however, will have a written record of what descendents we have been able to visit."

Xari knew the fairies had done their best to keep track of the descendents of the twelve Houses, believing it was these that would eventually reclaim their roles as speakers. It was probably the only reason the fairies ever left Fairlight Forest, to discover if any new children had been born. She had often wondered if that meant her mother—or even, possibly, her father—had been one such descendent.

Xari tugged on a braid. "Burin—"

"You need to go," Burin said gently.

"Yes. I need to try to get to Montressa before the fairies. I doubt I'll get there before Mortén, but—" She sighed. "I suppose I'd better head to the post and see what boats are traveling north in the next few days. The River Road will be the quickest way of travel." She pressed her lips together grimly. "Hopefully it'll be quick enough."

4

Running the entire length of the Eastern Continent was a series of waterways known simply as the River Road. It was, in fact, one of the things for which the Eastern Continent was famed. Large portions of the waterways were natural, as if a giant hand had carved them out of the land. The rest of the great canals had been laboriously shaped by men centuries earlier in order to connect the system. As a result, it was now one of the main thoroughfares of travel, used by everyone from vacationing nobles to merchants with wares. Posts were stationed all along the rivers, stopping points for boats, and departing points for travelers. Northbound travel, going upstream, was a bit slower than southbound travel, but it was still faster than other means.

Situated as it was at the mouth of one of the River Road's main branches, the small city of Urnii reaped the benefits of such prime geography. The harbor town never really slept, even when night fell. Since no sea captain could ever predict with certainty when he would be arriving in port, there was always a constant stream of travelers and ships at all times of day and night. Even so, when Xari arrived at the post after dark to learn when she might be able to get a ride upriver, she received her fair share of raised eyebrows. Busy and prosperous though things were in Urnii, the sight of a young woman walking about so brazenly alone was still some cause for speculation.

Some people in Urnii thought Burin an irresponsible, or perhaps eccentric, guardian for allowing Xari such freedom, not only in her appearance, but also in her wanderings. Some people said it must be because of his Southron upbringing, but the whispers about Burin rarely stopped people from coming to him with their business. The fact was that most residents of Urnii were accustomed to strangers and their odd ways—sojourning Southrons or Islanders—and were far more lenient than others in the Eastern Continent. If not for this, Xari might have worried that she was costing Burin his reputation.

Xari's trip was to take six or seven weeks, depending on the weather and other hazards. She quickly learned that the next boat would depart two mornings hence, and paid a small portion of her travel expense to secure a place on board. She would deliver the rest to the captain upon departure. Afterward, she cast a swift glance around the post; only two boats were tied to the river's dock, gently bobbing in the water. There was a man on board one of them, sorting through packages. Two elderly men were seated beside the river, fishing rods in hand.

Xari headed swiftly along the path upstream. The torches around the post soon became pinpricks of light in the distance, and then vanished altogether, leaving Xari to pick her way along the riverbank by the light of the stars. Ashe accompanied her in companionable silence, already aware of her destination.

The sense of the otters in Xari's mind grew as she neared their dens, a tingling in her head that was at once warm and sweet, a familiarity that lightened her heart and brought a smile to her face. She could never fully explain exactly what it was like to have this connection to the otters. They were a part of who she was, and would forever be, until the moment she died. It was meant to be that way; she was meant to be the otters' voice, if she could only get people to listen.

Sighing inwardly, Xari came to a halt on the riverbank. As problematic as Mortén's interference was, he was not the only obstacle to overcome if she wanted the speakers and their place in the world to be restored. People didn't want to believe that they were missing something; they didn't always want to hear, and unless they could open their ears and their hearts, Xari could shout for the otters from the highest peak in the Northern Mountain Range and still not be heard.

The otters were asleep, but when she reached out with her mind to them, she knew they would stir from their cozy chambers and emerge through the underwater entrances. As she had expected, she had barely come to a stop when several sleek heads popped out of the water. Xari met them in the water before they could clamber out onto the bank. She slipped into the edge of the river, wading in up to her waist, giggling as the otters twined around her, tickling her with their sensitive whiskers.

"Xari!" chirped Arie, the smallest of the three, rubbing her nose against Xari's hand. "It's very late—is something wrong?" She paused in her swim and gazed up at Xari with keen brown eyes. "You feel excited.

And nervous."

"Scared, really," the second otter, Riri, said shrewdly. "Even though you're trying to hide it from yourself, aren't you?"

It was impossible for Xari to conceal her emotions from the otters. Such was the gift of their House, a gift that she shared with them. Even now she could feel their growing concern and sympathy as clearly as if it was her own, and she smiled at them, knowing how deeply they cared for her.

"What happened, Xari?" Brand, the eldest and largest of the trio, and the only male in the group, nudged her hand. "What is frightening you?" He looked up at Ashe, able to see him even though he could not understand him. It was one of the ways that the brethren were set apart from the normal creatures of the world. "Surely nothing your Asheford can't handle?"

One thing Xari loved about the otters was their fierce loyalty and hope. They were strong and could be ferocious in protecting that which they loved, yet they maintained a joy that was never crushed. Pressed, tested, but never shattered. If the twelve brethren had different strengths, then the otters represented the childlike faith that so many people lost, or never seemed able to find.

"I have news for you," Xari said softly. "I'm going to be away for awhile." As she said this, she realized just how scared she was. It wasn't as though traveling was a novel experience, but this was a challenge she had not faced before. "There's been another choosing, you see," she continued quietly, half to herself. "I have to try to locate the person, and it's very near where Mortén will be, if not in the same city."

A surge of anger struck her from the otters, and Arie pressed close to her side, trying to offer comfort. The otters had as much reason to fight and fear Mortén as she did; if he had little patience and mercy for the dolphins because of their affiliation with Xari, then he was ruthless with the otters.

"And there are no otters in the mountains," Xari whispered. "Only mountain rivers, and I'll be cut off from the sea."

"You will not be alone, Xari," Riri said fiercely. "The Master goes with you, and who cares more for you than he?"

"Asheford isn't so bad, either," Brand added.

Xari laughed. "No, not so bad," she agreed. "It's mostly—I don't know what it is. Maybe the idea of another potential speaker. I can't quite bring myself to believe it could be true. Then what if this person turns out to be—" She shook her head, not wanting to speak her thoughts into words, as if it would somehow call them forth into being.

"Another Mortén?" Ashe asked, alighting on her shoulder and placing one miniscule hand on her face, a touch somehow as soft as a butterfly's wings and yet as solidly comforting as a tight embrace. "I trusted with you, my sprout, and we shall trust now together. Besides, we have something now that I did not have with Mortén, or even with you."

"What's that?" Xari asked, turning her head to look directly into his eyes, already certain she knew what he was going to say.

Ashe smiled. "You, and the gift you have. Is it coincidence that the otter and leviathan relics surfaced at the same time? Mortén might have physical strength because of his gift, but you have a different strength, Xari, and I'm sure it will be called upon many times during our journey."

"What did he say?" Arie asked curiously, and Xari, wiping tears from her eyes, quickly translated Ashe's words for the otters.

"He's right," Riri said stoutly. "All we can do is trust the Master. There is but one thing left for you to do, Xari."

"What's that?"

Riri turned and splashed into the water. When she resurfaced, she said, "Come swim with us one more time before your journey!"

Xari spent the next while splashing in the river with the otters. Others who lived along the riverbank swam down to see her. She finally tore herself away from them and bade them farewell. She was practically skipping as she headed back toward Urnii, and Ashe chuckled at her from beside her head.

"The Master has shown me so many times why you were chosen to be Otter Speaker," he told her, the smile still on his face. "When I met you, you were a child who did not know how to be one. The otters have been as good for you as you have been for them."

"They are a remarkable race," Xari said. Her heart was infinitely lighter than it had been an hour ago. "And I'm grateful I'm their speaker."

When she reached the post, she saw that the two men who had been fishing had departed, but there were now several men taking care of the cargo on board one of the boats. They stared at her as she walked by, and she could only imagine how she must look, dripping wet and alone in the middle of the night.

"Good evening to you!" she called cheerfully, waving a hand at them. She didn't wait for a response but continued down the road, heading toward home, a home that would be there for her no matter how long she was gone.

⌘ ⌘ ⌘

Flute was on discipline again.

Despite her protests that she was getting too old for discipline, Elder Hawthorne had told her that she would be young enough until he said otherwise, and had, of course, sentenced her to weaving baskets with old Henna. The baskets were made for various purposes, but the two that Flute was presently helping with were intended for the two new eggs that would eventually hatch into fairy young.

So rare was it these days that even one egg was bred that the arrival of two, one in Summerby and one in Northpine, had been cause for much hope and celebration, and the baskets were a tradition that went back as far as anyone remembered. Once Henna finished with the two baskets, she would send them to the expecting villages. Nobody had been able to understand the mysterious decline in the fairy population over the past couple of centuries. Flute could see just by the size of her own nursery space that it had once housed many, many more sprouts.

It was during her midday meal break that Jesper found her, jumping out from behind the bole of the elm where old Henna's nest was and practically scaring her out of her wings.

She yelled in surprise. *"Jesper!"* She darted around him in the air and slapped him on the back of the head.

Jesper grinned at her, his green eyes impish. "Wait till you hear what I've found out."

"What?"

Jesper danced backward in the air, still grinning.

"Jep, would you *please* tell me?" Jesper was taking advantage of Flute's deep and incurable sense of curiosity, which Elder Wisteria insisted would one day be the death of her.

Jesper pretended to think for a moment, until Flute flew at him and tackled him. Before he could move, she began to tickle him.

"Flute! Stop! Stop, all right, all right! I'll tell you, just *stop!*"

A grin on her own face, Flute fluttered backward. "All right, so tell!"

"I heard some of what the council was talking about during the meeting today."

Flute placed her hands on her hips. "You eavesdropped without me?"

The elders in the village would no doubt be scandalized if they knew how many council sessions Flute and Jesper had been privy to. Several years ago, they had managed to discover and enlarge a tiny hole in the Great Tree, and they always covered it back up so that no one could see it.

"You were weaving baskets!" Jesper said in his defense.

Flute sighed heavily, but then straightened with expectation. "Well? What are they going to do about the new relic? Do they know who was chosen?"

It had been yesterday that the fairies had felt, for the third time in the past few years, the Master choose someone to carry a relic.

Jesper shrugged. "I think they said somebody named Immen Corper. He lives somewhere called Montressa."

"I know where that is!" Flute exclaimed. "At least, I know where it is on the maps in the Great Tree," she amended. "But I bet I could find it! Are they sending someone to find the chosen one? A guardian?"

"Yes—they're sending Thornbee."

"Ha! *Thornbee?* How could they pick him? He's such a—a—" A stick-in-the-mud, that's what he was. "He's so *boring.*" She made a face.

"Well, he would make a good guardian, and if this Immen Corper is found, and he really is called to the relic, he's going to need one," Jesper pointed out mildly.

Flute snorted. "Thornbee would make a good guardian to a *rock!*"

"Well, he is a bit impersonal sometimes, but he doesn't even live in our village, Flute. Maybe he's not as bad as he seems when he comes to Westfern."

"Ha!" Flute repeated her earlier sentiment. "No, no, *no*, Jep. If there's going to be a new speaker, he needs someone who can protect him, but have fun doing it! He needs someone who is a conversationalist. Someone who's not so arrogant. Someone—"

"Like you?" Jesper laughed.

Flute paused and considered. "Yes! Someone like me!" She beamed.

"Great. Then we know how long that speaker would last."

Flute narrowed her eyes dangerously. "And just what do you mean by that, Jesper*?*"

Undaunted by Flute's expression, Jesper said, "Flute, anyone that you tried to guard would wind up vanished or invisible or sprout an extra limb or something."

"Hey! I have never made anyone sprout an extra limb!" Flute said indignantly.

"You know what I mean, Flute."

"You don't think I could be a guardian!"

"I think you could be, once you've learned to better control your magic. Besides, there's Asheford to consider too," he pointed out. "We still don't know what happened to him, except that he probably awakened whoever it was that connected to the second relic. Do you really want to deal with him?"

"Asheford doesn't bother me," Flute said irritably, moving backward in the air. "I could do it! I could—"

"Flute, look out!"

Flying backward, Flute didn't see the tree branch until she had slammed into it. Laughing, Jesper zoomed forward. "Come on, Fluttermouse," he said, taking her arm. "I'll protect you from yourself."

Flute made a face at him and pulled her arm free. "I can handle myself just fine, thank you very much. I may not be perfect at controlling my magic like Sir High-and-Mighty Thornbee or a former Grand Magi like Asheford, but that doesn't mean I'm incapable!" She was a little angry with Jesper. He knew her magical accidents frustrated her; she was very sensitive about them.

"Flute! Don't lose your acorns. I didn't mean it like that, and you know it." Jesper sighed heavily. *"I* wouldn't make a good guardian right now, because I still have a lot to learn. There are protection spells that a guardian needs to know."

"I can do protection spells," Flute retorted, glaring at Jesper. "And if you tell me that's one of the only things I can do properly, I'll—I'll make *you* disappear to the next village!"

Jesper laughed again. "You have other things to worry about, Flute. Like how to convince the elders to let you celebrate Rowan's naming day in Northpine next week."

The event Jesper spoke of was a gathering in honor of one of Flute's friends, to celebrate the day he had hatched and received his name. It was still a week away, but if Flute was going to be there on time, she would have to leave in the morning with the other sprouts in her village.

"Anyway, I have to go help in the nursery," Jesper informed her. With a wave over his shoulder, he darted away.

Flute took a seat outside and picked up a half-finished basket. As she twisted the strands of dried grass over each other, she thought about the things Jesper had said. Truthfully, despite his advice, Flute still wasn't convinced that she wouldn't make a good guardian.

Flute savagely poked a piece of grass through the basket. She could do it. She knew she could. Not that anyone would ever give her the chance. She was merely an accident-prone little sprout in the eyes of the elders.

She thought about it all the rest of that day—when she finally finished helping old Henna, when she went to splash in the river with Jesper, and when she retired to her nest in the nursery that evening. She curled up on her bed of cottony fluff from a cattail, and her mind continued running over the day's events. It wasn't fair to Immen Corper if he got Thornbee as a guardian! Anyone would be miserable with him, but no one would do anything about it!

A sudden idea struck Flute, and she sat straight up, her wings fluttering excitedly. "I could—no," she whispered. Her wings lilted against her back. The council would have her wings! Not to mention what Elder Hawthorne would do. Yet Flute could not contain her excitement at the thought. Why not, after all? She knew she could do it. She could prove it to them, and then they wouldn't see her as a joke anymore.

A giddy thrill ran down her spine. She *would* do it, and finally show everyone she was capable of doing something right. She would bring honor to her elders, her friends, and her village. She would be a guardian, just like her ancestors were!

Flute was careful to wait until she was certain all the other sprouts were sleeping that night before she got up and sneaked out of the nursery, as quiet as she'd ever been in her life. Her last thought before she left Westfern village in her wake was that Immen Corper would thank her for it when he found out who might have been his guardian.

If she could get to him before Thornbee did.

⌘ ⌘ ⌘

Xari was not, by nature, a morning person. In fact, Ashe had often said that the day she got out of bed with the sun would be the day the world ended. Even when she did get up, those who knew her well gave her wide berth until she'd had a bit of time, not to mention a strong cup of brew.

So it was a small miracle in itself that Xari was awake before dawn on the day she and Ashe were set to begin their journey. She had a few fitful hours of sleep—she couldn't get her mind off of the new relic's sudden emergence and everything it could mean for her. She finally dragged herself out of bed and trudged into the small kitchen.

Typically, Burin was already awake, making a pan of eggs. "Well! Look who's decided to grace me with her presence! Did the sun rise and I missed it?"

"Ugh," Xari grunted.

"And such a ray of sunshine," Burin added.

Burin, Xari decided, was far too cheerful for this early in the morning. She growled something incoherent under her breath and plopped down at the wooden table, laying her head on it and closing her eyes, while Ashe helped himself to some fresh fruit.

"Here." Xari cracked open an eye to see Burin set a plate of eggs and a steaming cup in front of her. "You eat these, and drink that. You'll feel more human."

Xari immediately grabbed the cup and downed the brew. The bitter drink was one of the only things that helped wake her up in the mornings. She sighed contentedly, feeling a little more alive. Tucking her knees against her chest, she scooped eggs into her mouth with her fingers, as was custom in the Southern Continent. She had grown used to eating that way since taking up residence with Burin.

"Are you all packed?" Burin asked once she was finished eating.

"Yes. I got everything finished last night, after going to say one last good-bye to the otters and dolphins," Xari replied. "I'm glad it's spring—I would hate to travel to Merenth if it were any cooler." She shivered, thinking about it. "I prefer the south, thank you."

After breakfast, Xari helped Burin clean up, then said, "Well, we have to leave." She always hated leaving this simple, beautiful place that was her home, and this time she had no idea how long she would be gone.

"I have something I want to give you before you go," Burin said.

"Oh? What is it?"

"That would be telling." Burin winked. "You'll have to come and see."

Curious, Xari followed Burin out of the kitchen and into the practice room, Ashe hovering over her left shoulder, still finishing his breakfast. Burin went into the corner of the room and retrieved a long case. He brought it back over to Xari and set it on the ground. Kneeling, he opened the case and folded back a corner of cloth.

Xari's eyes widened as Burin lifted a sheathed curved sword out of the case. He silently held it out to her, and she looked down at it. She hesitated, then grasped the hilt. It fit perfectly in her hand. Xari pulled the sword out of its sheath, running her fingers along the curve of the blade. Looking more closely, she saw the blade was engraved with tiny depictions of the twelve brethren. There she saw an eagle spreading its wings, an otter twisting its body around, a dragon surrounded by flame, a howling wolf, a unicorn with a beautiful long horn—

"Burin—" Xari's voice was choked, and her eyes blurred with tears.

"Here."

Xari blinked away her tears and saw that Burin was holding out another identical sword. "I couldn't send you off without swords, now could I? You need to practice, or you'll fall behind, and I'll spend six months trying to get you caught up again."

Xari let out a half-laugh, half-cry. "You couldn't have made these just last night."

"No, I've been working on them for a while. I finished them when you went off to see your friends last night," Burin explained. He closed the case and stood to his feet.

Xari threw her arms around him. "Thank you," she whispered.

Burin patted her gently on the back. "You're welcome, little one."

Half an hour later, Xari was ready to leave. She made it as far as the door before she stopped, turning back to Burin. "Be careful, all right?"

"You're telling me to be careful? You're about to travel clear to the other side of the Eastern Continent!"

"I'll be careful," Xari promised.

"Good. Because I expect to see you back here. You've yet to finish your training," Burin said, attempting to sound stern.

Xari saw through it and grinned at him.

Burin returned the grin. "Try not to take too long. Things will be far too quiet without you and Ashe around."

Xari experienced a wave of emotions—worry, sadness, and pride all at once. Resolve followed quickly as she realized that she needed to let go. She closed her eyes, knowing they were not her own emotions; they were Burin's. She hugged him tightly once more. "I'll come back." Her smile wavered. "You're the only family I have."

Burin had been more of a father to her than anyone had. He had told her once that it didn't matter she hadn't been born to him by blood; she was a daughter in his heart, and that was what mattered. He had even told her that since she didn't have a family name, she could have his. It had been the greatest gift anyone had ever given Xari. To have a name meant that she belonged to someone; it meant that she was no longer just Xari the orphan; she was Xari Oth'ilin, and she was loved and wanted.

"Hey!" Ashe said indignantly. "What am I, stuffed mushrooms?"

Xari made a face at him. "You know I love you, Asheford." Turning back to Burin, she took a deep breath. "Well, it's time to go."

"May the Master's hand guide and protect you," Burin said, pulling one of her braids.

Smiling, Xari straightened her pack, and she and Ashe started down the road toward the post.

5

When she reached Oriri, Xari was obliged to find a second boat, as the merchant's barge she'd first chosen had completed its northward trek. After two days of searching, she managed to find another going all the way to the base of the Northern Mountain Range, where the river nearest Montressa had its source. From there, Xari would have to walk for several days to get the rest of the way. Most of the journey was uneventful. Xari helped with what chores she could, and no one seemed to have any problems with her. It wasn't until they'd crossed the border from Threnphol into Merenth that anything noteworthy happened.

They docked about midmorning to exchange goods, and Xari took the opportunity to disembark and stretch her legs, though she didn't go far. When she returned almost two hours later and was about to board the boat again, she saw something that stopped her dead in her tracks. Fluttering several feet above the crowds, gold rays of sunshine flashing off of buzzing gossamer wings, was a fairy.

"Ashe!" Xari gasped and pointed. Ashe whirled in the air. When his sharp eyes spied Xari's discovery, they widened in surprise and then just as quickly narrowed.

"Jesper?" he murmured quizzically. Before Xari could move, let alone ask what he was talking about, he sped forward toward the fairy. By that time, the other one had seen them in return, and was quick to dash away, zipping between the shoulders of two people passing close to one another. He was temporarily lost from Xari's sight. She could only hope, as she hurried off after Ashe, that her guardian wouldn't lose him.

She wound her way through the people in the crowd, hoping she merely looked like another busy traveler who was late for an errand of business. It was difficult, though. The riverside docking area was crowded, heavy with trade, and the limit of her bond did not allow Ashe much freedom for pursuit, should she get held up behind.

She was rounding a corner booth stacked to the brim with potato cuttings ready to be planted when she finally heard them once more. The second fairy was making some kind of protesting cry, and her searching eyes found them just as Ashe caught up. She could now see that the other was a male. Ashe grabbed him by the arm, but just as he did, his captive made a final, valiant break for open air. His momentum carried them both headlong into the support strut of the awning protecting a potato seller's wares from the midday sun.

A corner of the awning came crashing down, and the impact caused several of the potatoes to go tumbling to the dusty street below. Xari, however, was more concerned about the sight the two struggling fairies were causing, trapped underneath the awning. Casting her thoughts about, she immediately went to the aid of the startled vegetable seller, helping him pick up his wayward merchandise, assuring him that not all of them were unsalvageable.

She tried enlisting the aid of some of the others about, though most of them were unwilling to leave their own wares for fear of theft. Hoping to make her presence less memorable, she even made a few quick, select purchases. Fresh bread would be a welcome change with their dinner anyway, she mused. By the time she'd finished all of this, Ashe had extricated himself and his new friend from the awning, and he watched her patiently until she finished, safely out of reach in the air near the first vendor's stall.

Xari stopped directly underneath them, and at this proximity, she could see that the other fairy looked horrified. She could also see that he looked much younger than Ashe. "Let me go, let me go, let me go!" he squealed, trying to pull his arm away.

"Settle down, Jesper!"

"You know him?" Xari asked, surprised.

"Of course I know him." Ashe dragged Jesper down until they were level with Xari's nose. "He was the worst troublemaker in my village."

"I was *not!*" Jesper exclaimed indignantly.

"Ashe, we need to get somewhere less crowded," Xari muttered, knowing from long experience that if she stood alone talking to herself for too long, people would begin to notice, no matter how much generous gold she'd paid them for vegetables and bread. She turned and headed to find a more secluded area. Ashe yanked Jesper along behind him, and Xari was almost positive he was using magic to keep him from escaping.

Xari stopped when she found a spot a bit down the river that didn't have a crowd. A single shop selling fishing supplies stood nearby, but it was closed for midday.

"You—can't—do this—to me!" Jesper grunted. "Let me go! The council will hear of this! You're a traitor! A traitor!" He was in the oddest position; Ashe was still gripping his arm, and he had twisted so he was facing away from Ashe. He looked as if he were trying to dive into the air. His wings were buzzing, but he wasn't going anywhere. After a long moment, he gave up trying that approach, and flailed his legs, arms, and wings frantically.

"We just want to talk," Xari said soothingly.

Jesper stopped throwing himself around and looked at Xari. "Talk!? You just want to *talk?* If you can see me, then you must be the—" here Jesper lowered his voice to a mere whisper, sounding even more horrified than he looked "—the speaker that Magi Asheford awakened!" He shot a look of venom at Ashe.

"Yes, I am a speaker, but it's not what you think," Xari replied.

"Not what I think!? I think Magi Asheford is a thief!" Jesper gasped. "And I think that he betrayed all of my people!" He wriggled in Ashe's grip once more. "Let me go!"

"If we let you go, will you stay here and talk with us?" Xari asked.

Jesper froze again, and paused. "Yes," he said after a moment.

Xari probed him with her gift and found that he was so frightened and in such turmoil that he would likely take off in an instant. She sighed. "He'll fly off as soon as you let him go, Ashe. Listen—Jesper, is it?—if you would listen to Ashe's side of the story, you might not think him a traitor."

"Ha!" Jesper glared fiercely at Xari. He seemed to have given up on fighting, and was doing his best to look unafraid, though Xari could feel his tension.

"If you'll allow me, Xari," Ashe said quietly. "Jesper, do you remember what I always told you sprouts about hearing the Master's voice?"

"You said a lot of things." Jesper sounded grudging, as if it was against his better judgment to answer. Then he glared angrily. "Not that anyone thinks about what you said anymore!" he said hotly. "Not since you ran away!"

Xari resisted the urge to grab the little fairy out of the air and give him a good shake. Jesper had no idea what Ashe had been through because of his decision, including long years of painful separation from the home and people he loved. He had no idea of the sacrifices Ashe had made—for his people, for the world, for Xari herself. She pressed her lips tightly together and strained to keep her temper in check.

"Jesper," Ashe continued with patience, "I have always told you that we have to keep our hearts open. Our people are very gifted, and we can be very wise at times, but we can also be very blind and foolish."

"You went against the council's wishes!" Jesper protested.

"And for that I am sorry, but there is a higher authority than the Grand Magi council!" Ashe sighed. "You've known me your entire life. I may have gone against them, but do you honestly believe that makes my decision to awaken Xari evil? I believe I made the right choice. What you choose to believe is entirely up to you."

"Ashe, the boat is going to be leaving," Xari spoke up. She wanted to know what was going on with this wayward sprout, but she had a mission to focus on. "You may see for yourself that Ashe speaks the truth," she added, speaking to Jesper. "We're heading north."

"We could also discuss just what you are doing so far from home," Ashe said pointedly.

Jesper twisted in the air rather guiltily. "Um—er—well, I'm lost."

"Lost?" Xari echoed.

Jesper sighed. "It's a long story." He still looked hesitant, but after looking back and forth between Xari and Ashe for a moment, finally sighed again. "I'll come with you—but just to talk. I have to find Flute."

"Flute," Ashe muttered. "I might have known."

"Who's Flute?" Xari asked.

"*She's* the worst troublemaker in my village," Jesper said, sounding half-proud and half-exasperated. "She's my best friend."

"I see."

"And what does Flute have to do with any of this?" Ashe asked.

"We need to get back to the boat," Xari reminded him. "Why don't we talk there?" She had a feeling this journey had just become a good deal more interesting.

⌘ ⌘ ⌘

Anathriel had been spending a few days with her father, but was now relieved to be returning to her duties in the palace. Home hardly felt like home these days. She was so rarely there.

As soon as she stepped through the front gates of the palace she made note of how much busier everything seemed since she had gone. Spring was a busy time of year for the court of Par Auspré. The opening of the mountain passes brought all manner of fresh trade and more news than the Windriders alone could bring.

She proceeded towards the banquet chamber, where she knew the lord and lady would be taking their morning meal. True to form, the hall was abuzz with activity when she arrived. Servants rushed to and fro, setting out breakfast dishes, while the courtiers chatted and gossiped over their meals. At the head of the great table, Lord and Lady Kavela sat together, and with them was Lord Darius Mortén, back once again from his home in faraway Réol.

Springtime also brought visitors to court, those few Montressa received. Of all their visitors, however, none was as persistent or perplexing as this mysterious southern lord. Réol was very far away indeed, but Mortén had been making a journey to their city nearly every year since Anathriel had come to Par Auspré. He had an inexplicable fascination with the eyries, one that bordered on eccentric.

He was a tall man, just beginning to show signs of age. His hair was cut short and neat, graying at the temples, and he was dressed in dark, heavy velvets. No doubt he found it unseasonably cold in Montressa; most visitors did. Anathriel found herself wishing he had finished his meal before she'd arrived. She really wasn't fond of the man, for reasons that were difficult to explain. While he was polite and genteel enough on the surface, he always struck her as patronizing and underhanded beneath, as though he were concealing a great secret.

As if the situation weren't awkward enough, Immen was standing at attention next to one of Lord Jassene's bodyguards behind the noble trio. Undoubtedly he had come to make his daily report of Windrider matters, but it seemed he was being forced to wait. His eyes were fixed resolutely ahead, yet Anathriel had no doubt he was aware of everything going on in the room.

Anathriel wasn't sure if she really wanted to be in Immen's vicinity just now. She'd been doing her best to avoid him as much as possible since the Festival of Winds, though he had never said or done anything that might embarrass her in public. Still, it wasn't easy to encounter him in the course of their respective duties and carry on as though their awkward encounter had never taken place.

However, there was nothing for it. She had to report back to her mistress before anything else. Lady Rillandra smiled as Anathriel stopped before them, curtseying gracefully. "Welcome back, my dear. Did you enjoy yourself?"

"I did, my lady, thank you," Anathriel lied. In reality, she'd seen very little of her father, and loneliness had made her anxious to get back to Par Auspré and her friends.

"You remember Lord Mortén, of course?" the lady continued, making a graceful gesture to the man on the other side of her husband.

Anathriel made another curtsey. "Of course. Good morning, my lord. Welcome again to Montressa."

Mortén leaned back in his seat and nodded at her with a smile. "As beautiful as ever, Anathriel. Another year and yet unmarried?"

Anathriel gritted her teeth before forcing her lips into a smile and concentrated very hard on not looking at Immen, standing only six feet away. "That is correct, my lord. I suppose the time is not yet right." She paused and couldn't resist adding, "Although I might ask the same question of you."

Mortén's booming laughter filled the banquet hall, causing a few people nearby to glance over curiously before returning to their breakfast. "It seems there is no lady in my realm willing to put up with me on a permanent basis. In your case, however, I daresay the reason is that there is simply no one deserving of you, my dear," said Mortén with a smile.

"You flatter me, my lord," Anathriel said calmly as Lord and Lady Kavela chuckled.

"Look at her, Rillandra," said Mortén, eyeing Anathriel specu-latively. "I think she's determined to be a maiden forever."

Anathriel's cheeks flamed, and Lady Rillandra regarded Mortén with an expression of mild disapproval, so brief Anathriel barely caught it. Then her features smoothed again. She looked back at Anathriel with a small, knowing smile. "Anathriel knows her own mind, I'm sure."

"I'm sure that when Anathriel does marry," said Lord Jassene, "my wife will miss her most keenly."

"No doubt, no doubt," agreed Mortén, glancing at Anathriel again. "She is unique."

"All of my girls are special," injected Lady Rillandra. "And though I feel none of them could be replaced, they are indeed always coming and going. Just this afternoon Jassene and I shall be considering a new young lady to fill a position that will soon be open here in the palace."

One of Anathriel's friends, Sedaille, was going to be married shortly, so it was common knowledge that a position was available, but Anathriel hadn't realized Lady Rillandra had progressed this far in getting it filled. To Anathriel's surprise, Lady Rillandra glanced back at Immen. "As a matter of fact, she is the younger sister of our newly appointed Captain Corper. This is an excellent opportunity for her."

Anathriel froze, a sudden wave of surprise coursing through her at these words. Immen Corper had a sister? It was a possibility she'd never even considered. The Festival of Winds was an important occasion for family; was it possible the girl in the courtyard could have been this relation? Furiously, she flew back in her memory to that horrible moment. It was not difficult to picture it again, for it hadn't exactly been easy to forget.

As she recalled the expressions of fondness that Immen and the girl had been sharing, she realized that they certainly could have been attributed to brotherly and sisterly affection. Still, Anathriel did not want to jump to conclusions. For one thing, if it was true, it still left the question of who had given him a favor to wear for the festivities, and she'd just begun to resign herself to the fact that Immen was firmly and irreversibly in love with some stranger. Yet the possibility was taunting.

Anathriel brought her attention back to the conversation before her. She wasn't about to overreact in such a silly manner to one little offhand comment.

"Ah, yes," said Mortén. He shifted in his chair to look at Immen with interest. "Captain Corper. How long have you been assigned to this post?"

Immen glanced at Lord Jassene for a moment before replying. "Seven weeks, my lord."

"Jassene tells me nothing but good things of you. I must confess, I'm most eager to hear it, for my interest in your eyries is no secret in Montressa."

"I am aware, my lord."

"Perhaps you'd be willing to take me on a tour? I have not yet had a chance to see the improvements made to the facilities since my donation last year."

Immen looked to Jassene again before nodding. "Certainly you of all people have a right to see them, my lord. I will advise you when it will be a good time."

Anathriel noted with some satisfaction that Immen did not seem to want to indulge Mortén's silly quirks any more than she did. At least they had *something* in common. Thankfully, Lady Rillandra saved Anathriel from any further idling with the man.

"Anathriel, have you breakfasted?"

"At my father's, yes, my lady."

"Very well. I would like you to attend to Taryn this morning. She awoke quite ill; I want someone watching over her today."

"As you wish, my lady." Anathriel turned heel and left them to their conversation. Heading out the door, she briefly met Immen's gaze. His expression was unreadable, and he soon averted it.

When she was safe and clear of the banquet hall she let out a long, relieved sigh. Then her thoughts turned once again to her new discovery. The news about Immen's sister was far more interesting to her than anything Lord Mortén had to do or say.

What if the girl she'd seen *was* his sister? It would be easy to find out. All she had to do was get a glimpse of the girl during the interview this evening, and she would know whether or not she was the same one. But that still didn't answer the question of what Anathriel should do if it was true. She was beginning to be sick of all this double guessing, but she still wanted to marry Immen very badly.

Anathriel frowned. If it was the same girl, she decided, then tomorrow she would track him down. She would confront him. She would ask him outright whether or not he wanted her. Then, either way, she would be done with him. After all, if the paré would not let her have

60

him, she would have to start trying to find someone else as soon as possible, before Anathriel Lelaine became the oldest handmaiden in living memory, as well as having been the youngest.

6

When Flute had been a small sprout, she'd often dreamed up stories in her head about adventures in other parts of the world, of guardian fairies that saw things and went places and did great deeds with their speakers. The adventures had been exciting, full of dangers and rescues and thrilling victories over evil.

So far, the only evil she'd defeated, if it could be called that, had been a swarm of large, black beetles that had chased her after she'd inadvertently flown straight into their secluded hive. Even that hadn't been any cleverness on her part, but another instance of her magic going berserk. As she had once done to her fellow sprouts, the entire swarm of beetles suddenly disappeared entirely. This had been a good thing for Flute, but she was a little bit worried about where she'd sent the beetles, and any unfortunate souls who happened to be on the other end.

All in all, the journey had not been very fun. Rather, it had been in turns both boring and exhausting. Flute flew hard, wanting to get so far away that anybody the council sent after her would not be able to catch up. She wanted to reach Immen Corper before any other fairy entourage did. Unfortunately, her inexperienced little wings were not used to long-range flying. As such, she was forced to take long breaks. Sometimes she tried to walk, as the humans did, upon the ground, but this idea was sometimes almost laughable, particularly in the high grasslands she crossed over, which some called the Plains of Urhil.

Next had come a vast stretch of moorlands, full of bogs and noisy nightlife. It had been hard to find places to sleep there, and Flute had missed her nest very much. She continued to miss it as the days grew longer and longer. Indeed, the moon had gone through its changes one and a half times before she finally beheld the mountains in the distance that were her destination. That had been a happy and relieving moment, until a few hours later, when they hadn't seemed any closer, and she'd come to realize exactly how far away they still were. For many long days and hours, they were nothing but a mirage in the distance, taunting her with the promise of proximity.

It wasn't until six days after Flute first saw the great northern mountains that she actually reached them. Now she hovered in the crown of a lone tree, gazing upon a human village settled at the foot of the first mountain. Having gotten this far, she was somewhat at a loss for what to do next. *Eagles,* she reminded herself firmly. *I'm looking for eagles.* The eagles would have nests in the tops of the mountains, she reasoned. Flute craned her neck back, staring up at the imposing peaks above her. She'd never flown so high before. And how would she know where to go once she got there?

Flute gazed back at the village longingly. She was incredibly tired; perhaps it would be wisest to delay her journey until she'd had some rest. And some food. She hadn't eaten much besides wild raspberries in the last few days, and it would be nice to find something new. Perhaps there would be something in this village she'd never eaten at all before! Besides, it was getting dark. If there really were eagles up there, she didn't want to be flying around in the dark, when they might mistake her for a midnight snack.

Her mind made up, Flute made sure she was invisible, then darted out of her hiding place and headed towards the village. Once there, she was completely enraptured by a myriad of new sights and sounds. Flute had very rarely ever seen a human, and when she had it was usually one or two of them alone, passing through the forest, unaware of the unseen eyes all around them. Here, she saw all sorts of humans, of all shapes and sizes all around her. Some, in very loud voices, were calling good nights to one another from across the streets. Some were chatting amicably to one another as they walked. Some walked alone, intent and focused on their own errands and agendas. Flute spied one pretty human girl walking hand in hand with a boy, both with dreamy expressions. This Flute found puzzling, but she didn't dwell on it long.

Of most fascination to her were the human sprouts, for these she'd never seen at all. Old Henna had told her that human sprouts had to be watched and taken care of all the time, that they couldn't sit or walk or do anything for themselves; they only ever cried and ate. Flute could never understand why anyone would want a human sprout if that were true. Fairy sprouts couldn't talk for a while when they were first born, but at least they could *fly*.

Watching the humans more closely, however, she realized old Henna must have been speaking only of just-born sprouts. Like fairy sprouts, they seemed to come in a variety of sizes, and while it was true that the very littlest ones weren't doing anything exciting, some of the medium ones, and even some of the bigger ones were laughing and playing games. Flute enjoyed watching the latter very much, recognizing many games that weren't all that different from what she and Jesper played with their friends.

The evening grew progressively darker, but it was a lazy, pleasant sort of evening. In the shadow of the mountains, the village was sheltered, and the grass there grew thick, cool, and dark. Flute would probably have no trouble finding something for a nest tonight. She watched stars peep on the horizon to the south and gave a contented sigh, feeling truly peaceful for the first time since she'd left Westfern village.

Eventually, most of the humans disappeared from the streets and paths, and Flute, too excited yet to go to sleep, observed what she could of them through open windows and doors. She learned that humans did not sleep in nests at all, but some slept on the ground, and some on platforms above the ground with soft coverings. Mostly it was the little ones that were asleep now, anyway. Some curled up in a proper sleeping position, but many of them slept stretched out as straight as a tree-branch, which Flute thought looked decidedly uncomfortable.

She also learned that human cooking tasted very nice indeed—except for something she heard one woman call *ham*. She didn't like that very well. As she'd hoped, however, there was a lot of good fruit she'd never tried before, and also something very soft, yellow-white, and slippery that the humans put on their bread, and that tasted so rich and sweet Flute was sure one of the elders would have chastened her harshly for even trying it in the first place.

She learned that dogs could sense fairies, even if they couldn't see them, much like the beetles she'd encountered. Every time she came to a house that had one, it would start barking and snapping loudly, to the confusion of its poor owners. One of the dogs nearly nipped Flute's heels off before she had the sense to get away, and she at last began to check for the annoying creatures before she went into a home, choosing only to visit those with no dogs.

At last even most of the big humans began to go to sleep, and Flute realized that if she wanted to get a good start up the mountain in the morning that she had better do the same. She headed towards the far north end of the village, where a strong mountain stream was tumbling over itself, bordered by many good-sized trees, which looked like a promising place for a comfortable nest. She had not yet reached her destination, however, when she noticed something very odd that she had not seen before. She paused, glancing at it curiously, and flew down for a closer look.

A large clear space was covered with flat wood not far from the stream, and in the middle was the oddest shape of metal that Flute had ever seen. It was round like a tree trunk, and thick enough that it would take at least four fairies to reach all the way around it, and smooth of any branches or knotholes. It rose from the wooden surface for a bit before it bent sharply to one side, so that most of it was going in the same direction as the ground beneath it. Flute flew around this strange contraption three times, more puzzled each time she surveyed it. What was it doing in the middle of a village? What was it for? It didn't seem to be *doing* anything. Just sitting there.

Off to the side was a building with words over the top of the door, but this did not help Flute, because she could not read human writing. A light was spilling from a small, square window beside the building's door, and she flew to it curiously to peer inside. There she saw a very skinny man, asleep with his head on a table—Flute had learned the word *table* in her exploration of the village—snoring so loudly that Flute could hear him easily through the open window. She giggled. His face reminded her of Magi Heath.

Flute frowned suddenly, realizing how much she missed Jesper. She'd never been apart from her best friend this long before. Come to think of it, she hadn't been apart from *anyone* she knew for this long. She even missed Elder Hawthorne a little bit, even though she knew he was probably very angry with her right now.

Feeling strangely lonely, Flute backed slowly away from the window of the building, leaving the mystery of the strange bent metal tree trunk for another night. Sudden weariness was overcoming her, and she decided that maybe it was too far to go even to the stream tonight.

Glancing down, she saw thick untrimmed clusters of that dark grass she'd been admiring earlier lodged against the corners of the building. With a smile, she fluttered down to one, and found that it was just the right size for a very soft and handsome nest indeed. She burrowed into the grass, curled up with an exhausted yawn, and fell asleep.

⌘ ⌘ ⌘

The morning and afternoon of Anathriel's return to Par Auspré were spent with a very sick Taryn, which turned out to be a rather uneventful task, as the young girl was asleep almost the entire time. Lady Rillandra's healer came to check on her every once in a while. Anathriel spent most of her time experimenting with thread colors for a new embroidery piece and talking to Taryn during the few times she was awake. At last, late in the afternoon, Taryn's fever broke and Lady Rillandra sent Rylli to overtake the vigil. Anathriel refreshed herself, put on one of her best gowns to help fortify her courage, and headed back downstairs to find her lady.

She was stopped by a member of the guard before she entered the reception hall. "Not yet, Miss Lelaine," he said calmly. "They're doing an interview."

He hadn't needed to elaborate. As it had been for Anathriel's own interview, Lord and Lady Kavela greeted all handmaiden candidates alone, with only guard members present outside the doors. Anathriel wasn't sure of the reason for this practice, except she supposed it might have made the hopeful girl in question more nervous if she'd been in the presence of actual handmaidens. It didn't really matter, though. Anathriel only needed to wait in the corridor outside for the interview to be over.

She didn't end up waiting alone. Lost in thought, the arrival of a newcomer took her by surprise.

"Are we banished, then?"

Anathriel stood up abruptly. "My Lord Mortén," she said quickly, bowing her head slightly.

"Sit down, lass," he said calmly. Though his voice was gentle, Anathriel was surprised by the automatic manner with which she complied. He seemed oddly distracted. "May I join you?" he asked, indicating a small chair not far from hers.

Slowly, Anathriel nodded, and together they waited in the silence. She folded her hands in her lap as he sat, wishing she'd brought her needlework to hold her attention.

Mortén didn't say anything for a long time. He must have been awaiting the end of the interview, as well, and not sitting there simply because she was. Before long, however, his brooding silence began to make her more nervous than his usual outgoing behavior, if only because it seemed so oddly out of character. He mostly stared straight ahead, eyes focused on something that perhaps only he could see, lost in inward thoughts. Whatever he was thinking on was something captivating, for he seemed to forget she was even there.

When she could bear the eerie quiet no longer, she finally broke it of her own accord. "How are you enjoying your time in Par Auspré this season, my lord?"

He glanced at her, almost surprised, before his features reverted into their usual appearance of jovial affability. "Very much. I look forward to this time of year almost more than any other."

"What is it about our eyries that interests you so?" Anathriel asked. This question had long puzzled her, for though she knew the eyries to be both unique and central to Montressa's way of life, she'd never seen them as anything worth making a long journey across countries to come and see, particularly on an annual basis.

"Not the eyries," he amended lazily, reaching up to hook a finger in the iron curl of a sconce above his head. "It is the eagles I come to see. I find them of particular interest. Magnificent creatures, aren't they?" He ran his thumb along the metal absentmindedly, and once again, Anathriel got the impression he hardly noticed or cared she was there.

Still, she didn't want him to revert back to his previous introvert manner. "Many have used that word to describe them," she said, shrugging, feeling suddenly cranky. "Myself, I've never seen them as anything more than what they are. Strong, useful beasts."

At this, Mortén did look at her, his eyes briefly flashing something between contempt and amusement. "You don't find their intelligence to be singular?"

"Captain Corper does, but I believe he's biased."

"Ah, yes. Captain Corper." Mortén glanced at the closed doors nearby, still flanked by attentive guards. "He's due to take me on that promised tour. I've come by to remind him."

Anathriel set her chin and hardened her eyes. "Captain Corper does not forget promises, Lord Mortén," she said sharply.

Mortén looked back at her, surprised. "Well, well. That was somewhat a passionate response, my dear." He cocked his head at her and laughed quietly. "So I see," he said, almost to himself. Then he shrugged dismissively before turning his attention once more on the closed doorways.

"As you heard this morning," Anathriel said stiffly, "Lord and Lady Kavela are interviewing the captain's sister just now. I've no doubt he will wish to escort her back home when the interview is complete. I'm afraid you shall not likely get your tour this evening."

"Perhaps I may just get permission to go on my own."

Anathriel highly doubted this but did not press the issue. Just then the doors to the reception chamber finally opened, and both she and Mortén rose to their feet and headed inside. It was several paces to the end of the hall where the small conference had been gathered, but Anathriel's eyes instantly sought out and spotted the young woman at Immen's side.

Numbly, Anathriel tried to keep from staring. It was the same girl Anathriel had seen in the street during the Festival of Winds. For a few moments she couldn't decide if she was more shocked, hurt, or angry.

"Welcome, Lord Mortén, Anathriel," called Lord Jassene from his seat, where he was standing up.

Lady Kavela also stood up with a smile. "Anathriel," she said kindly, taking a couple of steps down from the dais and extending her hand warmly. When Anathriel reached her, she accepted the hand, curtseying as she did so. "I am very pleased to introduce to you the captain's sister, Areen Corper. She will soon be joining us here in Par Auspré." She placed her free hand on the other girl's shoulder and smiled.

"A pleasure to meet you, Miss Corper," Anathriel mumbled.

All she could do was sit and stare dumbly as the girl smiled prettily and replied, "And you as well. Please, call me Areen."

Immen was gazing with fondness and pride at Areen; the same expression that he'd given her on the first day, and the affection there was so strong that Anathriel felt justified in her previous assumptions. Anathriel thought about the favor Immen had promised to wear to the festival. *This* girl's favor.

The inner battle within Anathriel ceased, and anger emerged victorious. Anathriel was no fool. She could tell when she had been deliberately hoodwinked, and Immen Corper had obviously sidestepped her in this matter. How dare he mislead her like that?

Distantly, she noted that Lord Mortén was requesting Immen's time for a private word outside in the corridor. The two men walked off together, leaving Anathriel alone and feeling very awkward in Areen Corper's presence. She coughed a little and turned to Lady Rillandra. "My lady, I'm pleased to inform you that Taryn appears to be recovering from her sickness."

The lady gave a relieved smile. "That is excellent news. I should go and check on her. I presume," she said, gathering her skirt in one hand, "someone is with her now?"

"Rylli, my lady. She took over the watch so I might come inform you."

"Very well. Would you be so kind as to remain with Areen here until her brother is ready to escort her home?"

"Certainly," Anathriel replied, though it was the last thing she wanted to do.

Somehow, the two girls kept up a steady stream of trivial conversation as they headed towards the door and back out into the corridor. Anathriel hoped that Mortén wouldn't demand too much of Immen's time so she might have a chance to get away soon. As they approached the door, however, both girls paused in surprise to hear muffled sounds of what seemed like a very heated argument taking place between the two men. They exchanged bewildered glances with each other before Immen burst into the room without warning. Anathriel glanced out into the corridor behind him but could see no trace of Mortén beyond.

Immen took a deep breath to compose himself before looking at the two girls. "Are you ready, Areen?" he asked quietly.

His sister peered at him closely before nodding. "Yes, Immen, thank you." She turned to Anathriel. "It was a pleasure to meet you, Anathriel. Good night."

Immen also gave her a curt bow. "Good night, Miss Lelaine."

Anathriel watched them leave, grateful he hadn't expected a reply. She was still full of hurt and anger towards him, and she wasn't yet prepared enough to call him to account for his actions, though she had every intention of doing so soon enough.

Anathriel headed in the opposite direction than that of Immen and Areen, further into the palace itself. It would soon be time for the ladies to convene for their evening needlework and conversation, though she'd never understood why Lady Rillandra liked to do this in the evenings when the lighting was so poor. Still, Anathriel had little say in the matter.

She hadn't taken two steps when she heard furious swearing in a male voice coming from not too far ahead. She paused, recognizing the voice as Lord Mortén's. It seemed to be coming from the small alcove where the two of them had been waiting together a little while before. She could see their seats from where she stood but could not see Mortén. Instinct held back Anathriel's progress. She wasn't sure she liked the idea of intruding upon such an angry man, and she retreated slightly for good measure. A moment later, there was very strange noise, like a loud crack, followed by what sounded like something heavy and metal being thrown to the stone floor with a clang. Very puzzled and more than a little frightened, Anathriel waited until she heard Mortén's voice and footsteps fading away before she proceeded.

When she passed the little alcove, she noticed that the sconce Mortén had been fingering earlier had been torn from the wall and was now lying on the ground in two pieces, as if someone had snapped it like a tree branch. This bizarre sight filled her with considerable unease. Cautiously, looking around to make sure she was unobserved, Anathriel knelt down and picked up the two pieces, studying them with trepidation.

She looked worriedly in the direction Mortén had gone. How could he possibly have managed such an unnatural thing?

Between the sconce and the matter of Immen, she did not sleep very well that night.

7

Flute was jarred from her sleep by something very loud and very close. With a gasp and a start, she sprang out of her burrow of grass, only to be met by an onslaught of brilliant morning sunshine. She instantly closed her eyes. As such, she didn't see the windowsill that had been just over her sleeping place and flew straight up against it, hitting her head hard.

"Ow!" Flute cried, clutching the injured crown of her head through its cap of feathers. Only then did she remember where she was. Her eyes snapped open, already adjusting to the light, and she looked around quickly. Then the sound that had awakened her repeated itself, and when Flute saw its source, she forgot everything else, hurt head and all.

It was a great, piercing scream, a cry from above. Descending towards her was a beautiful golden eagle, easily the largest bird Flute had ever seen. She gasped at its speed as it soared before her, and almost before she realized it, the eagle had landed. Even more surprising, it landed on the strange bent metal tree trunk she'd been wondering about the night before.

Of course, she thought amazedly. *It's a perch.* She noticed appreciatively how it was just the right width for the grip of the eagle's claws, and how strong it would need to be to support the great bird's weight.

The eagle nestled his wings to his sides as he found a settled position on the perch. Only when he'd stopped altogether did Flute notice the young man climbing off the eagle's back. He was dressed in red and gray, and some papers were sticking out of a bag over his shoulder. When his feet hit the ground, the young man pushed something from his eyes that had been covering them, and put them up on his forehead. Then he shook his hair a little, patted the eagle fondly, and began walking towards the small building.

"Good morning, Regen!" The sound of a voice close by made Flute jump again. She hovered around the corner and peered at the door of the building. The skinny man who looked like Magi Heath was wide awake now, waving with a smile at the young man approaching.

"Good morning, Veris," greeted the one called Regen in return. "Are you feeling better? I missed you last week."

"It's strange how I suffer less from a sour stomach when my wife is not at home," the man called Veris replied.

Regen laughed as he approached the doorway, and together they stepped inside.

Flute zoomed back around the corner and dashed into the window.

"Is it the cooking or the wife herself?" Regen wondered, sitting heavily in a chair across from the table where the skinny man had been sleeping the night before.

"You, sir, have no wife, so I don't think you're the one to be asking me," said Veris, making a sour face, which caused Regen to laugh yet again.

"Still unmarried and safe," he confirmed. "Do you have any dispatches?" he asked, straightening in his chair and eyeing the papers scattered across the skinny man's table.

"Plenty," Veris said, waving his hand at the mess. "All this and two bags more besides. This is the busiest time of year for news."

"You should see the mail coming in from the northern villages," Regen said with a nod.

"Do you often get assignments up that far north?"

"I used to," Regen said. He stood up and began helping Veris gather the papers off the desk. "But I think Captain Corper knows I prefer the southern runs to the northern, so he lets me have them. Good man," he added thoughtfully.

At the mention of "Corper," Flute paid even closer attention to what the men were saying.

"Of course," Regen added, "I'd like to get out of the mountains altogether. Take Eulaie and see other parts of the continent. Maybe even go as far as Threnphol and the coast." He sighed and shook his head sadly. "But you know how that is. My family would never stand for it. They say it's too dangerous." He rolled his eyes. "As if riding thousands of feet above the ground on an eagle's back wasn't dangerous already."

"You heading back to Montressa, then?"

72

"Yes, as soon as we're finished here," Regen said. "I spent the night up in Pensa, and the captain's expecting me back as early as tomorrow, so I really shouldn't waste any time."

Flute licked her lips eagerly. He was returning to the captain. The captain named Corper. What a fortunate chance!

She left the men to discuss their dispatches—which really held little interest for her—and went back out of the building to look at the eagle again. He was still on the perch, his eyes closed almost lazily, but there was no sign of relaxation in the way he held himself with powerful pride and dignity. Suddenly, Flute was overcome with the magnitude of what she was seeing. This was a great eagle, one of the twelve brethren! One of the ones the Master had chosen above all other creatures in the world, and endowed with thoughts and wisdom. She suddenly felt very small.

Unbidden came the memory of something Asheford had said, long ago, before he'd disappeared from the village. He was angry that the great eagles were treated as dumb beasts of labor. Flute stared at the beautiful eagle, waiting patiently and obediently on the perch, and she too was filled with anger. The humans had no right to do that to him—treat him as if he were some common horse or mule!

She willed herself to calm down, remembering that her goal on this adventure was to eventually help change all that. The thought was sobering, and it did serve to soothe her. Yes, she wanted to help the eagles and all the other brethren regain their proper place in the world, but to do that she was going to have to find Immen Corper, and to do *that*, she was somehow going to have to hitch a ride on this eagle. She wasn't nearly fast enough of a flyer to follow him.

The problem, however, was how to go about it. She knew from the old stories and her history lessons that the eagle would be able to see her, even if she was invisible to humans, so how to get to him without him knowing? She would have to sneak up from straight behind him, she decided. Most birds had a very wide range of sight to either side of them, but they were blind in the back.

Flute cut herself a large swath of space in her circuit, flying almost all the way to the stream before she began to circle back towards the great eagle, coming up upon his broad gold back. Her stomach curdled nervously inside her. What if he turned his head? Would she know what she was if he saw her? Or would he think she was something good to eat?

She gulped. Hopefully the former, but she had to take the chance. Hopefully he wouldn't see her at all.

When she was close enough to touch the eagle, almost paralyzed with fear, she began studying the strange human devices strapped to the eagle's back, looking for a comfortable place to hide. Just then, Veris and the eagle-rider named Regen emerged from the small building, still chatting, their arms laden with rolled-up papers.

Flute paused, hovering slowly in place. The two men walked around to the far side of the eagle and began stuffing the papers into a large satchel, which Flute had not noticed before. Quick as a flash, as the eagle-rider put in the last batch of papers, she dashed inside it and watched the flap close over her head.

Well, now you're really in for it, Flute, she thought, taking a deep breath. *If this is wrong, then you might not be able to find the way back.*

There was no chance of changing her mind, though. A few moments later she felt the thrust of powerful wings beneath her, making her hiding place rock and shift, fairy and all. There was a sort of jolt, and Flute realized that the eagle had taken off. They were flying.

It wasn't long before Flute discovered that this mode of travel was far from fun. The sack itself was stuffed full of rolled papers, which kept poking her in uncomfortable ways and didn't leave her much room to maneuver. To make matters worse, about half an hour into the flight it started to rain heavily, something that caught her by surprise, considering how sunny it had been when they'd taken off.

Flute usually enjoyed rain, but that was when she could fly freely through it, feeling the raindrops splash on her face and breathing in the freshness of the washed earth and trees all around her. She did *not* enjoy being stuck in a dark, cramped space while being incessantly dripped on. The sack itself seemed to have been oiled to protect the documents within, so she avoided the openings as best she could, but to little avail. It also seemed to be colder here than she was accustomed to, and the combination of cold and dripping made her very miserable.

A familiar heave, which Flute had come to recognize as the great eagle beating its wings, shook her hiding place. It jostled her up against the top of the thick sack and then gracelessly back down on top of the papers again, where she slipped and slid into a damp corner. The impact caused a shower of collected rainwater from the outside, plastering her head with dampness. Instead of absorbing the moisture, as a human's hair might have done, the water slid right off of Flute's feathers and down her face and back.

"That is *it*," Flute whispered fiercely. "I can't fly just now, but surely I can do something to get warm." She struggled to a halfway sitting position with a grunt and closed her eyes. "What was the spell for heat again?" she wondered aloud. She concentrated. Elder Osprey had taught this lesson to all the sprouts her age, including herself and Jesper, only seventeen days before she'd left Fairlight Forest. Ignoring the little voice in her head that tried to remind her she hadn't really managed to succeed with the spell during the lesson, Flute tried to remember the exact technique.

"The Master's materials are in all of us," she heard the voice of Elder Osprey saying. "All magic in the world is from him, and the fairies are charged to care for the magic of the earth. The things you see and touch. The wind, the sunlight, the force of a river or a stream."

"But Elder Osprey, how can we be as powerful as a river?" asked Whisper skeptically.

"Patience," said the Elder with a smile.

As if that were any kind of answer, Flute reflected, shaking her head. Why must the elders always insist on being so cryptic and superior? She sighed and went back to trying to remember his words about the heat spell.

"You have all learned much about your magic," he said. "You know that you are made up of the Master's material. Light, water—" He paused and looked carefully at one or two of them before adding, "Fire."

There was a quiet but collective gasp from the gathered sprouts. "We're going to learn a fire spell?" Jesper asked eagerly. His wings fluttered rapidly, causing him to raise a small space from the grass clearing where they were gathered. Flute pulled him back down with a gentle tug on his coat and a laugh.

"Yes, Jesper, it is finally time. The council has decided you are ready. But don't get too excited; the spell itself is nothing especially spectacular." He chuckled. "Just a little something to help warm the bones on occasion, which," he added, "at my age is sometimes appreciated.

"The fire inside you," continued Elder Osprey, "is very difficult to find at first. It is in pieces so small you would never see them if you did not know to look for them. Most of us, however, eventually find it in our hearts. There you will see it with your inside eyes. Concentrate. When you find the fire, imagine that you are pulling it through your bones as if they were veins. But only a little bit. Only a strand no larger than a cat's hair. You do not want to burn yourself up, yes?" He chuckled again.

"Can we *really* burn ourselves up with our heartfire, Elder Osprey?" asked Whisper.

"No, but you can make yourself unconscious or do any other number of unforeseen things if you handle too much of it."

Flute licked her lips and took a deep breath, once more positioning herself on the rolls of paper, trying to get to the best possible position before she tried this. "In my heart," she recited to herself. She turned her mind's eye inward, as she had learned to do many years ago. Young sprouts knew water spells aplenty, as the water inside all the Master's creatures was very easy to find. Fire, though—as Elder Osprey had said, she would have been skeptical such a thing was even there, had not every fairy before insisted that it was and that they had once shared her disbelief, and that she would find it if she kept trying.

Heartfire. It meant so much more than just the Master's element inside of her. It was a symbol—a thing of special reverence among the fairy kindred. Sometimes it took years to find one's heartfire. Flute had heard people say this was because it was smaller in some fairies than in others, but Asheford had used to say that maybe it was because in some the heartfire burned brighter than in others—so bright that it was not immediately recognized for what it was. She didn't necessarily want to believe in things Asheford had believed in, but she rather liked the idea of her heartfire being brighter, as opposed to being smaller, because she was having trouble finding it.

Elder Hawthorne had scoffed at this idea after Asheford had gone away. "Brighter indeed," he had said, darkly. "He fancies his heartfire so bright that he thinks himself above even the Master's will, I wager." Nobody ever spoke of Asheford or his ideas much anymore, though it wasn't strictly forbidden. But Flute remembered. She remembered many things.

It probably was small, her heartfire. After all, she was a naughty fairy, who disobeyed her elders and did things such as go on adventures without the council's approval. But she wanted to help so very badly, and she was afraid that by the time she was old enough, things would be over and all chances for helping or adventures would be gone.

For several minutes, Flute searched her heart with her magical eye, as she'd learned to do with the rest of her body many years ago. She did her best to be patient, and concentrate, and go slowly, but after several minutes she still found nothing. She was just about ready to give up and try again later, when she realized that if she wanted to be a guardian, she was going to have to learn to do this eventually. Guardians had been very strong in magic, some of the strongest of all fairies. Only Grand Magi were stronger, it was said. Flute was certainly nowhere near strong enough to be a guardian, at least traditionally. If she was going to prove to the council that she truly had the potential, she'd best be persistent in her studies, no matter how frustrating.

Flute sighed and settled down to try again. She listened to the rain pattering against the side of the oil-skinned sack. It was a pleasant sound, despite her less than comfortable position. It reminded her of music. Softly, and almost without realizing it, she began humming her favorite song, usually sung in a circle on a sprout's naming day.

Songs a rain,
Songs a sun,
Some a come,
Some a gone.
Sing again,
Sing a come,
Songs a rain,
Songs a sun.

The tune helped her remember many naming days, most recently Jesper's, and she smiled. They'd played lots of fun games. Flute enjoyed games, but Jesper could usually beat her at anything. He was terribly cocky about it. Flute laughed aloud midsong. As she laughed, she saw something flare before her sight, like a bright white light. She gasped and peered closer, almost diving to where she'd seen it, though it hadn't strictly come from anywhere. Instantly, her mind's eye was overwhelmed with brilliance.

This was it! She'd found her heartfire, without even trying! Was that the secret? To relax and not try to find it? No, it was more than just that, she knew, but she'd have to puzzle it out later. Right now she wanted to try her spell and she wasn't entirely sure how quickly she'd be able to find her heartfire a second time. Somehow, she knew it would be much easier now that she'd been here, but she didn't want to take the chance.

Gingerly, she touched the brilliance with a tendril of her mind and grasped a piece of it. Elder Osprey had said to take the smallest of threads. She licked her lips, determined to follow directions as best she could. Slowly, she spun a twine of the heartfire away from the rest like a strand of flax. Then she began pulling the twine gently away from the main part of the brilliance.

Another beating of the great eagle's wings beneath her sent her tumbling forward. She was so shocked that she forgot about the twine of heartfire onto which she still held. Instead of letting it go, she only twined it faster. A searing flash of heat zipped through her small body. Flute panicked, and without thinking, reached for her water magic to douse the flames. It was the last thing she remembered as she slumped into a heavy sleep.

⌘ ⌘ ⌘

The skies threatened rain as Anathriel stood on the grand balcony, gazing at the eyries below her and the mountains beyond. Regen and Eulaie were due back home today, and she kept an eye open for Eulaie's golden wingspan as she pondered the events of the previous evening.

Learning of Areen Corper would have been distracting enough, but combined with her strange encounter with Lord Mortén and his puzzling behavior, it wasn't exactly conducive to a peaceful night's rest. Each circumstance clamored for dominance in her thoughts, confusing her even more, for she would have assumed the situation with Immen to naturally hold greater weight in her mind. Why did she care two coppers for what Lord Mortén said or did? In three weeks or so he would be gone anyway.

Perhaps it was because she couldn't find a logical explanation for his actions. Anathriel prided herself in her ability to read the subtleties of court life, but she could not determine Mortén's motives, or any plausible reasons behind his superficial actions. The man was a walking pillar of contradiction. For example, not five minutes ago she had seen Immen leading Mortén into the eyries, clearly giving the promised tour. Why then had Mortén been so angry the previous night, presumably because Immen had denied him an instantaneous viewing? Was being asked to wait one night such an unbearable thing?

In truth, the sight of the broken sconce was what had set her most ill at ease. She wasn't sure how it had been shorn in such an unnatural way and it frightened her. Whatever the reason, she was suddenly having wild and horrible ideas that Lord Mortén was, in fact, quite mad.

Raging a furious, competitive battle with all these strange thoughts and fears was a mounting frustration with Immen. Hurt and disappointment were swift to transform themselves to anger when met with an element of deception, and Anathriel was fairly certain she'd been deliberately deceived by the illustrious captain of the Windriders. Strictly speaking, he hadn't lied about anything, but Anathriel wasn't stupid. He had quietly and graciously shuffled himself away from her by hiding behind his sister. Although she considered this to be rather cowardly of him, she was beginning to think that the slave Zeth's words had in fact been true. Immen really had no interest of any sort in being with her.

Anathriel drew in a deep, angry breath at the memories of everything that had happened. She might not like the fact that he didn't want her, but did he have to be so underhanded about it? He couldn't even show her the respect to tell her straight to her face?

At the first drop of rain on her arm, Anathriel turned and began heading back indoors. There was much to be done today, including making preparations for the remainder of the guests who would soon arrive for the summer, and no doubt she would be asked to assist Taryn in her recovery. Anathriel could not shirk her duties to Lady Rillandra, no matter how much her heart wasn't in it just now.

Stubbornly, she wiped at furious tears that threatened to form in her eyes and squared her shoulders. She wasn't about to let this dampen her spirits or her resolve. Now that she knew the truth, she wasn't going to let Immen get away with it. He was going to answer for his behavior. It was just a matter of when. She needed an opportunity to confront him, preferably alone.

Preferably today.

8

Flute was never certain if she woke because of all the jostling or of her own accord. She suspected the former, as the severe headache that accompanied her revival suggested she probably should have remained unconscious a good while longer. It took her a moment to regain her bearings before she realized that a searching human hand was reaching repeatedly into the bag where she was hiding. The hand, presumably that of the man who had been riding the eagle, was collecting the rolls of paper in great bunches, and Flute was right in the way.

She dashed aside just in time to avoid the fingers closing over her small legs. Then she made a furious scramble for the far corner of the satchel and plastered herself against the side of it until at last it was empty and the flap above closed over her head. Flute gave a sigh of relief. That had been a little too close. Her power to make herself invisible did not extend to making herself insubstantial. She was still very much solid.

There were muffled voices coming from outside the bag. Flute recognized the tenor of the young man who had unwittingly brought her here—wherever here was—and it sounded as though he were greeting someone, but she could not discern the words. Licking her lips, she opened her wings and hovered up towards the opening, pushing aside the flap slightly and peering carefully outside.

"We've been expecting you since last night," said another young man, dressed similarly to Regen. He was holding several of the scrolls that Regen had just removed from the bag, examining the variously colored seals on their sides.

"Actually, I'm a little early," said Regen. His back had been turned to Flute, but now he changed direction and made for the eagle's head and out of Flute's line of sight. "I was forced to bypass Littath altogether. I didn't have room for any more dispatches."

"Not uncommon for this time of year," observed his companion dispassionately, still shuffling through scrolls.

"Is Immen here?" Regen asked. Flute could hear faint sounds of clinking metal coming from the same direction of his voice, and the eagle's body beside her shifted. "There you go, boy," Regen said more softly. "That feels better, doesn't it?"

"He's at the palace, escorting back that lord that was here this morning. You know, the one that came last year? I've never been good with names."

"Mortén?" Regen asked knowingly.

"That's the one."

"Ah, yes, I suppose it is about the right time for his visit."

When she heard the name, Flute covered her mouth with a hand to stifle a gasp. She knew very well the name of Mortén, of course. It had been whispered as a synonym for evil and bad fortune in her village for many years. He was *here?* Panicking, she ducked back completely inside the satchel. Mortén could see fairies. This scenario had never been part of her glorious daydreams. She wondered desperately if there could be more than one Mortén. But if not, how could he be friends with Immen Corper? What if the Magi council had been altogether wrong about Immen Corper, like they had been with Mortén?

Regen's voice became louder again as he approached her hiding place. A shadow fell over the sliver of light seeping into the bag. "It's a good thing, Mavah," he was saying. "Lord Mortén is a bit eccentric, but he always donates to the eyries, although only the paré know why. As such, I never make a big issue of it."

"I agree," said Mavah. "The captain doesn't seem as tolerable about it as you, though."

"Immen's never taken well to humoring the whims of nobles," Regen replied in a wry tone. "At least not those he doesn't respect." There was more jarring as he began loosening the riding things attached to the eagle's back.

"Meaning he doesn't respect this Mortén?"

Flute strained her ears to catch every word of Regen's reply, which was difficult, considering all the shuffling he was doing with his gear. "I'm not sure. We've never discussed it, exactly. Maybe I've got him figured wrong." Abruptly, the motion of the bag stopped. Cautiously peering around an opening with one eye, Flute was able to discern that

Regen had hung it on the wall. "At any rate, I've got to get going. I have a couple of urgent messages here that need to be taken directly to Lord Jassene as soon as possible."

Regen patted his eagle affectionately on the neck before he and Mavah headed out of Flute's sight to the left. By now she had determined that the satchel was hanging in what seemed to be a special area for this eagle. There was a large perch like the one she'd seen in the village before, and a great nest in the corner. The nest was so large that all the sprouts in her village could have assembled inside with plenty of room to spare. Some distance straight ahead she could see another similar space across from the one where Regen's eagle was perched, but it was empty. There was a great open section in between the two areas.

A moment after the men had departed, the great eagle himself stretched his wings lazily and took off out of the nest area in the opposite direction than the two men had gone. Carefully, noting that there were two solid walls on either side of this nest area, Flute dashed out of the satchel and made a beeline for the nearest, darkest corner. She looked up then and smiled at what she saw there. The top of this human place seemed to be full of wooden beams—many convenient places for a little fairy to hide.

At the thought of Mortén, Flute backed more fully into the shadow of her corner. She must remember that there was a good chance he was here. Shivering, she slowly began ascending towards the top of the building. When she cleared the walls that separated this nest area from the others, she could see that the building was very large and very long, with many nest areas on either side for a very long way. Several were occupied by eagles.

Reminding herself yet again that they would be able to see her, Flute thought about what to do next. Now that she had come above the partitions of the nest area, she would be visible to anybody that could see her, be it Immen Corper, Mortén, *or* an eagle. After a glance around to ensure that nobody seeming to match any of these descriptions was watching her, Flute looked up, made a dash for the nearest beam, and alighted atop it. Then she flew along its length until she came to a place where two beams came together to make a corner. This, she surmised, would be an excellent place from which to observe.

There were many people walking about below her, dressed in

clothing similar to Regen's. For a long time she watched them with interest. Every so often, an eagle would swoop in from the outside and land in the middle of the building or exit in the same manner, sometimes bearing a rider, sometimes not. The people came and went as often as the eagles, and Flute studied them all carefully, searching for signs of which one might be Immen Corper. Soon, she realized, she was going to have to figure out a way to eavesdrop on the humans, because from this high up she couldn't make out what any of them were saying.

Still, there were plenty of very interesting things to see, most of which Flute didn't understand, but she watched in fascination nonetheless. Besides the men dressed in red and gray, other humans were coming and going. Young boys and girls in plain clothes rushed about, almost in the same way as the eagles themselves, no doubt on very important errands of some kind.

Whenever an eagle and rider flew in, they usually brought bags of rolled papers just like the one in which Flute had stashed away. The papers were taken into a large doorway in the middle of one side of the building, which appeared to lead into other, smaller rooms. Sometimes papers were carried out from the door and given to a rider who was just departing. Once, a flurried-looking young girl with dark hair, dressed in much prettier colors than the other humans, had come rushing in, calling at the rider who was mounting an eagle to leave and waving a piece of paper frantically at him. When she delivered the paper, he gave her a pleasant nod and tucked it in his bag with the others, whereupon she gave a smart bob and exited the building again much more calmly than she'd entered.

Some words *were* able to reach Flute's small ears, such as those that had been shouted by the young girl with the last-minute message. She paid attention to whatever she could pick up, but heard no references to "captain" or "Corper," nor did she spy any person who might be in charge as he apparently was. Regen came back a couple of times. He returned to his eagle's nest area and went over his gear with practiced care—polishing some things, straightening others. Then she watched him make a round of the whole building, very often visiting certain eagles, giving them affectionate strokes and helping them feed their young. Flute was rather disappointed to see that the sprouts of the great eagles were just as ugly as those of every other bird. She'd rather hoped that a creature as important as one of the twelve brethren would be more impressive when born. Still, they would all grow up impressive enough, so she supposed it didn't really matter.

Pounding on the wooden roof above her head, she could hear the rain outside persisting on and off all day, and see the gray sheets of it through the patches of sky visible on either side of the building. Whatever else was out there she couldn't tell, for it seemed thick and foggy all day.

Finally—she estimated late afternoon or evening, but the sky was so darkened it was hard to tell—a very tall, young man came walking with a quick and confident step from the southern end. Flute might not have paid him any particular mind at first—he was nondescript in a thick cloak of dark gray over his clothes, but she couldn't help but take note when six of the nearest people instantly rushed to him and demanded his attention.

She followed him with her eyes as he made his way down the corridor, addressing in turn each of the people that came to talk to him. When he was directly below her, she strained her ears and thought she might have heard one of the men call him "captain." She smiled. This looked promising. She began to follow him from above, staying out of sight as best she could. If this *was* Immen Corper, she wanted to see and observe him for a while before revealing herself to him. After all, he might be a wicked man like Mortén. This seemed unlikely, as he was the only known descendent of the twelve Houses in this area and someone had been chosen, but she knew well the bitter lesson the fairies had learned when they'd awakened Mortén.

Like Regen, the man paused to visit several eagles along the way as he walked, though unlike Regen he wasn't able to spend very long with them. He seemed to have time only for a short word or a pat before moving on, still conversing with those all around him. At one point he took off his cloak and draped it over his arm, and Flute saw that his clothes, though also red and gray, were much fancier than the others' were. Finally, the young man and his entourage disappeared into the middle doorway.

Biting her lip in hesitation, Flute hovered above her beam of safety for a moment. The door would close soon. What if she lost track of him? She had to find out if he was the one. Heart hammering, she stole a glance around, hoping desperately that none of the eagles would spot her. Then she took a deep breath and plunged with all speed towards the door, dashing inside just as it clicked shut, nearly clipping her wings off with it.

It was very dark on the other side. For this, Flute was grateful. Although nobody was able to see her, she somehow felt safer in the shadows. This was a strange place and no matter how fascinating she found these people, they didn't believe in fairies. Therefore, she flew up as high as she could and hovered along the top of a small, stone corridor, which was lined with doorways. She could see that the dim gray light coming from the outside was spilling from those doorways that were open.

Some feet ahead of her was the group of people she had been studying, and they were walking farther away. Flute began to follow. The curious part of her wanted to know what was in all of these rooms they were passing, but the smart part of her knew she'd better focus on one goal at a time. If she didn't, she might get lost or lose the person she was trying to follow. Wouldn't that be embarrassing?

Other various corridors branched out from this main one, but the group Flute was following continued to proceed straight. She was now able to hear what the people were saying, and she was pleased to discover that this did seem to be the captain after all.

"Willowbreath appears to have an injured leg, Captain Corper," said a short man, handing over a scrap of parchment.

The captain glanced over it quickly, though Flute couldn't tell how he could see anything in this dim light. "Get the tender to come and see her tomorrow," he instructed distractedly, handing the parchment back.

"The tender is in Valedyne, visiting family," said the short man worriedly.

"Then have Regen take a look at her—he has a knack for that kind of thing."

"Yes, sir."

"Speaking of Regen," spoke up another man, "he returned about four hours ago."

"Yes, I saw him at the palace before I returned."

"He was unable to make it to Littath on his tour. Too many dispatches; plus he was running late."

"Phanesh is making a northeastern circuit tomorrow, isn't he? Add Littath as the first stop on his list."

"Already done, sir, I only needed your approval."

"Is Zephyr back yet?"

"No, no one's seen her since the day before yesterday. Should we send out anyone to search for her, sir?"

"No, she's been gone longer before. I simply wanted to see her." There was a note of sadness in the man's voice as he said this. Then he gave a short laugh. "I think she knows I can't fly as much as I used to."

"She's a smart one, all right."

The captain stopped at a closed door that looked no different from any other. He put his hand on the latch and turned to the group. "Is that everything?" he asked as he eased the door open beyond. "With Lord Mortén dragging me around by the nose all day, I'm very behind on all this wretched desk work."

"Of course, sir," replied the short man with a quick bow of his head. There was a round of similar assurances from the others, and they soon dissipated from the doorway, heading in various directions. Flute held her breath, watching the captain carefully. In the fading light coming from the now-open doorway, she could see that his expression was extremely regretful as he gazed inside. Then he stepped over the threshold and out of sight. Just as Flute was making up her mind whether or not she should follow him, he came out again, bearing a short candle stub in his hand, and began lighting the torches on either side of his doorway. Flute took this as the opportunity to make her move. She ducked smoothly and silently into the room beyond the door and again headed for the nearest shadow.

The captain returned, shutting the door behind him. He blew out his candle and set the stub on the table in the middle of the room. Though she had seen many tables in the village the previous evening, none had been exactly like this one. It was full of compartments in different sizes, some of which the young man began opening and closing as he sat down. There were papers all over the tabletop, which he began moving and shuffling. She watched him at this strange activity for several minutes, her heart seeming to pound louder and louder in her ears as her nervousness mounted.

Suddenly, the captain stood up again, his chair scraping on the floor.

He walked over to what seemed to be a tree with short branches and no leaves behind his table. He pulled off his cloak and hung it on the tree, and as he did so, something glittering on his vest caught Flute's attention. Squinting, she saw that it was a silver pin in the shape of an eagle. She gave a small gasp. *The relic!*

At the sound of her gasp, the young man's head whipped around towards where she was hovering. She didn't think he'd heard her accurately, though, because he wasn't looking high enough. "Hello?" he asked quietly, but not as if he expected a response.

Flute swallowed. This was it. If she ever needed a better opportunity, she probably wasn't going to get it. It seemed she had found the Immen Corper of whom the Magi council had been speaking. It seemed he had a relic. There was only one more thing to test. Without speaking, Flute flew straight out of her corner and into the middle of the room, settling herself directly in front of the young man's eyes.

There was a couple seconds' shocked pause. It was clear that he saw her, for his blue eyes fixed upon her directly, widening in amazement. Then he whispered, "Sweet paré defend me" and took three steps backwards, toward the crackling fire behind him, reaching blindly at his side for something long and black that was propped up beside it.

"You can see me!" Flute cried happily. "It *is* you!"

"It is me?" he repeated dumbly. At last his fingers clasped the long object and he quickly hoisted it, brandishing it in Flute's direction.

She dashed backwards. "Hey, watch it!"

"What are you?" he demanded. "What are you doing here?"

"You're Immen Corper, right? I've come a very long way to find you."

"What do you want with me?"

"The fairies need your help," Flute said in her best dramatic voice. She wondered if that was how one of the Grand Magi would say it.

"Fairies?" he repeated. "Fairies are a myth."

"You're not blind, are you?" she snapped, flabbergasted. "I'm here, aren't I? Fairies are real; you humans merely don't remember anything. Would you please put that down? I'm not going to hurt you." She didn't add that she wasn't sure if she *could* hurt him. Slowly, he lowered it, still watching her with wary eyes. Curiously, Flute flew closer and studied it. "What is it, anyway?"

"It's a fire poker," he replied.

"What do you do with it?"

"You poke the fire."

Flute glanced up. His tone of voice was the very patient sort that she always got from her elders. How did he learn it?

He met her gaze with confidence, his initial alarm apparently receding. "What do you want?" he asked again, more slowly and deliberately.

She decided he was in no mood for an elaborate tale. She swallowed. "I've come to bring you to one of the Grand Magi. They will awaken you."

"I'm not going anywhere. What is a Grand Magi?"

Flute frowned at his ignorance. "The greatest and most skilled at magic among my people. Only they can awaken a speaker."

"A speaker?" he repeated, now giving a short, incredulous laugh. "I have no idea what you're talking about."

Flute put her fists on her hips and hovered level with his face, doing her best to look authoritative. "You've been living up on this mountain by yourselves for a very long time. Those eagles out there," she brandished an angry finger back the way they'd come, "are one of the Master's twelve brethren of the earth." She glanced at the brooch on his vest again. "And you are to be their speaker," she finished.

Before Immen Corper had a chance to respond, there was a knock on the door and a loud, insistent voice calling from the other side, "Immen!" It was a woman's voice.

Immen Corper rolled his eyes and muttered something indecipherable under his breath. He looked desperately around the room, then at Flute, then back at the door. Before he could do anything, however, the door burst open and the woman walked in. She was on the tall side for a human woman, and very pretty, with long, wavy, blond hair almost to her waist.

"Immen, I'm sorry to bother you, but I really need to ask you about something, and I'd appreciate it if you—"

She never got any further. Her eyes clamped on Flute, and she let out a very loud, very long scream.

9

Anathriel's fright and distraction were so overwhelming that when Immen's strong hand clamped around her mouth, she jumped in shock again. His action, however, probably did not have the effect he desired. Rather than quiet down, Anathriel began squealing more insistently against his fingers and wriggled violently until she broke free.

"What is *that?*" she cried in a quaky voice, pointing a finger at the little person. Or was it a bug? Anathriel knew what to do about bugs. She glanced around frantically and noted the poker Immen was holding in his other hand. "Kill it, Immen!" she cried.

"Now just a minute!" The tiny little person still hovering in the middle of Immen's office was staring back at her, and it looked angry.

Anathriel jumped again and emitted another petrified cry. It could *speak?* She took two paralyzed steps backwards, then spun around and made a beeline for the hallway outside. Out of the corner of her eye, she could see Immen dash after her.

"No, wait!" cried the bug creature, but Anathriel kept running. She hadn't gotten far, however, when something very odd happened. Just as Immen reached out and grasped her elbow, a wave of something strong and imperceptible surged towards them, a strange pulse of power, which caused both of them to stagger. Immen was knocked to the ground, but Anathriel managed to wrench her elbow free of his hold and catch herself on the opposing wall. An instant later, the sensation was gone.

Anathriel whirled back towards the door. The bug creature was flitting in the doorway now, small hands outstretched, looking very shocked.

"What was that?" Immen wondered in a low voice.

He glanced up at Anathriel, and she could see in his eyes that he was feeling as unsettled as she was. She did not respond to his question. Honestly, she wasn't sure if he was truly expecting a reply, but now she was really afraid. Without another word, she regained her footing and darted down the hallway once more. She would go find Regen and tell him about this. She would—

Any further plans were jolted from her mind as something odd tugged through Anathriel's chest, as if someone was yanking at her from behind with a giant hook. Her body slammed soundlessly into a nonexistent wall, and she fell onto her backside with a loud smack. She would have cried out, but whatever had just happened seemed to have robbed her of her breath as well. Instead, she sat there in the middle of the floor in a most embarrassing position, gasping for breath and trying to overcome her shock.

"Miss Lelaine!" Vaguely, she heard Immen scramble to his feet, then heavy footsteps rushed toward her. "Are you all right? What happened?"

Anathriel stared at him for a moment and finally managed to catch her breath. Instead of answering his question, though, she turned back in the direction of Immen's office door, which was now several doors away. The bug creature was heading toward them, looking—amazingly—very distressed about something.

"What did you do!?" Anathriel shouted.

Immen tried to pull her to a standing position. "Miss Lelaine—" he began.

She accepted his help until she was on her feet but immediately shrugged him away and cut off his words. "What did you *do!?*" she repeated more loudly.

The little creature looked positively desperate now. Its little hands were wringing frantically. "I'm sorry! It was an accident. Oh, I am going to be in so much trouble!"

"You little... mosquito!" Anathriel shouted. She made a lunge for the creature, but Immen held her back.

"Miss Lelaine—"

"What did you do? I demand that you fix it! You did something to us! We both felt it!"

"Anathriel!"

Within Immen's grasp, Anathriel wriggled furiously, but he was holding onto her much more tightly than before, and her efforts were futile. She tried to turn on him instead. "Let me go, Immen. What in the name of Pathon is going on? I'm going to go tell Regen. I'm going to—"

Once again, Immen clapped his hand over her mouth, and his grip on her arm tightened none too gently. "Shut up, Anathriel," he hissed.

Shocked, she obediently closed her mouth. It wasn't so much that she was disposed to be obedient just now, but rather that Immen had raised his voice. He'd never behaved like that towards her before.

Before Anathriel had any sort of chance to complain, urgent footsteps heading towards them from down the hall made the trio all turn their heads as one.

"Captain?" called a concerned voice from around the corner.

Immen turned to the bug creature. "Hide," he told it firmly.

"But—"

"Hide!" he repeated, looking very stern.

The creature gulped and nodded, then whizzed off towards the nearest open doorway. It flew so quickly that Anathriel had a hard time following it. Immen tightened his hold on Anathriel's arm, though not as painfully as he had the first time. "Keep quiet, or so help me, I swear I'll tell Lady Rillandra who it was that threw Rylli's good silk into the kitchen scraps last summer."

Anathriel blinked indignantly and scowled. How did he know about that? Still, the threat was a heavy one. She certainly wouldn't want Lady Rillandra to find out about the incident. She nodded slowly, though she vowed she was going to get him back for this, somehow.

He released her arm just as the footsteps rounded the corner and an aide rushed towards them looking concerned. His eyes took in the sight of Anathriel and Immen standing there, undoubtedly looking piqued. "Is everything all right, sir?" he asked worriedly.

"Yes, Dobbs. We're fine," said Immen calmly, as if he were mentioning that the pass up to Montressa had been unseasonably dry this spring. He nodded at Anathriel. "She saw a mouse." He gave the young man a meaningful expression.

Concern dropped instantly from the aide's stance to be replaced by amusement. "Very well, sir." With a polite but mirthful glance at Anathriel, he added, "I trust the problem has been taken care of?"

"It has, thank you."

"Very well, sir. Is there anything you need?"

"No, that will be all, Dobbs."

With a final nod, the aide retreated. Anathriel opened her mouth to speak, but Immen held up a warning finger and she closed it again. Immen stood still for several minutes, head cocked, listening to the retreating footsteps. When they were sufficiently far enough away, he called to the doorway where the bug had hidden. "He's gone. You can come out now."

"Immen, what in blazes is going *on?*" Anathriel demanded. She was feeling angrier than she had in a long time. When she'd come in search of Immen she had already been annoyed, but now she'd also been frightened out of her wits, experienced weird, invisible feelings coming over her, been physically pulled around by strange forces, and subsequently humiliated in front of an aide.

"I'm not sure," Immen said softly. "But we can't discuss it here. Come on." He reached out for Anathriel's arm once more and jerked his head at the bug. He led them all back into his office and shut the door. Then he bolted it firmly in place.

Almost immediately, the bug started buzzing around the room frantically. "This is not good. This is not good. This is not good."

Anathriel and Immen both stared. It continued to mutter to itself, holding its small head in its hands and shaking it in distress. "What's not good?" Anathriel asked, unthinking.

The little creature's head darted up, looking at Anathriel. "Everything! You can *see* me, and you're not supposed to! I messed up on the binding, and I'm going to be in so much trouble!"

"Of course we can see you," Anathriel huffed, confused.

"But only he's supposed to be able to!" cried the creature again, pointing a despairing finger at Immen.

"All right, just a moment," said Immen, clearly as frustrated and bewildered as Anathriel. He peered closely at the creature. "Please calm down Miss—Fairy. I'm not going to know what you're talking about until you explain it better."

"Fairy?" Anathriel echoed.

"My name is Flute," said the creature indignantly. She sighed slightly and her shoulders slumped. "Actually, it's Fluttermouse, but they call me Flute."

"They?" Immen asked.

"My village. My elders."

"How many of you are there?"

"Lots, Immen Corper! Most of us live in Fairlight Forest. That is where I need to take you."

"Take him?" Anathriel repeated incredulously. "Why in the world would you need to take Captain Corper anywhere? Immen, what is going on?" she asked for what felt like the hundredth time.

"I have no idea," he replied with a weary sigh. He seemed to be speaking almost to himself. He looked at Flute again. "Maybe you'd better start from the beginning."

"No, first I want to know what happened to us," Anathriel snapped, pointing an accusatory finger towards the hallway.

The fairy looked mournful. "I didn't mean for it to affect you. Only him. It was a binding spell."

"Spell?" repeated Immen.

"That's right. To bind a fairy guardian to his or her speaker."

Anathriel wondered if this was making any sense to Immen, because she was lost. "All right, fine, start at the beginning," she said, dropping into one of the chairs in front of Immen's desk. It wasn't particularly comfortable, but her recent screaming, running, struggling, and being tossed about by invisible forces was leaving her feeling very tired.

"When the Master created the world, there were fourteen great races," Flute began, as though she were reciting a lesson back to a teacher. "The fairies to care for the earth and guard its peoples, the twelve brethren to care for its creatures, and humans to bring them all together, and to live and love in his will and his image."

Anathriel laughed. "This is ridiculous. Everyone knows the Master stories are just that—stories. I don't see how any of this—"

"Miss Lelaine—Anathriel—let her talk, please?"

The fairy glared at Anathriel. "The Master is not a story," she said hotly. She glared another moment longer before looking at Immen again. "With our magic, we fairies know when the Master has called a speaker. And that's why I came to find you, Immen. I need to take you back to the Magi council. They said you had been chosen."

"Wait, wait. Chosen? Magi council? Speaker? What are you talking about?" Anathriel asked, irritated. If this little creature was going to talk, the least she could do was make sense.

"You mentioned a speaker earlier," Immen said slowly, his eyes on Flute. "You said I was one of them. What did you mean by that? What are they?"

The fairy gave a tiny sigh of impatience. "There are twelve speakers, one for each of the twelve brethren."

"And what are the brethren?"

Flute straightened importantly. "They are intelligent beings of the earth. They have feelings and thoughts just like you and me. No one can talk to them except the speakers."

"Who are human," Immen said slowly.

"Yes. And you're one of them," Flute replied. "Or you will be, anyway."

"You said the eagles were one of the brethren." Immen studied Flute with narrowed eyes.

Anathriel stared at him in disbelief. "Immen! You don't actually believe all this, do you?"

"Anathriel, there's a fairy in my office," Immen said, giving her a very pointed look.

"Exactly! A fairy you know nothing about! Who knows what she really wants? She could be trying to trick you into something! She could be lying! She—"

"I am not lying!" Flute burst out indignantly. "Immen Corper is the only person who can help the magical world. We need him!"

Immen looked confused. "But you said there are twelve speakers. If what you're saying is true, why do you need me? Can't one of the others help you?"

Flute shook her head adamantly, her eyes huge. "No, no, no! There are only two others right now. The rest of the relics are missing, and—"

Anathriel groaned and buried her head in her hands.

Flute twirled a full circle in the air and ran her hands over her feathers. "You have to understand. One of the other two is here now. I didn't know he would be. He is a very, very bad man—oh, and he can't find out I'm here, or you'll be in so much trouble! And one—"

"Wait!" Immen held up a hand. "Here? In Montressa?"

Flute scanned the office cautiously, as if expecting someone to be hiding in the shadows. A shiver ran through her tiny body. "Mortén," she whispered, her voice so quiet that Anathriel had to strain to hear her. An unexpected chill came over Anathriel, and the unnaturally shorn sconce flashed briefly before her eyes.

"Mortén? Darius Mortén?" Immen asked, a dark expression on his face.

Flute squeaked. "Yes! Yes, he's an evil, horrible man, and he doesn't deserve to be a speaker. The fairies made a mistake with him. And if he finds out about you, I don't even know what he would do to you. We're in so much danger!"

Of everything Flute had said thus far, this for some reason disturbed Anathriel the most...especially because she couldn't bring herself to discredit it.

Immen looked equally unsettled. He rubbed his eyes wearily with one hand before looking at Flute once more. "All right. Let's skip that part for now. Tell me about the eagles. You said they're part of these twelve brethren?"

"Yes, and you ought to be ashamed of yourselves for treating them like animals!" Flute said, pursing her lips indignantly.

"They are animals," Anathriel retorted.

"They are not," Flute exclaimed vehemently. "They can talk, except you can't understand them. Only the speakers can understand them."

Immen frowned. "I can't understand them."

"You won't be able to until I take you to the Grand Magi," Flute explained.

"This is the most ridiculous—" Anathriel drew a deep breath, straining for a semblance of calm. She turned her narrowed eyes on Flute. "Let's get to the part where you tell us what you did to us!"

Flute sighed again. "I did a binding spell."

"You said that earlier," Immen said, with far more patience than Anathriel was feeling. "What does it mean?"

"I had a very hard time finding you," Flute said desperately. "When you ran off, I was afraid I wouldn't be able to catch up, and I cast the spell so I wouldn't lose you. It connects you to me," she said, pointing at herself and Immen in turn. "That way, no matter where you went, I'd be pulled along."

"And Anathriel?" Immen prompted.

Flute looked embarrassed. "It was an accident," she mumbled once again. "The magic hit her at the same time it hit you. It's not supposed to be used for two humans. I'm not sure what I did, exactly, but I think you're both bound to each other, too. And since the spell is designed for a human to be an anchor, neither of you can go anywhere without the other."

"What!?" Anathriel jumped up from the chair.

"That was why you couldn't go very far down the corridor," explained Flute hastily.

"I can't believe I'm hearing this."

"Anathriel, calm down, please," said Immen, placing a strong hand on her shoulder. He coaxed her firmly down until she was sitting in the chair once more. Then he looked at Flute. "Obviously this hasn't been a good experience, but all you have to do is reverse the spell, right?"

There was a painful silence as Flute hovered before them, suddenly looking even guiltier than she had before. She mumbled something very quietly.

"What's that?" Immen prompted.

This time they could hear her words, but barely. "I don't know how. I'm still kind of learning magic."

"Oh, fantastic." Anathriel scowled. "We're stuck to a novice fairy." She made a face and looked up at Immen expectantly. "Well, now what?"

He closed his eyes for a moment. "All right."

Anathriel knew Immen well enough to see that his patience was starting to stretch as well, long as it was. He opened his eyes again. "Is there anyone who *can* fix us?" he asked, very slowly.

For the first time Flute looked relieved. "Yes! One of the elders could fix you, but I will have to take you there."

"Listen," Immen said, very tiredly, "we can sort through this speaker matter later. First and foremost, we need to fix this binding spell. It won't do either of us any good if we can't be separated."

Anathriel was forced to agree. At the moment, she was very disheveled and irritated with Immen. There was the practical point to all of this, too—how would they eat, or sleep, or work, or do anything else if they were yanked back by unseen energies every time they tried to part ways?

"And where are these elders of yours?" Anathriel demanded.

"In Fairlight Forest," Flute said promptly.

Anathriel stared at the wretched little creature in shock.

Immen exhaled. "I was afraid you were going to say that."

"You want us to go all the way to the other side of the continent!?"

Anathriel cried, whirling on Flute. "I don't think so. That kind of journey takes weeks and weeks. It might well be near winter by the time we returned!"

"What else do you suggest, Anathriel?"

"I think she can jolly well fix us on her own. If she stops and thinks, maybe she'll remember how."

"I can't remember what I never learned," Flute insisted. She appeared on the verge of tears. "If I tried, I might make things worse."

"Well then, go get your fairy guru and bring them *here* to fix us."

"And what, Anathriel?" Immen pointed out. "Wait for who knows how long until they get back? Not counting all the time it might take her to convince them? It wouldn't take long for people around here to discover the binding. How are we going to explain it, especially without Flute here for proof? And if she's right about Mortén—"

"Do you know what's going to happen if we leave?" Anathriel said, glaring at him. She put her hands on her hips. "Think about it: the newly appointed captain of the Windriders and one of the Lady's best handmaidens mysteriously disappear from Montressa on the same day. Witnesses saw them conversing in private on the day in question. Doesn't paint a very responsible picture to you, does it?"

To her satisfaction, there was a grim set to Immen's lips.

"When and if we returned," she continued, "I'd be back to manning my father's shops, forever disgraced and shunned, never to marry, the subject of whispers and rumors. And you—you know the consequences of abandoning the Windriders. You would—"

"I know," Immen said swiftly, cutting her short. He looked thoughtful. Then he shook his head. "But the way I see it, we have little choice."

"No, Immen, I refuse to believe that. Surely we can work out some way that—"

A strong knock on the door caused all three of them start. Flute immediately zoomed to the bookcase and hid between two books propped loosely against one another. "Captain Corper?" called a voice.

Anathriel froze. She recognized the voice, and she could see by the set of Immen's shoulders that he did, too. "Who's there?" he called warily.

"Lord Mortén, Captain. I had another matter on which I wished to speak to you."

Immen said something below his breath that Anathriel was sure he didn't usually say in the presence of a lady. She was too alarmed, however, to take offense. Lord Mortén was here? Why? She glanced at Immen fearfully. Somewhere in the back of her mind she wondered why they hadn't detected his approach.

"I'm a bit preoccupied, Lord Mortén," Immen called. "You'll have to come back later." He winced. Clearly, he knew how flimsy the excuse sounded.

The only reply from the other side of the door was a strangely heavy silence that caused Anathriel to shiver. Then, without warning, the door shook hard on its hinges. It heaved with a great, splintering *crack*, and the heavy bolt split away from the door and the stone wall where it had been anchored. Anathriel gasped and jumped backwards, covering her mouth with both hands. The bolt fell to the floor with a clang, and the door swung swiftly open.

Lord Mortén wasted no time idling in the corridor. He stepped into the room with cool authority, closed the door behind him, and turned around to look at the two of them. He chuckled. "Preoccupied, Captain?" he repeated with a smirk. He looked meaningfully at Anathriel. "Well, I suppose I can understand such a form of preoccupation."

Immen's jaw was set hard, and he stared angrily at Mortén with fire-lit eyes. If he was going to respond, though, he never got the chance.

"How dare you!" Anathriel cried. Her hands were balled into fists.

Mortén only laughed again. "I dare. You look very fetching when you're angry, Anathriel." He turned to Immen. "Now," he said, matter-of-factly, "there was a third. Where is she hiding?"

"I told you to leave," Immen said in a cold voice, ignoring Mortén's question.

"There is no need to play ignorant, Captain. I've been listening to your conversation for the past five minutes. Where is the little meddlesome shvri?"

Anathriel looked at Immen, alarmed. His eyes warned her to keep quiet, though, so she said nothing. In this instance, she was only too happy to comply.

"What are you doing here, Mortén?" Immen asked, glaring.

"That's an interesting question." Mortén did not look so amused now, rather a little angry. "I came here to enlist your aid in my search. Just when I arrived at your door, what should I hear but my name being spoken from the other side? Naturally, I waited to hear what was said, but what I discovered was more enlightening than I could possibly have imagined. Now, where is the fairy whelp?"

Instead of answering his question, Immen grabbed his sword from the side of the desk, and before Anathriel could blink, he had it drawn and pointed at Mortén's throat. "I don't know what you're talking about. Now leave, or you'll make me guilty of spilling noble blood."

Mortén sighed, shaking his head. He drew his own sword, but instead of engaging Immen, he threw it at Immen's head, causing Immen to duck and Anathriel to flinch. While Immen was still distracted, Mortén took three steps across the room and grabbed Anathriel by the shoulders. He dragged her back to the door and spun her around. Then he twisted her arms behind her back, locking his own arm behind them, crushing them to his chest. The other hand he enclosed around her throat.

Immen had regained his footing, and now had both swords in his hands, standing in a ready battle stance, coiled and set. He glared challengingly at Mortén, but looked at Anathriel and made no move.

"I don't need a sword to kill her, Corper," said Mortén coolly.

Anathriel tried to struggle, but it was as if she were encased in a steel trap. Mortén didn't so much as flinch. She was terrified. Mortén continued speaking without regarding her. It was as if her efforts were so laughable they didn't even deserve the honor of his derision. "I can crush her throat before you had time to even nick me. And she would die quickly."

Anathriel was thinking once more of the shorn sconce. She also noted the heavy bolt that had been pulled clean from its stone moorings. She swallowed and closed her eyes, trying to think of anything but the cold fingers clamped about her neck.

"What do you want?" Immen asked, slowly lowering the swords. He did not relax.

"That's better. Where is the relic?"

"I don't know what you're talking about," Immen replied.

Mortén tightened his grip on Anathriel's throat, and she made a desperate, choking sound. She might have more elaborately voiced her protest, but she was incapable of words.

"I told you I don't know!" Immen shouted.

Mortén relaxed his grip slightly. "Interesting. Where is the shvri, then? Apparently, she didn't tell you everything you needed to know."

With a buzzing blur, Flute dashed from her hiding place. "I'm here," she said, in a way that she probably hoped sounded courageous. It was clear, though, from the way her body was violently trembling from head to tiny toes that she was terrified. "And that's the second time you've called me a shvri. I'm *not* shvri."

Mortén watched Flute with a satisfied smirk. "I don't know what's more surprising. Finding that the captain of the Windriders talks with fairies, or that the Grand Magi council can't keep track of its brats. I know you are not the one they sent; he was easily disposed of. It seems the standards of the guardian race have been getting lax these past few years."

"We know what you are, Mortén!" Flute said bravely.

"Where is the relic?" he asked her, very hard and serious. Anathriel could feel Mortén's head and shoulders shifting as he looked around for whatever he was talking about. He turned back to Flute. "Where is it?" he demanded.

But Flute did not appear to be listening to him. Instead, she was staring at her hands with intense concentration. Then, suddenly, she glared fiercely at Mortén and thrust her hands toward him. A shot of something like brilliant, hot fire sprang from her fingertips and directly into Mortén's face. He screamed in fury and dropped his hands from Anathriel.

"Run!" Flute screamed.

Although Anathriel was paralyzed with fright, Immen wasted no time in acting. Just as the fairy shot fire at Mortén again, he dropped one of the two swords he was carrying, rushed over, seized Anathriel by the hand, and jerked her into motion. They fled out the broken doorway into the cool, dark hallway beyond. Mortén's screams could still be heard echoing behind them, but Immen did not stop to look back.

At some point, Anathriel's sanity seemed to snap back into place, for she shook herself and began running of her own accord. A second later she felt a strange weight on her shoulder, and turned her head slightly to see that the fairy had alighted upon it and was barely hanging on.

Unthinking, Anathriel reached up, grasped the small passenger in her hand, and transferred her to a front dress pocket.

"We can take the hillside path into the city," Immen said as they ran. He was leading them through little-used corridors in the eyries barracks. They hadn't seen another soul since they'd taken off. "Somewhere away from Par Auspré. I need a little peace and quiet to work this out."

"No!" Anathriel argued. "We need to go tell Lord Jassene what happened," she managed to say between heavy breaths. She wasn't accustomed to so much running, or running so quickly.

"I don't think that's such a good idea."

"He was going to kill us, Immen!"

"Anathriel, be quiet and do what I say," Immen said warningly. "If Flute is right about all this magic and legend, then it might not do to go spilling everything to the higher-ups."

Immen slowed momentarily to seize a torch from the wall. Then he turned another corner and led them down a short flight of stairs. It was very dark at the bottom. A long tunnel with a door was barely visible at the far end. Immen had slowed to a brisk walk, but he still kept throwing wary glances over his shoulder.

When they reached the door, Immen enlisted Anathriel's aid in lifting the heavy wooden beam from across the center that barred it from outside intrusion. As he opened the door, Anathriel was surprised to see that night had completely fallen outside. When she'd set off in search of Immen—which now seemed a lifetime ago—it had been only early dusk. She thought briefly about the reason she'd sought him out and found that it now seemed rather silly.

Anathriel looked longingly at the lights coming from the windows in Par Auspré, looming above their heads. By now, Lady Rillandra would begin to wonder where she was. With great regret, Anathriel peeled her gaze away and focused on keeping up with Immen in the enshrouding darkness. He led her to a small, rusty gate that headed a steep, slightly overgrown trail down into the city.

"What is this for?" she asked.

"Windrider shortcut," Immen said, taking her hand once more to help her over some particularly rough footing. "Honestly, I'm not sure of its initial purpose. We rarely use it, but it comes in handy."

"Where are you taking us?" Anathriel asked, thinking of the courtyard and his sister. Was that where they were going? His home?

A large boulder in the middle of the path created a drop in the trail of about three feet. Immen nimbly leapt down, then turned back to face her. "I'm not sure how desperate Mortén will be to find us once he recovers." He passed her the torch and held her firmly by the waist to lower her down off the boulder. "I don't think we should go any place obvious, such as my home or yours."

"Where then?" Anathriel prompted.

"I know somewhere we'll probably be safe."

10

Immen's sanctuary was in a part of Montressa Anathriel had rarely been. It was hard to recognize anything in the dark, and it wasn't until she was ushered through a narrow back gate and saw large bundles of rough wool stacked in a small lean-to that she realized where they were. It was a craftsmen's alley—a place where carpenters, smithies, and the like kept both their homes and their businesses.

"What are we doing here?" she finally dared to whisper. They hadn't said another word their entire flight down the mountaintop, and her edginess was finally getting to her.

Immen did not bother to reply. Instead, he clambered as silently as possible up a thick wooden trellis on the side of the nearest darkened house. When he reached a very small, narrow window on its second floor, he knocked quietly and waited. Many long moments later, the window pushed open and the shadow of another person was barely discernable in its frame. Down below, Anathriel was too far away to make out the face of the person, and the whispered conversation he and Immen shared likewise failed to reach her. She waited, rubbing her arms against the chilly night and feeling frightened and annoyed.

When at last Immen descended, he finally seemed in the mood to talk. "We're in luck. The master and mistress are in Valedyne for the week seeking trade."

"So who were you talking to?"

"A friend of mine. He should be down to let us in any second." As he spoke, Immen started looking around, puzzled. He turned to Anathriel. "Where's Flute?"

Anathriel realized, with some surprise, that in her panic she'd completely forgotten about her little stowaway. She reached into her pocket. The weight of the small, limp body in her hand as she pulled it out felt distinctly odd. The little creature was smaller than a doll, and perfectly made, right down to ten small fingers and ten small toes, and a pair of fine gossamer wings tucked against her back. She was also unconscious.

"Oh, no," said Immen worriedly, taking the fairy from Anathriel.

"I don't think she's dead," Anathriel said pragmatically. "She's breathing, and she flew to me on her own before she passed out."

She didn't want to vocalize any form of sympathy for the creature, although she was grateful the fairy was still alive. Like it or not, she was their only means of fixing their predicament.

"How long has she been like this?"

"I don't know, Immen. I stuck her in my pocket, and I've been climbing down half of Montressa in the dark with you!"

"Shhh!" he hissed as the door unbolted beside them. It opened from inside. "Come on," Immen instructed her firmly.

Anathriel scowled. When had he become so bossy?

It was mostly dark in the room, but Anathriel could make out the outlines of furniture from the dim, orange light left by the dying embers in the large fireplace nearby. She stepped closer, eager to absorb whatever heat could be had. The sound of a flint being struck behind her caught her attention, and she turned in time to see a young boy lighting a lantern on a simple but smoothly worn wooden table.

"You!" she cried, instantly recognizing him. It was the tailor term-slave who had insulted her on the day of the Festival of Winds. "What in the name of—? Immen, what are we doing here?"

The boy snorted. "I was going to ask the same, thing, actually." He raised his eyebrows meaningfully at Immen.

"It's a long story, Zeth," Immen said. He glanced between them. "You two have met?"

Anathriel and the boy shared a mutual glower before she crossed her arms and tossed her head. She even found herself grinding her teeth, a habit she'd thought she'd rid herself of when she was eleven.

"Not officially," the boy replied, giving a short, sardonic laugh.

"In that case, Zeth, this is Anathriel. Anathriel, this is Zeth."

"He's a term-slave, Immen." Anathriel turned her glare to Immen.

Immen was a long moment in replying, during which he stared back at her so coldly she was forced to look away. "He's my friend," she heard him say in a dark, challenging voice. "And he might be able to help us. That should be enough for you."

It was Zeth's turn to speak up. "Immen, what's going on?"

Slowly, Immen pulled the small figure of Flute from behind his back where he'd been holding her and laid her gently on the table, not far from the lantern.

Zeth's eyes bugged. "Mighty Pathon and Auspré," he whispered, leaning in closer. "What is that?"

Anathriel helped herself to one of the table's four uncomfortable chairs while Immen explained, as summarily as possible, everything that had happened in his office, including parts Anathriel didn't know, such as what had taken place between him and Flute before she'd arrived.

"Incredible," Zeth murmured, shaking his head when Immen had finished. "I always knew there was something special about the eagles." There was a strange light in his eyes, unmistakable even in the nighttime shadows.

Anathriel, getting grumpier by the second, emitted a very unladylike snort but made no further comment.

Zeth seemed to think arguing with her was not worth his time. "Immen, what do you need from me?"

"Honestly, all I really needed was a place where no one would think to look for me."

"'No one' meaning this Mortén?"

"Right. I need time to decide what to do."

"Well, time you have, I think, though it'd be hard to say how much. I guess it depends on how hard he decides to search for you, if at all."

"Oh, I have no doubt he'll search, it's just a question of how openly. I'm thinking he'll have to be discreet to avoid any odd questions."

"All right, so we'll be discreet back," Zeth said.

Anathriel wondered exactly at what point Zeth had decided to include himself in a "we." Maybe he thought he sounded clever, but she noted he hadn't made any useful suggestions so far.

"You're going to have to leave the city?" Zeth continued.

"The sooner the better; I just don't know how. At the very least, Mortén will be keeping tabs on the city gate and the eyries."

"We could always just tell the Kavelas the truth about what happened," Anathriel insisted. She was frustrated that Immen did not see that this was the most sensible course of action. "It's not as if it's our fault. Then they could kick Mortén out and give us an armed escort to this Fairfield Forest place."

"Fairlight," Immen corrected. He looked thoughtful. "No, Anathriel. It might work, but I don't think we could take the chance. Too many people admire and believe Mortén. I'm not sure who we could convince. And if we could expose him, there's no knowing what damage he might do to others before he was apprehended. *If* he was apprehended."

"Oh, so you're saying we just leave and let him go free?" she retorted.

He leaned in closer to her and spoke intently, capturing both her and Zeth with his gaze. "Whatever he's after, we either have it, or he thinks we do. If we leave, I'd say there's a pretty good chance he won't be a danger to anyone else, including our families. It's too risky for a man as high up as he is."

Zeth was nodding sagely, but Anathriel crossed her arms again, more tightly across her chest. But fight as she might, she could not prevent a single, inevitable tear from escaping onto her cheek.

"Oh, great," Zeth muttered.

Anathriel stared at him with narrowed eyes before turning to Immen. "So, what? I'm supposed to leave—just like that? Flee in the middle of the night to a country I've never been to, get un-spelled, and then what? What am I supposed to do then, Immen? Hmm? Have you thought of that?" The tears were falling freely now.

"Do you think he's stupid?" Zeth spat. "He's giving up his life too. Are you really this selfish?"

"Zeth," Immen chided quietly. To her satisfaction, he did seem genuinely sympathetic. "I'm sorry, Anathriel. I've thought it over, and I don't see how we have any other choice. And I think you're smart enough to see that too."

Two more hot tears slipped down her cheeks and Anathriel bit her lip. She closed her eyes for a long moment before finally—and most reluctantly—nodding. "I think I know how to get us out of the city."

⌘ ⌘ ⌘

Humiliation was not something Anathriel was accustomed to dealing with, nor did she handle it very gracefully. The worst of it was, from the way the scrawny slip of a term-slave radiated smugness at every step, that he found her mortification more than amusing.

Since conceding to flee Montressa with Immen, Anathriel's evening had gone from bad to worse. The first part of the bad news had been Zeth's declaration that he was going to come with them. She had really raised a tempest over this decision, and was shocked that Immen had seemed nonchalant, even sympathetic to the child's decision.

"He's a term-slave, Immen," Anathriel said, wondering how many times she was going to have to point out this very obvious fact. Couldn't Immen understand what that meant? "It's illegal for him to run away. He has, what, another four years at least before he's free? I'll not be a partisan to helping slaves escape. Do you know what they do to people who abet fugitives?"

"Zeth isn't—" Immen began.

"None," Zeth interrupted forcefully. His eyes were proud and hard as he spoke.

"What?" she asked dumbly.

"None," he repeated. "That's how many years of service I have left. As far as I'm concerned, I never had any. I'll not be a slave. Term-slaves are supposed to be made so by choice. I never made a choice. I was a slave against my will."

Anathriel laughed. "That's not possible."

"Isn't it?" Immen murmured as he gazed into the newly crackling fire. "By law a person can be made a term-slave as young as five years old. How is a child so young capable of understanding the full extent of such an agreement?"

"But—" she started.

"They're not," said Zeth firmly, cutting her off. "Parents who are desperate and hungry enough can sell their children into service." He pulled a rough sack off a nearby shelf and began collecting certain articles from around the small kitchen. "Or how easy is it to nip orphans off the street, manufacture papers, and have them branded before they know what's going on?" He paused and fingered the tattoo on his wrist with a brooding expression. "They justify themselves by saying they're doing the children a favor." He laughed bitterly.

"Perhaps they are," Anathriel managed, trying to ignore the uncomfortable fact that what Zeth was saying seemed to be his own story. "If this be the case, the child in question would learn a useful trade. They would have a good home, and when their term of service was up, they'd be able to make their own way in the world."

"That's not the point, Anathriel," Immen said. "To be a term-slave is supposed to be a matter of free will."

Now Zeth brandished the offending wrist directly at her. "See this? It's a twenty-year brand. I won't be free by law for another eleven years at least. And after that, what? In Merenth—and its bordering countries—people recognize this brand. Even after my term was filled, even if I dutifully served my time, would my life be so much better? Everywhere I went I'd be questioned and looked down upon because of what I am. This is my chance to have freedom. I'm coming with you."

"People will recognize you as a runaway," Anathriel pointed out. "Your mark will betray us. I'm sure Mortén and probably the Kavelas will be searching for us for a good long while. Are you trying to make it harder?"

"I can cover it with a tunic."

"You're not allowed to do that," she said, scowling.

Zeth rolled his eyes. "I'm not supposed to run away, either."

"And what if someone sees it?" Anathriel raised an eyebrow.

"We'll manage," Immen said, cutting them both off with a weary voice. "Added to that, Anathriel, only a handful of the Windriders know of my friendship with Zeth. His master and mistress are gone for four more days, so he likely won't be missed until then. I doubt anyone will entertain the idea that our disappearances are connected. He can help us."

Their next stop had been Anathriel's father's store for supplies. The streets were wet and quiet as the three of them slipped across the nighttime city. The paré seemed to be favoring them. One of Montressa's seasonal fogs was filling it with damp, murky shadows, making it difficult to see more than a few feet ahead of them. Anathriel spent the journey clutching the back of Immen's cloak and taking careful mind of her feet.

It had been her suggestion to take supplies from her father. She felt a little bad about it, but she figured the things they were taking could indirectly be considered hers, so it was a little bit better than outright stealing. It took her a few minutes to dig up the spare key for the back door, but soon enough they were in.

The main room of the store was rather larger than most—her father was, after all, one of the wealthiest tradesmen in Montressa.

"We need to be quick," Immen had said. "If Mortén is searching the city, he'll come here eventually, but I think he'd probably search your home before he thought to look here."

"Right," she agreed. "We hurry."

For the first time since it had happened, Anathriel and Immen had opportunity to realize the limits of their bond. The fairy had been correct. It seemed they could only go about twenty feet apart from one another, at most. On more than one occasion, one or the other would forget about it, such as when Immen climbed a ladder on the far wall to retrieve spare flints from the top shelf. Anathriel felt herself being tugged in his direction, and had to catch her footing to keep from tripping.

Zeth seemed to have elected himself chief of supply gathering. He had a very good grasp on what sort of supplies they'd need, which he packed into three sacks with efficient care as they went along. "You're going to need a better dress," he told Anathriel pragmatically, as he tied up the first bag when it was full. He glanced at her, and then at Immen. "Actually, both of you are going to need different clothes."

"I hadn't thought of that," Immen said, frowning.

"What's wrong with my dress?" Anathriel asked. She glanced down at her gown. It was pale sky blue, with a ruffled skirt that teased her ankles—rather longer than the typical Montressa style, but still easy enough to move around in. A day dress, really. She hadn't planned on going anywhere or participating in anything special when she'd chosen it that morning. "All my better ones are at the palace, and I don't think it's a good idea to go back to my quarters anymore."

Zeth rolled his eyes. "I highly doubt anything you own would be right. By better I didn't mean fancier. You need something that doesn't make you stick out like a gaudy blue jay." When Anathriel stared at him blankly, he added, "A peasant dress."

"I don't have one," she replied automatically, a little appalled.

"I thought as much." His eyes fell on bolts of fabric near the front door, and he tapped his fingers on his arm thoughtfully. Then he nodded. "Does your father sell shears?" he asked her, as he marched over to the fabric.

"Yes," she replied indignantly.

"Get a pair," he ordered. "And a needle. Actually, get several needles, different lengths. And a good book for them—preferably leather." As he spoke, he began pulling several colors of fabric off the wall.

Anathriel scowled and did as he directed. She couldn't believe she was taking orders from a fourteen-year-old term-slave.

"Bring the shears here," he continued when she'd retrieved them.

"What is all this?" she finally asked when she and Immen joined him.

"You don't have a plain dress, so I'm going to have to make you one. We need to blend in. The problem is what to do in the meantime. I wish we had thought of this back at my master's. We had a couple of plainer skirts in the shop I was working on. And things Immen could have used, as well."

"My father keeps work shirts in stock," Anathriel said. "We don't sell many, but they should be..." She stepped around the work counter where Zeth was trimming a bolt of dark gray wool and knelt down to pull four or five plain white linen shirts from a cubby shelf in front of the counter. She plopped them on top the counter.

"Does he keep trousers as well?" Zeth asked, not looking up.

"Yes."

"Good. Immen, find one of those that fits you. Anathriel, you grab a shirt, too, and a pair of trousers."

"What!?"

He looked up. "We have to sneak back into Par Auspré, don't we? It'd be better, I think, if you went as a boy. For now. We need to hide you."

And so she had changed. The trousers were the source of her humiliation. She was sure Zeth was taking secret delight in every step she took wearing the scandalous things. As for Immen, he was impassive about the whole matter. He hadn't been saying much the entire course of the night, mostly just adding insight where it was needed, and more often being a voice of calm when the tempers flared between Anathriel and Zeth, which happened often.

Despite her annoyance with the boy, Anathriel secretly had to give Zeth credit for knowing his trade. At his direction, she bound up her hair as tightly as possible, winding it in braids around her head so that it lay flat, while Zeth quickly basted together a crude page's cap to hide it. By this time, they'd already lingered at the shop longer than any of them had hoped to, but Anathriel was reassured by how prepared they seemed to be for an escape and subsequent journey.

It was during this part of the preparation that Flute finally woke up. Immen had settled her in a nest of handkerchiefs on the main counter, right next to where Zeth was assembling their packs. Anathriel was carefully folding the material Zeth had chosen and putting it in the third bag when the fairy stirred. With a small groan, almost indiscernible, she awoke, sitting up in her kerchief nest and holding her head.

"Flute," said Immen, walking over and smiling down at her, "I'm glad you're awake. How do you feel?"

She did not reply immediately but rubbed her head and looked around. "Where are we?"

"We're getting supplies for our journey," he told her. "You need to take us with you, remember?"

Flute's eyes widened excitedly. "You're coming?" she cried with a big smile. She looked at Anathriel. "Both of you?"

"Of course both of us," Anathriel said, rolling her eyes a little.

"Right," said Flute, shaking her head. "I knew that." She scrambled to her feet on the countertop and looked around. "Wow," she muttered. "There're all kinds of human things in here." As she turned, she finally spotted Zeth.

"Hello," he said, giving a small wave.

Flute's eyes flew open even wider. Her wings buzzed and she sprang two inches off the counter. "Who are you?"

"Flute, this is my friend Zeth," Immen said. "He's coming with us."

Flute looked troubled. She stared at Zeth a long while. "You can see me, too?" she finally asked, sadly.

"Yes," he said slowly, looking around as if verifying it was him to whom she was talking.

"I must have hurt myself, somehow," she continued, frowning even more.

"What do you mean?" asked Anathriel.

"Fairies are invisible to humans unless we don't want to be—they can't see or hear us." She sighed. "But I guess I must have broken my magic somehow, because that's how I'm supposed to be right now."

"Back in my office you said only I should be able to see you," Immen began.

Flute nodded. "Someone who is chosen to be a speaker can always see and hear fairies, no matter what."

"And we're back to the speakers," Anathriel muttered. She tied the bag closed with an emphatic tug.

"Are we almost ready?" Immen asked, straightening from his conversation with Flute.

"Just about," Zeth replied, tying his own bag. He picked up the finished page's cap from beside his hand and tossed it to Anathriel. "Put that on. We should all get cloaks too."

"I'm going to leave my father a letter," Anathriel said. "Let him know what we took."

"What, so he can show it to Lord Jassene's men?" Zeth asked. "I don't think so."

"He won't if I ask him not to," Anathriel replied, glaring. "I'm not stupid, despite what you think. I'll ask him not to report the loss and then burn the letter."

"And you think he'll do it?"

"Yes." It was true. Her father had always had a blind spot for her.

"Well, hurry up with it then."

Anathriel composed the letter quickly and stowed it in her father's office, in a place she knew he would find it soon. At last they were ready to go.

"All right," said Immen, turning to Anathriel. "Tell us about this secret route. What part of the palace is it in?"

"Kitchen cellar," Anathriel replied. "I've only seen it once, but it should be pretty quiet down there this time of night."

Immen nodded. He looked at Zeth. "There's a wall in the kitchen gardens we can climb over. Let's go."

He headed towards the door, and just as he did, a shadow filled the front window, then another. There were voices. "Get down!" Immen called as softly as possible, ducking quickly. He scuttled back towards Anathriel, Zeth, and Flute. "Back door," he whispered. "Flute, you ride with Anathriel."

Flute fluttered over to Anathriel and tucked herself inside the hood of her cloak, buzzing on her shoulder until she came to a rest. Just as they all reached the back door, the front burst open. "There they are!" shouted a guard.

"Run," Immen urged, taking the rear and shuffling them all out the door. Zeth was in the lead, putting Anathriel between the two. She could hear Flute's tiny breaths next to her ear, which were almost drowned out by the panicked pounding of her own heartbeats.

Once they were out in the street, she was forced to admit to herself that it was much easier to run in the trousers, but they didn't go very far before Zeth stopped, causing Anathriel to nearly run into him.

"Watch it!" she hissed. "Why are we stopped?"

"Shhh," he ordered, holding up a hand.

Coming up behind her, Immen leaned in closely so she could hear his whisper. "Walk slowly," he instructed. "Be as quiet as possible. In this fog, they won't be able to see us, so we need to take advantage of it."

"Thank the Master for the fog, then," Flute whispered back.

It was clear that Zeth knew the streets of Montressa very, very well. Anathriel had no idea how he was able to determine their position at all, let alone know which direction to go. They walked as noiselessly as possible, giving her time to reflect upon the utter strangeness of the situation. She was in men's clothes, in the middle of the night, fleeing her home. She was probably friends with some of the guards chasing them. She would be taking advantage of Lady Rillandra's trust in her by showing Zeth and Immen the secret tunnel. There was a fairy on her shoulder, and she'd witnessed magic twice now. How had this happened?

To keep her anxieties at bay, Anathriel focused only on Zeth's footsteps in front of her, the swish of his cloak against his back ankles, and making sure she didn't trip over anything in the dark.

Anathriel found the kitchen garden wall Immen had spoken of far more imposing than Immen seemed to think it. Anathriel decided that this difference of perspective must have been one of gender, however, because both of her companions scaled the stones with no trouble. When she failed climbing more than a few feet in several strained attempts, Immen was forced at last to climb back down and lift her onto his shoulders while Zeth pulled her up from above. The experience was unflattering at best, but somehow they managed.

Finally, it was Anathriel's turn to take the lead. Once inside the lower levels of the palace, they took more care not to be seen, as they no longer had the advantage of the enshrouding fog. Anathriel got turned around a couple of times trying to locate the unobtrusive door, but at last they found it. Zeth and Anathriel slipped through, and Immen brought up the rear, a torch he'd borrowed from a wall nearby in hand. When he pulled the door firmly shut behind them, it echoed down the stone passageway with a resounding thud. Anathriel couldn't help but think the door was closing forever on her life as she'd known it. The thought was not altogether cheerful.

11

"This—is—way—too—high." Xari stopped to take a deep breath. "And the higher it gets, the more lightheaded I feel. And colder. How does anyone breathe up here?"

"Look on the bright side—coming down will be much easier," Ashe consoled.

"You get to fly or ride my shoulder, so don't even start," Xari said crossly.

"You're just grumpy because you haven't had any brew this morning," Ashe said pointedly.

Xari made a face at him. The brew Burin had packed for her was long since gone, and Ashe probably had a point. "I'm glad we're almost there. Shouldn't we be there by now? Jesper? You said we had three bends in the road to go. Haven't we already gone around three?"

"Two." Jesper was perched on top of her head. He kept standing up and bouncing around, trying to see everything, which meant she kept feeling little feet dancing on her scalp.

Xari clenched her teeth and pressed one hand against her forehead. She'd had a headache all morning, and it was steadily getting worse. She blamed it on the elevation, but she wished it would go away. Besides that, her mind kept going back to Mortén. She had been checking his location through their connection since beginning the journey. She had known the moment he arrived in Montressa, and he had yet to leave. She wondered if he knew she was also coming to Montressa—it depended entirely on whether he bothered to check her whereabouts. She hoped to avoid him while she was in the city.

Collecting herself, she picked up her feet and started off again. "One more bend," she repeated. "I can do that." She pulled her long-sleeved tunic more snuggly around herself and shivered.

When she finally got around the next wide turn in the road, she stopped and stared. The entrance to the city of Montressa was between two high cliffs, an ornate golden gate built into the stone. It was presently hanging open, but according to the tidbits of information that Xari had picked up on her trek, the gates would close during the night.

Four guards posted at the entrance were standing at attention, but didn't hinder Xari as she passed through, though she noted the usual odd glances at her out of the corners of their eyes. As soon as she was inside, she stepped out of the way and stopped again. She stared up at the peaks of the city, at the roads meandering and twisting upward and sideways, some going straight into the mountains. Buildings were perched everywhere, built on ledges and slopes. The highest peak wasn't terribly far away, and Xari could make out the outline of towers with golden spires.

"That must be Par Auspré. That's where I feel Mortén's presence." Pulling her eyes away from it, she surveyed her surroundings in amazement. "This place is huge. Look at all the roads. I think we're going to get lost."

"How can we get lost when we don't even know where we're going?" Ashe pointed out.

Xari rolled her eyes. She turned her head so she could see him, feeling the pitter-patter of Jesper's feet on her head again as she did so. "Do you have any idea where to start looking for Immen Corper?" Trying to find one person in a city of strangers was a perplexing task.

"I haven't a notion," Ashe said, "but at least we know who we're looking for."

"That's true," Xari agreed. It was Jesper who had provided them with the name of Immen Corper. According to the fairy historians, he was a descendent of the House of Wolves through his mother's side. Once the name had roused Ashe's memory, he'd been able to recall some of the details Jesper had not known.

And then there was Jesper himself. Xari did not believe in coincidence, and she couldn't help but wonder what providential purpose had crossed his path with theirs.

"We have to hurry," Ashe said, drawing Xari's thoughts back to the present. "If there isn't a fairy here seeking him yet, there could be one any moment."

"Our best bet is probably to find a tavern or an inn and ask about him," Xari decided. "Surely someone in the city knows who he is."

Ashe shrugged his tiny shoulders. "That sounds reasonable. Where do you want to go first?"

Xari gazed at the numerous wandering pathways. "This way," she said, heading off toward the right.

She stopped at the first inn she came to, a tall place built into the side of a mountain in the middle of a twisting road. She stepped inside. It greatly resembled most other inns she'd seen in her lifetime, but for the staircases that adorned all edges of the room, climbing to higher levels, from which Xari could hear more bustling activity.

"Can I help you?" The matron of the establishment was bone thin and very clean. She studied Xari cautiously, taking in the braids and the breeches. Xari sensed the woman's fierce pride. Xari had met people like her before; she probably wasn't sure what to make of this savage-looking stranger, but she wasn't going to turn down good business without cause.

"A room, if you have one," Xari said, pulling out some coins. "One night at a time. I'm not sure how long I'll be staying."

"Very well, miss. Anything else?"

Figuring it was as good a time as any to broach her purpose, Xari ventured, "I'm looking for someone. A man by the name of Immen Corper."

Several people turned their heads in her direction at her words, and Xari felt a mild sense of surprise coming from them, and the matron as well.

"Immen Corper?" the matron repeated. "You and everyone else. If you want to find him, you won't have much luck here in Montressa. He's gone."

"Gone?" Xari asked, alarmed and disappointed. Had the fairies beaten her here, after all?

"It's been all over the city, miss," piped up a laundress carrying an armful of bedcloths nearby. "Terrific scandal. He ran away with one of the Lady's maidens."

"Mind your chores, Tilda," chided the matron. She turned back to Xari. "She's right, though. There's been talk of little else around here these past few days. Captain of the Windriders with a promising career—not even noble, but he made something of himself. Until he ran off with that young handmaiden." She shook her head.

A man nearby who'd been munching noisily on the wing of some

117

type of fowl jumped into the conversation. "Irresponsible, if you ask me. Young Lord Feldstone has had to step in as acting Windrider captain. Of course, Lady Kavela certainly cannot be happy with that Lelaine girl."

"Certainly not. A merchant's daughter, you know!"

"The most confusing thing is why they eloped at all. From what I'm told, they were a perfectly suitable match for one another. They would have met with little objection."

Xari glanced at Ashe, who appeared rather unsettled. Was it possible? She certainly knew nothing about the man, so she couldn't refute it, but given the circumstances surrounding Xari's arrival in the city, she was willing to bet there was more to the story than met the eye. "When did this happen?"

"Oh, not a week gone, miss. No one knows where they went, either, or how they got away."

Xari questioned the woman until the woman finally began to wonder about Xari's interest in the matter, and began asking questions of her own. Then Xari politely drew the conversation to a close and asked to retire to her room.

"What's eloped, please?" Jesper asked as soon as the matron had shut the door to Xari's room behind her, leaving the three companions alone at last.

"Eloping is when two people sneak off and get married in secret," Xari said.

"What's married?"

"When two humans become lifelong mates," Xari said simply.

Jesper's eyes lit up in understanding. "Oh!"

"Well, this is just great," Xari said, sighing heavily. "All this way for nothing."

"I'm certain it won't be for nothing," Ashe advised serenely. "I think you and I both know this can't be coincidence. We're going to have to see if we can learn anything else."

Xari, in great need of rest, took advantage of Jesper's presence by sending him off into the city to see if he could learn anything else. Ashe wasn't thrilled about letting him go alone, but they all agreed it was best if Xari remained more or less unseen until nightfall. He gave the young fairy a strict word of caution before he disappeared. Xari very much hoped Jesper would learn something more helpful, because despite all the gossip and rumors, she wanted more substantial information. Knowing where Immen and his unexpected female companion had gone would be helpful, for starters.

By the time the young fairy returned, Xari had awakened from her rest and bought a dinner, which she took alone up in her room.

"So what did you learn?" Ashe asked Jesper, sounding prepared to be very disapproving.

Xari smiled.

"Well, I found the eyries!" Jesper said excitedly. "Up by that big building on the high peak—Par Osprey, I think? You should have seen all the eagles, Magi Asheford! They're *so* big!" He helped himself to a bowl of nuts on the table. "There were a lot of humans talking, too, in the eyries—the humans who ride the eagles. They don't think that Immen snuck off and eloped. They said Immen wouldn't have done that. They were talking about how they can't believe he left, because that's not something he would do, either. But he did leave, and he did have a girl with him. That girl with the funny name. Alanrie—"

"Anathriel?" Xari supplied, recalling part of her downstairs discoveries.

"That's it!" Jesper agreed, crunching a nut as he talked. "Why do humans have such funny names?" He shrugged to himself. "Anyway, that was all. I still don't know if Flute made it here!" he said dejectedly.

Xari rubbed her temples tiredly. "Immen was Windrider captain. If his fellow Windriders don't think he would have run off, or eloped—well, let's suppose for a moment that he didn't. He must have had a very good reason for leaving. Perhaps one of the fairies reached him—Thornbee or Flute, but one of them. Still, why would he have taken a handmaiden with him?" She shook her head. "We really can't be certain until we find Immen, but there are still other questions that need to be answered. I really need to talk to the eagles; they might have a lot more insight."

"There's a great risk of running into Mortén up there," Ashe pointed out.

"I know."

"Oh! Oh! I can help!" Jesper jumped off of the table and fluttered excitedly in the air. "I know how to get into the eyries!"

Ashe grabbed Jesper by his foot and pulled him back down to land on the table. "Oh, I don't think so."

"But—"

"Even if the eagles did know something about it, how can we be sure that knowledge will help us? What we need—" Xari's eyes lit up as an idea struck her, and she looked at Ashe. "What we need is to track them."

Ashe blinked, considering. "Track? But what do you—?" Then his eyes filled with understanding. "Oh, I see! That may work, but only if you can find—"

"What might work? Find what?" Jesper asked.

Xari and Ashe exchanged glances, and Xari replied, "Wolves. They're hunters; that's their gift. They can find almost anything they're searching for, and they might agree to help us track down Immen, if we can find them. That's something the eagles definitely *can* help us with."

"That still leaves us with the problem of reaching the eagles," Ashe said.

Xari tugged on a braid thoughtfully. "I say we risk it."

Ashe frowned. "Well, I could use my magic to hide you from other people, but you know that it wouldn't work on Mortén."

Xari nodded. With magic, Ashe had the capability to conceal her for a short time, as long as she didn't touch anyone. The reason it wouldn't work on Mortén was because of their speaker connection. Just as they could find one another mentally, they couldn't be hidden from one another through magic, or so Ashe had always believed.

"Oooh!" Jesper breathed. "You're going to shade her. Can I watch?"

Ashe rolled his eyes. "Well, you're certainly not going anywhere away from us! Besides, you just pointed out that you can get into the eyries, so you'll be our guide." Under his breath, he muttered, "I can't believe I suggested that."

Jesper flew up and landed on Xari's shoulder. "This is such big magic! We're never allowed to do things like this!"

"That's because this is something that Grand Magi learn to do," Ashe replied tartly.

"Oh. Right." Jesper's wings drooped for a moment; then he brightened. "Maybe one day I'll get to be a Grand Magi."

Ashe landed on Xari's other shoulder, and Xari heard him mutter, "Master, preserve us should that ever happen."

Anathriel could hardly believe how much her life had changed in only six short days. She hardly recognized herself. She was learning things that she had never expected to ever need to know. She knew how to pack a bedroll neatly and carry it comfortably, and which parts of a rabbit were most tender and how to cook them, just to name a few. It seemed that far longer a period of time had passed. The only thing that remained constant was her bickering with Zeth, and even then sometimes they were too tired to speak.

Anathriel longed for a hot bath and a comfortable bed, but Immen had told her they couldn't risk detouring or staying in any towns. They had been traveling in the forest at the foot of the mountains for four days now, led along by Flute's sense of direction, which Anathriel was not at all certain about, especially after Flute had let it slip that she had gotten "slightly lost" on the way to Montressa.

"I merely went a bit too far north in the grasslands. They all look the same, you know. I won't get lost this time, though. I know the way now," the fairy had said cheerfully.

From what Anathriel had seen of the fairy's capabilities, this did not instill confidence in her. At least Immen was keeping track of their whereabout, and said that he knew where they were, and that yes, they were headed in the right direction, which was a small comfort to Anathriel.

"Immen?"

Immen was slightly ahead of her as they walked through the trees, and didn't even bother to stop. "What, Anathriel?" he asked wearily.

"I would appreciate it if we could stop for a bit. I am tired, and hungry, and my pack is getting heavier by the moment." Despite herself, tears stung Anathriel's eyes. Not only had this journey been physically draining, but it had also taken its toll emotionally. She would never have admitted it, particularly in front of Zeth, but she was terrified. Her life, so certain only a week ago, would never be the same. She was doing everything she could not to think about it, yet it was impossible not to. All she could do at this point was try her best to keep the despair and fear from consuming her, so she wouldn't be immobilized by it. She was afraid that if she gave into the hopelessness of everything that had happened to her, she would go completely insane. She had already cried herself to sleep several nights—silent tears, for she would not give anyone the satisfaction of hearing her weep.

"I know, Anathriel, but we really need to keep going. It's only two hours past midday."

Anathriel blinked away the tears that threatened to fall. "We're going to be in this—" Anathriel's shirt snagged on a branch and she stopped to untangle it "—accursed forest for well over another week at our fastest pace. Why can't we go slowly?"

Anathriel had suggested taking the River Road, but both Immen and Zeth had vetoed the idea, saying it would be more difficult to go unnoticed on such a public transport. On foot, it would take *ages* to reach Fairlight Forest. From what she understood, they had to cross the moors and the plains. Then they had to go over Jier Ré, the Great River. That in itself scared Anathriel. The western countries in the Eastern Continent bordered some very dangerous and strange wilderness lands, if any of the stories she had heard were true. Judging from Flute's sudden appearance, at least some of them had merit, and she was frightened to find out which other ones were. To leave the safety of the habited parts of the continent was something she had yet to come to grips with.

"We are going slowly," Zeth retorted from behind her. "Maybe if you didn't complain so much—"

"Complain? Excuse me? I didn't ask for this! I—"

"—never shut up!" Zeth inserted.

"Zeth," Immen said, just as wearily as he had sounded a moment ago.

Zeth promptly fell silent, and Anathriel gave him a fierce look over her shoulder. He glared right back.

"We'll stop in a couple more hours, Anathriel, and we'll eat and camp for the night," Immen assured her.

Anathriel drew a deep breath and stopped to lean against a tree. A moment later, she experienced the familiar sensation of an invisible hook pulling at her. She was still startled by the sudden yank and quickly stepped forward, just managing to keep her balance.

Immen wasn't so fortunate. He was thrown backwards and promptly fell onto his backside. He stayed on the ground for a moment, and then pushed himself to his feet as Anathriel rushed forward. "Oh! I'm sorry, Immen. I keep misjudging the distance!"

The stupid, stupid bond. Not so long ago, she would have given anything to be close to Immen, but not like this. Not without the freedom to go anywhere alone.

"That's all right." Immen's eyes met hers. "Anathriel, I know it has been a long, hard couple of days, but we have to get as far away from Montressa as possible. The deeper into the forest we can get, the harder we'll be to find."

"Yes, until we come out and wander off into the moors!"

"Well, we'll never get to the moors if we don't get through the forest, now will we?" Zeth muttered, walking past her toward Immen.

"Stop, stop, stop!" Flute's shrill voice rang through the air, and she appeared from behind Immen.

They had discovered that she was bound only to him, so she had to stay as near to him as Anathriel did. The little fairy had been taking turns riding on their shoulders or on the tops of their heads, or flying along beside them. Anathriel had even caught her singing to herself at one point—something about songs a sun and rain and singing again—a happy little tune that had made Anathriel even more frustrated with Flute. How could she be cheerful after everything that had happened? Didn't she realize how she had turned their lives upside-down?

"You're never going to make this journey if you can't get along!" Flute cried now.

"Anathriel, can we please go on for a little while longer?" Immen asked. "Just a little longer." He came toward her and offered her his arm.

Anathriel gazed at him for a moment, then pursed her lips, too exhausted to argue. "All right, Immen."

They ended up walking for another four hours before they set up camp in one of the many clearings in the wood. Anathriel immediately collapsed by a tree and sighed in relief.

"What's wrong?" Flute asked, popping up in front of her in a way that never failed to startle Anathriel.

"The same thing that was wrong yesterday, and the day before that, and—" Anathriel stopped herself, trying to get a grip on her irritability. "I'm exhausted."

"It's too bad you don't have wings."

"Yes, well, not all of us can be so fortunate," Anathriel said waspishly, closing her eyes.

"Although I got tired with all the flying I did at first, I got used to it," Flute continued. "I bet you'll get used to all the walking, too!"

"Fantastic," Anathriel muttered. "I simply wish I didn't ache as much."

"Hmm. It's too bad there are no unicorns around."

Anathriel's eyes snapped open. "Unicorns? You mean they're—they're real?" When she was little, she had always loved the stories and drawings of the horned white horses in the books her father had.

"Of course they're real! They're one of the twelve brethren!" Flute exclaimed. "I told you all about the twelve brethren right after we left Montressa! Weren't you listening?"

Anathriel vaguely remembered hearing Flute talking about different animals and creatures, but she couldn't remember all the details. Of course, considering it had been pouring rain for half of the day, and she had been picking her way down a mountain, she thought it wasn't fair to expect her to pay attention to the conversation.

"Unicorns pretty much keep to themselves," Flute went on. "They never come near humans anymore. They're healers, though. They could take away your pain."

"Healers?" Zeth asked with interest. He looked up from the fire he had started. "What do you mean?"

Anathriel scooted over to the fire, glad for its warmth. Her stomach clenched with hunger, and she dug a piece of flatbread out of her pack while Flute continued talking.

"Well, all of the brethren have a special gift," Flute said, flying over and landing on his shoulder. "The unicorns can heal."

"What can the eagles do?" Zeth asked curiously.

"Um, they have far sight."

"Of course they do," Immen said, moving to sit beside Zeth. "Eagles can see much farther than humans."

"No, no, not that kind of sight! They can *see,* you know. They have visions. They can see into the past or the future. And you'll be able to, too!" Flute told Immen.

"What do you mean, I'll be able to?"

"You'll be speaker for the eagles, and that means you'll have the same gift they do."

Immen blinked. "I—really? Is it like that for all of the speakers?"

"Yes. The speakers share a special bond with the brethren they speak for. Why do you think Mortén is so strong? The leviathans have the gift of strength, and so does Mortén, because he's their speaker."

"You said there were two speakers," Anathriel stated. "Mortén and Immen, so—"

"No, no, Immen's not a speaker yet. He has to see the Grand Magi first. Mortén is the speaker for the leviathans, and there's another speaker for the otters." Flute shook her feathery head. "None of the fairies know who the Otter Speaker is."

"Why not?" Anathriel asked.

Flute shook her head again. "One of my people did something…" She said simply, "We don't talk about it."

"What is the otters' gift?" Zeth asked.

Flute shrugged. "I don't know. Some of the gifts we remember, but it's been so long since there were speakers that the rest of them have been forgotten." She bounced off of Zeth's shoulder and into the air.

Immen stared at her. "So there's another speaker out there, with a gift that could be a curse for us, if it's anything like Mortén's."

Anathriel wondered if Immen was thinking the same thing she was—was the other speaker like Mortén? From everything she had seen of the man, she knew for certain that she didn't want to come across another like him. When Immen became a speaker, what was he going to have to face?

She shivered and turned her mind away from that thought, fixing it again on the business at hand. She turned pointedly to Zeth. "Well?"

"Well, what?" Zeth replied.

"You told me you would make me a dress. That was six days ago. You cannot possibly give me any further excuse. It's not raining, you're not going hunting, you're not fussing around with Immen and that sword—if I have to go in trousers one more day—"

Zeth rolled his eyes. "It'll be harder for you to walk in a dress."

"And exactly how would you know?" Anathriel snapped, more than fed up with Zeth and his wretched attitude.

Zeth simply looked at her and raised his eyebrows.

"For your information, I can do anything in a dress that I can do in trousers, and I'll be far more comfortable," Anathriel continued. "So if you wouldn't mind, I would appreciate—"

"Oh, so you're asking now?" Zeth interrupted.

"Oh, for goodness' sake!"

"Zeth," Immen called quietly. Zeth stopped and turned his eyes upon Immen, who waved the younger boy over. Zeth shot Anathriel another hostile look before going over to Immen, who spoke softly to him for a moment. Anathriel was positive they were discussing her, since Zeth sent several glances her way, but she tossed her head and tried to ignore both of them.

Zeth finally moved away from Immen, snatching his pack off the ground and pulling out a bolt of gray material. Within minutes, he was expertly taking Anathriel's measurements and laying out a pattern on the cloth. Before long, he had the pieces cut out, and he was stitching them together.

Anathriel moved nearer to him to observe and was immediately infuriated. "Excuse me! What are you doing?"

"I'm making you a dress," Zeth said, in the patronizing tone that had become long familiar to Anathriel.

"You—" Zeth's stitches were extremely sloppy, and Anathriel was sure he was doing it intentionally. She had seen him sew, and if he had truly been a tailor's term-slave for years, then he could sew well, but he was deliberately being careless on her dress. "You irritating little—" Anathriel snatched the dress away from him. "If you're going to be so impertinent about it, I'll sew it. Give me the needle."

Zeth relinquished the needle and thread, then sat back with a smug expression. Anathriel resisted the temptation to throw something at him. She turned her back on him and carefully began stitching the dress together. Gray definitely wasn't her color, and the pattern was unflattering at best, but it was better than trousers. She worked until there wasn't enough daylight to comfortably see her work and put it away. It would take a few days to finish the garment.

By the time she was done, Zeth had gone to bed and Flute was curled up on his stomach. Immen was lying on his bedroll, but his eyes were open. Anathriel walked over to her pack and untied her own bedroll. She was exhausted and knew that Immen and Zeth would want to get an early start, no matter how much she protested.

"He's had a rough life," Immen said unexpectedly from behind her.

Anathriel smoothed out her bedroll and spared Immen a glance over her shoulder. "He's a runaway term-slave, Immen." A horribly rude, conceited, mulish, incorrigible one at that.

"He's a human being, Anathriel," Immen replied quietly.

"We're each born into our position, and if we have the initiative, we can work our way into something greater. I can't help it if he was an orphan. That doesn't give him an excuse to be so belligerent."

"And being a handmaiden doesn't give you the right, either."

Anathriel whirled on him, her eyes flashing. "How dare you! I—"

"You've always had everything you wanted, Anathriel," Immen interrupted, but without any venom in his voice. "Listen, I'm sorry you have been taken away from the life you loved. I'm sorry you have been pulled along on this. I know you've had a hard time these last couple of days, and I understand. This isn't an easy journey to make."

Despite her aggravation at the situation and everyone involved, Anathriel felt her resolve to be angry with Immen waver slightly. She had sought his approval for so long that hearing any of it now, particularly in the midst of Zeth's criticism, was like a breath of fresh air—until she remembered her grudge. Before she could stop herself, she was asking, "Why didn't you tell me the favor was your sister's?"

Immen looked startled by the abrupt change in subject. "What?"

"The favor, during the spring ceremonies. You said you couldn't take my favor because you already had one, and then I found out it belonged to your sister." The memory brought on a wave of fresh hurt. "Why couldn't you simply tell me you weren't interested in me?"

Immen's forehead creased in a frown. It was a long moment before he spoke. "I had already agreed to wear Areen's favor during the ceremonies when you asked."

"You still could have told me that, instead of leading me to believe that—" Anathriel broke off and shook her head. "Don't try to tell me you didn't know what I was thinking."

He was quiet. "I did," he confessed at last.

"So you wanted to discourage me."

There was a very uncomfortable silence, filled only by the hum of stirring nightlife. "I didn't know I would hurt your feelings so badly," he finally replied.

"Well, you did," Anathriel said, tilting her chin slightly. "And I hope that in the future, you will be more straightforward. I'm not brittle, you know."

Immen considered her carefully, then slowly nodded. "So it would seem. I promise."

"Good. Apology accepted." Anathriel sniffed. She laid down on her bedroll and closed her eyes. Perhaps this expedition would be good for one or two things. Maybe she would be able to show Immen that there was more to her than he thought. She couldn't guarantee that he would ever return her feelings for him, but she had an opportunity to try, and Anathriel Lelaine had long ago learned not to waste opportunities.

Sighing, her mind drifted back to her home. Her fellow handmaidens would have fits if they could see her now. She wondered just how they were doing. Was Lady Rillandra furious with her? What did her father think? What had happened to Mortén? Just what was going on in Montressa?

⌘ ⌘ ⌘

Entering the eyries was one of the stranger experiences of Xari's journey. She, Ashe, and Jesper waited until late into the night, so that most inhabitants would have gone to bed, and then made their way up to the second-highest pinnacle in Montressa. A thin mist had descended upon the mountains, so Xari treaded carefully. They finally reached the large gate surrounding the eyries, and Xari had to scale it while Ashe hid her from the sight of the guards. She thanked the Master for every time she had hammered metal in Burin's forge; if it weren't for the strength she had built up, she never would have made it over the gate.

There were several entrances to the housing of the eagles, but at this time of night, all were closed save for the southern one. It was this that Xari approached. The shadows of the mountains covered her, making it easier for Ashe to shade her. Xari knew that it was straining him; he couldn't make her invisible; he had to use air magic to screen her from the vision of the people they passed. She also had to move as quietly as possible, because though Ashe's protections temporarily kept her from being seen, they didn't keep her from being heard, the way the fairies' invisibility did. Ashe had performed this magic for her benefit once or twice before, and it had always tired him afterwards. She wouldn't have asked him to do it if she didn't think it necessary.

Jesper had said that there was a path leading out of Par Auspré to the eyries, to make it easier for the Windriders to deliver messages to the Lord and Lady of the High House, and he pointed it out as they passed. "Everything goes right through the mountains here!" He sounded impressed. "I don't know how they built all of this without it all falling on their heads! And I don't know why anyone would want to live in stone. How can they stand not living with lots and lots of trees?"

Ashe hushed Jesper, and Xari continued stealthily toward the south entrance, passing into the eyries between two guards. Neither of them stirred as she passed. She touched her link with Mortén one more time as she stepped into the eyries. He was close, so very, very close inside the palace of Par Auspré.

The sheer size and breadth of the eyries made her pause in awe, but only for a moment. The next instant, she was immediately scanning for signs of humans in the building. She didn't see anyone, though there was a large door in the center. Xari guessed it might be a hallway or an office of some sort, and she hurriedly moved as far away from it as she could, walking down the length of the enormous nests. The eagles were asleep; their beaks tucked into their wings, and only the sound of a few shifting wings could be heard.

The eagles had always been on her side. Their gift of foresight had saved Xari from the need to convince them of her intentions. Mortén had tried to gain their trust, but they had seen right through him, unlike some of the other brethren.

Choosing one of the eagles, Xari took a deep breath and approached him slowly. She glanced over her shoulder at the closed door, then beyond to the entrance she had come through. She was far enough away from it now that the guards shouldn't hear her. Letting out her breath, Xari whispered, "Excuse me."

The eagle she stood in front of snapped its head up, as did several of the eagles nearby. All fixed Xari with piercing stares, and she bowed her head slightly. "Good evening. Please forgive me for interrupting your sleep."

"Speaker," the eagle two nests to her left spoke, "we have been waiting for you, but you must leave at once. You are in danger here."

Xari didn't bother to question; she knew better. "I will leave immediately, but can you please tell me if you know where any of the wolf clans reside?"

"Of course we know," the eagle in front of her said, a bit sharply. "And we will send one of our brothers to show you the way, but you must leave now. Watch for our brother at the entrance to the city; he will lead you."

Xari nodded again. "Thank you." Picking up on their haste, she turned on her heel and made her way back to the entrance. She stopped when she realized that a contingent of guards now blocked it and were peering into the eyries with a frown. She couldn't walk past them, so she stood quietly for a moment, straining to hear what they were saying.

"…alerted us to an intruder in the eyries," one of them said.

Another guard raised an eyebrow. "I assure you, no one has come into the eyries. And do you see anyone?" He waved an arm to gesture at the building, looking right past Xari as he did so.

"Well, something's afoot," his compatriot said more doubtfully. "The beasts are stirring."

Xari's eyes darted to the large door nearby, but she couldn't open it without it being seen or heard, so she continued to remain still, a flutter of trepidation running through her. Who would have known she was here, save Mortén? Her anxiety increased when she again checked to see where Mortén was, and realized he was not far away at all, and he was rapidly moving closer, and she knew instantly that this was why the eagles had warned her. Mortén had sent the guards to block her escape— she doubted he knew the guards couldn't see her.

"What's going on?" Jesper asked in a loud whisper, as if the guards would be able to hear him if he spoke any louder. She felt him on her shoulder, pushing braids out of the way so he could see past them, tickling her neck with his wings.

Xari didn't answer—couldn't, or she would be heard. The door she had eyed moments earlier opened, revealing a young man with tousled blond hair standing in a long hallway. He held a stack of parchment, and it seemed he was leaving for the night. He considered the group of guards with a puzzled expression. "What is going on?"

"Xari! I cannot hold the shading much longer!" Ashe said urgently.

Xari turned fully and rested her hands on the hilts of her swords. Was this what it was going to come to? Fighting her way out of the eyries? Mortén had nearly reached her, and how would she get past him? He could snap her swords like twigs if he got a hold of them. She knew that he was a practiced swordsman; perhaps not a swordmaster like Burin, but he was very skilled, and he had many more years of experience under his belt than she did. *Dear Master, what am I supposed to do now?*

Xari glanced over her shoulder. Unfortunately, the only way out was through the huge open side of the eyries that she assumed to be the eagles' entrance. It was fairly close to the southern entrance, for which Xari was thankful. Had it been anywhere else, it would have taken her longer to reach it, given the enormity of the eyries. She moved swiftly toward it. The fog had thickened, and she couldn't see the ground. She knew even if it were visible, it wouldn't have helped. It would certainly be too high for her to jump.

Gasps drew Xari's attention back to the guards and the blond man, all of whom were staring in disbelief straight at her. "I lost it, Xari," Ashe said, frustrated.

"It's all right," Xari replied, her voice steely.

"Who are you? How did you get in here?" the blond man demanded.

"Master Feldstone, this must be trickery of some sort!" one of the guards exclaimed. "She did not come through the entrance, I swear it!"

"I—" Xari stopped when an eagle in the nest to her right spoke.

"Speaker! Listen quickly! You must move to the side of the entrance. I will fly out, and then you must jump. I will catch you."

Before Xari had time to acknowledge the eagle, the magnificent brethren had hopped gracefully onto the edge of his nest and down onto the ground, cutting the men off from Xari.

"Eulaie!" the man, Master Feldstone, cried out.

Xari threw herself to the left, holding onto the wall as the eagle spread his huge wings and leapt out of the eyries, catching himself in the air and gliding downward. She could just make out the vague shape of the eagle in the swirling gray blanket of fog.

A final glance backward showed her that the guards were running toward her—and behind them, a tall, stately looking man with graying hair had appeared in the open entrance. Despite the distance, her eyes were drawn almost magnetically to his. When they locked, Xari felt such a surge of loathing that she physically reeled backwards. With it came an onslaught of terrible anger, wrapped up in an undeniable and unavoidable connection. It was, without a doubt, Darius Mortén in the flesh.

That, if anything, spurred Xari into action. "Ashe, Jesper, grab onto me and hold on tight!" she called.

She felt her braids tugged as Jesper held more tightly to her hair, and didn't bother looking for Ashe. He would know what to do. Ripping her eyes away from Mortén's, Xari took a deep breath and launched herself out of the eyries into thin air. She heard someone scream something, but the rush of wind in her ears kept her from hearing their words.

For a sickening moment, Xari dropped, and her stomach seemed to be pushed into her throat. Then, with a *thwump,* she landed on a mass of feathers and clutched instinctively. With a wordless shriek, the eagle she was riding dove into the night.

12

Xari had come to the conclusion that solid ground was one of the Master's greatest gifts to humankind. The journey through the air had been long—much longer than she had expected when she had landed roughly atop the eagle's slick, feathered back. She had nearly fallen off at first, clutching handfuls of feathers in desperation, and it was clear that only the creature's keen sense of tilt and balance—as well as a seeming awareness of Xari's exact position on his back—had saved her. When she'd finally established a secure position—or as secure as she imagined was possible—she'd dug her face into the feathers, eyes tightly shut, and hung on for dear life. She hadn't looked up for a single moment, not even when she'd felt Ashe and Jesper shifting about to get a safer hold on her.

She lost track of how much time they flew, long into the night, while she desperately staved off the sleepiness that began to creep upon her. At last the eagle made a swift descent into the forest below. When Xari felt leaves and branches brushing her neck and back she dared to look up. A wizened, gnarled stump on the edge of a very small clearing made a landing perch for the great bird, and soon Xari was eagerly sliding off his back onto the forest floor below.

"Head south and you will come upon our brethren the wolves," said the eagle, "but I do not know what sort of reception you may expect."

"I do not know, either," Xari said. The wolves were very aloof and suspicious creatures. She'd spoken with one or two in Ithrin, but they rarely ventured so far south. Overall, her experiences with them could hardly be called successes. Although they had never harmed her, neither had they warmed up to her completely. They were admittedly slow to trust. On the other hand, this meant they had not aligned themselves with Mortén, either. She turned her full attention back to her rescuer—Eulaie was the name he had been called by humans. "Thank you for your help."

"It is my honor, Speaker. We hope that your arrival is a sign that the Master's ways will once again be honored in our land."

"Why do the eagles allow themselves to be used by humans as common mules?" Xari asked sadly. She reached up to stroke his sleek, beautiful neck.

"The humans have forgotten us, but we will not forget them. They are still the Master's children, and the Windriders of Montressa love us, in their own way."

"Soon they will know you for what you are," Xari promised. "That is what I hope to accomplish."

"It will come to pass, but it will not be you that brings it about," said Eulaie sagely. "The one we wait for is the one you pursue."

"Immen Corper."

Eulaie paused. "Immen Corper will be very important in your life, Xari of the otters. He will be missed."

"What do you mean?" Xari asked curiously.

The eagle did not reply. Instead, he spread his wings once more. "Due south," he repeated. Then, with two great beats of his wings, which created a breeze strong enough to stir Xari's braids, he was soaring up and out of sight.

"Well, that was interesting," she said aloud.

"What?" Jesper asked eagerly.

"Nothing. It's merely that eagles can be annoyingly cryptic when they want to be."

"Did he prophesy something?" Ashe asked. "Xari, what did he say? You should tell me; it could be important."

She shrugged. "That's the trouble. I'm not sure. But we're on the right trail, apparently. We'll camp here until daybreak. Then we head south."

⌘ ⌘ ⌘

After more than half a day's walk, Xari fervently began to wish that being awakened gave her the ability to locate all of the brethren, not just the otters. The trees became progressively older and taller, creating darker shadows in the forest, and everything was eerily quiet. All in all, not an inspiring way to search for a pack of predators.

"Yes, I can imagine there being a large passel of wolves lurking around here," she muttered to Ashe. "It resembles the evil forests from children's stories, doesn't it?"

"It feels like we're being watched," Jesper said.

"Well, that's what we want, isn't it?" Xari pointed out, trying to convince herself. "I don't know how to track a parade, much less a wolf."

"Which is why we need them to do the tracking for us," Ashe said.

She laughed a little. "Yes." Then she sighed.

"What are you worried about, little Xari?"

"How am I going to convince them I need their help? When we met Naris in Ithrin four years ago, she wasn't exactly polite. She treated me like I was a child."

"You *were* a child."

"Somehow I don't think it would have made a difference if I'd been thirteen or sixty-four. And then there was that other wolf, who wouldn't even bother telling me his name, remember?"

"Xari—"

"I think he must have met up with Mortén first, because he seemed angry with me."

"Xari—"

"He said something about not giving up trust again so easily, and then—what!" Ashe had flown directly in her face and stopped her gently in her tracks with a nudge of magic. He fixed his eyes somewhere behind her, and they were full of alert and meaning. Xari turned around slowly, with trepidation.

There were two great, gray wolves behind her, one sitting on its haunches, the other still on all fours. Both were staring at her with very calculating expressions in their dark eyes.

Xari's heart was suddenly beating very fast, and she took a deep, steadying breath. Her first instinct was to make herself less of a threat, so she slowly removed her sword belt from her waist, then lowered the belt and swords to the ground, kneeling as she did so, and bowing her head respectfully at the wolves. "I come in need of aid," she said quietly.

She could feel the movement of the wolves' heavy paws in the ground below her knees. Out of the corner of her eye, she saw them circling her. Jesper, who had lowered himself down to her head level when he'd seen Ashe do the same, was trembling violently as the great brethren sniffed him appraisingly, but to his credit he did not move or speak.

"It was not common, in the old days, for a speaker to travel with two guardians," one said at last.

Xari dared to look up. The one who had spoken was sitting on her haunches again, peering at Xari shrewdly. She was the larger of the two, with a full chest of white fur. "Ashe is my guardian," Xari replied, nodding where Ashe hovered on her left. "Jesper merely my companion." Another nod, this time at Jesper, who was shaking with fright. "My name is Xari. I am the Otter Speaker," she continued.

"We have heard reports of you," replied the great wolf, eyes fixed upon Xari's face. Her eyes drifted to the fairies, then back to Xari. She studied her for another moment, then finally said, "I am Appleseed. This is White Paw."

Xari blinked. Appleseed didn't strike her as a very wolf-like name. White Paw, on the other hand, was easy enough to understand. He was smaller; his coat was more matted than that of his elder. One of his front paws was white, the other gray. He finally stopped his pacing to look at Xari again, as if still trying to decide something. Whatever conclusion he came to, it must have been good, for he finally relaxed and opened his mouth, sticking out his tongue and panting. Xari almost got the impression he was smiling at her.

"What is it you require?" Appleseed asked in a shrewd tone, drawing Xari's attention back to her.

Slowly, Xari rose to her feet but left the sword belt on the ground. "Almost a week ago a man fled the city of Montressa. Do you know it?"

"The city in the sky? Yes. The mountain is on the northern border of this forest."

"That's correct. I need to find this man. I don't know for certain which way he's gone, but it's very likely he's heading for Fairlight Forest, along with another of Asheford and Jesper's people. I am also almost entirely sure there was another with him. A woman."

White Paw put his tongue back in his mouth and the wolves exchanged significant glances. Finally, White Paw spoke for the first time. He seemed amused. "Yes, they passed this way," he said. "I'm not sure we could have missed them. They traveled so loudly an ass could

136

have found them. They, too, traveled with a fairy, but we knew that they were not speakers, as we could not understand their speech. There was also another with them. Another male."

"Another?" Xari echoed. She turned to Jesper. "Did you hear anything in Par Auspré about anyone else missing?" She and Ashe certainly hadn't heard anything about it.

He sighed reluctantly, as though he was being quizzed on a lesson by an elder. Then he screwed up his face in concentration. "A boy ran away. They said he was a slave," he said at last, and Xari sensed the unfamiliarity of the word on his tongue. "About four days after Immen Corper and the lady. Or at least it was four days after that they found him missing. The eagle riders—"

"Windriders," Xari inserted.

"Yes, those people mentioned it." Jesper shook his head. "I'm sorry, it didn't seem like it was very important. Most people wanted to talk about the eloped."

"Elopement," said Xari and Ashe at the same time, unthinking. Then Xari added, "I suppose maybe there could be a connection." She addressed the wolves again. "These are all? No others?"

"Going the way you asked? There was one other, but there were none with him—only a dog."

Xari paled and relayed this information to Ashe. "Hunter," he muttered softly.

"Mortén could have sent someone," she agreed, her mind racing. "I had wondered why he would've still been sitting up in the city so calmly. I don't think his desire to capture me would have been enough to dampen his need to pursue the others."

"What is it you require? If it was information you sought, I believe you could have found it elsewhere." Appleseed repeated her earlier question in a tone that suggested she was still trying to size up the situation, or Xari. Or perhaps both.

"I came to ask you to help me find them. The man I'm seeking has been chosen to carry a lost relic—I'm not certain which relic. He must be intercepted before his life is threatened."

"You would not wish this man awakened?" asked the large wolf. She seemed suddenly more threatening.

"I would," Xari assured her. "But not until the proper time. Do you know of Mortén?" she asked carefully. She had no idea what these wolves thought of her adversary. She was trying to feel out the situation as much as the wolves were. "If you've heard reports of me, then surely—"

"Yes, we know his name," said White Paw.

"Mortén would not wish this new speaker awakened. I must protect the new speaker from him," Xari said. "He will have much to learn, and the more he knows what he's getting into, the better."

Appleseed and White Paw were quiet for a very long time. At last, the former spoke. "What is it you seek, Xari of the otters?"

Xari's brow furrowed in confusion. "What? I told you, I'm looking for—"

"No," the large wolf cut her off. "What is your grander purpose? Why do you wish so badly to thwart Mortén? We have heard reports, yes, of both you and Mortén, but why should we believe that you have come to us in honesty and integrity? Why should we trust you, let alone help you?"

Xari considered her words carefully before she spoke. "Mortén seeks to thwart me, therefore I am forced to deal with him, but more than that, I wish the ways of the speakers and the brethren to be restored to the Master's earth. You must know that the balance between the races is in danger of being lost forever."

"Yes," agreed Appleseed.

"I know that you have no reason to trust me—you do not know me, any more than I know you. I hope, though, that for both of our sakes, you will allow me the chance to show you that I am trustworthy. Unfortunately, I fear my time to find the chosen speaker is short."

Appleseed considered Xari for a long moment. "We will take you to rejoin the rest of our pack, and we will see what will be done with you."

"Thank you," Xari said respectfully, hoping this was a step in the right direction.

"Hooray!" cried Jesper when Xari announced they would be joining the other wolves. He paused. "I mean, that's good, right?"

"I think so," Xari said.

"Then hooray!" Jesper said again. He gave a yelp of fear, however, when White Paw ran by and snapped at him playfully with his jaws.

"Careful, Jesper," Xari said, laughing as she donned her swords again.

"White Paw says he likes fairies for snacks when they get too loud."

She was sure the wolf smiled at her again. Feeling a bit more at ease now than she had an hour ago, Xari hitched her pack up more securely on her shoulders and increased her pace to match the wolves, who were already moving steadily south through the thick trees.

It took only a short while before Xari and her small troupe met up with Appleseed and White Paw's pack, and the reception that met them was mixed. There were seven other wolves in the pack—three of them pups. A black and white male wolf approached first and sniffed at her. "Why have you brought her here?" he asked.

"She is the Otter Speaker. She is seeking aid," Appleseed said frankly.

"And you agreed to give it?" the other wolf asked in disbelief.

"No. I agreed to bring her here," Appleseed replied calmly. "She is called Xari. Xari, this is Dagger, the leader of my pack."

"It is in honor to meet you," Xari said, bowing slightly. She was distracted when the pups darted up to her and started sniffing at her breeches. "It smells like a bird!" one pup cried.

"Does that mean we can eat it?" another asked.

"It doesn't look like a bird," the third pup put in.

"She's not an 'it,'" Appleseed told the young wolves. "She is a 'her,' and no, you may not eat her."

"Perhaps we should hear what she has to say," a small white and tan female spoke up.

"She is a speaker," a gray male growled. "Our experiences with—"

"Perhaps she is different," the female interrupted, leaving Xari to wonder what their experiences with Mortén had been.

"Still, why should we help her? What help have speakers—or anyone else, for that matter—been to us?" the gray male demanded. "We have always had to help ourselves!"

"Maybe that can change," Xari said quietly. Nine pairs of eyes fixed upon her. Feeling the heavy tension in the air, Xari gathered her courage and spoke again. "That's why I'm here. Because it must change. You—all wolves—are part of the twelve brethren, and you are needed as much as speakers are needed. I want to help—"

"And how do you suppose you can help?" the gray male asked incredulously. "Look at you! You're a scrawny pup! How do you expect to—"

"Appearances, Blue Moon, can be very deceiving, which you would do well to remember." It was Appleseed who spoke this time.

"We will discuss this privately," Dagger cut in. He turned to Xari and spoke to her for the first time. "You. If you attempt any treachery, you risk your life. Do not think we will be unable to find you."

Xari nodded, her stomach fluttering nervously. She sat carefully on the ground. "I won't move."

The wolves disappeared into the forest, leaving her alone with the fairies. Ashe immediately flew to where he could see Xari's face. "What is going on?"

It took a minute to explain, and when she finished, she fell into apprehensive silence. Jesper seemed even more nervous than she was, hopping from her shoulder to her head to her other shoulder. "I thought coming here was a good thing," he said.

"We don't know that it isn't. If I can make headway with the wolves here, well, it could do wonders for the future," Xari replied.

"What if they try to eat you?" Jesper asked.

"Wolves don't eat people," Xari said quietly. "That's a myth that ignorant humans have concocted." She rested her arms on her knees. "And I don't think they'll harm me—unless I try to run away," she added. "They're simply trying to figure out what to do with me." She glanced at Ashe, and a small smile crossed her face. "Besides, this is definitely going better than our meeting with the dragons."

"Why?" Jesper asked, wide-eyed. "What happened with the dragons?"

"*They* tried to eat me."

⌘⌘⌘

It was awhile before the wolves returned, and when they did, it was Dagger who came to speak to her. Xari remained seated as he approached, hoping that in doing so she was showing him that she truly posed no threat. The wolf stood over her for a long moment before he said, "It has been decided that we will grant you our assistance."

A relieved smile crossed Xari's face. "You have my gratitude."

"Know this," Dagger said, a low growl of warning in his voice. "We are allowing you this one chance to prove yourself. Should it be revealed that you are speaking false, or that you are dishonorable, you will not get another opportunity to spread your treachery."

Xari studied the great black and white wolf. "I understand."

"Good. You will leave first thing in the morning. White Paw will accompany you." The leader of the wolf pack turned and trotted away without giving her a chance to respond.

Despite the wolves' agreement to help her, Xari still felt the tension as the wolves went about their business—at least one of them was always present to watch her. She could feel the weight of strain upon the wolves, and she could not get her muscles to relax. She suspected that some of the wolves were not happy with the decision to help her, and that was causing stress in the clan.

Some of this tension was alleviated when one of the wolf pups, a small female, decided that the fairies were fascinating, and that chasing them was a splendid new game. Ashe thought she was funny, and would play right along with her, but Jesper was less than pleased and spent his time constantly flying from her keen little nose, not realizing that the pup seemed to think he was playing games, as well.

"How easily the young are amused." Appleseed's voice distracted Xari as the large wolf sat down beside her.

Xari smiled. "It must be nice to be so carefree."

"You speak as though you do not know what it is like, but if I am not mistaken about human age, you are not that old yourself," Appleseed said.

"You're not mistaken," Xari said softly. "I'm not that old, by way of human time. But I never really had a carefree childhood. And being a speaker can be—" She broke off and shook her head.

"Can be what?"

Xari twisted a braid around her finger, absentmindedly watching Jesper dart into the leaves of a tree branch and refuse to come out, while the little pup yapped at him from the ground. "It can be a bit frightening," she said at last.

"And what is it about being a speaker that you fear, Xari of the otters?"

Xari contemplated a long time before replying. "Failure," she confessed. She drew her knees up to her chest and rested her chin upon them. "I mean, sometimes I feel like everything's depending on me, you know? Then I feel like I'm the only human in the world that believes the truth. And I'm supposed to convince everyone else? All by myself?"

"If you find this other that you seek, you will not cease to be alone?"

Xari rubbed her arms against the night chill. "I'm not sure," she murmured. The fears she had expressed so long ago to the otters came flooding back to the surface. She knew, as Ashe had told her, that they had the advantage of her gift to aid them in determining what the new speaker was like, but doubt continued to poke at her mind. The closer she came to reaching Immen Corper, the more she wondered what would happen when they met.

"I have to determine if he is anything like Mortén. You may not believe me, or trust me, but I know Mortén is malevolent. If this new speaker is like him, things may become twice as bad when this is over." It was still her greatest fear.

Appleseed was quiet for a moment before answering. "If you truly seek and follow the Master's will, then do you not think he will lead you rightly? That he will give you what help you need?"

"Well, yes."

"Then why do you fear?"

The question was simple, and for a moment Xari suddenly felt as if she were back at home with Burin, listening to him advise her with his simple faith and common sense, or swimming with her otter friends and feeling their encouragement. She'd missed them all greatly over the long weeks on the road. They had always been a bolstering influence. "Thank you," she said quietly. "I am not always—that is, trust is not always easy for me." She closed her eyes tightly. "You would think that after everything I have done and seen, I would find it easier to trust the Master. I fall short in so many ways."

"So do we all, and that is why we are not the Master," Appleseed replied. There was a long pause, and then she said, "You should rest. You have a journey ahead of you. You leave with White Paw very soon."

Xari nodded, but though she was tired, she doubted she would get any rest. All of the mixed emotions she was feeling from the wolves and from herself were keeping her awake. Besides that, she didn't feel completely safe with these particular brethren. She was very glad that

White Paw had been chosen as her traveling companion, because he actually seemed to like her. She would have been a lot more nervous if Blue Moon had been the one to accompany her.

As if sensing her thoughts, Appleseed said, "White Paw is young, and very brash and vain, but he is one of the best trackers in this pack, or any other. He will find those you seek."

The wolf trotted off, and Xari sat quietly, thinking over the conversation. Appleseed was right. Though the wolves didn't fully trust her, they did not fully distrust her, either—not all of them, anyway. She was headed in the right direction; even the eagle had said so. And she knew the Master would provide for her needs—not necessarily as she saw them, but as he saw them. And the Master's will was always enough.

In the end, Xari did manage to sleep during the night, with some encouragement from Ashe. "Xari, the last thing we need is for you to be exhausted. Besides, you know how you get when you're tired. Sleep. I'll watch over you." With that assurance, she slept more soundly than she had thought she would.

⌘ ⌘ ⌘

Xari's trek with White Paw began as the sun above the canopy was creating gray shadows between the trees. The wolves saw them off, and as she got farther from them, the emotions she had felt from them ran off of her like rainwater. The tension in her muscles slowly eased, and she began to relax slightly.

White Paw kept silent for the most part, and Xari did not mind. She did have difficulty keeping up with him, though, as he kept a steady pace all morning. He kept circling back to find her when she would lose sight of him in the underbrush. He seemed surprised when Xari finally asked if they could stop for a bit.

"Do you not wish to find these humans quickly?" White Paw asked. He seemed extraordinarily puzzled.

"Yes," Xari assured him. "But I have limits. Don't wolves also need rest?"

"Yes," said White Paw. "But not yet. However, for you, I will stop. I will hunt, and you may rest."

About midday the trees began to get thinner again, the light more yellow and green than it had been before. She noticed that White Paw became more cautious about proceeding, which slowed down their time, but that was almost a relief.

"There aren't many humans who come this far into the forest, but there are a few roads," he explained. "I don't like humans, mostly. I do not wish to meet up with any besides those we are hunting."

As the afternoon progressed into evening, they found the charred remains of a fire in a clearing. White Paw sniffed it carefully before speaking. "Good. We have found their direct trail at last. They are closer than I thought. They camped here last night. We should find them tomorrow."

"Xari," said Ashe worriedly from the other side of the fire pit, "come look at this."

There were large paw prints in the cinders near the charred remains of the firewood. "Perhaps another wolf?" Xari asked, although she was hardly convinced of that.

White Paw came over to investigate. "No. It is the dog. The hunter still seeks your quarry, as well, and he is very close."

Xari looked up at Ashe. "We cannot stop tonight. We must keep going, with all possible speed."

She only hoped they would not be too late.

13

Just over a week after their departure from Montressa, Anathriel awoke to the gentle shaking of strong hands. "Time to wake up," Immen said quietly. She could tell by the sounds and the feel of the air that it was still early, probably just before dawn.

With a groan of protest, she rolled over with her eyes still closed, trying wistfully to remember what it had been like to wake up in a bed at a decent hour of the day. Perhaps today she might have been asked to play her viol for visiting dignitaries or joined Lord and Lady Kavela for a game of maquette in the green atrium within the palace. Soon, she estimated, the whole court would be departing for the annual summer holiday at the lodge to the north, where a beautiful blue lake lay nestled among the craggy peaks, cold and clear and serene.

But not Anathriel. No, she was now doomed to forever awake upon the knobby ground on cold, wet mornings with nothing to look forward to but the endless, wearying trek through the forest.

Immen had wandered off already—probably dousing the lingering embers from the fire and other such things he did every morning. Anathriel sat up, propping herself with one hand behind her and using the other to rub her eyes. Then, wordlessly, she climbed out of her bedroll and began going through the morning motions. She'd made up her mind to stop wondering how long they would be at this, because otherwise she would drive herself crazy.

Anathriel had assembled together all of the things she was responsible for carrying—a load significantly lighter than either Immen's or Zeth's. Immen had insisted she not be required to carry as much, something Zeth hadn't been very happy about, but Anathriel was grateful. Shouldering it with practiced ease, she made her way over to where Immen was strapping on his quiver. "I'm ready," she said quietly.

He nodded. "Zeth went to fill up the canteens."

"Where's Flute?" Anathriel asked, peering around. In a half-light like this, it was sometimes hard to find the little creature, who could be surprisingly stealthy when she so desired.

"Over here," came a whisper, barely discernable. "Shhh."

Immen and Anathriel exchanged mystified glances and walked toward Flute's voice. It took Anathriel a minute or two to find her—she was hovering several feet above their heads.

"What is it?" Immen called softly up to her.

Flute flew down to eye level with Anathriel and Immen. "I think something is out there," she said worriedly. "The birds are too quiet."

"Sometimes travelers come to this part of the forest," Immen told her. "After all, we're here."

Flute shook her head. "The quiet part of the forest—it's behind us. From the way we already came."

Immen's eyes narrowed, and he peered in the direction Flute was indicating.

"Mortén?" Anathriel whispered fearfully.

"We have no way of knowing," Immen assured her. "It could be nothing more than another innocent traveler, but all the same we should avoid meeting up with anyone. Let's go find Zeth. We should get a move on."

⌘ ⌘ ⌘

"We are very close," said White Paw suddenly. The growl in his throat was so low and quiet that Xari almost did not hear him.

Abruptly, she halted and the wolf stopped with her. She knelt down near his head. "The hunter is just over this ridge, but the ones you seek are even nearer to him than we are."

Xari felt herself pale. "What are we going to do?" What if, after all her efforts, she fell short?

"The hunter's dog," began White Paw. "She is very strong, very intelligent. Leave her to me."

Xari nodded slowly, understanding his meaning.

He continued, "I will circle around and assist you from the other side." Without warning, White Paw dashed off speedily and silently into the dark underbrush.

146

"Wait!" Xari called as loudly as she dared, but he was already too far gone.

"What was that all about?" Ashe asked, flying to hover beside her face. He too watched the place where White Paw had disappeared.

"I'll explain later," said Xari, swiftly rising to her feet. "We have to hurry."

In addition to swordplay, Burin had taught Xari some of the basics of stealthy traveling, but she'd never really perfected the skill. As such, she figured her quarry would probably be able to hear her coming a mile away, but she determined at this point secrecy was less important than speed.

The morning had now become fuller and brighter, the pink-orange sunrise tinting the damp undergrowth all around her. All in all, the beauty of the forest belied the state of high nerves and alert senses that Xari was feeling. Brambles snatched at her breeches as she crested the small ridge and immediately dropped to a crouch. "Ashe," she said quietly.

Her guardian did not even need to nod to convey his understanding. For so long he had been her closest companion that by now their thoughts often merged seamless. He flew high—high as the bond would allow, surveying the glen before them with a liberty Xari did not share.

"What's he doing?" Jesper whispered at her elbow.

"Shhh," Xari chided him. This was no time for fairy children to be inquisitive. Fortunately, the sprout seemed to interpret her scold correctly and did not speak again.

A moment later, Ashe flew down near them once more. "White Paw was right. He is down there—and about to spring his attack upon them. They do not suspect his coming. I see the girl and two men, but I cannot see Flute or Thornbee. The hunter—Xari, he is clearly quite skilled at his trade. I do not know whether or not Mortén would wish these people dead or alive, but my guess is the former. We must go now. I will shade you again."

"No, Ashe," Xari argued. "That will weaken you. You—"

"Do not argue, sprout. I will only hold the shading until you have made your attack. Jesper, you stay here. Xari, go!" Even as he spoke, Xari knew he was employing his magic, and that further argument would only waste precious time. With a dancer's grace, she sprang up from the underbrush and began to run. It did not take her long to catch sight of her quarry. In the next glen—about a hundred feet ahead of her—three people were walking steadily, unaware of the man crouched in the thicket behind, an arrow notched to his bowstring.

Just as he pulled back to fire, Xari dashed noisily through the remains of a dying sapling, and a loud crack reverberated through the morning air. Shocked, the hunter turned around. So did the three travelers.

⌘ ⌘ ⌘

"Get down!" Immen cried.

By the time he spoke, Anathriel had spied the man as well, a hulking figure dressed in greens and browns with an arrow pointed straight at them. She let out a frightened gasp and immediately did as Immen said, dropping to a crouch and then lowering herself to her hands and knees.

"Who are you?" Immen demanded. His bow was strapped to his back, as he had not expected to need it, and he now had no time to untie it.

There was a frightened squeak from the vicinity of Anathriel's right ear, and she turned her head slightly to see Flute hovering very close to her, her right hand stuffed in against her mouth and her eyes terrorized.

But she was not looking at Immen or the hunter.

Nervously, Anathriel turned her head slowly to see what had captured the fairy's attention. She was met almost face-to-face with the dark eyes and bared teeth of a very big, very ugly dog about eight feet away from her. It was staring at her intently.

"Don't move," she heard a frantic whisper from behind her.

She whipped her head to see Zeth some feet behind them, crouched low on both legs, his gaze switching tenuously back and forth between Immen and the dog. Anathriel was only too happy to comply with his suggestion, although truth be told she wasn't sure she would have been able to move even if she'd wanted to.

"Who are you!?" Immen demanded again.

The hunter did not reply. He acted as though Immen's challenge was the least concerning thing in the world. He kept glancing out of the corner of his eye, and Anathriel was very curious as to what he was looking for.

Immen took two steps forward challengingly, a very brave move considering he had no weapon in hand. "What do you want with us?"

"Kadesh, *vajé!*" the hunter cried, his voice harsh. Anathriel screamed as the dog suddenly lunged, heading straight toward her. She covered her head with her hands and closed her eyes tightly, screwing her face into the dirt and hoping to all higher powers that she wouldn't die here in this forsaken forest without a single friend.

Instead of the blow she was expecting, however, Anathriel heard the scrambling of feet and paws, then a loud *thump* and heavy grunting. She looked up quickly and saw Zeth standing a few feet away, facing off with the dog—who was growling back at him menacingly. Zeth picked up a big stick nearby and began dancing with the great beast. "Go away!" he ordered, waving it frantically. Anathriel was only able to watch transfixed, her mouth hanging open in paralyzed fascination.

"Come on!" she heard Flute's voice and felt the little creature tugging on her sleeve. "We have to get up!"

Numbly, Anathriel scrambled to her feet. Flute dashed forward and began zipping in and out, trying to distract the dog on her own.

Beyond this melee stood Immen, also watching as if mesmerized, his expression disbelieving.

"Immen, look out!" Anathriel cried, spying the hunter still behind him, preparing to make his shot.

On her warning, Immen spun around in time to see the arrow released. At that instant, however, something very strange occurred.

There was a loud, rushing sound, and a voice cried, "No!"

An invisible force struck the hunter from his right side and the arrow was knocked askew. There was more strange scuffling. Anathriel gasped in shock and surprise as, out of nowhere, a dark-haired girl appeared on the forest floor beside him. The girl was just coming out of a somersault, but before Anathriel could blink, she was on her feet again with a long, slightly curved sword in her hand, breathing hard and glaring back at the hunter challengingly.

"White Paw, now!" the girl cried, calling back into the forest. Anathriel turned to see to whom she was talking, but all she saw were Zeth, Flute, and the dog still snapping and revolving around each other.

Zeth had scratches on his arms and tears in his clothes. Anathriel winced.

Everything around her was happening so fast she could hardly keep up. Her eyes jumped from scene to scene—the hunter had abandoned his bow in favor of a long dagger and was sparring with the dark-haired girl, who now had two blades. Anathriel goggled at the speed with which she wielded them. She could barely see the girl's hands.

Immen, too, was staring at the pair, his own sword half-drawn in his hand. He looked entirely unsure of what to do.

Anathriel ran up and grabbed his sleeve, jarring him out of his stupor. "Immen, the dog," she said insistently, turning him with urgency towards where Zeth was still struggling.

Even as they watched, the great beast lunged underneath Zeth's makeshift club and bowled him over. Anathriel let out a sharp gasp.

Flute had stopped trying to help him. Instead, she was suspended about halfway between, looking frantic, wringing her hands. She noticed Anathriel and Immen and flew over. "I can't get there! The bond, come on!"

Immen clenched his sword. "Come on," he echoed to Anathriel. "Stay back a little."

Anathriel swallowed and followed obediently behind him as he started forward.

Before they reached Zeth, however, a massive gray form hurled out of the nearby underbrush and slammed into the dog. Anathriel jumped back with a shriek, and even Immen stepped away. The figure was a large wolf—even larger than the dog—and the two beasts were now locked in a furious conflict.

Zeth scrambled to his feet and limped as fast as he could over to them, wiping his hand on his mouth.

"Are you all right?" Immen asked him urgently, eyeing the dog and the wolf worriedly, and shepherding the group farther away.

Zeth winced. "As well as can be expected. What is going on?"

Immen swung his head around toward the girl and the hunter. Zeth and Anathriel followed his gaze. The other pair was also still fighting.

Zeth gaped. "Where'd she come from?" he asked.

"Nowhere," Anathriel replied, but her explanation was cut short by Zeth.

"What the—?" Zeth began, squinting hard at the scene before him.

Then his eyes widened.

"What is it?" Immen asked.

Flute hovered down between Anathriel and Immen. "Asheford?" she whispered fearfully. She pulled closer to Immen.

"What are you talking about, Flute?" he asked her.

She pulled back. "There, see him?" She pointed.

"See who?"

"Immen—" said Zeth, placing an urgent hand on the man's opposite shoulder. "Look."

The large hunter seemed to be having sudden trouble moving his limbs. He stumbled heavily, and Anathriel watched, transfixed, as the girl with the braided hair kicked him hard in the chest and then the stomach, finally knocking him to the ground. She then kicked his dagger out of his reach, placed her foot on his stomach and one of her swords at his throat. The girl turned her head and spoke some words softly, seemingly to no one. Anathriel could not hear them.

Suddenly the forest seemed very, very quiet. Anathriel looked behind her. The dog and the wolf had inexplicably stopped fighting. The dog was lying on the ground, tense and coiled, staring at the wolf, who stared back, looking stern.

"Just stop right there," said Immen's voice, and Anathriel turned around again. He was pointing his sword at the girl and the hunter. "Who are you? Why were you following us?"

The girl did not look at Immen when she spoke but kept her eyes squarely on the man trapped below her. "I've been searching for you. So has this man. Mortén sent him to find you."

"What do you know of Mortén?" Immen asked carefully.

The girl finally looked back at them but tightened her foothold on her captive. She glanced to the side again before saying clearly, "Mortén is my nemesis, and I am his."

"She is the speaker, Immen," said Flute urgently, tugging on his sleeve. "The other speaker." Then she snapped her head back towards the scene, her face paling.

"What's wrong?" Immen asked her.

"Asheford," she whispered again. "He's the one who betrayed my people, Immen."

"A fairy?" Immen asked, his eyes roaming the place where Flute was staring so avidly.

"A Grand Magi," she said. "One of the most important ever, before he went away. But I don't understand something."

"What?"

She looked dazed. "You should be able to see him."

"I can see him," said Zeth quietly. He was peering dispassionately at an empty space in midair.

As one, Flute, Immen, and Anathriel turned to stare at him incredulously. "What?" they all asked together.

"What?" asked the braided girl, staring between Immen and Zeth with equal bewilderment. "But I thought—" Whatever else she was going to say was cut short as the large man still pinned beneath her tried to heave to the side. The girl gave a grunt and struggled to regain control, gritting her teeth and bearing down harder when she did so. She glared fiercely at her captive. "White Paw," she called loudly, "could you come help me, please?"

There was a low, throaty growl from behind them, and Anathriel, Immen, Flute, and Zeth glanced behind to see the wolf still glaring at the dog. Then he turned his attention across the clearing to the braided girl and abruptly began trotting towards them, passing the four of them without even seeming to notice they were there. Anathriel gulped and sidled closer to Immen, noting that his sword was still unsheathed in his hand.

"Did you—?" Anathriel began faintly. "Did you tell that wolf what to do?" She continued to eye the beast warily as he reached the girl and the hunter. The girl stepped aside, and the wolf pinned the man firmly into place with his two heavy forepaws.

"I asked him," said the girl, turning to face Anathriel squarely. "It is a gift."

"The wolves are one of the twelve brethren," Immen said slowly, almost to himself.

At these words, Anathriel couldn't help herself. She made a face.

The girl turned her gaze to him and nodded. "Ashe," she said calmly, "you should probably go ahead and make yourself visible. I have a feeling this will take a long time even with everybody being able to see you."

A patch of sunlight suddenly grew brighter and then, with a tremor of light that made Anathriel feel as though she had blinked without even closing her eyes, there was another fairy floating in the middle of the clearing where he hadn't been a moment before. She yelped in surprise.

The girl, meanwhile, had slipped the pack from her back and was pulling out a coil of long, thin rope. "My name is Xari Oth'ilin," she said matter-of-factly. "I am speaker for House Otter. This is Asheford, my guardian."

Anathriel, Immen, and Zeth looked at Flute, who was staring dumbly at Asheford as though she couldn't see a single other thing.

"Flute?" Immen said softly.

She jerked and gazed at him as though surprised to see him there. "What do we do?" she whispered nervously.

"Oh, for goodness' sake, Fluttermouse," said the other fairy, speaking for the first time. "I'm not here to harm you or these people." Behind him, the girl who called herself Xari had turned away and was binding the hunter's arms and legs tightly, with the wolf looking on vigilantly.

"How can I be sure of that?" Flute said back to the other fairy challengingly, looking a little bit angry now, despite her fear.

Asheford paused and glanced back at Xari. She nodded without saying anything, then returned to her work. "Jesper," Asheford called into the forest, "you can come out now."

Mystified, Zeth and Immen stared at each other in confusion as Flute's eyes widened. "Jesper?" she echoed in a whisper.

There was another bright shimmer of light that streaked out of the nearby underbrush.

"Oh, there's another one," Anathriel muttered as the third fairy blinked into view.

"Jesper!" Flute cried joyously, and she dashed forward. "What are you doing here?"

"I followed you," he said proudly as the two fairies clasped hands. "I got lost but found Magi Asheford and Xari. We went to Montressa, but you were already gone. And guess what? Magi Asheford is safe—he's not going to hurt you, I promise. Oh, and you are in so much trouble!"

"Jesper," said Asheford patiently.

Both the young fairies turned and looked at him sheepishly.

Despite herself, Anathriel couldn't help but smile a little. It made for an amusing picture.

Asheford turned back to Immen. "There is much to say," he said sagely. "But there is something we must clear up first."

He glanced back at Xari, who straightened from her crouching position. The hunter was now bound and gagged on the ground behind her, and the wolf had settled down beside him. Xari rubbed her hands on her breeches for a moment, then focused on Immen. "You, I'm going to presume, are Immen Corper."

Anathriel, startled, looked at Immen. He seemed uncertain but nodded.

The girl returned his nod, as though confirming speculation. Then she cocked her head toward Zeth. "And you are not," she said in a tone that said she knew she was pointing out the obvious.

"No," Zeth confirmed.

"But you could see Ashe before he made himself visible?"

"Yes."

"Then we have a very interesting mystery on our hands."

14

Xari found herself watching the boy intently. She saw instantly that Jesper had been right; he was a term-slave. The tattoo on his wrist was evidence enough. He couldn't have been any older than fourteen or fifteen, but Xari felt anger nonetheless on his behalf. The practice of indenturing a servant was common in the three northernmost countries of the Eastern Continent—Merenth, Threnphol, and Demuant. She highly disapproved of this practice. There were some people who chose to become term-slaves in exchange for something, but a great many were indentured against their will, though those of higher status often turned an oblivious eye to this fact.

Her eyes met his, and something in their wide, gray depths caught her attention. She suddenly had an overwhelming sense of loneliness and a desire to be more than she was. A tight knot of pain formed in her stomach, and she experienced an ache of realization that everyone saw her only as a lowly servant, and that's how they would always see her—

Xari pressed a hand against her forehead and tore her eyes away from the boy's. *Those aren't my feelings, they're his.* She felt a pang of sympathy for him; she knew exactly what it was like.

She cleared her throat and scanned the clearing. First things first: introductions. White Paw would probably be offended if she didn't introduce him. "This is White Paw." She nodded graciously at the wolf some feet away, dutifully standing sentinel over their captive and still glowering at the now-cowed dog.

"I'm Immen Corper," Immen said. "This is Anathriel Lelaine, and this is Zeth Rellwyn. That's Flute." He motioned at the fairy with Ashe and Jesper.

Xari repeated the introductions for White Paw, who was pleased. "At least some humans still have manners," he said.

At Ashe's suggestion, the seven travelers sat down, and Xari was grateful. Now that the rush of trying to stop the hunter was over, her hunger and exhaustion were setting in. The stars above had faded as the sun rose higher.

"I think it would be easiest if we told our respective stories before we try to figure this out," she said.

Everyone agreed, albeit warily. Xari could see that Immen Corper was still reluctant to trust them completely, but he was willing to listen. She would have to be satisfied with that for now.

Flute spoke first, and Xari couldn't help but be entertained—not only because of the little sprout's lively passion as she spoke, but also because of the mixture of frustration, exasperation, amusement, and reluctant fondness that kept emanating from Ashe during her tale. He was halfway between laughing and scowling the entire time, it seemed, and she noticed his wings twitched more than usual—sometimes they were easier to read than his face.

For her part, Flute still seemed unsure of how to behave around Ashe. At first Xari thought she was merely clinging to her belief that Ashe was a disgraced traitor, not to be trusted. However, as time went on Xari realized this was not the case. In an admirable display of blind faith, Flute seemed perfectly willing to accept the commendation of Ashe's character based upon nothing more than Jesper's word. It was a testament of how close their friendship was. Instead, Flute's reluctance towards Ashe seemed more to do with being once again subjected to the supervision and scolding of one of her elders.

"You tried to do a fire spell on your own?" Ashe asked, interrupting Flute's narrative.

"I found my heartfire," she insisted sullenly, frowning. Her head tilted proudly. "I bet I could do it again, too. The spell would have worked if that eagle hadn't jumped at the wrong time."

At her words, Immen let out a quiet chuckle.

"What?" she asked, frowning at him.

"Eulaie is one of the smoothest of fliers," he told her with a smile. "I can assure you, his 'jump' was entirely at the moment he intended."

"It's a wonder you didn't kill yourself," Ashe muttered to Flute. He rose up from Xari's shoulder and flew around the younger fairy, scrutinizing her through narrowed eyes. "You've also got your magic all twisted up in here, and now I realize why. I'll have to get it straightened out when I can."

Flute's eyes widened knowingly. She glanced quickly at Anathriel. "Is that why—?" she began.

"What?" Ashe asked her.

"Magi Asheford," she began excitedly, "when I found Immen and Anathriel, I didn't understand why both of them could see me, because I thought I was invisible. Something was wrong."

Understanding filled Ashe's eyes and he nodded. "I see," he said almost to himself. "Tell us more, sprout, but don't jump ahead."

Flute explained how she'd tracked Immen down—more through chance than anything, Xari decided privately—and how she'd confronted him with the knowledge about speakers. "I did everything right, Magi," she said grouchily to Ashe when his expression appeared particularly disapproving. "I made sure he could see me. I even made sure he had a relic."

Xari perked up with interest now. This was an element about which she'd been most curious. "Where is the relic, Flute?"

"We thought it was this," said Immen helpfully. He reached for his bag and rummaged around for a moment. Then he held out something— a pin in the shape of an eagle. "I received it upon being made Windrider captain."

He passed it to Xari, who studied the brooch carefully, then held it up for Ashe to inspect. "I do not believe this is a speaker relic," he said after a moment's study. "It is old but not old enough."

"What about this?" Zeth asked.

Everyone turned to look at him in surprise. The boy had been mostly quiet up until now, but he had observed the proceedings with a calm sobriety that made Xari suspect he knew what was going on more than any of his companions. He reached up to his neck and pulled a long chain from beneath his tunic. Dangling on the end of the chain was a medallion—a pendant—made of silver. There were engravings on it and Xari got to her feet, moving with Ashe to peer at it closely.

"I found it in Zephyr's nest weeks ago," he said quietly. "On the day of the Festival of Winds. I tried to leave it there, but I—I just couldn't. And Zephyr, she—" he shook his head confusedly—"she kept looking at me like she wanted me to have it. So I took it."

"Zephyr?" Ashe asked, looking up briefly from his study of the medallion.

"The eagle Immen rides," Anathriel supplied.

"Well, this is certainly an interesting twist," Xari said. The medallion was engraved on one side with an eagle soaring in flight and the other with an eagle's head, the eye staring out piercingly to the side. So it was the eagle relic that had been recovered. "We set out to find Immen Corper, and we have done that—but he is not the one we should have sought." She gave a half-smile and glanced at Ashe. "Burin always says there are no such things as accidents."

Anathriel sniffed. "This Burin obviously hasn't met Flute."

"Hey!" Flute protested.

Xari set her lips in a thin line and moved back to her place in the circle. She looked between her three fellow humans with a serious expression. "Immen Corper was not chosen to be speaker." She indicated Zeth with a nod. "Zeth was."

Anathriel gave an incredulous laugh. "Zeth?" she repeated. "But Flute said it could only be Immen. She said it was because of his family. Zeth is—"

Zeth gave Anathriel a murderous glance and looked like he was going to say something, but Ashe beat him to it.

"Fluttermouse," he said, "would have known this had her magic not been tangled. As it is, it was only through providence that she brought the right person along with her." Ashe shook his head. "My people," he began, "have assumed that the speakers would always be descended from the twelve ancient family lines. I am beginning to believe this isn't so. Perhaps the legacy of relic passing from generation to generation was simply tradition. The fact remains: this boy has the relic of House Eagle, and he has been chosen."

"Zeth could see Asheford when you were fighting the hunter!" Flute cried knowingly, understanding dawning on her face. Zeth nodded.

"And Anathriel and I were able to see Flute because—?" Immen asked Ashe.

"Because she performed magic she wasn't ready for and somehow rendered her power of invisibility ineffective," Ashe explained. "It's a wonder she wasn't seen by anyone else before she encountered you." He looked at Flute. "So you found Immen and you thought you'd proven him the one you were looking for. I guess I can partly understand your mistake. One thing I do not understand is how Fluttermouse arrived in

Montressa and found Immen before Thornbee did."

Flute turned large eyes on Ashe. "I think something happened to him, Magi Asheford. I heard Mortén. He said he knew I wasn't the one that had been sent; that he had been easily disposed of."

Ashe's eyes narrowed, and Xari knew he was wondering the same thing she was. Exactly how had Mortén disposed of Thornbee? "I see. And what else happened with Mortén?"

At this point, Anathriel, Immen, and soon Zeth were able to help Flute tell the rest of her story, all the way up until the moment Xari had crashed through the forest and stopped the hunter from killing them.

"Why didn't you stop him before then?" Immen asked curiously when they'd finished.

Xari looked sympathetic. "I would have, had I been able. As it was, I only found you just in time."

"To tell our story, we must go further back," Ashe said. "In fact, I must go back even before I met Xari. If you are to be a part of this, you must understand about Darius Mortén and how he came to be where he is now." He sighed. "And the hand I played in getting him there."

⌘ ⌘ ⌘

Anathriel tried to pay attention as the fairy called Asheford began his explanation. She still wasn't at all sure what she thought about all of this, but knew if she was going to understand any of what had happened to her in the past week and a half, it would probably be a good idea to listen.

Asheford perched on Xari's shoulder, looking pensive. "This is a tale known to all fairies, but the details have been closely kept and harbored by the Grand Magi, of whom I once belonged. It began even before my time.

"It began with the deaths of the twelve speakers, which is a long tale in itself. All you need to know right now is that many, many years ago—nearly nine hundred years—the Houses of the twelve speakers were strong and flourishing. While the world still had its disputes, there was much peace. The fairies were caretakers of the speakers, and the twelve brethren lived in harmony with the humans and each other. For years upon years, the mantle of speaker had been passed from generation to generation within each House. When one speaker died, the choosing of the relic passed to another in the family. We fairies always felt a choosing, and always knew who was chosen because we could be seen by the chosen one.

"It was in the final days of the twelve speakers that the newly appointed speaker for House Leviathan was murdered. She had yet to receive a fairy guardian, and a man we later learned was named Maehdron Vittes killed her. He craved the magical power of a speaker, and only obtaining a relic could give it to him. But he could not get it until she was dead."

"Um, excuse me, Magi Asheford?" Zeth said, raising his eyebrows. "I thought a speaker couldn't be a speaker unless the relic chose him."

It was Xari who answered. "The choosing is the way in which the *Master* selects the speakers. It is possible, however, for a person who has a relic to be awakened as a speaker even if they are not chosen, as was discovered when Maehdron Vittes took the leviathan relic."

Zeth nodded, and Ashe continued his tale. "With the assistance of the shvri, Vittes was awakened to the leviathan relic, and he massacred the other speakers. We are not sure precisely when he was awakened, but we know that it happened."

"What are the shvri?" Immen asked. "That's what Mortén called Flute, back in my office in Montressa. She was quite indignant."

"As she would be," Ashe said, with a look at Flute, who was sitting beside Jesper on Zeth's knee. "Years before the speakers' deaths, there was a great rift between my people. There were some who questioned the ways the Master had taught us. They believed the fairies should not be so compliant, but should live life for themselves. They didn't believe the peace between the twelve speakers would last, as there had been trouble among the Houses before—in one such instance, they had been fractured and it had taken great effort and diligence to bring them back together.

"Eventually, the rift among the fairies became so great that those who questioned the Master's teachings left. They joined together and became what we called the *shvri*—which, in old tongue, means 'forsaken.' They did their best to undermine what we worked for, possibly in an attempt to prove that we were wrong."

"Fairies did that?" Zeth asked in disbelief.

"Shvri," Flute and Jesper said at once.

"And so the shvri were able to undermine the defenses of the fairy guardians, for they were great in number, and each speaker had only one guardian," Ashe said heavily. "It was terribly wrong, but it happened very quickly. So quickly, in fact, that the rest of my people were not able to aid in time. As the speakers were overcome, Vittes gathered each of their relics for himself.

"But before he could fulfill his plans for them, he was killed in the great earthquake that caused much of the landscape we know to drastically change. An entire portion of the Northern Mountain Range sank into the sea, creating Narimni Bay. The island upon which House Leviathan stood sank into the ocean. The relics were utterly lost. So was some of our knowledge of the speakers. During Vittes' pursuit of the speakers, those fairies that were able left Fairlight to confront the shvri and attempt to protect the speakers, as it was clear that the guardians were no longer enough. Many were also lost in the earthquake, and it was given to those left in Fairlight to rebuild and remember. We have since kept meticulous records of everything we could recall, including those descendants we could track. However, my people ventured out of the forest much more often in the beginning. The seclusion, as well as the long passage of time, makes it far more difficult to keep thorough records."

There was a long silence, and then Zeth asked, "What did Vittes want with all of the relics?"

"As far as we know, he was attempting to awaken the power of all of the relics into himself, a feat which I am not sure is possible. If the shvri succeeded in awakening him to more than one relic, it has never been learned. We have not seen or heard from the shvri in hundreds upon hundreds of years."

"So how did Mortén wind up with the leviathan relic?" Zeth asked.

"I'm coming to that," Asheford said patiently. "A little over eight years ago, the fairies felt a choosing. As I'm sure Fluttermouse explained to you, all fairies can sense when a speaker has been chosen. We immediately know the area in which the choosing has taken place. In this instance, we felt the occurrence take place in Réol. We traced it to a man who we knew to be a descendent of House Leviathan—and he was able to prove his bloodline."

"Mortén," Immen said.

"Yes."

Anathriel suppressed a shiver. Zeth leaned forward slightly, careful not to disturb Flute and Jesper, and focused intently on Ashe's words.

"I was the Grand Magi chosen to visit Darius Mortén and ascertain that he truly had been chosen as a speaker. Things seemed to go well at first. He could see me, and those who had accompanied me. After explaining to him what it was he carried, and what being a speaker was, he agreed to the awakening. After the awakening, we stayed to help him and teach him. For a while, everything seemed fine, and we believed that Mortén might be the beginning of the restoration of speakers."

Ashe shook his head, looking terribly sad. "We finally had some hope that balance would be restored to the world, and that Mortén might have some success in locating the missing relics—perhaps with the brethren's aid. We were grievously mistaken. We saw small things that showed us his true nature, but it culminated one day when we observed an atrocity so horrendous that we knew Mortén could not possibly be well-intentioned."

"What was it?" Flute breathed, and Anathriel looked at her in surprise. She had thought Flute knew all of this.

Asheford shook his head. "He killed one of his servants," he said gravely. "My people and I left immediately for Fairlight, and I brought with me the otter relic, which we also had found in Mortén's possession. How he came by it, I cannot say."

"So why didn't you just kill Mortén right there and save the world a whole lot of grief?" Zeth asked pointedly.

Flute jumped up and turned around on Zeth's knee so she could stare up at him. "Fairies don't kill!" she said in a shocked voice. "We defend and protect!"

"Yes, but wouldn't killing Mortén defend and protect the rest of the world?" Zeth shot back.

"You must understand, we are bound by our own laws, and there are some lines we will not cross," Ashe said.

"The shvri crossed them," Zeth persisted.

"What the shvri have become is another matter," Ashe said.

"What about the otter relic?" Immen asked.

"The others of the Grand Magi council felt the risk of exposing the relic to the humans was too great. I disagreed. I made the decision to take the otter relic from my people and leave Fairlight Forest. I knew they would think me a traitor, but I saw little other choice. I had to believe that someone would be chosen who might stand a chance of battling Mortén's corruption."

"And so you found her?" Anathriel asked, looking at Xari skeptically.

Xari gave a pragmatic smile. "Unintentionally. We crossed paths— well, by the Master's will, I believe, and I was chosen to carry the otter relic. Ashe awakened me as a speaker, and assisted me in the duties of being one. Unfortunately, I also had to contend with Mortén. He knew immediately that I had awakened—"

"How?" Zeth interrupted.

"You have not been told?" Xari asked in surprise, glancing between Flute and Zeth. "That is something you will need to know if you are to be a speaker. The speakers share a mental connection. Even now, I share this with Mortén."

"He can read your mind?" Anathriel asked. She wasn't sure she'd ever heard of anything more distasteful.

"Not exactly. It's more like strong emotions and sensations," Xari explained. "And they're generally only transferred willingly."

"We believe it was a means by which speakers worked together over a distance," Asheford said.

"Yes, but I doubt most speakers in time gone by were mortal enemies," Xari agreed, giving her guardian a wry look. She turned back to the others. "I can also find Mortén, and he can do the same of me— that is, when I want to know where he is, I can reach out with my mind and locate him. I cannot, however, tell what he has planned, or know or feel anything that he does not wish me to know or feel."

"So when you said Mortén is your nemesis, you meant it literally," Immen said quietly.

"Yes," Xari said. Silence fell for a moment, then Xari reached into her pack. "Excuse me; I haven't eaten since sometime yesterday." She unwrapped a dried fruit and nut mixture.

Anathriel didn't fail to notice the way Flute and Jesper immediately perked up, Jesper going so far as to stand on Zeth's knee and lean forward slightly, his wings fluttering.

Xari noticed as well and rolled her eyes. "Yes, you may have some too." She laughed.

Both fairies immediately converged on the food, and Xari continued her story, briefing them on her travels. She had apparently come all the way from Ithrin as soon as Ashe felt the choosing. Anathriel supposed that this must explain her peculiar dress; she knew very little of the country, but perhaps other women in Ithrin dressed and behaved like Xari. If that was the case, Anathriel was quite happy remaining oblivious and exceedingly grateful for her own proper upbringing.

Xari told of her encounter with the guards in the eyries, her meeting with the wolves, and exactly how she had ended up in the clearing fighting the hunter.

When she was finished, Asheford turned his attention on Immen and Anathriel. "Now, let's see what can be done about all of this tangled magic."

15

The fairy called Asheford did much to endear himself to Anathriel. As the bizarre morning progressed, she took a deep, secret satisfaction in the authoritative way he upbraided Flute, who, as far as Anathriel was concerned, was the author of all her many recent troubles. Although Anathriel knew Flute wasn't intentionally troublesome, she had always had a distaste for reckless children, and Flute was certainly that. It was relieving to know that Asheford seemed to share this opinion.

His first step had been to free Immen and Anathriel from the binding spell, a process that required considerable patience for all parties concerned. He was polite enough to warn them before the exact moment the enchantment was lifted, which Anathriel thought was exceptional of him, as she knew she wouldn't have liked to endure the experience without forewarning. It felt as though someone were tugging all her skin hard in one direction, towards Ashe, and it was more than just uncomfortable. When the feeling vanished, Anathriel found herself breathing hard and a little dizzy. Still, all discomfort was forgotten when she and Immen tested their now-accustomed boundaries and discovered that they were finally free of one another. It was something for which Anathriel knew she'd be forever grateful.

With the binding lifted, both Immen and Xari had been eager to interrogate the hunter. Anathriel had watched this process from a safe distance away. Immen and Xari tied the man more securely to a nearby tree of decent size before Immen released his gag. "Who sent you?" he began as soon as he'd tugged it free.

"If you lie to us, I will know," Xari added. She stood before the man, somehow towering over him despite the fact that, had he been standing, she might have reached his breastbone. She was posed defiantly, her swords belted to her waist.

Immen rose to his feet and came to stand beside her, mimicking her posture. "Who sent you?" he repeated.

The strange man only glowered and did not reply.

Immen exhaled. "Very well, let's start with something simpler. What is your name?"

Zeth was sitting near Anathriel as he watched the proceedings. She leaned towards him and whispered, "How did Immen learn to interrogate someone?"

"How should I know?" he retorted.

Anathriel scowled.

The sullen man still had not replied to Immen's question.

Xari took over the questioning. "White Paw," she called, never taking her eyes from the man's face. The wolf, who had also been watching these proceedings, licked his chops shrewdly and growled something. "Maybe you'd better kill the dog."

The man scowled. "It's Cane," he spat.

She narrowed her eyes at the man. "I said no lies."

Now he looked positively livid. "Very well," he bit out. "My name is Roglio."

Immen looked over at Xari, who nodded slowly, her mouth set grimly. "Who sent you?" he asked for the third time.

"How does she know he's telling the truth?" Anathriel asked Zeth.

"Shhh!" he insisted.

Anathriel glared at him crossly.

Roglio opened his mouth, then glanced at Xari, obviously torn. He hesitated a moment longer before scowling further. "Lord Mortén," he muttered darkly.

Anathriel inhaled slowly, letting her breath seethe through her clenched teeth and leaning forward to hear what else their captive might have to say.

As it turned out, not much. After a bit more threatening and cajoling, all they were able to learn was that the man was a mercenary of sorts, whom Mortén had paid good money to track down and hire on short notice. In the end, Xari had freed his hands long enough to let him choke down a hard piece of bread and drink some water from a canteen before tying him up once more.

After that, Asheford suggested they all take some time to rest, a suggestion Xari proceeded to take literally. Apparently, she'd been awake for an entire day and night before she'd found them. Anathriel wasn't tired enough to sleep, but she was thankful for a day that didn't involve any arduous traveling. She sat and listened, somewhat bored and morose, as her two companions asked Asheford more questions, or chatted with Flute and Jesper, who were in no short supply of conversation.

Xari slept without stirring, well into mid-evening, only to find herself alone with Anathriel upon waking, as Immen and Zeth had gone off to procure the evening meal.

"What is that dog doing?" Anathriel asked, staring at the edge of the clearing.

It was getting darker. A fire was cracking and sputtering in the center of the clearing, and she was supposed to be tending it. She was distracted, however, by the hunter's dog, which kept skirting around the encampment, watching them with shifty eyes.

"She won't hurt us," Xari said somewhat testily, throwing a couple branches onto the small blaze. She was sitting cross-legged on the opposite side, her guardian perched on her head. A yawn escaped her lips, and she shook her head as if to clear it of sleepy cobwebs.

Anathriel wrinkled her nose. "That's not what I asked." She wasn't thrilled about being left alone with this girl. It was bothersome that Immen and Zeth had taken to being so friendly toward her. The girl dressed like a savage, fought like a barbarian, and talked with a wolf! Why was she so special that they wanted to hang onto her every word? Just before her nap, she and Immen had shared an animated conversation, and Anathriel had rarely seen him so enthusiastic. He had told Xari about the eagles, about riding on the winds, and all about Zephyr. And Zeth was actually civil to her. It was uncanny the way she brought something to life in both of them. It bothered Anathriel immensely.

"I daresay she's watching to see what will happen to her master," Xari replied.

"How do you know she won't hurt us? She tried to kill Zeth and me."

It was not Xari, but Asheford who answered. "White Paw constrained her not to harm us. She is beholden to obey him."

White Paw? Anathriel frowned, and turned to peer at the great gray wolf now curled up in sleep some feet away, his chest rising and falling

167

calmly. He looked rather bored and superior. "I don't understand," she said with a snip, turning again to the pair by the fire.

"The Master appointed the twelve brethren to be the caretakers of all the world's creatures," Xari said with exaggerated patience. "They each have their own domain, you might say." She nodded at the dog, whose eyes were once again visible, reflecting the firelight sharply in the fading twilight. "Dogs, foxes, jackals…are all answerable to the wolves."

"You don't have to be so rude," Anathriel said, glaring.

"You must forgive her," said Asheford. "She is not very personable when she wakes up. Xari?" he added in a chiding tone.

"Sorry," Xari muttered, throwing another twig in the fire, though she didn't exactly sound it.

Anathriel set her chin and decided to force herself to be polite, simply to prove she could do it better than Xari. "So, you're telling me the dog has to do what the wolf says, whether or not she wants to?"

"In the simplest sense, yes," said Ashe.

Anathriel frowned at the wolf once more before turning back and sitting down herself, albeit much more ladylike than Xari. She spread her skirt carefully around her legs, mindful to keep it out of range of the sparks from the fire. "Then why doesn't he just tell her to go away?" she asked with another irritated glance into the shadows. "She's making me nervous."

"Because there is no need," said Xari. She regarded Anathriel shrewdly. "You don't want to believe in any of this, do you?"

Anathriel looked up sharply. The other girl's tone was not speculative. It was as if she somehow knew how Anathriel was feeling. She pressed her lips together. "I don't like it," she conceded curtly. "But I won't waste my breath trying to tell myself it isn't real." Idly, she flicked two pieces of ash off her skirt.

"You were surprised that the chosen one was Zeth," Xari said.

"So were you," Anathriel pointed out levelly.

Xari looked subdued at this and did not reply.

"What makes me curious, though," Anathriel continued after a strained pause, "is how you weren't surprised he was with us. Or that I was, for that matter."

"We suspected. There was much talk of your and Immen's disappearance in the city. Talk was that you'd eloped."

Anathriel clamped her teeth together and began flicking at the charred flakes of ash with more vehemence. She had known that was probably what would happen, but the confirmation made it harder to bear. The irony was that she gladly would have married Immen, but he didn't care three feathers for her, not in that way. In any case, she never would have consented to such a scandalous elopement to *any* man. The taint on her reputation was more painful than ten thousand blisters could possibly have been.

"And what about Zeth?" she asked. "How did they explain his disappearance?"

"A runaway," Xari replied. "According to Jesper, who was our source—" here Xari appeared slightly skeptical—"nobody was sure when Zeth had actually run away. There wasn't any evidence to suggest your respective disappearances were connected."

"Yet you suspected."

"The wolves said there were three humans traveling this way. What we didn't understand until now was why either you or Zeth would have accompanied Immen."

"Zeth is running away," said Anathriel disapprovingly.

Xari's face was stony upon these words.

"As for me," Anathriel continued, "well, you know why I'm here."

Xari nodded stiffly but made no further comment. The threesome sat in awkward silence, listening to the snapping of the fire until Immen and Zeth returned, a handful of squirrels in tow. Immen proceeded to clean and dress them for eating. To their surprise, Xari made an offering of salt and spices for seasoning, something heretofore they'd been without.

"Where did you learn to cook?" Immen asked appreciatively, licking his fingers as they ate.

"My father taught me," Xari said. A little time awake and some food in her stomach seemed to be having a positive effect upon her mood.

"Your father?" Anathriel repeated. She was slightly surprised, but she didn't know why. It seemed odd to think of Xari having parents; she couldn't imagine any proper parents allowing their daughter to grow up learning to fight and wearing breeches.

"His name is Burin Oth'ilin," Xari said calmly, scooping food into her mouth with her fingers, which caused an appalled Anathriel to frown deeply at her.

Immen froze. "Burin Oth'ilin?" he repeated.

"Mm-hmm," Xari replied, her mouth full.

Immen continued to look amazed. "Burin Oth'ilin," he said again. "When you said your name was—I didn't think—"

"Who is Burin Oth'ilin?" Anathriel demanded.

"He's one of the best swordmasters in the Eastern Continent!" Immen said, sounding awed. "And the Southern Continent, or so I've heard—that's where he's originally from, isn't it?"

Xari swallowed and nodded fondly. "Yes, his credentials are why I first sought him out. Burin is my adoptive father," she clarified, noting Anathriel's confusion.

"No wonder you fight so well," Immen said, grinning at the other girl.

Xari seemed rather pleased by his praise. "What about you?" she asked, nodding at his sword. "Have you been trained?"

"Yes."

"Would you care to spar?" Xari asked.

Anathriel's mouth dropped open, and she stared at the two curved swords at Xari's sides. She couldn't possibly be serious! Anathriel was pleased to see that Immen looked doubtful. "Spar?" he repeated uncertainly.

Zeth looked interested. "Come on, Immen, are you afraid of being beaten by a girl?" he asked with a grin.

Immen still looked hesitant. "Are you sure? I don't want you to get hurt."

Xari smiled platonically. "I'm sure you're very skilled, and you might be able to best me, but I've been hurt training more times than I can count. I'll be fine."

"Immen!" Anathriel said, shocked. "You cannot seriously be considering fighting with this—this—" She trailed off, not sure what to call Xari without sounding unladylike.

Xari's eyebrows rose. "Yes?"

"Anathriel," Immen said warningly.

"What kind of proper swordsman would teach a woman to fight?"

"One who is a better man than any I've known," Xari said. There was a quiet challenge in her tone, and her dark eyes lingered on

170

Anathriel before she turned back to Immen. "So what do you say?"

"Well, if you're sure," Immen said dubiously.

"I am."

Anathriel objected again, but neither Immen nor Xari paid attention to her outburst. She watched in frustration as Xari pulled one of her swords out, and Immen drew his. She clenched her hands as Xari bowed, and Immen copied her. Their swordplay started out slowly, as Immen seemed hesitant, but then Xari flicked the point of her sword across the back of Immen's hand so fast that Anathriel wasn't sure what she'd done until a thin red line of blood appeared there. Immen stared at his hand in surprise.

Anathriel jumped to her feet. "Look what you did!"

"Anathriel," Immen murmured, "it's all right."

"Immen, you have to stop!" Anathriel pleaded, glaring at Xari.

"Anathriel, shut up," said Zeth.

Immen actually grinned. "It's only a scratch. And I learned my lesson." He grinned at Xari and then attacked without warning.

After that, it was hard to keep up. Anathriel resisted the urge to cover her eyes and hide as they practiced. When the two had finally finished—the fight ended when Xari held her curved blade at Immen's throat—Immen smiled and nodded respectfully. "I fear, Miss Oth'ilin, that your skill far outmatches my own. How are you with a bow?"

"Far from exceptional," Xari said, laughing, lowering her sword. "I'd be fortunate if I didn't end up shooting someone by accident." She bowed gracefully to Immen. "Thank you very much. It's been weeks since I've been able to practice with anyone. I've missed it."

"Where's Flute?" Anathriel asked, in an effort to get them off this particular line of conversation. "And Jesper?" she added, almost as an afterthought. She realized she hadn't seen the two young fairies since before Immen and Zeth had gone hunting. She pulled a handkerchief out of her pocket to wipe off her fingers, wondering how long they would be staying in this spot and if she could attempt getting some things washed. All her handkerchiefs were filthy.

"Over there," said Zeth nodding to his left a little bit, his mouth full.

Anathriel scowled at his uncouth display but craned her neck in the direction he had indicated. "Where?" she asked, frowning. It was fully dark now, and she wasn't sure what he was looking at.

Xari laughed as she sat down again. "They're playing tag." She was also watching the spot where Zeth had nodded. "A two-person fairy variation, anyway. I think," she added. Anathriel must have still looked mystified, because Xari then said helpfully, "They're likely invisible."

This was a practice to which Anathriel would have to become accustomed. It didn't seem to be polite, popping in and out of invisibility all the time. She wondered why Asheford hadn't done so. Presently, he was flying back and forth near Xari, seemingly lost in thought. He hadn't eaten any of the squirrels, explaining that fairies didn't eat meat.

"Ashe?" Xari finally asked, after the four humans had studied this quizzical behavior for a moment. "What's on your mind?"

Ashe landed on Xari's shoulder and looked at Zeth. "Now that we have found you," he said to the boy, "there only remains one thing to do."

"What's that?" Zeth asked.

Ashe looked surprised. "Why, to awaken you. Whatever else any of us here decides to do come tomorrow, that much was never in question. If you consent to it, of course."

16

It was silent for a long time after Ashe made this announcement, but it was neither a shocked nor an uncomfortable silence. Rather it was heavy and thoughtful, filled only by the sounds of nightlife and the popping fire that reflected brightly in everyone's eyes.

It was Zeth who finally spoke up. "When?" he asked quietly, focused on something far away. The firelight dancing in his eyes seemed almost mystical, his face a picture of fierce thought.

"I'd like to perform the awakening in the morning, if you'll allow me, after a good night's rest. I worked a great deal of difficult magic already today, and the rite of awakening is the longest and most draining."

Zeth wrapped his arms more tightly about his knees, his chin resting atop them, and continued staring avidly into the fire. "And then?"

It was Xari who answered. "And then you will need a guardian. Ashe?" She turned to her own guardian questioningly.

Ashe's face was a mask of sobriety. "Xari is correct. It is imperative that you have a guardian. That means going to Fairlight, though, which is going to be tricky."

"But Magi Asheford," Flute burst out, "I can be his guardian!" She spun around and looked at Zeth.

"Fluttermouse, you cannot be a guardian right now. Have you even left the nursery in the village yet?" Ashe asked pointedly.

"Well, no, but I can do this! I came all this way to—"

"Flute, you have not yet mastered your magic, as was evidenced by your inability to correct the binding spell—which you did incorrectly to begin with—and your invisibility problem."

Xari could definitely see the merit to Ashe's objections. As sweet as the little fairy seemed, it was crucial that Zeth have a guardian who would be able to sufficiently protect him.

"I can do protection spells, really I can! Just ask Jesper! I may mess up on some things, but I've never had an accident with any protection spell!" Flute gazed longingly at Ashe. "You taught me protection workings, Magi Asheford. You know I did well with them."

"There is more to being a guardian, Fluttermouse, than knowing protection spells."

"You can help me learn more," Flute said. "If we're traveling together anyway, then you can teach me."

Zeth watched this exchange for a moment, then cleared his throat. "Magi Asheford, she really has done well with us."

Anathriel scoffed almost inaudibly in disbelief.

"That may be, at least to some degree, but she is not ready to be a guardian. End of discussion," Ashe said firmly, as Flute opened her mouth to again protest. "You are returning to Fairlight, and I'm certain the elders will decide what to do with you then."

Flute looked equal parts crestfallen and frustrated. She opened her mouth, closed it, and zipped off into the leafy branches of an oak tree. Jesper pelted off after her.

Ashe watched them go, then turned back to Zeth. "As I was saying, I do not know what sort of welcome you may expect among my people, but I certainly know the sort of welcome I will get if Xari and I accompany you."

Xari continued to watch Ashe. "Well?" she prompted after a long moment. "Are we going to accompany him?"

Ashe sighed heavily. "It may be that the time has come for me to return. It would certainly be best if we stayed with Zeth for now, as he will have many questions that you will be able to help him answer."

"What about us?" Anathriel said, her voice suddenly alarmed. "Are we supposed to come along, too?"

"No," said Immen. Xari looked over at him, surprised at the wistfulness in his voice. He glanced back at her, then at Zeth, then at Ashe. "Not that I wouldn't be honored to join you, but I have responsibilities in Montressa, and—" he hesitated, then gestured toward Anathriel—"I owe it to Anathriel to see she gets back home safely. With the binding lifted and Mortén gone, the reason for our flight no longer exists."

Anathriel brightened considerably at these words; a large smile blossomed on her face. "Oh, Immen, thank you!"

Xari winced. "Actually—" she began.

Anathriel whipped her head around with accusation. "What?" she demanded, frowning.

Immen looked confused.

"Mortén is still in Montressa," Xari said simply.

The other three humans stared at her for a minute before understanding filled Immen and Zeth's eyes. No doubt they were remembering Xari's ability to sense Mortén's whereabouts. Xari wasn't sure if Anathriel remembered this detail, but it was clear she understood the seriousness of Mortén's presence back home, because her face fell, crushed.

"Why would he still be in Montressa?" Immen asked, thinking aloud.

"He always stays three or four weeks," said Anathriel miserably. She mimicked Zeth's posture and laid her head on her arms, which were wrapped around her knees.

As an overwhelming wave of homesickness and heartbrokenness emanated from the girl, Xari felt sympathy for her for the first time. It wasn't Anathriel's fault she'd been dragged on this journey.

"Maybe he doesn't want to raise any speculation by leaving before he's supposed to," Anathriel continued. She loosened her arms to bat away an errant tear from her eye and sniffed a little.

"He's probably confident in his hunter's ability to find us," Immen pointed out, glancing over his shoulder, where the hunter was still tied to the tree, presumably asleep. Xari reached out with her ability to make sure he was. It wouldn't do for them to be overheard, no matter how securely the man was tied.

"Maybe," Xari said doubtfully, "but he can sense my whereabouts just as easily as I can his. I've no doubt he's been tracking my movements. You can always stay in a town somewhere until Mortén has left Montressa, and then return. You do not have to come along. However, I will warn you: you know what he is. I do not believe for a moment that he will forget it. You may not be safe in a town, or going back to Montressa, even if he is not there. Staying in one place may not be the best course of action right now."

Anathriel's jaw tightened. "But he will be actively seeking you and Zeth," she said, almost accusingly.

"I don't know," Xari replied honestly. "Maybe. He has never tried to harm me directly, but then he knows I have a guardian. I can make no guarantees as to what he will do now."

"There can be safety in numbers," Immen said quietly. "I say we face the problem instead of hiding from it." His eyes slid to Anathriel. "Unless you want to be chased by him your entire life."

Anathriel shuddered. "No."

"We were headed for Fairlight in the first place," Immen said with an ironic smile.

"So you're coming?" Xari asked, looking between him and Anathriel.

"Apparently so," Anathriel said through stiff lips. She stared into the fire, depressed.

Xari nodded her acceptance. "As soon as Ashe awakens Zeth, Mortén will know. That is why when the deed is done, we must move with all possible speed towards our destination."

"Meanwhile, I think it is high time we all got some rest," Ashe said. "The Master has afforded us this day of reprieve, but I do not believe it will be long-lasting. Jesper! Fluttermouse! Come down here; it's time to go to sleep."

Xari smiled as she reorganized her bedroll, watching the two young sprouts argue with their elder. Deciding it would be prudent for someone to stand guard of their camp from here on out, Xari offered to take first watch, considering she had just had a full day's rest already. She didn't think she would be able to sleep, anyway. She needed some time alone to prepare herself. Searching for another speaker had been one thing; actually coming to the point where there was going to *be* a third was entirely different. It was a bit frightening. She was going to be sharing her life with another person, having a bond that went stronger and deeper than anyone could understand. She already had that bond with Mortén, and she hated it. When there had been twelve speakers, how had they managed experiencing eleven others' lives, memories, and strong emotions?

It would be different with Zeth, she knew, but the thoughts, excitement, and uncertainty still roiled about in her head. For starters, he was so young. Not much younger than she was, but she had lost her childhood, first to the orphanage, and then to being a speaker. It was a huge and awesome responsibility, and while she had always wished for someone to share it with, she was also regretful that Zeth must now share the burden.

In the end, however, her concerns were secondary to more long-term considerations. Zeth would be gaining his own very useful talents as a speaker, talents that Xari and Ashe hoped would give them some guidance.

Xari kept vigilant eyes and ears trained on the surrounding trees for four hours, then roused Immen as she promised she would do. By that time, her thoughts on the matter had run their course several times, and her eyes were beginning to get drowsy, so she was grateful for the chance to rest. Her sleep was dreamless, and she awoke to the pale gray-green light of the forest morning. She immediately knew it had rained at some point after she'd retired, for there was a layer of damp on her bedroll that was attributable to more than just dewfall, and a faint and steady dripping could be heard among the trees.

"Good. I was just about to wake you," said Ashe, mere moments after she opened her eyes.

Xari struggled to a sitting position and rubbed her eyes. Everyone else seemed already awake. Anathriel was stirring something at the fire. Zeth was sitting nearby, idly fingering his relic and talking quietly to Flute and Jesper. Immen was restringing his bow. Xari blinked and looked back at Ashe.

"Are you ready?" she managed to croak. She coughed slightly to clear her throat. Cool, damp weather always had a poor effect upon her.

Ashe gave a small nod, his face grave. "Then let's get this started," Xari said.

She scrambled out of the bedroll and stood, giving a good, long stretch.

"Zeth, we're ready," Ashe called.

All three of the other humans looked towards him. Anathriel and Immen merely looked curious, but Zeth appeared very nervous. He gave a shaky nod and stood up, wiping the palms of his hands on his trousers. In the distance, even the hunter was watching them shrewdly, and Xari remembered with a twinge of annoyance that she was going to have to figure out what to do with him soon.

She gave a nod to Anathriel and Immen, indicating that they should join Zeth and the other fairies, who had already reached Ashe. "Have you eaten?" she asked Zeth. "This could take awhile."

"Yes, I have."

"Good. Awakening is a huge work of magic," she began, addressing them all. "It will take a lot out of Ashe, and I must stress to you all that he must not be interrupted."

"What do I do?" Zeth asked.

"Just sit still," she instructed. "Actually, as far as you're concerned, it's a bit boring. That is, until the spell is complete." She gave a small smile. "Then, I assure you, bored is the last thing you'll be."

"Magi Asheford, can we watch?" asked Flute eagerly. Though she had been disgruntled with Ashe the night before, it seemed that it had passed—or at least been set aside at the prospect of watching a huge magical working. Jesper eyed the space between Flute and Ashe in trepidation, but managed to look supportive of this request.

"I don't think there's much you'll be able to understand, Fluttermouse."

"Please?" she asked longingly.

"Very well," Ashe said. "But I must warn you both, you cannot ask me any questions or interfere in any way. You may harm both Zeth and me. This is not a game."

Both sprouts nodded seriously.

"Thank you, Magi," Jesper said, giving Flute a meaningful look.

She seemed to come to herself. "Oh! Yes, thank you, Magi."

Xari turned to Ashe. "All right. I'll wait over here. Are you ready?"

"Yes." Ashe flew forward until he was level with Zeth's face, and soon she recognized him to be lost in an intricate web of magic.

Xari carefully assembled her own bedroll and pack and asked Immen to see that their captive was fed and watered—something she could not do herself at present without disturbing Ashe.

Anathriel seemed pensive and unsure. She kept watching Asheford and Zeth with odd, troubled expressions. Finally, she took it upon herself to do some washing, and Xari was grateful the girl had found something with which to occupy herself. Xari took a cue and spent a good deal of time slowly sharpening the blades of her swords. It helped her ignore the pounding of her own heart. Very shortly, there would be an Eagle Speaker, and she would no longer be alone.

When the moment came, it was unmistakable. It was as if something had suddenly slammed into Xari's brain, bringing with it flashes of Zeth's life. She saw a small child being plucked off of the streets, slapped with a tattoo, and enslaved. She saw a lonely boy being shunned by others because of his status, growing more resentful and alone—until he met Immen Corper. She hadn't realized just how much Immen meant to Zeth until this moment. Immen had taught Zeth how to shoot a bow, how to catch food in the wild, and had even taken him out for a ride on an eagle in secret. He had welcomed Zeth into his home.

Xari saw several memories that included Immen and another person, a young woman who was perhaps around Xari's own age. Zeth did not have many friends or companions, but Immen and this woman—*Areen Corper,* Zeth's memory told her—had counted strongly among them.

At the same time she saw this, she had flashes of Mortén's life—something with which she was already very familiar. She hadn't expected it, but she supposed that awakening one speaker must bring all of them together in mind, all at once, and she knew, without a doubt, that Mortén was seeing the same of Zeth and her.

Another thing she hadn't expected was that the connection to Zeth would feel so natural. She was so accustomed to the conflict of her bond with Mortén, which had never been embraced by either of them. With Zeth, something indescribable fell instantly into place. It was amazing and refreshing after eight years with only Mortén in her mind. She sensed a great deal from Zeth and felt that she had known him for years rather than two days. He had a good heart—he was confused and angry about a great many things, much as Xari had been in the past, but he certainly didn't have the taint of darkness that Mortén carried.

Almost simultaneously, Zeth and Xari straightened, and their eyes locked. Zeth was the first to speak, and it was as if he was completely oblivious to any presence but Xari's.

"I—" He shook his head, his eyes wide. "I can sense the eagles, like a buzzing in the back of my mind. There are so many. It's amazing, and strange, and—" Zeth hesitated for a minute, continuing to gaze at her. "And I saw your life. And Mortén's, and his thoughts, and—is it—?" He took a deep breath.

Xari nodded, more than a bit dazed. "It's not always like this," she assured him, taking a deep breath of her own. She pressed her fingers to her temples. "The only other time I've seen Mortén's memories was when I was awakened."

She straightened up, suddenly realizing they had observers. Immen and Anathriel were staring at them, as were Flute and Jesper. Ashe had collapsed onto the ground, his eyes closed, though Xari could tell from his breathing that he was still conscious.

"Should we help Magi Asheford?" Flute whispered.

"No, Flute. Ashe needs to be left alone. Thank you, though." Xari looked down to assure her guardian seemed somewhat comfortable. "Mortén is aware of what we've done. He knows Zeth and I are together, and he knows his hunter has failed. With his fire fueled, I do not know what he will do now."

When White Paw returned to the camp, he didn't seem all that surprised that Zeth could understand him. "We have awaited the days of the speakers for a long, long time," he said, sounding more solemn than Xari had yet heard him. "I am honored to truly meet you, Zeth of the eagles."

Zeth appeared taken aback. "Wow," Xari heard him whisper. He cleared his throat. "I am honored to truly meet you, too," he managed.

The wolf turned his attention on Xari. "I have given some thought to the hunter, and I believe I may have a solution."

White Paw proceeded to suggest that if Xari kept all of the hunter's weapons and released him, he would escort him to the edge of the forest. It would take a good week to complete the task, but White Paw didn't seem bothered by the time. "Just tell him that if he tries anything, he won't like the consequences. And his dog will be under my influence at all times. I will assure that he takes the path back to the mountains, because you have said you will not be going that way."

Xari nodded thoughtfully. "That might work."

"It sounds like the best idea we've had so far," Zeth agreed.

"You may also assure the hunter that while he might not see them, others of my clan will be joining us." White Paw gave a very toothy grin.

Xari wasn't sure whether or not White Paw was bluffing, but she would relay to the hunter exactly what he had said. She heard Zeth briefly discussing the plan with Immen and Anathriel, and she strode over to Roglio, carefully unbinding his eyes and mouth. "I am going to untie you," she told the hunter. "And White Paw is going to take you and your dog out of the forest, back toward Montressa. If you try to harm him, or if you try to escape, I will feel no sorrow for what White Paw will do to you. Others of his clan will be joining him, though you may not ever see them, so there is no point in trying anything. "

Roglio gave her a look full of loathing and ground out, "And what makes you think I wish to go back to the mountains?"

"I don't care one way or another what you wish," Xari replied calmly. "Be glad you're leaving with your life." She glanced back at White Paw. "When do you want to leave?"

"Now."

Xari turned around, kneeling so she was eye level with the wolf. "Thank you so much for everything you've done. And please thank Appleseed and the others for me. I'll never forget it."

White Paw nuzzled her shoulder, then gave her another grin. "Neither will I forget you, Xari of the otters. May the rest of your hunt be successful! Should you need our aid again, you know where to find us. You have proven yourself to be trustworthy."

"Thank you. I hope all of your kin feel that way."

"They will see reason eventually."

A small smile crossed Xari's face. "I hope so." She turned back to the hunter and used a knife to slice through his bonds. Roglio stayed on the ground for a moment, rubbing his wrists and ankles. White Paw came to stand over him and gave a wordless growl low in his throat. The hunter scowled fiercely as he stood carefully to his feet, but Xari sensed the fear he was trying to cover. Within moments, he had disappeared into the forest, shepherded by White Paw, while his dog trailed along at his side.

Xari turned back around. "That's one thing taken care of, anyway. We'll stay here the rest of the day." It was already midday. "If we leave tomorrow morning, Ashe should be recovered."

⌘ ⌘ ⌘

The first drowsy hour of darkness was broken by a strangled cry of uncomfortable fright. Xari sat up quickly. She could feel Zeth's distress with her gift and also through their newly forged bond. "Ashe?" she muttered, trying to find her guardian in the darkness with still-sleepy eyes.

"I know," said Ashe reassuringly.

"What is wrong?" Anathriel's half-curious, half-annoyed, very lethargic voice came from across the glowing remains of the fire.

Xari had already reached her fellow speaker's side. "What is it, Zeth?" She could see him a little better now. Out of the corner of her eye, she also saw Immen sit up slowly, watching them with thoughtful eyes.

"I saw—" Zeth began. "I saw—" He swallowed.

"You had a vision?"

He nodded vigorously. "I don't know what else it could be."

"We told you about them."

"I know," he said, still trying to catch his breath. "I just didn't think it would be this soon."

Xari and Ashe exchanged looks. She couldn't quite make out his features, but she knew they both were thinking the same thing. "Nor did we," she confessed to Zeth. "Was it frightening?"

He finally seemed to be calming down. "No," he said slowly. "Not in itself. It merely took me by surprise."

"What are we talking about?" Anathriel said crankily, finally sitting up herself.

"Visions," Xari told her. "Of the past. Of the future." She faced Zeth. "You might call them missives from the Master himself. It's certainly a more direct method than I'm used to, but it remains to be seen if it will be any easier to deal with."

"What was it like?" Immen asked.

"Otherworldly," Zeth explained. "Not like a dream. It was so much more powerful. And I was aware, you know? I absolutely knew I wasn't dreaming, and I was looking at something that had happened in the past."

"How do you know it was the past?" Xari asked.

"Because I know."

"What did you see?" asked Ashe.

"Am I supposed to tell you? Just like that?"

"Unless you think—"

"Honestly," Ashe interjected, cutting off Xari's argument, "we don't know, Zeth. Xari and I have long hoped for guidance from what your gift would show or tell us. But maybe it was never meant to be used as such. That's the problem. We don't know."

"I think it might be sometimes."

After a moment of silence, Ashe asked again, "What did you see?"

In a low voice, Zeth said, "We have to go to Réol."

"What? Why?"

"Because Mortén left the leviathan relic there when he went to Montressa."

Xari froze, staring at Zeth. "Really? But he always takes the relic with him when he's away. Else Ashe and I would have tried to take it long ago."

Zeth shrugged. "I don't know anything about that. I saw him hide it before he left for Montressa. He has a private study in his house, and he hid it underneath a loose floorboard, below his desk. I don't think you could even guess that it was there. The way it looked—"

Xari tugged on a braid. "How do you know it was *this* trip? He's gone every year since he became a speaker."

"I can't explain it. I just know that the relic is at his estate. You said the relics are important, didn't you?"

"Yes," Xari said slowly, already pondering the full impact of this change of circumstance.

"Are you mad?" Anathriel broke in, disbelieving. "You want to walk right into Mortén's estate? He's already hunting for us! He wants us dead!"

"I'm telling you what I saw, and I think it's important that we try," Zeth insisted.

"And how do you know it wasn't the future?" Anathriel shot back sardonically.

"Because I know, Anathriel!" Zeth shouted back. "Did you not hear me the first two times I said it!?"

"Stop it, both of you," Immen said, shooting both Anathriel and Zeth stern looks.

"You said you wanted to know what to do, and you said you wanted to look for the other relics. I'm telling you there's a leviathan relic left alone and unprotected on Mortén's estate, and it's ours for the taking if we move fast," Zeth said firmly.

"I hardly think it would be unprotected, Zeth," Anathriel began, "and if you think—"

"Anathriel," Immen warned darkly, "please." He asked Xari, "Is it possible to awaken another Leviathan Speaker if you have the relic?"

Xari shook her head. "No. No speaker can be awakened to the leviathan relic until Mortén is dead. Still, if we could get our hands on it, it would prevent Mortén from hiding it or putting it somewhere forever beyond our reach. Besides, Mortén can't live forever."

"You would have our help on this, Xari," Immen said kindly. "We have reason to fight Mortén now, too. You're not alone."

Xari looked at Ashe.

"This is a choice you must make without me," he said.

Xari had expected him to say something like that. She glanced around at the circle of faces in front of her. Zeth's fervor was compelling, and Immen was also correct in saying that she was no longer alone. Zeth was not her only companion on this journey, nor the only other one who had a personal stake in Mortén's fate. Every single person and fairy seated in this circle could be in danger because of Mortén, but if they went to Réol, it would not be without consequences. It was very likely Mortén would pursue them the instant he determined their intentions.

Xari had spent years avoiding Mortén and still didn't feel completely ready to confront him, no matter how much she had tried to prepare for the eventuality. He had always been more powerful, and she had never been in the right position to deal with him outright. Was she ready for it now? Was Zeth, so new to his power, ready? What if they got to Mortén's estate to find the relic and found a trap instead?

"You still need a guardian," she reminded Zeth.

"The relic is more important. You know that," Zeth replied. "I know I've only been a speaker for—well, for less than a day, but I know that. We might never have another chance to get it. Besides, we'll be traveling with three fairies. That should be enough protection until we can actually get to Fairlight Forest, right?"

"You may be right, Zeth." Xari looked at Immen and Anathriel. "As I said earlier, you don't have to come with us."

"I don't believe this," Anathriel said, shaking her head and resting her fingertips on her temples. She turned a hard stare on Xari. "What else do you expect us to do? You've already made a point of saying that we're not safe anywhere!"

"And as I said earlier, I don't want to run from Mortén the rest of my life," Immen said with quiet determination. "I think we'll be coming along."

17

It was quickly decided that they would turn southeast. If they continued that direction, they would hit the section of the River Road that went into Merenth—the same river that Xari had traveled up only recently. Mortén's estate was far, far down the river, almost to the eastern coast of Réol. The journey would take several weeks, but Xari's consolation was that even if Mortén left Montressa immediately, he shouldn't reach his estate before they did. Besides, he probably wouldn't even guess exactly where they were headed until they got into Réol.

Despite the day of rest, the journey did not start out well the next morning, at least not for Xari. She became vaguely aware that Ashe was calling her name, no doubt with his usual ridiculous suggestion to get up. Xari groaned and rolled over. "Go away," she muttered.

"Come along, Xari. Everyone else is already up and ready. We need to begin early," Ashe said, his voice sounding slightly muffled.

Xari cracked open an eye and realized she had pulled her entire head into the bedroll sometime during the night, and it didn't take long to determine why. The pattering of raindrops on leaves and the top of her bedroll met her ears. "It's raining,"she moaned.

A moment later, the top of the bedroll was yanked completely off of her, exposing her to the chilly, wet air. "You'll feel better when you get moving," Ashe said unsympathetically, from the point where he was hovering above her. "Come along." He waved his hand, and her bedroll tipped to the side, as if someone were picking it up with invisible hands.

Xari rolled off and found her feet, rain striking her on her head. "Fine," she said grouchily.

As Ashe had said, the others were already dressed, packed, and wearing their rain cloaks. It wasn't long before Xari managed to stuff everything into her own pack. When she was ready, they started out through the forest, following Immen's compass southeast. He had apparently been keeping track of their direction since he had left Montressa, which was how he knew where they were in the midst of the forest.

Xari ate some breakfast as they walked, but it did very little to improve her mood. Despite her own rain cloak, she was getting wet, especially as the droplets began to fall faster. Unlike the warm rains that fell on Ithrin, this rain was freezing. Water leaked into her hood and ran down her neck, and soaked up the bottoms of her breeches. Immen, Anathriel, and Zeth were equally damp, and Anathriel complained on several occasions but continued to press on. Had Xari been more inclined to whining, she might have complained as well, but she simply gritted her teeth and shivered her way along.

It really helped that she had company; not that Ashe wasn't company, but it was nice to have other people to talk to, especially when she could be completely free with what she said. The only other person with whom she had ever had that liberty was Burin. She spoke a great deal with Zeth and Immen. Anathriel was a bit harder to approach, as she seemed to have nothing in common with Xari, and Xari had the distinct impression that Anathriel disapproved of her. Still, Xari did try.

She had developed a bit of a cough by the end of the day, which only made things worse. She was going to take first watch again, but Zeth quickly offered to do so, and Immen said he would take second watch. Xari nodded her thanks and collapsed into her bedroll.

The next few days brought no improvement. It continued to rain steadily, without a single break. "It's common to have quite a bit of rain during the summer," Immen pointed out.

That did nothing to console Xari. Ashe couldn't do much with his magic to keep her dry, because the rain never ceased. All of her companions seemed to be handling the moisture better than she was, even Anathriel, despite her protests.

At night, they pitched a makeshift tent and crammed their bedrolls underneath. Between that and the waterproof covers on their bedrolls, they stayed relatively dry. They were not, however, able to make a fire of any sort, and so ate only their dried foods, along with whatever edible plants Immen found.

When they reached the edge of the forest, everyone was excited to be in a different landscape.

Despite the rain, Immen continued to spar with Xari every evening, which was one thing that brightened her disposition. She had so missed this nightly routine, and it did her well to continue it. During their travels, and sometimes when huddled under the tent, Xari taught Zeth of the brethren, offering what insight she had learned over the years about being a speaker, and answering his numerous questions.

The high point of the journey was when Xari awoke on the fourth morning to discover that the rain had actually stopped. Everyone was in better spirits as they continued, and moods improved as the rain held off, though the sky remained overcast and gloomy.

By that night, however, the temperature had dropped drastically due to all of the rainfall, and Xari's cough was worse. She was feeling rather achy. She took first watch, and sat awake in the grassy knoll where they had camped. Things were still too wet to start a fire, so she wrapped her arms around herself and shivered. Ashe, while still keeping an eye and ear out for her, was in one of his contemplative moods, and Xari knew it was best to leave him alone while he was meditating.

They had pitched their tent in case it began raining again, but now a large, pale moon was flittering in and out of the clouds. Xari sat at the edge of the tent for a while. Finally, too cold to sit still any longer, she turned and tried to creep around Anathriel toward her pack.

"Are you all right?" Immen's soft voice came from his bedroll. Xari had quickly learned that he was a very light sleeper, and awoke at the slightest changes or noises, very unlike her. Burin had always said she could sleep through a herd of stampeding elephants.

"Cold," Xari managed. She grabbed an extra tunic and pulled it on over the one she already wore. She twisted back around and climbed carefully over Anathriel's legs, settling again at the edge of the tent. "I'm sorry to wake you," she said over her shoulder.

A gust of cold wind blew over her, and she shivered, hunching down as far into the folds of her clothes as she could.

"It's not a problem," Immen said. Xari heard him scuffling around but assumed he was merely getting comfortable in his bedroll, until she suddenly heard his voice right behind her. "Are there any fairies on you?"

"What? No, why—" She was halfway through turning around when she felt something being draped across her shoulders.

Immen smiled at her and tucked his heavy cloak around her arms. "It's always chilly up north, even during the summer." He took a seat beside her, seeming far warmer than she was, though he only wore a single layer of clothing. "I suppose I'm used to it. It doesn't bother me. Now *winters* are cold."

"I know." Xari shuddered. "It snowed every winter when I was in the orphanage—not as much as up here, I guess, because it was southern Threnphol, but I hated it. It was hard to stay warm. Given the circumstances, it's not surprising I moved to Ithrin."

Immen shot her a sideways glance. "You sound as if you miss it."

"I do. I miss Burin, and the forge, and the otters. And Diegan."

"Who's Diegan?" Immen asked curiously.

"A dolphin. He brings me news from all around the ocean once a week or so." Xari smiled longingly. She pulled Immen's cloak more tightly around herself as another draft of chill wind struck. "I used to travel all the time when I was younger, before I met Burin. It was hard sometimes, trying to find places to stay, but Ashe and I managed. I've still traveled on and off during the last five years, but it's not as easy to pick up and leave the only place that's really been home. And now everything has happened so fast." She made a face. "I'm sorry. I'm sure this has to be far stranger for you than it is for me."

Immen chuckled. "Perhaps. I would never have imagined I would be fleeing Montressa at all, let alone with Anathriel and Zeth."

"Zeth certainly seems to be in his element." Xari glanced over her shoulder and saw Zeth sleeping with his mouth wide open. "He took to being a speaker without even blinking."

Immen was silent for a moment. "I'm not really surprised. Zeth—he was meant for so much more than a slave's life. He's always been waiting for something to happen. He was ready for this. I'm glad he was the speaker—I think he's more cut out for it than I would have been."

"Oh, I don't know. I think you would have made a pretty good speaker. It took a lot of courage to leave your life in Montressa." Xari wrapped her arms around her knees. "Do you miss it?"

"Mmm, sometimes, when I think about it. I was happy there, but I can be happy in a lot of places. I do miss being around the eagles. More than anything, I miss Areen."

"Your sister?" Xari hazarded a guess, recalling the girl she had seen in Zeth's mind when she had witnessed bits of his life through the awakening.

"Yes." Immen's brow furrowed. "Did Zeth or Anathriel—"

Xari shook her head. "I saw her. About sixteen or seventeen, brown hair, hazel eyes. She wears a gold necklace in the shape of a flower."

Immen looked a bit surprised. "Yes, but what do you mean you saw her?"

"In Zeth's memories," Xari said quietly. "You were usually in them, too."

Immen's face smoothed in understanding. "Yes, Zeth knows her," he agreed, with a backwards glance at the sleeping boy. "He came to our house at times, when his master and mistress were away."

That was true, but Xari knew there was more to it than that. There had been nights even when Zeth's master and mistress were in residence that Zeth had sneaked out to visit the Corpers' home, times when he was so lonely and frustrated that it seemed the only refuge in his small world. "Is she your only family?"

"Yes. My mother died when I was very young, and my father remarried. Areen's mother died in childbirth. The necklace you mentioned—it belonged to her mother, a wedding gift from our father." Immen was quiet for a moment. "He died several years ago. Areen just became a handmaiden at Par Auspré, like Anathriel. I was offered a home at Par Auspré with the other Windriders long ago but refused until I knew Areen would be looked after. I'm—I'm worried about her, and I've no idea what she thinks of my disappearance. I wanted to leave her a message when I fled Montressa, but I was afraid if it were discovered, I would put her in danger with Mortén." His jaw tightened, and Xari got a sharp, hot flash of his fear and guilt.

She worked one of her hands out of the cloak and laid it on his arm.

"She—" Immen swallowed hard and shook his head slightly. "There were so many things we were talking about, like whether or not we should sell our house now that we were both going to be living at Par Auspré, or whether we should hold onto it for other reasons. And other plans we had, things we wanted to try to do. I've left her with so much to handle."

More guilt rushed over Xari from Immen. "If she's anywhere near as resourceful as you, I'm sure she's fine," Xari said with a smile.

Silence fell.

At last Immen nodded. "She is very resourceful," he agreed.

"Will you go back, then, if things with Mortén ever conclude?"

"I don't know," Immen said thoughtfully. "I suppose I'll walk that road when I reach it. I'm beginning to wonder if my life holds a different path, as I seem to have been pulled so quickly out of the one I was living. You would probably say it was your Master's design."

"And do you believe that?" Xari asked curiously.

Out of all of them, Immen had been the most willing and open to discussing the Master, and she thought he was beginning to truly believe in the Master's existence.

"Strangely enough, out of everything on this journey, it makes the most sense," Immen replied, offering her a lopsided smile. "I want to see Areen, but if I do return to Montressa, it may only be to sort out affairs, depending on where this road takes us. I just wish I could take Anathriel home. She was happy there, more or less." Suddenly, his expression brightened. "I forgot!" he said excitedly.

"What?" Xari asked, puzzled by this strange transformation.

Immen reached into the inside of his vest and groped blindly into a well-concealed pocket, drawing out something from within. He handed it to Xari.

Curious, she unfolded it, a square of linen with an intricate scene of a silver eagle, majestic in flight against a setting sun. Even in the dim moonlight, Xari could appreciate the craftsmanship. "Oh," Xari breathed. "How beautiful."

"That's Zephyr," Immen said proudly. "It looks just like her."

"Where did you get this?" Xari asked.

He paused, and flashed her a strange, half-amused expression, as if daring her to believe his next words. Then he jerked his head back to Anathriel meaningfully. "Anathriel made it for me."

"Really?" Xari examined the needlework again. Suddenly, she felt very strange. "Immen, did you and Anathriel ever—?" She almost choked on her words. "I mean," she continued clumsily, "this is—" She held up the needlework meaningfully. "It's a lot of work for a gift between friends," she finished hastily. Why was this bothering her so much?

He appeared uncomfortable. "That's a story for a private time," he said significantly, once again sending his glance the other girl's way to

190

indicate his meaning. Then he locked eyes with Xari. "But I promise I'll tell you."

"You don't have to," she said automatically, although inside she desperately wanted to know. "It's not my business."

He turned his attention toward the night sky. "What about you? Will you be returning to Ithrin when this is over?"

"Well, I promised Burin that I would. I also have a duty to try to find the rest of the relics, even if nothing turns up at Mortén's."

"What if you spend your whole life searching and never find them?" Immen asked.

"Then I'll spend my whole life searching. And Ashe, who will most likely live far beyond my years, will take the otter relic, find a new speaker, and keep looking." She cocked her head. "But I don't think it's coincidence that three of them have been recovered in the past decade. Still, no matter how much I search, I hope I can always go home."

They fell into a relaxed silence, then Xari glanced sideways at Immen. She found it a bit strange, and a bit disconcerting, how comfortable she had come to feel around him—perhaps even more comfortable than she was with Zeth. While she felt that she understood Zeth in a lot of ways, and while she shared a connection with him, there was a part of himself that he kept locked away and didn't allow anyone to see. It was a place deep in his mind and heart, and Xari wasn't sure he even realized it was there. She understood it and knew that prying would only make it worse.

Immen, on the other hand, was the most open and honest person she had ever met, save perhaps Burin. He always treated her courteously, but it wasn't mere politeness. He honestly cared about her, and not just her—she sensed he cared for everyone on this trip. He was as respectful to her as he would be to any lady of great standing, which might have normally made her feel awkward, but Immen's very nature barred discomfort, especially since he didn't act as if she were incapable, but treated her as an equal.

"Xari? Is something wrong?" Immen asked, his eyebrows rising.

Xari suddenly realized she was staring at him and quickly shook her head. "Just thinking."

"It looked like very serious thinking."

Xari shrugged a little but chose not to comment.

Immen nudged her shoulder with his own. "You can go to sleep for a while, if you'd like. I'm not feeling particularly tired."

"And I am," Xari admitted. *And not feeling well,* she thought, but she refrained from mentioning that. She started to take off the cloak, but Immen shook his head.

"Hold onto it. It'll keep you warmer tonight."

Xari smiled. "Thank you."

18

The group of travelers was reminded of the urgency of the situation the next morning when Xari, who had been keeping track of Mortén's position, suddenly sat up straight. "Mortén," she said.

Everyone froze instantly, and Immen asked, wariness in his voice, "What is it?"

Xari locked eyes with Zeth, who regarded her grimly with a knowing expression. He then took in the gaze of everyone else. "Mortén has departed from Montressa."

Anathriel wrapped her arms around herself. "He left early? Why did he leave early? Is he trying to catch us?"

"We should still keep well ahead of him, if everything goes as planned," Immen said firmly.

If there was one thing that Xari had learned over the years, it was that even the best-laid plans could only be held at arms' length. She was already very grateful—and a bit amazed—that things had gone as well as they had. Though they had faced obstacles, everything had thus far gone in their favor.

The next day, however, their fortune began to decline, and it was entirely her fault. She awoke feeling even more poorly, with an almost constant headache. Even her body felt weaker than usual, but she went about her day as normally as possible.

They reached the river about midday, and came across the nearest post that evening. It didn't take long to find a boat traveling south, and Xari still had plenty of money left to pay their fare. It was wonderful to be on a boat, without the need to force her feet to keep moving. Her strength had been waning with every step she had taken that day.

Come nightfall, they made their beds on the deck. The sky was completely clear, and the moon shone down on them. Xari fell asleep almost instantly but woke up in the middle of the night, shivering unstoppably. Her bedroll didn't seem to warm her at all. She sat up, which set her head to pounding and made her feel dizzy. She blindly groped for her bag but ended up smacking Zeth on the head. Zeth just groaned and rolled over, which woke the fairies and Immen instantly, and Anathriel peeked open tired eyes.

"Xari?" Immen whispered, sitting up.

"What's going on?" Anathriel mumbled, as Ashe's worried eyes appeared in front of Xari's face.

Xari's hands finally landed on her pack, and she opened it, yanking out her extra tunics. She pulled two on quickly, then collapsed back into her bedroll and pulled it up around her ears. She willed her head to stop pounding so she could talk.

Immen's concerned face came into view over hers a moment later. "You don't look well." He laid a hand on her forehead. "Sweet Auspré, you're burning up."

This pulled Anathriel out of her bedroll, and she knelt beside Immen, resting the tips of her fingers on Xari's forehead. "Are you feeling any pain?" she asked briskly, sounding much more awake.

"My head hurts, and I feel really shaky. And I'm cold," Xari managed.

Anathriel frowned. "Did it just start? You've been coughing a bit lately."

"Yes. And I've had a headache since yesterday."

Anathriel glanced at Immen. "It seems a pretty serious fever. We should probably get her to a healer; they would have herbs to help alleviate the fever and her aches."

"Can't we simply buy the herbs?" Ashe asked.

Anathriel shook her head. "Only from a healer. I'm not sure how it works where you're from, but here, medicinal herbs aren't available to the general public. I know what she needs, but I don't know what I'm looking for as far as gathering our own."

Immen nodded. "I'm going to speak to the captain and find out where the next post is. Hopefully the next one will have a town with a healer."

Xari finally managed to find her voice. "No, no." She waved a hand. "I'll be fine."

Immen had to step over her, and he stopped midstride, straddling the bedroll and looking down at her. "I'd rather be safe than sorry."

"We don't have time for this," Xari objected. "We need some time at Mortén's before he arrives; we still need to find a way to get onto his estate and locate the leviathan relic. We can't afford detours."

"We're going to make time for this one," Immen said firmly. Ignoring Xari's further protests, he disappeared in search of the captain.

⌘ ⌘ ⌘

Never in all of Anathriel's wildest imaginings would she have guessed she would be in this situation. She couldn't believe she was headed for Mortén's estate, of all places. Still, her reasoning was that it might be safer than being anywhere else. After all, Immen was an experienced bowman, the fairies had their magic, and the crazy warrior girl had her swords. Sometimes she still hoped she would wake up and find herself asleep in her warm, dry bed in Par Auspré, and learn that she had dreamt all of this.

Instead, she was traveling down a river on a merchant boat—which reminded her painfully of her father—with people who seemed to have accepted all of this as normal. Zeth, for instance, acted as if he had been a speaker his entire life. Immen had always seemed completely comfortable traveling, and despite the dire circumstances they found themselves in, he almost seemed to be enjoying it. He had spent a great deal of time talking—not to mention sword-fighting—with Xari lately, which was a source of frustration to Anathriel. She had been surprised, and strangely hurt, when Xari had awakened one morning wrapped in Immen's cloak. Yes, the girl seemed inordinately cold all of the time, and yes, Immen was a gentleman, but the fact remained that Xari had been in Immen's cloak.

That same Xari now lay curled in a bedroll, shivering and fevered. Oddly enough, it was one thing that grounded Anathriel in some sense of sanity. She could deal with illness. Learning to care for the sick was inbred in the women of Anathriel's society. She had always been taught that it didn't matter who the person was; if you had the ability to help, you did. So though she didn't particularly like Xari, she did her best to help, dipping cloths into the cold river and laying them on Xari's forehead, trying to get her fever to go down.

They reached the next post midmorning, crossing the border into Threnphol.

"We're getting off here," Immen said.

"We can't," Xari protested weakly, turning fevered eyes on Immen.

Anathriel huffed. "Oh, for Pathon's sake! If this is more—"

"Don't—understand," Xari said miserably. "We're in Threnphol. "

"Yes! And they have healers, like anywhere else!" Anathriel said, exasperated. "Your fever hasn't gone down—in fact, it has worsened. You need medicine."

"Don't—" Xari coughed and winced.

It was Immen who looked at Xari with understanding. "She's a Westerlon," he said quietly.

"You noticed," Xari murmured, trying to smile and instead grimacing.

"A what?" Anathriel glanced between Immen and Xari, baffled.

"Sweet Auspré, don't you know about anything outside of Montressa?" Zeth asked in exasperation.

Before Anathriel could retort, Immen, watching Xari very carefully, explained, "The Westerlons are from the Western Continent, Anathriel. They attacked Threnphol a long time ago—"

"There was a lot more to the attack than most people know," Xari whispered. "But the people of Threnphol always hated me because I'm at least half-Westerlon. I was born after the war." She seemed to be having difficulty breathing and began coughing again.

"No matter. You have just as much right to medical treatment," Immen said firmly. "And we're getting off here."

Xari had a hard time standing and had to be supported by Zeth and Anathriel as they got off the boat. Immen quickly went to speak with a local baker, then he came running back. "The healer's the next street over. Zeth, would you wait here and watch our belongings?"

"Sure."

Anathriel and Immen managed to get Xari to the next street. The healer's building would have looked simply like a house, were it not for the small sign with a healer's symbol on a stake in front. The symbol was a unicorn, which Anathriel had never thought much of before, but it now held an entirely new meaning for her.

They knocked on the door, and it was opened by a middle-aged woman. She glanced at them, her eyes locking on Xari, and Anathriel saw a surge of hatred flare in the woman's eyes.

"What are you doing bringing that abomination onto my doorstep? Take her away!"

Anathriel blinked at the woman in shock. "Excuse me?"

"You heard me! Get that filthy Westerlon off of my property!"

Anathriel was temporarily at a loss for words, so stunned was she by the woman's rudeness.

Immen, however, spoke sharply. "We only need—"

"I don't care what you need! I do not treat, nor would I ever help, a Westerlon!" With these final words, the woman slammed the door in their faces.

Immen's jaw knotted in anger, and Anathriel stared at the door, indignant and disbelieving. "She can't refuse her aid!" she exclaimed.

"She just did," Xari said, wincing as she spoke. "I told you this would happen. It's all right."

"It's not all right," Immen said. "You need medicine."

"I know what herbs she needs, Immen," Anathriel said as they walked away from the healer's. She knotted her jaw and glared at the house. "Where are Flute and Jesper?"

"With Zeth," Xari whispered.

"Then let's get back there. I have an idea."

They went as quickly as they could back to the post where Zeth was waiting for them. Immen gently helped Xari sit while Anathriel enlisted the fairies' aid. "Jesper?" she asked, keeping as quiet as possible so she wouldn't attract the attention of onlookers. "Flute? Are you around here? I need your help."

The little fairies appeared in whirs of light directly in front of Zeth. "What do you need help with?" Flute asked.

"The healer should have a cupboard or a room or something with herbs in it, and I need you to find it."

Jesper frowned at her. "Why?"

"Because I need you to get medicine for Xari. The herbs should be labeled—"

"Labeled?" Flute wondered.

"Yes," Anathriel said impatiently. "They should have their names written on them."

Jesper shook his head. "But we can't read human!"

"All right," she fired back, "then here's what we're going to do: you're going to distract the healer while *I* go in and find the right herbs." At this point, she realized everyone was staring at her in surprise. "I'm not going to steal them!" she snapped. "I'll leave money in her house, perhaps somewhere she won't find it for a few days. I will *not* stand around while someone who claims to be a healer refuses to give treatment. Jesper, Flute, will you help me?"

Jesper and Flute both glanced to the side—probably at Ashe—then nodded determinedly.

"Anathriel, I can do it," Immen said, considering her with a strange, bemused expression.

"No, I'll do it. I know exactly what I'm looking for. It'll be quicker. You wait here. I'll be back shortly."

"Why don't you take Zeth? He can see Flute and Jesper even when they're invisible," Immen suggested.

"Fine," Anathriel said. "Come on, Zeth."

As Anathriel turned back to Jesper and Flute, she caught sight of Zeth giving her an odd look as well. Not one of respect, certainly, but there was something in his eyes that was more than the contempt he usually showed her.

⌘ ⌘ ⌘

Flute and Jesper caused a splendid distraction, making a potted plant on the healer's front porch crash to the ground and shatter, which brought the woman out of her home. Anathriel had already determined there was a back entrance—Jesper had gone to check—and while the healer woman went out the front door, she sneaked in the back. She hoped the two little fairies were keeping the woman sufficiently distracted, and from the cries of surprise and anger coming from the front, it sounded as if they were.

The healer's home was small, and as she had predicted, the healing herbs were all in a cabinet. It took only moments to find the herbs she needed and then to deposit money Xari had supplied in a jar near the back door. The woman might not deserve the money, but Anathriel could not in good conscience take the herbs without paying.

She crept back out of the house and waited several minutes before she heard the front door open. Knowing Flute and Jesper had stopped whatever they had been doing, she hurried around front.

Zeth, who had been waiting across the street, grinned when she arrived. "You should have seen it."

"Where are—"

Before she could finish the question, there were two more blurs of light, and Jesper and Flute appeared in front of her, huge grins on their faces. "Did we do it right?" Flute asked.

"You were splendid," Anathriel said, not quite believing she was saying that to Flute. "What did you do?"

"We just kept making her flowers fall over," Flute replied. "She was mad!"

"And confused," Jesper added. "She was muttering about the neighbor's cat, which I thought—"

"Wait!" Zeth's urgent tone cut Jesper off, and he whipped around toward the direction of the post.

"What is it?" Anathriel asked at the arrested expression in his eyes.

"Xari's in trouble," he said.

19

"We need to find another boat traveling south," Xari murmured from her position on the ground. She was leaning against their pile of baggage, waiting for Zeth and Anathriel to return from their escapade to the healer's. Immen was standing beside her, but when Xari began speaking, he crouched down to better hear her. This particular post wasn't very busy at the moment, but there were several people loading a fishing boat, and a couple of merchants talking nearby.

"We'll take care of it," Immen assured. "There aren't many boats here right now. We may have to wait a little while."

Xari closed her eyes, exhausted. She hadn't been sick like this since she was fourteen and a pox had been going around Urnii. Why did she have to come down with something now, when it was so vital that they continue their journey? How was she going to be in shape to do anything if she could barely stand?

She had spent years training her body to do what she wanted it to, to move and fight with everything she had available. She was used to having aches; during sword training and working in the forge, she had been bruised, burned, cut, and had even broken an arm once. But an illness was something she could have no control over, and it was incredibly frustrating. She hated feeling useless.

She also kept feeling waves of great concern coming from Immen, which was distracting. "I'll be fine," she told him.

"I didn't—"

"I know you didn't say anything. You didn't have to." On top of his concern, a strange feeling tingled at the edge of her awareness. Cautiously, she opened her eyes, focusing instead on pinpointing the sensation, as it didn't seem to be coming from Immen. She often had different, outside emotions strike her, especially in crowded areas, and was used to it, but this particular emotion was so exact, so focused.

Emotions were usually tumultuous and uncontrolled. This was more like the sense she got from White Paw when he was hunting, intent on a goal.

After only several moments, Ashe asked quietly, "What is wrong, Xari?"

It still astounded her how Ashe was able to read her body language. He didn't even have a gift for such things as she had.

"I'm not sure," she replied, eyes still darting around subtly. The merchants had been joined by several townspeople. Striding toward the post were two men dressed in uniforms of the local law enforcement, one lean, one burly. "I'm getting a strong sense of—" She screwed her eyes shut and concentrated hard, trying to put a name to what she was feeling. Her eyes opened again. "Anticipation," she concluded. "Determination."

She opened her eyes as the lawmen came closer, and it was only as they turned toward her and Immen that she realized the sensation was coming from them. Something was wrong, though. "Immen—" Her words died in her throat, all thoughts of the officers vanishing. Coming out from hidden areas around the post—behind a wooden pole, over an empty tent that normally sold fish—were at least three dozen fairies.

Xari's only experience with Ashe's folk were those now traveling with her, and certainly none of them had been like these. Physically, they were the same, but they wore strange garments—including armor, of all things, but what it was made of she wasn't near enough to tell. And they carried weapons. Small, perfect little bows and arrows, no doubt fashioned after human war gear. The arrows were more like darts, or large needles, with barbs on the end so they seemed clumsier than any arrows Xari had ever seen.

Shvri. The word arose unbidden from her memory. The forsaken ones of Ashe's race. The lost. Although she had no certain proof, somehow she knew her instinct was correct. If nothing else, she might have known merely because all of their weapons were pointed at Ashe, and they wore expressions of utter disgust and loathing. The shock of this unexpected sight made Xari forget every sensible thing Burin and Ashe had ever taught her.

Ashe leapt into the air, circling in place, trying to eye the ring of ill-kempt shvri all at once. This was difficult, as they were completely surrounding him, from above and below as well as from the various sides.

"Can we help you?" Immen was asking the officers in a puzzled voice. Xari vaguely realized that the two men had stopped several feet away.

"You're under arrest," one of the men said.

No! Everything in Xari screamed that these men were not who they claimed to be. She knew, too, that Immen couldn't possibly see the shvri. This, if anything, snapped Xari to her senses, her thoughts flashing to her swords. Unfortunately, they were on her belt, which she had folded into her pack earlier. She could just see their hilts peeking out of the pile of packs, behind her and on her right.

"What? On what grounds—?" Immen's question died as Xari grabbed for the nearest sword, just as the two men lunged. The burly one went after Immen and the lean one darted toward Xari. Her reflexes were slowed by her illness; she couldn't reach her weapon in time, and as she tried, the sudden movement sent a horrible pain through her already aching head. The next instant, she was sprawled on the ground with the strange man pinning her down, trying desperately not to throw up or pass out as stars sparked in front of her eyes.

"Xari!" Immen called, but he seemed far away. By the sounds of it, he was still trying to ward off his own inconvenience.

Xari began struggling furiously, making it as difficult as possible for her captor to keep her secured. It cost her dearly. Parts of her body that hadn't yet ached started to hurt. She was angry because she was being attacked and she was too weak to do much about it. With an extra-hard twist, she managed to free an arm and enough of her torso to get a quick, better view of the invisible crowd all around.

Ashe's hands were clenched at his sides, and while some might have taken this as a sign of fear or anger, Xari knew better. Certainly, Ashe might be a little bit afraid, and probably very angry, but he had lived for many years and knew well how to conduct himself in unexpected situations. Instead, she knew he was preparing himself for a great spell, perhaps even one that would fend off so many small attackers.

Her captor managed to wrest her back into a more manageable position, and Xari was swiftly losing the strength to resist. Her body couldn't handle this right now, and her heart was full of fear for Ashe.

Through their bond, she could feel Zeth's shock and confusion. He realized she was in trouble, since she was projecting her emotions to him, and she sensed that he was trying to make his way back to her, but she could not bother to discern where, exactly, he was. Her mind was entirely too occupied with the plight of her guardian.

"Do not wait for him to strike!" shouted one of the shvri angrily. "Fire, now!"

Xari screamed as several of the small creatures let their arrows fly. Ashe tried to dodge out of the way, but too many shots had been made, and all around him. She could not see how many of the small, dart-like arrows actually hit him, but his cry of pain made her feel as though someone had ripped her stomach out.

"No!" she screamed. "No, Ashe, no!"

Immen, whom she still could not see, let out a sound that was a half-grunt, half-snarl, particularly loud. Xari did her best to twist again, and could just barely see him. He was half-kneeling on the ground but had managed to get his hands around a large, wayward rock. In the few seconds she watched, he stalled his opponent with a hefty backwards elbow jab to the stomach. This gave him a brief moment with which to step free of the man's arm, which reached out vainly to grasp for Immen, even as he tried to gasp for air. Immen sprung up on his knees so that he was completely standing, kicked the man over, and cracked him soundly in the head with the rock until he slumped all the way to the ground.

He glanced around frantically, but his eyes did not see the small army of shvri impeding his way. His eyes took in Xari, lying pinned to the ground, and her captor, and immediately headed towards them, full of determination.

"The human!" shouted the first of the shvri again.

"Immen, no!" Xari screamed. In her fury, she was able to once again wrench her arms free, catching the wiry man by surprise. She jabbed the heel of her hand sharply into his face, first his chin, then his nose, causing him to let her go completely as he reached out for her, shouting a curse. Xari struggled to get to her feet, but her legs gave out from under her and she collapsed, head throbbing, stomach roiling.

She managed to stay conscious long enough to hear the tiny twang of bows letting loose once more. The small projectile weapons struck Immen full on. She watched despairingly as his eyes rolled closed and his lanky form toppled gracelessly to the ground, the hovering shvri dashing away to avoid his path downward.

⌘ ⌘ ⌘

Halfway back to the dock, Zeth came to a dead halt.

"What is it?" Flute asked, stopping beside Zeth's head. She and Jesper had turned invisible again, to keep out of sight of any of the humans in town.

"Xari's unconscious."

Anathriel grabbed Zeth's arm. "What about Immen? What sort of trouble was Xari in?"

Zeth shook off her arm. "I don't know! I can't read her mind."

Flute was very used to Anathriel and Zeth's bickering and didn't pay it much attention. In fact, something else had caught her attention, and she stared for a long, long moment, eyes wide. Jesper must have seen it, too, for he was frozen beside her.

"You don't have to snap at me!"

"Zeth," Flute whispered.

"I'm—"

"ZETH!" Flute and Jesper cried as one.

Zeth finally turned to them, halting as he saw the same thing that had captured Flute and Jesper's stare. A being had come from seemingly nowhere and was hovering only a few feet from Flute. She knew, instantly, that it was not a fairy; fairies didn't carry weapons and wear armor.

"What in the—?" Zeth murmured.

"Shvri," Jesper whispered, terror in his voice.

"What?" Anathriel sounded confused. "Is something wrong?"

"Shut up, Anathriel," Zeth hissed. He stepped up to Flute and Jesper. "What do you want?" he asked the shvri.

Jesper darted back to Zeth's shoulder and landed on it. Flute wanted to follow him, wanted to hide from the shvri. She couldn't, though; she had to protect Zeth—it didn't matter that she wasn't really his guardian, or that she was terrified. Ashe wasn't here to help, and Zeth was a speaker, one of the first in hundreds of years. She had to make sure he was all right.

Swallowing back her fear, she flew in front of Zeth's face, hands clenching into fists, her mind racing through all of her magic lessons to try to think of something that would be useful against shvri. It didn't help that she kept thinking that the shvri had killed all of the guardians once—why should it be any harder for them to do it again?

"Who are you talking to?" Anathriel whispered. "Is there someone here besides Flute and Jesper?"

The shvri—a female with a red and orange cap of feathers that puffed out around her head—held up her hands. Her weapon was hanging at her side. "My name is Heron," she said in a sturdy voice. "I mean you no harm."

"What do you want?" Zeth repeated.

Flute was glad that he was asking, because she wasn't certain her voice would work at the moment.

"To help you. You must come with me, now."

That brought Flute's voice back quicker than lightning. "No!" She held up her hands. "Stay away from him!"

Barely thinking, she pulled as much air around her as she could, then pushed it at the shvri. To her surprise, Heron went flying backwards as if an invisible wall had slammed into her—which, in essence, it had. Flute just hadn't expected it to affect her so much and quickly decided she must have caught her off guard.

Jesper seemed equally shocked. He leapt off of Zeth's shoulder and zoomed over to her. "What did you do, Flute?"

"Just a simple air spell!" Flute whispered. If it had worked, she wasn't going to question it. She whirled around. "Zeth, run!"

Flute was thankful Zeth didn't question. He shot a glance at Heron, who was trying to recover and fled back toward the post. Anathriel was right behind him, looking equal parts confused and exasperated. "Zeth! Wait!"

Zeth ignored her, coming to a halt only when he was within sight of the post. Flute saw instantly what he was staring at, and fear overwhelmed her. Numerous shvri were in the air, too many for Flute to count, and there were two men dressed in matching clothes. One was dragging another large man in the same clothing back toward a wagon. The other was right behind him, carrying Xari. Flute didn't see Immen at all—perhaps he was already in the wagon.

"They're being arrested!" Anathriel gasped.

Flute's voice was determined, if a bit shaky, when she declared, "We have to help them!"

"Too late," Zeth whispered, as the shvri spotted them.

"There they are!" one shrieked, and the entire group of shvri raced at them.

Trembling, Flute once more positioned herself in front of Zeth. She gathered her courage and closed her eyes, frantically calling on her magic to do *something.* She heard yells of surprise and opened her eyes to find the shvri right in front of her—but they were only half the number they had been before. The other half had vanished.

Before she had time to react to that, or anything else, something sharp hit her from behind. She gave a cry of pain, and then the world went blurry around her. Within moments, it had faded out completely.

20

A nathriel was very groggy when she came around, and thoroughly confused. Her head ached, her mouth was dry, and her eyes felt as though tiny weights had been placed upon them. Where was she? What had happened?

The first thing she felt was an incessant bumping beneath her. She was moving, somehow, but the sensation was unfamiliar. Then memory returned, and she recalled Xari being loaded into a wagon by officers of the law. She must be in the wagon as well. Had something happened that now they had the law looking for them?

The last thing she remembered was feeling stinging, needlelike pains on her arms and shoulders. She was lying on her side. She tried to move and quickly discovered that her hands were bound tightly behind her back.

Carefully prying open her eyes, Anathriel took in her surroundings. Zeth was sprawled out beside her in the wagon. He was on his side, facing her. His arms were pulled behind his back, no doubt tied as well. She twisted her head around to try to get a better glimpse of her surroundings. She quickly saw that Immen was opposite her, but he was awake. Despite his own bonds, he had managed to get himself sitting. Xari was beside him, and she didn't look to be in any position to move, bound or not. Her breathing was feverish and sweat rolled down her face. She looked, if possible, worse than she had when Anathriel had last seen her, however long ago that had been.

There was also a bulky man sprawled, unconscious, toward the back of the wagon. He wasn't tied; in fact, he appeared to be an officer of the law. Part of his head was bloody, as if he had cracked it on something. Piled next to him were all of their belongings.

The wagon was covered, and Anathriel couldn't see out the back, nor see who was driving, though she heard low voices coming from the forward end. "Immen," she whispered, trying to swallow back her fear.

"Where are we?" She slowly worked her way to a sitting position, wincing as her head protested the movement and the ties twisted at her wrists, digging into her skin. She wriggled her hands in an attempt to relieve some of the tension, but her bonds were tight and she had little success.

"I don't know," Immen whispered back. "I only woke up a few minutes ago. I—"

A gasp from Zeth stopped him midsentence, and both Immen and Anathriel turned to see Zeth's eyes snap open. He looked around frantically for a moment. "Where—?" He abruptly stopped speaking, his eyes roaming slowly around the wagon—not, Anathriel realized, at those tied on the ground, but up near the roof. "Shvri," he murmured, twisting his body around until he was seated, as well.

"Shvri? Those evil fairies?" Anathriel asked. "You mean they're here?" Her eyes went wide, and then flicked up toward the ceiling, but she saw nothing.

"Yes."

Anathriel shrank back, still looking around. She hated not being able to see what was truly happening around her.

Zeth was silent for a moment, eyes still fixed aloft. "Where are they?" he demanded.

Abruptly, Anathriel realized Zeth must have been asking about the fairies.

Zeth's mouth tightened and he turned back to Immen and Anathriel. "The shvri say they have the fairies, and that we had better not try anything."

Anathriel shivered. "What is going on? What happened to us?"

"Them," Zeth muttered, glancing upward. "They must have attacked Xari and Immen, because I saw the shvri by the post." He looked at Immen for confirmation.

"I don't know," Immen said. "We were jumped by two of those men, the lawmen; they said we were under arrest."

"I seriously doubt they're lawmen," Zeth said, eyes narrowing.

"You don't think Mortén had something to do with it?" Anathriel's whisper became even more hushed as she said Mortén's name.

"I don't know. It's certainly possible," Immen said. "If these men only pretended to be lawmen—well, nobody questioned it. They pulled us right away from a post and any bystanders must have thought they were arresting crazy criminals. When they grabbed us, Xari started screaming about Ashe, then I managed to hit that guy with a rock." Immen nodded at the unconscious man at the other end of the wagon. "Then I felt like I was struck with pins. The next thing I knew, I was waking up here."

"The shvri carry bows and arrows," Zeth murmured, speaking so softly that Anathriel had to strain to hear. "Or darts of some sort. I think they were poisoned with something to knock us out. They came at us, at Anathriel and me. Flute did something—I don't know what, but about half of the shvri suddenly disappeared before she was hit with an arrow, or a dart, or whatever. Then they were shooting at us, and like Immen said, we were here."

"We all woke up, though," Immen said, glancing worriedly at Xari. "Shouldn't she be awake?"

"She's sick." Anathriel's voice came out harsher than she had intended it. She was trembling, and not, she knew, from the after-effects of being drugged. She was terrified, horribly sick of being terrified, and worse, of being in a position that brought constant threat. "If her fever hasn't gone down—" she trailed off. "She needs medicine." The thought of the herbs brought to her the realization that there was a lump in her pocket, but she kept the knowledge to herself. The fact that there were unseen ears all around her did not escape her.

Zeth leaned in close. "There's something else," he murmured, his mouth barely moving. Anathriel and Immen bent forward. "I don't think I should talk about it right now, but later, if I have the chance." He glanced back up at the roof, and Anathriel knew he'd thought the same about the shvri.

Zeth raised his voice to speak to them directly. "Where are we going?" There was a pause, and then he replied, "Well, if we're going to see soon anyway, there's no point in keeping it a secret." Another pause, and Zeth glowered at the ceiling. "It's no use," he told Anathriel and Immen, still glaring. "They say we're almost there, but won't say where."

Despite the shvri's claim that they were almost to their destination, the ride seemed to go on forever. A hundred scenarios of what they could be riding into ran through Anathriel's mind, each worse than the last. She couldn't help thinking that this had something to do with Mortén.

Who else would want them? Who else would have known their location? Granted, she couldn't figure out how Mortén could have sent anyone to get them so quickly; he was on the road traveling, wasn't he?

After what seemed like ages, the movement of the wagon finally stopped. The wagon rocked as the drivers disembarked, and moments later, the cloth at the back was ripped aside, revealing two shapes silhouetted against the early afternoon sun. *Afternoon. That means we've been traveling for several hours.* Then another terrible thought occurred to her. *If it's still the same day.*

One of the men climbed into the wagon and yanked Zeth to his feet, shoving him unceremoniously toward the end of the wagon, where the other man grabbed him and pulled him out. Anathriel was thrust after Zeth, tripping from the force with which the man pushed her. Unable to use her hands to stop the fall, she fell onto the floor, scraping her cheek on the rough wood. She didn't have time to move before she was hauled back up and out of the wagon.

Anathriel found her feet and bit her lip angrily. Now that she was outside, she had a better glimpse of the men. They were no longer dressed as law officers. The one standing outside had a swollen nose, obviously recently broken—likely from the struggle with Xari and Immen, Anathriel thought with some satisfaction.

As the man in the wagon roughly grabbed Xari, Anathriel stepped forward. "Be careful with—"

A sound backhand to her face from the man with the broken nose silenced her. Her already stinging cheek suffered a fresh wave of pain.

"Nattan!" A new, sharp voice cut in. Anathriel tore her eyes away from the men and the wagon to see yet another individual approaching. This one was a very tall, broad man of middling years with a full, neatly trimmed, dark red beard and pale blue eyes. He was adjusting a tabard across his chest and two servants trailed behind him. The tabard was dark red and silver and featured the emblem of a hawk.

A noble. Anathriel didn't recognize the emblem, but that was no surprise. There were far too many nobles to know all of their emblems, and she knew only a few from Threnphol, if, indeed, they were still in Threnphol.

Right now, the nobleman looked angry. "What do you think you are doing?" he demanded of the ruffians.

"Delivering, as promised," the large thug in the wagon replied, jumping out with Xari in his arms. He dumped her none too gently on the ground.

The nobleman's blue eyes flashed. "I said they were to be unharmed. And why are they bound? Didn't I say—?"

"Pardon, my lord," the man with the broken nose said in a tone of scorn. "But we saw fit that they be bound. They caused enough damage as it was."

The nobleman turned to examine Xari, whom Immen was crouching beside on the muddy ground. "This one appears to be very ill. I hardly think she poses much of a threat to men such as you in her condition."

"She did this," the man retorted, jabbing his finger at his nose. "That was enough of a threat for me."

"Enough." The noble held up his hands, looking no less angry. "I will speak with the two of you later. Right now, unbind them at once."

The two thugs exchanged dark glances but complied. Anathriel was spun around, and moments later, her hands were free. She stepped back shakily, rubbing her sore wrists in an attempt to get the blood flowing again. As soon as Immen's hands were free, he lifted Xari's upper body off of the ground, and then looked up at Anathriel. "Are you all right?" he asked in a low voice.

Anathriel swallowed, not sure how to answer him. She was terribly confused as to what was going on, that was for certain, and her fear had not abated, even at this nobleman's insistence that they not be harmed.

"Wait for me in the hall. I will be there shortly," the noble told the two men sharply. They hesitated for a moment, then walked away in the direction from whence the nobleman had come.

It was only then that Anathriel looked around. They had come through a gate, which punctuated a high iron fence topped with sharp points. The fence encircled a large courtyard. Beyond it she glimpsed wooded grounds. It wasn't anything like the estates she was used to in Montressa, especially Par Auspré, which cleaved to its mountaintop like a cloud-trimmed crown. This seemed lackluster in comparison. The main hall was built of stone, but all the outbuildings were wooden, with slate roofs.

"Who are you?" Immen demanded, still supporting Xari. "What do you want with us?"

"I am Lord Jopherus of Nanaene."

"We're still in Threnphol," Immen said.

"Indeed you are." Jopherus surveyed them almost warily for a moment. "I apologize for the way you were treated. Unfortunately, hired help is not what it once was."

"Hired mercenaries, you mean," Zeth said boldly.

"What do you want with us?" Immen repeated.

"That, I'm afraid, requires a long explanation, which I do not have the inclination to give at the moment," Jopherus replied. "For now, you will remain guests in my house."

"Prisoners," Zeth muttered.

"If you choose to see it as such. You will be given a room, and I must ask that you stay there. You will be watched over—you, I believe, are the runaway?" Jopherus looked pointedly at Zeth.

Zeth's eyes narrowed, and he didn't answer.

"And from what I understand, you can see my small friends," Jopherus said frankly. He did not take his gaze off of Zeth, but gestured to the vicinity of the air around his head.

Anathriel's eyes widened, but she didn't know why she was so surprised. The shvri had been helping the hired men, whom Jopherus had hired. It stood to reason he would know about the shvri, too. "You can't see them, though," she said slowly.

"Not at the moment, but I know they are there, and you know they are there. That, for now, will be enough." Jopherus turned and motioned his servants closer. They approached, and Jopherus spoke to them too softly for Anathriel to hear. They nodded, and one disappeared back to the estate. The other moved to retrieve Xari, but Immen's arms tightened around her protectively, and he refused to relinquish her. "I'll take her," he said sharply. He gathered her up in his arms and stood.

"Follow me, please." Jopherus turned, clearly expecting full compliance.

Immen and Anathriel both looked at Zeth, who shook his head slightly, discreetly moving his eyes upward and around in a circle, indicating that the shvri were still present. Immen's mouth pressed in a grim line, but he nodded. With only a moment's hesitation, he followed after Jopherus, Xari's head lolling against his chest, Zeth right beside him.

Anathriel hurried to fall into step on Immen's other side. "I can't believe this," she hissed, nervously scanning the deceptively empty air around her.

"There's not much we can do at the moment, Anathriel," Immen whispered. "Even if we could escape, we wouldn't get far, and Xari needs help."

The rumble of livestock pervaded throughout the small estate as they made their way towards the main hall. Once inside, Jopherus turned and led them up a flight of stairs, emerging into a corridor with numerous doors off to the sides. He stopped at the second door to the right and opened it. Inside were two beds and two sleeping pallets.

He was expecting us, Anathriel thought with a shudder. In the middle of the room, chairs rested around a circular table, which was spread with food.

"Your belongings will be brought up soon—all save your weapons, of course," Jopherus said, ushering them into the room. "And a healer has been called for Xari."

Anathriel started at Jopherus's use of Xari's name. This man was certainly well-informed, which made the mystery of who he was and what he was up to all the more foreboding.

"Again, I must request that you stay here," Jopherus said. "I trust you will be comfortable." He said it in a way that made Anathriel think they would be comfortable whether they wanted to be or not. He shut the door behind him, and Anathriel heard the subtle click of a lock. Just to be sure, she grabbed the handle and tried to open it, but it didn't move.

"A gracious kidnapper. Can our journey get any stranger?" Immen muttered. He laid Xari carefully on one of the beds, frowning as he brushed a braid out of her face. He turned, his mouth a firm line. "Zeth, did you see Flute, Jesper, or Ashe anywhere?"

"No, but that doesn't mean they're not around. The shvri could have put them anywhere. They could have kept them in the front of the wagon, and brought them out before us."

Immen shook his head. "If Ashe is still alive, he has to be close by. They can't take him far from Xari."

"If," Anathriel echoed, a slight tremor in her voice as she came to stand at Immen's side. Her eyes flicked to the room's two windows, both of which were covered with iron grating. There would be no escape through that route. "And Flute and Jesper—"

She hoped they were all right. She had never thought she would be desperate to see them. Pulling her mind to other thoughts, she dug into her pocket and pulled out the herbs she had gone to such lengths to acquire. "Zeth, check the table and see if there's any hot water. Healer or no healer, Xari needs help."

The girl had not stirred at all during the entire trip in the wagon. Her breathing was shallow, and she burned to the touch.

"Are the shvri in here?" Immen asked.

"No, but a whole lot of them were outside the door when Jopherus shut us in here." Zeth walked over to the table. "There's hot water—do you need it in a cup?"

"Some in a cup, some in a bowl. And I need a cloth," Anathriel said, not bothering to turn around.

"Hold on—" Anathriel heard some bustling, and Zeth returned a moment later, carefully carrying the requested materials. He also had a roll crammed half in his mouth.

"Zeth!" Anathriel cried. "What if it's poisoned?"

"If Jopherus wanted to kill us, he could have done it well before now," Zeth mumbled around a full mouth. "I'm hungry."

Anathriel glanced back at the food, her stomach clenching. She was hungry, as well, and the table held victuals that she hadn't seen in weeks—fresh fruits and juices, milk, bread, honey and nut pastries. It was enough to make her mouth water and her stomach growl. And Zeth did have a point; Jopherus could have killed them before now. Still, she would worry about food later. Xari's situation took much higher priority.

While Anathriel expertly mixed herbs in the hot water, Immen reminded Zeth of the news he'd wanted to convey in the wagon. Zeth spoke softly of his first encounter with a shvri called Heron—not at the post, but on the way back. Anathriel recalled his odd-looking conversation with midair.

"It's odd. I didn't know the shvri were at the post, but looking back, it was like she was trying to help us, though I can't for the life of me imagine why."

"This gets odder by the moment," Immen muttered.

"Here, tear this into strips?" Anathriel passed Zeth the cloth, and for once, he complied without snipping at her. She then made Zeth and Immen turn around while she pried off Xari's outer tunic. After dunking

214

strips of material into her hot herbal mixture, she wrapped them around Xari's upper body, and then covered her with a blanket. "That should help, but I also need to get her to drink something for her fever."

This proved more difficult. Immen had to hold Xari propped up while Anathriel tried to get the comatose girl to drink a hot tea. Xari gagged at first, then swallowed reflexively, and Anathriel managed to get her to drink all of it.

"There," Anathriel said, wiping her hands on a cloth. "That's all I can do for now."

21

It was dark. And hot. Flute couldn't breathe very well, and she wasn't accustomed to so much blackness. Even at night she could discern every leaf on a tree—something she had learned on her journey that humans couldn't do—yet it had taken a long time for her eyes to find the tiny cracks of light that lined one wall of her prison.

When she had first awakened in this frightening place, she'd sat on the hard floor, very scared, and tried not to cry. She could hear someone else breathing beside her, and this was more fearsome than anything else. She sat still until she had seen the cracks, and only then had she been brave enough to try to explore.

She was not alone. She discovered Jesper and Magi Asheford almost immediately, and recognized them by their clothes more than anything else. They seemed to be all right, but she couldn't wake them. Though she wasn't as scared of the dark with their presence, Flute still *felt* very much alone.

"No one is ever, anytime, anywhere, alone."

Flute suddenly remembered the most important of her lessons. The one she had forgotten. The one that was far more powerful than any magic of fairy or speaker, older than the stars or the forest—older than anything.

"I'm not alone," she declared with a strong voice to the darkness, as though the darkness itself was her enemy. "The Master is with me wherever I go."

The sound of her voice uttering this truth made her feel much better, and then she felt strangely sad. She had not thought much about the Master in her travels, save for getting angry with Anathriel for not believing he was real.

"I'm sorry that I forgot," she said softly. "I'm sorry I disobeyed my elders. I'm sorry I didn't listen." Guilt pricked her slightly. "I know I'm not ready to be a guardian," she confessed in the smallest, most reluctant voice imaginable. "I promise, when we are free and safe again, I will wait until the right time to be a guardian." After one more hesitant pause, she added, *"If you want me to be a guardian."*

The silence that followed didn't seem so threatening anymore. Rather, the warmth enveloped her in a strange sense of freedom, though she was by no means less captive than she had been a moment before.

There was a great, sudden creaking, and Flute started, letting go of her knees and falling back onto her hands to catch herself. Before her, the cracks she'd seen had split and given way to a great frame with a wooden door, and pulsing firelight was flickering in from a huge room beyond.

On the other side of the doorway were five shvri. Angrily, Flute jumped to her feet and then raised a couple of inches off of the floor, trying to glare at all of them at the same time. Two of them raised their weapons—Flute still couldn't believe members of her own race were using *weapons*—and glared warily back. Knowing there wasn't much she could do in this situation, at least without getting Jesper and Magi Asheford hurt or in trouble, Flute backed up slightly but kept glowering.

The center shvri, a female, held up a hand and made a small, pacifying gesture to her two armed companions. They slowly and reluctantly lowered the small bows, and the female narrowed her eyes at Flute. "I have a candle. I'm going to come inside."

All at once, Flute recognized her. She had called herself Heron. Flute had used the air spell to push her away just before they had been captured. "I know you," she declared. "You're—"

"Hush, sprout!" the shvri named Heron scolded. Flute blinked. She sounded very much like Elder Hawthorne.

"Why should I hush?" Flute asked, crossing her arms. "You're not an elder of my village. You're not an elder of anybody's village. You're a shvri!" She spat the word like the insult it was.

Heron gave a heavy and over-patient sigh, rolling her eyes slightly. "Here," she said, turning to one of the other shvri, a second female, and holding out her hand. The second female handed her what Flute recognized as one of the humans' fire devices, called candles. She'd never seen one so small before. It was skinny, and only half as tall as a fairy.

Heron accepted the candle, then flew straight through the doorway to join Flute on the other side. Flute backed up slightly but kept her chin up. "Do you know fire magic?" Heron asked.

Flute found this question very odd. Why did it matter whether or not she knew fire magic? "Yes," she said proudly. Then, remembering that the results of her fire magic had not always been successes, she added, "Sort of." Then, resuming defiance, she asked, "Why?"

"I want you to light this candle for me."

"Why don't you do it yourself?" Flute said spitefully.

"I asked you to do it."

"Why should I?"

"Because I have friends with poisonous darts outside the door," Heron snapped. "Light it, please?"

Flute gave a curt nod and flew hesitantly forward. She stared at the stringy thing where the fire was supposed to go, trying to calm down, trying to find her heartfire again. It wasn't so difficult. Magi Asheford had insisted on continuing her and Jesper's lessons once they had begun traveling with him and Xari. She still couldn't call upon her heartfire as quickly as she'd like—certainly not as quickly as air or water magic—but she was getting faster. As soon as she'd found the familiar brightness, she focused its energy cautiously into her fingertips and touched the candle as carefully as if it were a cobweb.

Instantly, the candle flared, and Flute was so surprised and pleased that she could only stare for a second. Unfortunately, she forgot to take her fingers from the flame. "Ouch!" she cried half a heartbeat later, snatching them back and sticking them in her mouth.

Heron didn't seem to notice or else she didn't care. She, too, was staring at the flame, and soon gave out a very pleased sigh. "Very good," she said at last, turning to Flute with an approving smile. She turned back to her companions. "Close the door," she instructed, as one of the weapon-bearing shvri flew up, handing her one of his small darts. "Signal me if anyone comes."

"Yes, Heron." Together, the other four shvri closed the big door, and Flute was alone with Heron. Well, and Jesper and Magi Asheford too, but they weren't much help.

"The smoke is going to fill up the room," Flute said, looking with displeasure at the candle.

"No, it won't," Heron assured her. "Look closer."

For the first time, Flute was able to see the extent of her prison. It wasn't very big. Square on all sides, and all made of wood. To her right and left, the two walls perpendicular to the door had holes in them. Curious, Flute flew up to one of them and peered out, but all she could see was more blackness. She could, however, feel a breath of air seeping in through the hole. She turned back to Heron. "What is this place? Where are we?" She wondered if Heron would actually answer her questions.

"You are on the estate of Lord Jopherus, a human noble of Threnphol. This is a specially designed cage, of sorts, for fairy kind."

Flute was astonished. "How would any human know how to make prisons for fairies?" she blurted. "And *why?*"Except Mortén, she realized. "Are you helping Mortén!?" she accused.

"No," said Heron. "That is the last thing I am doing. Now be quiet a moment." She turned away from Flute to Magi Asheford, flying down by his side and kneeling there. Then Flute watched in horror as she lifted the poisonous dart she still carried in her hand and brought it to bear on the Magi.

"Hey!" Flute cried. "What are you doing!? Stay away from him!"

Heron's hand jerked slightly, and she pulled it well away from Asheford, then glared up at Flute. "I said be quiet!" she scolded.

"You think I'm going to sit back and watch you kill Magi Asheford?" Flute demanded. Then, horrified, she clapped her hands over her mouth.

Heron smirked slightly. "Don't worry," she assured Flute. "We already knew who he was. And I'm not trying to kill him."

"Then what are you doing?"

"Keeping him unconscious, for now. A Grand Magi has enough power to break out of this cell, or so we strongly believe. There's not really any other way to keep a fairy captive. Believe me, sprout, if we wanted you dead, you would already be so. Our arrows are designed exactly like the humans'."

Flute rubbed the spot on the lower part of her back where the shvri dart had struck her in the ambush. She had seen Immen's sharp arrows and had considered how much damage they could do. "Shouldn't I be hurt more, then?"

"If we had used our normal arrows, then yes, but we designed special arrows for your capture. We did not wish to kill you."

"Are you going to prick Jesper, too?" Flute asked, worried. "Are they going to sleep forever?"

"Your little friend should wake up before too long," Heron said. "And no, I'm not going to prick him, at least not unless you give me cause."

Flute watched apprehensively as the shvri carefully poked the pointed end of the dart into Magi Ashford, on the soft, outside part of his arm. Uncomfortably, Flute reached around and again rubbed her lower back.

"There," said Heron, straightening when she'd finished. "That should keep him under for at least another day." She looked up at Flute. "Now, little sprout. What do you say you and I have a chat?" She got up and walked over to an unoccupied area on the floor, sat down cross-legged, and held out a hand to the space across from her.

"I'm not going to tell you anything," Flute said stubbornly, crossing her arms again.

"Very well. I'll do the talking then, shall I? Please sit down. Hovering makes me nervous."

In response, Flute smirked and rose a couple more inches, fluttering her wings harder.

Heron rolled her eyes again. "All right. Wear yourself out, if that's your choice. My name," she began, "is Heron. As you know, I am of the shvri."

"Traitors," Flute retorted.

"For the most part, yes," Heron agreed coolly. "Many of the reasons my people left Fairlight Forest still stand. I do not know what you have been told of the rifting."

"I know the shvri didn't want to serve the Master anymore," Flute said. "That's enough for me."

Heron was quiet a moment. "Indeed," she finally said. "That was the first of reasons. Since that time, the shvri have become a great race, greater in number than the fairies of Fairlight Forest. We have thrived in the world. We have built lives on all three continents and the island nations. We are very mighty."

"If you're so mighty, then why haven't the fairies ever known of all this greatness?" Flute asked, unconvinced.

Heron's chin rose slightly, and she smiled. "If the fairies left their forest more than they do, then perhaps they would. More than that, though, we have learned better than any fairy the art of concealment."

Flute considered these words. She didn't know about the concealment thing, really, but it was true that her people rarely left Fairlight Forest. Of all places in the world, it was the most alive with life and magic. Most fairies felt very uncomfortable venturing outside its borders. Flute had felt very strange and empty at first after she had left, but she realized now that she'd made such good friends—Immen, Zeth, Anathriel, and Xari—that she didn't feel so lonely for the forest anymore.

"But lately something has been happening," Heron continued. "Our numbers are dwindling. Fewer and fewer sprouts are born each year."

A funny sort of coldness washed over Flute, and she made her face straight. It was the same with the fairies, of course, but did Heron know that? For some reason, the fact that the same problem was happening to the shvri worried Flute.

Heron's eyes narrowed again, and she seemed to be thinking very hard. She looked thoughtfully at Magi Asheford a couple of times, then back to Flute. Finally, she nodded slightly, almost to herself, and leaned forward. "What I'm going to tell you now is a very great secret. Some of my fellow shvri would kill me if they knew I was going to tell you."

"What is it?" Flute blurted, her curiosity overriding everything else.

"You were able to fend off my people in the village," Heron said.

"Yes." Flute nodded fervently. "I remember." She would never forget it, in fact. The shvri should have been able to easily resist her attack.

"Sprout," said Heron slowly, "the shvri have lost the art of magic."

It took a moment for the full meaning of these words to sink in. "Lost?" Flute repeated. "But—" She wrinkled her forehead in confusion. "But how is that possible?" she said, remembering her history. "Some of the greatest of the Magi joined the shvri after the rifting." Finally tired of hovering, she slowly lowered herself to the ground and mirrored Heron's cross-legged seat.

"All of our Magi were destroyed in the great earthquake attempting to help Maehdron Vittes retrieve the final two relics from the northern mountains." It was very strange to hear stories Flute had known all her life from the point of view of a shvri. "The rest were cut off, both from instruction and from the life of the forest. We believe our disconnection from both these things is responsible for the decline of our kind."

Now Flute was really glad she hadn't confessed the fairies' similar problem. At least the fairies, though they had lost some knowledge over the centuries, had not lost the art of magic. Feeling rather proud of herself, she asked, "Was that why you wanted me to light the candle?"

"Yes," said Heron. "It is clear that even the youngest of your kind has far greater power than the greatest of the shvri."

And serves you right, Flute thought, secretly pleased. "Why are you telling me all this?" She couldn't really think of a good reason.

"I am not sure," Heron said. "I have long sought a means to make peaceful contact with the fairies, but certainly not like this. Certainly not with one as young as you."

"Peaceful?" Flute echoed, amazed. "What do you know of peace? You carry weapons! You attack people in the street!"

"You cannot possibly know the subtleties and conflicts among the shvri," Heron countered, voice rising. "You're only a sprout."

"Well, then stop poisoning Magi Asheford and talk to him about it," said Flute.

"I had considered it," Heron confessed, ignoring Flute's sarcasm. "But I do not know how much time I have."

"Do you know where our humans are? Are they all right?" Flute dared to ask.

"They are in the room on the other side of this cell. The bond between the Magi and his speaker prevents them being very far separated."

"I knew that," Flute said, rolling her eyes.

"Then why did you ask such an obvious question?"

"Is Xari still sick?"

"I have not seen them. I do not know."

"Anathriel was going to try to help her," Flute said sadly.

"I hope for her sake she recovers quickly. She will need her strength."

"Why?"

"Mortén is coming."

Flute nodded. "We know. We think he was following us."

"You don't understand," Heron replied sharply. "Mortén and Jopherus are allies. They have been using the Windriders to send messages. That is how we knew where you were coming from—Mortén kept Jopherus informed of your direction."

"What!?" Once again, Flute's wings snapped open, and she rose several inches in the air, fright and anger coursing through her. "Allies?" she repeated. "You said you didn't have anything to do with Mortén!" she continued, railing. "I should have known you were lying. Stupid shvri!"

"Sit down!" Heron said in a firm voice. When Flute had done so, she went on. "I never said I wasn't associated with Mortén. I said that helping him was the last thing I am doing. Do the fairies not teach their young any patience?"

"Yes, but they never taught me to listen to a shvri or believe one," Flute replied.

"Well, I'm asking you to do both," Heron said, still firm. "You really have little choice. I'm the best chance for saving your friends—and the relics Jopherus now has in his possession."

Flute's wings jerked reflexively again, but this time she managed to hold her seat. "Jopherus took the relics?"

"House Otter and House Eagle," Heron confirmed, nodding. "I have seen them both. Without my help, you will not get them back."

Flute wished that Magi Asheford were awake. She wished that Immen or Zeth were here, or even Elder Hawthorne—somebody grown up who would know what to do. Someone who could tell her what *she* should do. She wanted to do what was right.

Master, show me what to do.

Still a little bit afraid, Flute reached for the peace she'd found earlier and nodded slowly. "All right. I promise to listen. Only to listen, for now."

"Very well," said Heron, looking pleased and relieved. "If my trust in you is kept, and if you help me with what I ask, I shall give to the fairies' keeping something they've long sought."

Flute thought hard but couldn't think of anything to which Heron could be referring. "What?" she finally asked.

Heron's eyes sparkled, and she leaned forward. "The dragonfly relic."

22

Two days and nights had come and gone since Anathriel, Immen, Zeth, and Xari had been brought into this confining room. Though they'd had ample opportunity to eat and rest, they were still exhausted, as though all their travels had finally caught up and were now taking their toll. The healer had come, as promised, and tended Xari's fever with detached expertise. Anathriel wondered if he harbored the same prejudice the first Threnpholin healer had, but it was difficult to say. If that was the case, he was compelled in some way by this Jopherus to do the job despite any personal conflicts.

However, it had been Anathriel who maintained vigil next to the girl's bedside, made her drink, kept her skin cool. Immen and Zeth were eager to help, of course, and sometimes when Anathriel was too worn out to continue, she allowed them to take her place, getting some rest on the second of the proper beds, which Immen insisted should be hers.

Anathriel awoke now from such a rest, and wondered how long she had slept. She glanced automatically to the grated window above her head. Several hours had passed. The sky outside was dark, and the sounds of summer nightlife peeped in from somewhere beyond. Immen speculated there was a pond or a stream or some such nearby, that the animals created such a racket every night. He said it was that way in Valedyne or some of the other valley villages up in Merenth. Anathriel wondered how anyone could ever sleep soundly through such a clamor.

She glanced around the room, not yet willing to move anything but her eyes. Zeth was snoring softly on the nearby cot. His head was on his arm, his mouth hanging open, and he hadn't even bothered to get beneath the blankets. Instead, he was stretched out atop them, fully clothed. Anathriel supposed she could sympathize a little bit. It was appallingly hot and muggy here, but really. Did he have to be so uncivilized?

Soft voices had been coming from the direction of Xari's bed since

Anathriel had awakened, and she looked that way to see Immen sitting, as usual, very close and comforting to Xari's bedside, but instead of his usual fretful concern, his face was relaxed and happy. He was talking to Xari, who was sitting propped up against her two pillows, looking better than she had since before they'd boarded the riverboat.

Immen was speaking too quietly for Anathriel to hear his words, but from the way Xari began laughing softly, they must have been highly entertaining. A sad envy came over Anathriel, and she wondered if she should simply try to go back to sleep.

Xari glanced over, noticed Anathriel watching them, and smiled a little. She touched Immen's shoulder and nodded. When Immen saw her, he smiled much more broadly. "Anathriel," he said, still keeping his voice hushed. "Look who woke up."

Anathriel pushed the covers off her legs and pivoted up to a sitting position. "So I see." She stood, reached for her cloak, and stepped over to the pair.

"She's not so hot now," Immen informed her as she gently put the back of her hand to Xari's face. Indeed, the skin felt cool and healthy, beaded slightly with sweat.

"The fever's broken," Anathriel said, pleased. "How long have you been awake?"

"A couple of hours," Xari said tiredly. She gave a contented sigh. "It's wonderful to feel so human again."

"Yes, well, don't be dancing any jigs yet," Anathriel said calmly. "You're going to need rest. Your body may be on the mend, but you're still weak. Fortunately, getting you good food won't be a problem."

"Immen has been telling me what's happened," Xari said seriously. "It is a very strange thing, isn't it? I've never before heard of or encountered this Jopherus in my travels. Yet he seems to know of relics and fairies and everything...very puzzling." Her eyes were troubled. "I wish I knew what they've done with Ashe."

"Well, now that you're awake, who knows? Maybe we'll get a little more attention." Anathriel moved to stare out the window into the night.

"I feel so disgusting," Xari said, wriggling slightly. "I don't suppose this Jopherus will provide a bath?"

Anathriel, who hadn't washed her hair in over a week, was inclined to agree, but it was Immen who answered.

"I doubt it."

Xari frowned. "Well, do I at least have a change of clothes?"

"Yes, our bags are all here," Anathriel said.

"Shouldn't you get some rest?" Immen asked in concern, glancing between the women. "Anathriel said—"

"Oh, for goodness' sake, Immen. She can change her clothes. I'll help her. Besides, she should move around a little bit. It's not good to be still in a bed for so long."

"Thank you, Anathriel," Xari said as Immen reached over to help her get to her feet, one arm around her shoulders, the other grasping her left hand.

"Well, afterward, he's right. Straight back to bed," Anathriel said, slightly grouchy at the sight.

After banishing Immen to the other end of the room and making him turn his back, she helped Xari change into another set of clothes, wrinkling her nose in disgust at the dirty set. "We should probably just burn these," she said, not in jest, as she held the offending clothing well away from her. When Xari did not respond, Anathriel looked over to see what had muted the other girl.

Xari had sat down on the bed again and was staring sadly at her hands. A circle of pale skin on her naked forefinger marked the white shadow where her otter relic had been for so long. She began rubbing it slightly, nervously, and looked back at Anathriel. "I've never been without them," she said. "For eight years. My ring. And Ashe." She seemed frailer than Anathriel had ever seen her, even when she had been in the throes of fever. "I hope he's alive," she continued, voice breaking slightly.

Immen had probably realized he could turn around now, for he too was watching Xari worriedly from the other end of the room, but he did not move. Instead, Anathriel sat down cautiously on the edge of the bed beside Xari, this girl with whom she shared so little, and placed a hesitant arm around her shoulders. "Well," she said slowly, thinking, "remember, if he is alive, he's not far, right?"

On their first night here, Zeth had walked the edges of the room, calling quietly for the fairies and listening intently, in hopes that if Ashe was alive, they would be heard. There had been no response, or if there had, they had been unable to hear it. She, too, hoped Asheford was all right. She was becoming very fond of the stern, fatherly fairy.

Xari nodded wordlessly and relaxed slightly into Anathriel's embrace. "Right," she finally said softly.

"Now that you're getting better, Xari," Immen said, stepping closer, "it's high time we looked to how to get away from here. Zeth says Mortén is getting closer."

Xari nodded again. "He'll be here within days."

⌘ ⌘ ⌘

Silence followed Heron's declaration, and Flute could only stare at her in disbelieving shock. "A—relic?" she finally squeaked. "You have a relic?"

"It has been in my ancestors' possession for a very long time."

"But—" Flute began. "How—?"

Most believed that all but a few of the relics had disappeared in the earthquake along with Vittes. Magi Asheford said he had to believe this wasn't true, but Flute wasn't sure what to accept as true.

"To protect the relics," Heron said, "Maehdron Vittes split them up. Some he entrusted to the shvri. Maybe all of them," she added. "It's hard to say. The problem is that he did not disclose the locations of all to any one person or shvri. They've been hidden. Who knows where? Who knows what's happened to them since?"

"But you have one?"

"Yes, I told you. That of House Dragonfly."

"And you want to give it to us," Flute repeated, somewhat skeptically.

"Not without a price," Heron said.

"What price?" Flute asked.

"That you take me and a few of those under my leadership to Fairlight Forest to learn the ways of magic."

Flute drew her breath in hard, the way Anathriel did when she was displeased with something Zeth did. "I don't know," she said at last. "How do I know I can trust you?"

"I tried to warn you of your impending capture, if you'll remember. But of course you wouldn't listen."

That was true, Flute reflected. Of course, what if it had been a trick?

How could she be sure? "Don't the other shvri know about your relic, if you really have one?" she finally asked.

"Not aside from those under my leadership," said Heron. "If they did, they would likely inform Jopherus, and that is something I do not wish, either."

"But why would they tell him? Why are the shvri working with Jopherus? What does he want, anyway?"

Heron opened her mouth to reply, but before she could, there was a soft tapping at the doorway, and she stood up abruptly. "I can say no more for today. Please tell your Magi what I have said when he awakens. I do not know when I may return, but I will try to at least learn what I can of your human friends' treatment."

"But you said he wouldn't wake for more than a day!" Flute cried. "And we're hungry!"

"Someone will be by to bring you food in the morning."

Heron did not leave the candle with Flute, for which she was very sad—sad to go back to the darkness, and sad that she could not sleep. She hoped Jesper would wake up soon, as Heron had said. She had so much she wanted to discuss with him, and he would have distracted her from her hunger, her fear, and her uncertainties.

She knew that her elders would tell her absolutely not to trust Heron, but Flute was surprised to find how very much she wanted to. If it was true that Heron had the dragonfly relic, it was worth the risk of making the promise, wasn't it? The Grand Magi council, Flute realized, would be very happy to learn that the shvri didn't know much magic. Would they ever agree to help?

Flute didn't know what to believe anymore, but one thing was for sure. She wasn't playing a fun game of being a guardian anymore. This was very serious.

⌘ ⌘ ⌘

Unfortunately for the captives, there was no time to make escape plans. They had barely finished eating their breakfast the next morning when the door burst open with an unmistakable sense of authority. Xari was on her feet as quickly as she could manage, on her guard from years of old habit. Still weary, she wavered slightly, catching herself with a hand on the edge of the table. She sensed and saw out of the corner of her eye Immen move to help her, but she held up her other hand slightly, warning him away.

Coming through the doorway was an entourage led by a man who could only be the mysterious Lord Jopherus she'd heard so much about. He had three attendants, all male, and seven shvri hovered around the group as well. A glance at Anathriel, who was staring at them wondrously, told her they were not at present maintaining invisibility.

Xari did not hesitate in reaching out with her gift to gauge the man. She sensed great pride and confidence, a healthy dose of calculative, prudent caution, but nothing that gave her any clue to his intentions. The only thing she could be sure of was that he was concealing something, but she rather thought that would have been clear without a magical gift.

Jopherus stopped, studying each of the four young people in turn before he spoke. "I am glad to see you so recovered, Xari Speaker." Though forewarned by Immen that Jopherus knew her name, it was still startling to hear it from his lips, and she congratulated herself on not betraying the fact. Jopherus went on, "And now I must ask you to come with me."

Behind her, Immen stepped forward. "What do you want with us?"

Jopherus regarded him calmly. "Not you. Just Xari." He turned to the men behind him. "Bring her," he instructed. Without another word, he walked out of the room.

One of Jopherus's men came forward and took Xari by her upper arm, not cruelly, but firmly, in such a way that warned against resistance. Xari shivered. This man had taken lives.

"Xari—" Zeth began.

"It's all right," she said, doing her best to reassure him, though she was beginning to realize her own uncertain fear. Without Ashe's presence, she felt naked and incomplete. She could not sense him, and that was most frightening of all.

Jopherus's men led her out into a long, morning-lit corridor lined with doorways. Xari began to look around further, but the first of the men holding her reached down and pulled her chin back to face forward. "Keep your eyes ahead," he said. His voice was bland, but his fingers said otherwise. She mutely nodded her obedience.

As they walked, the architecture of the building reminded Xari in odd ways of the Nebraeth orphanage she'd left behind so many years ago, though more richly furnished. The layout of the rooms, the proximity of the great room to the living quarters, and the craftsmanship of the doors and trimming all whispered of her long-lost childhood. Ironic, she thought, that the last time she'd been without Ashe had been in Nebraeth.

She didn't think he was dead. Somehow, Xari had the feeling that if Ashe were dead, she would know, which meant he had to be close. The only other possibility was that the shvri had somehow convinced Ashe to release the binding, and Xari knew he would die before giving into that demand, especially if she hadn't been around to try to persuade him otherwise. This led her to the conclusion that he was somewhere nearby. It was undoubtedly why she was not being allowed freedom of movement. The thought was slightly encouraging.

She did her best to study the shvri. It did not require much focus to read their emotions, which varied in drastic ways. They were a mixture of determined, curious, and in some cases, hostile. And proud. Fierce, fierce, independent pride emanated from each and every one.

Ashe had never been able to tell her much of the shvri. The fairies knew so little of the lost ones that they might as well have disappeared altogether. One of them, she noted, seemed to stick out as the leader. The feathers that capped his head were a dusky, dull shade of blue, and he had sharp eyes that never stopped moving—from Xari, to the other humans, to his shvri comrades, to the shadows in the corners of the room. The hostility from this one was the greatest, and Xari decided right away that she neither liked nor trusted him.

At last, they reached an office of sorts, lined with heavy laden bookshelves, where Jopherus had already arrived. He stood casually on the far side, scrutinizing a piece of parchment that he folded and set aside as soon as Xari stepped in the room.

"Please, take a seat, Xari Speaker," Jopherus said politely, indicating a cushioned settee nearby. "We have much to discuss."

Xari, who was still feeling tired from her bout of fever, did not argue. She sat down warily, and her escort took vigilant places beside her.

"I'm sure by now you must have questions about your presence here," Jopherus continued.

Xari looked around suspiciously, wondering why Jopherus would make such an inanely obvious statement. Was he trying to play some sort of joke? "Of course," she said at last, turning back to him.

"The reason is actually simple," Jopherus said. He glanced beyond Xari and gave an indicative nod.

She turned around and gasped softly. "Ashe," she whispered, half in relief, half in concern. So he had been behind her. Three shvri were toting Ashe's limp form between them. Xari watched them fly him right over her head and land on the top of Jopherus's desk, carefully laying him down. "What did you do to him?" she asked, unable to tear her eyes from her guardian.

"Don't worry. It's nothing but a simple herb that the shvri discovered long ago will keep a fairy sedated. Or any living being, for the most part, if enough is administered. Some care is required, of course."

Xari took note of the weapons the shvri carried and remembered Immen's form falling to the ground so unceremoniously.

"As with anything," Jopherus continued, "too much of the substance is detrimental, but you needn't fear for Magi Asheford's life. The last thing the shvri wish to do is kill him, believe me."

Xari wondered if the shvri ever spoke for themselves. The one with blue feathers merely hovered a few feet from Jopherus, watching impassively. Occasionally, his eyes would scan the room with watchfulness again, but he didn't seem inclined in any way to speak.

"What do you want with us?" Xari asked, eyes returning to Ashe.

"For myself, not much," Jopherus said dismissively, taking a seat behind the desk and leaning back to regard her. "But the shvri want Magi Asheford, and they presume if you're alive, he'll be more cooperative. How else does one control a Grand Magi, after all?"

Xari's eyes widened. "They want—?" she began, staring at Ashe in a new light. "But why?"

"That's their business."

"If you're not interested in me, then why did you take my relic?" Xari challenged. She took in the parameters of the room, suddenly wondering if the ring was hidden there somewhere.

"That's *my* business," Jopherus said. He rested his elbows on the arms of his chair and brought his hands together, tapping his forefingers against one another, looking like a housecat very pleased with itself.

Xari gritted her teeth. "I can see you don't really plan on telling me anything," she retorted. "I guess what I can't figure out is why any human is helping the shvri, or even knows of them, for that matter." She glared over at the blue-feathered shvri, who narrowed his eyes in return.

"I suppose that's something you'll have to ask them," Jopherus said. He, too, turned his attention to Ashe. "When will he wake?"

At last the blue-feathered shvri spoke. "Heron said it would be a day."

His voice was surprisingly tenor for someone so malicious, Xari thought.

"Perhaps we should bring in an increased guard, just to be cautious," Jopherus said thoughtfully. Then he looked around. "Incidentally, where is Heron?"

"Elsewhere, on my orders," the shvri replied in a voice discouraging further query.

To Xari's surprise, Jopherus considered the information shrewdly for a moment, peering at the fierce shvri with calculating contemplation, before nodding. "Very well." He turned back to Xari. "You will be moved to a separate room with your Magi Asheford. The shvri, I'm certain, will see fit to keep you company."

"What are you going to do with the others?" Xari asked, not taking her eyes off of Jopherus. She probed him but still wasn't getting much from him aside from the confidence and caution she had felt earlier. The feel was different from most people, though. His emotions were well-controlled, composed, just like his conduct. Strangely enough, it reminded her vaguely of Burin, who had disciplined himself to keep his emotions in check. She strongly suspected that Jopherus knew about her gift and was doing his best to keep her from applying it to him.

"The Eagle Speaker will be kept here. Though I have no immediate need of him, he's much too dangerous not to keep at arm's length. The other two—I kept them here because I was sure they wanted to assist in your recovery, which made it easier for everyone involved. Now that you are gaining strength, there is really no purpose in keeping them."

Fear surged through Xari, and she pushed herself to her feet, planting her hands on the desk in front of her to keep her balance. "I don't know what you're after," she said forcefully, "but so help me, if you do anything to—"

Jopherus held up an appeasing hand. "You misunderstand my intentions. I have no wish to harm anyone as long as I'm given no reason."

Despite the thinly veiled threat, she was slightly relieved. Though Jopherus clearly did not intend to disclose his plans for Immen and Anathriel, it seemed, for the moment, that he wasn't going to kill them.

Jopherus nodded at Xari's escort. Two of them took hold of her arms and began to usher her toward the doorway. The meeting was over. Xari went willingly. She was in no position to fight at the moment, especially as the shvri still had Ashe. She did wonder exactly what Jopherus had gained from the conversation. Perhaps he had simply been trying to gauge her. Well, he could try all he liked. It had given her the same opportunity. She hadn't learned much, but at least this new obstacle now had a face.

Xari was not taken back upstairs; instead, she was led to a small, windowless room not far from Jopherus's office. It was bare of everything save a pallet and a chair, and a lantern resting on the floor. It looked very much like a large pantry back at the orphanage. The walls were made of broad stone, designed to keep the room cool and dry. If Ashe woke up, he would have a very difficult time trying to break out through the thick walls.

Unlike the room upstairs, the shvri were not content to wait outside the door. Six of them entered, though the one with blue feathers had disappeared. The three carrying Ashe deposited him on the pallet, and then took up positions around the cramped room, all silently keeping their eyes on Xari. She stared right back, refusing to fear them. When she was sure they knew she wasn't going to be intimidated, she pulled her eyes away from them and slowly sank down onto the pallet beside Ashe, finally getting a good look at him.

He looked so small and powerless, and it almost brought tears to her eyes. Though he had always been the one who protected her, she felt, absurdly, that she had somehow failed him, that she should have been able to do more.

Strangely, her human escort did not shut the door. They stood outside, and before long, Xari realized why. The blue-feathered shvri returned with several dozen more shvri in tow. It was evident that the men could see them, but they did not comment as the shvri filed into the room. As soon as the last was inside, the door was shut and locked.

In the dim light from the lantern, Xari watched the shvri take up various positions on the floor, the back and arms of the chair, and the edge of the pallet. The shvri with blue feathers flew directly up to Xari and stared her defiantly in the face.

Xari finally deigned to speak with them. "What do you want with Ashe?"

The blue-feathered shvri's eyes hardened. "I don't see why I should tell you."

"Well, let's start with the fact that you shot my guardian, helped kidnap me and my friends, and are keeping us prisoners," Xari retorted, her tone matching his. "I mean, really, if we're stuck here, what could possibly be the harm in telling me?"

"You are not my concern," the shvri retorted. "What you do and do not know is unimportant. The only reason you are here is so we can be sure that he will cooperate." He jabbed a tiny finger toward Ashe. As he did so, Xari got a sense of something emanating from him, so strong and strange that it took her a moment to sort out what it was. *Jealousy?* What in the world did the shvri have to be jealous of, especially concerning Ashe?

The blue-feathered shvri abruptly whirled and took point in front of the door. None of the other shvri said a word, leaving Xari feeling uncomfortable in the eerie silence. Frustration threatened to overwhelm her. There were mysteries surrounding this place and these people, and the only thing left in her power was to wait and wonder. And pray.

⌘ ⌘ ⌘

Xari had been gone for almost two hours before anything happened. Through his speaker bond, Zeth had been doing his best to keep track of Xari, though all he was really able to assure to Anathriel and Immen was that she was still alive, seemingly safe, and somewhere very close. Anathriel first assumed, therefore, that Zeth's sudden, sharp intake of breath had something new to do with Xari.

"No," Zeth said, standing up after Immen asked. "It's not her." There was a strange, almost excited expression in his eyes. "It's—"

Whatever it was, Zeth didn't get a chance to tell them, as the door to their room suddenly opened. Anathriel turned to see Jopherus again standing in the doorway, the same three thuggish servants that had been with him earlier still behind him.

"What have you done with Xari?" Immen demanded.

Jopherus's eyes drifted over to Immen, then to Zeth. "I presume you know," he said to the latter.

Zeth crossed his arms and stared at Jopherus. "She's still in the house," he said, his voice laced with suspicion and distrust. "Downstairs, opposite side of the building. It still doesn't tell us what you did with her."

"Rest assured that she is safe. She will remain where she is for the time being. You two, however, will be leaving now." Jopherus motioned to Anathriel and Immen.

Anathriel blinked in surprise. "Leaving? But—"

"I'm not going anywhere without Zeth and Xari," Immen said firmly.

"I'm afraid you don't have a choice. Your presence is no longer required. You need not worry; you will be given safe passage."

"Safe passage to where?" Anathriel asked, full of trepidation.

"Montressa." Jopherus waved dismissively and stepped out of the room.

Montressa? He's sending us back to Montressa? Anathriel was baffled, not to mention torn. While it was true she wanted more than anything to go home, it certainly didn't seem right to leave Xari and Zeth in this predicament. Mortén was still on his way.

From the determination on Immen's face, Anathriel suspected that he might try to put up a fight, but before he could do or say anything, Zeth stepped forward and grabbed his arm.

"Go," Zeth hissed, his eyes flicking over to Anathriel to include her in his command.

"Zeth—"

"Immen, trust me. Just go." The look of anticipation was back on Zeth's face, and Anathriel wondered what, exactly, he knew. His eyes gave her strange chills. He clasped Immen's arm more tightly and muttered, so quietly that Anathriel almost didn't hear, "Whatever you do, stay in the wagon. It will be awhile."

She didn't have time to give this much thought. The next moment, the three men were leading her and Immen out of the room and back down the stairs. One man stayed in front, and the other two in the rear, swords in their hands. Very quickly, Anathriel and Immen were ushered out of Jopherus's estate, to the same covered wagon they had arrived in several days earlier.

"Get in." The man in front motioned to the back of the wagon.

Immen hesitated, glancing uncertainly back at the house. A second later, he sighed, and resolution settled on his face. He held out a hand to Anathriel, assisted her into the wagon, and then clambered in after her. Two of the men climbed in behind them. Anathriel wagered that there were shvri around as well. There would be, wouldn't there? Or would Jopherus trade on Anathriel and Immen's inability to see the shvri to bluff them into fear?

It didn't escape her notice that Zeth had told them to stay in the wagon—which suggested that he'd had another one of those visions. She certainly hoped that he had, and that whatever he had seen would be of some assistance, because she felt utterly helpless.

⌘ ⌘ ⌘

Flute had been frightened when shvri had come to collect Ashe. The one with blue feathers looked dreadfully mean, and Flute had shrunk back against Jesper in the dim light from the room beyond. It had been a long, long time, and Ashe still hadn't been returned.

The darkness was stifling, and the quiet was almost unbearable. When Flute finally heard a groan escape Jesper's lips and turned to see him stirring, she thought she would burst into tears of relief. "Jesper!" She flung herself on her friend. "Thank the Master!"

"Flute?" Jesper sounded very confused and groggy. "I can't see anything!"

"You will in a minute. There are cracks of light around the door."

"What door? Where are we?"

"Oh, Jesper, I have so much to tell you!" As quickly as she could, Flute explained what had been happening. She was so relieved to have her friend conscious that she spoke too quickly and jumbled things together a few times, and Jesper had to stop her and ask her to clarify, but she finally managed to tell him everything. "And I don't know what to do, Jep. Heron wants me to trust her, and if she really has the dragonfly relic, then what should I do?"

Jesper sighed. Flute couldn't make out much of his face, but could imagine the expression he would be wearing while he tried to puzzle this out. "I don't know. What do you think Magi Asheford would do?"

"I've been asking myself that, too, and I don't know! I'm not Magi Asheford. I know what the elders would say, but, but I—I don't know if they would be right."

It struck Flute, suddenly, how Magi Asheford must have felt all of those years ago when he chose to take the otter relic. In that epiphany, she also knew how difficult the decision must have been. She buried her hands in her feathers. "If I ever see Magi Asheford again, I need to apologize to him," she whispered.

There was concern in Jesper's voice when he spoke. "Do you suppose Heron will come back?"

"She said she would," Flute replied, twisting her hands together. "She never said Magi Asheford would be taken, though!"

"They must have moved Xari, too," Jesper said thoughtfully, peering at the air holes in their prison. He stood up and poked his finger into one of them. "Flute," he said slowly, "if the shvri don't know much about magic—"

Flute heard the beginnings of an idea in Jesper's voice. "What?"

"You said that Heron thinks Ashe might have been able to break out of here, because of his magic," Jesper stated. "She knows he's very powerful."

"Yes," Flute said, a bit impatiently. "And?"

"I think *we* might be able to get out of here."

"What? How?"

"Remember the hole we made in the Great Tree, so we could listen to the council?"

"Yes, but we didn't use magic to do that. We—"

"I know, but I was thinking—Flute, you found your heartfire. You can do fire spells now! You could burn a hole through this wall." Jesper pointed at the blank wall opposite the door. "If Zeth and the others are really on the other side, maybe we can get to them."

"I might catch everything on fire!"

Jesper shook his head, sounding perfectly confident. "Not if we do an air spell as soon as we have a big enough hole," he said smugly.

"What are you talking about?"

"Remember during our fire lessons, when Elder Osprey showed us different ways to put out the fire? Oh, wait—you missed that part of the lesson. You accidentally made Taley—"

"I remember," Flute cut him off, not wanting to rehash her mishaps.

"Well, Elder Osprey showed us that you can put a fire out by taking the air away from it. A fire needs air to live," Jesper explained, sounding very superior.

Flute was beginning to feel rather cranky with him. "All right, all right!"

"If you can do the fire part, I'll do the air," Jesper said.

"Do you think we should do it now? What if we get caught? What are we going to do if we find the others? The shvri might be on the other side of that wall, for all we know!" Of course, the shvri didn't seem to want to kill them, but she really didn't want to get caught and poked with a dart again.

Still, she wasn't doing anybody any good sitting here. "All right. I'll try it." Flute stood and nervously faced the wall. Concentrating, she searched for her heartfire until she had it in her mind's eye. Then she carefully reached out and touched the wall until she felt it heat under her finger. Not wanting to burn her hand again, Flute carefully pulled it away. Reminding herself for the thousandth time that she didn't need physical gestures to work magic, she focused her attention on the wall. Within moments, a small flame was burning on it. Flute watched it smolder right through the wood, growing larger with each passing moment. She backed up farther as the heat increased.

"Um, Jep—"

"Got it."

Flute felt a tiny bit of air stir, but wasn't sure exactly what Jesper was doing. Seconds ticked by, and then the fire grew smaller, dying out completely. Flute stepped up to the charred edges of the hole now burned into the wall, and her heart sank. "There's stone behind the wall!" she exclaimed. She rubbed her hand on the second, impenetrable barrier.

"There's no way we can burn through that," she said miserably.

Jesper sighed sadly. "Well, it was a good idea."

Flute sighed as well and sat on the floor. "We could burn out the other side, but I think the shvri are out—"

As if the shvri had heard her, the wooden door to their prison creaked open. Both fairies jumped to their feet, turning to face the door. Flute was strangely relieved to see Heron on the other side, along with the same shvri that had accompanied her earlier.

Flute crossed her arms. "What's going on with Magi Asheford? Where is he?"

"He's safe," Heron said, her eyes flicking to Jesper. She sniffed the air. "What have you done?" She landed in the small room, peering at the charred wall. "Well. Inventive of you, I must say, but I'll tell you now that there are stone walls on all sides of your prison save for the one we are guarding. Most of this house is stone." Heron turned to face them, an odd, almost approving expression on her face. "I don't have much time. My people are guarding you right now, but shifts will change very shortly."

"*Your* people?" Jesper said, sounding equal parts suspicious and uncertain.

"It's a very long story, and I do not have the time to go into the particulars of the situation in which you find yourselves. I need to know: where is the leviathan relic?"

Heron's question was met with surprised silence from Flute and Jesper. They exchanged wary glances. "Why do you think we know where it is?" Jesper asked.

"I have exactly no time for games."

"We still don't know whether we can trust you!" Flute exclaimed.

"No more than I can be sure to trust you," Heron returned. "It is a leap of faith on both of our parts. It's vital I know where the leviathan relic is. There is information you fairies don't have, and if you want any chance of finding the other relics, I must know where to find this one."

"Answer Jesper's question. Why do you think we know where it is?"

Heron sighed impatiently. "Because I listened to your human companions. I went into the room when the Otter Speaker was removed and heard them speaking of getting to the leviathan relic before Mortén."

"You spied on them!" Flute accused.

"Isn't that what I just said?" Heron asked, sounding exasperated.

Flute sank backward, even more uncertain of Heron's intentions. "But—"

"How many times must I tell you? There are things going on here that you don't understand. The important thing is to get to the leviathan relic before Mortén, if, indeed, that is what you and your companions were trying to do."

Flute glanced at Jesper, who looked back at her just as hesitantly. He gave a tiny shrug. It all came back to whether Heron was being truthful. If she really wanted to go to Fairlight Forest with them, then she wasn't likely to do anything to betray them. If. And that was what Flute really had to decide, wasn't it?

For a brief moment, she desperately, terribly missed her old life, where the elders told her what to do and the biggest decision she was entrusted with was how to care for the younger sprouts. She didn't know if she could make decisions that would affect the speakers, the brethren, her own race, possibly all of the magic in the world!

Well, a tiny voice in the back of her mind said, *could the shvri having the leviathan relic be any worse than Mortén having it?*

Master, please, please, let me make the right decision.

Flute drew a deep breath. Her eyes flitted again to Jesper, who took her hand and squeezed it, silent reassurance that he would support whatever decision she made. Finally, her eyes landed steadily on Heron. "All right," she said. "I'll tell you where it is."

⌘ ⌘ ⌘

When Ashe woke up, Xari was almost as relieved as when she had first seen that he was alive. The shvri, who had remained eerily silent the whole day, had only paused in their vigil to partake in the meals that were deposited inside the room, and even that was done in shifts. Xari did her best to eat, to help regain her strength, but had a hard time forcing the food into her clenched stomach.

She had little concept of day or night, but guessed that it must be late into the night when Ashe opened his eyes—she had been brought lunch and dinner, and she was exhausted.

It took her a moment to realize he was awake. He laid completely still, his eyes roving over the shvri, and then landing on her. Very carefully, he stood up on the pallet, his hands clenched into fists.

The shvri, too, noticed that Ashe was awake. There was a faint stirring among them, and Xari heard several whispers, though she couldn't make out the words. Xari knew that Ashe had to be disoriented, but he showed no sign of it. He kept his gaze fixed on the shvri. "Xari," he said, his voice steady. "Are you all right?"

"I'm not hurt, Ashe," she whispered.

"Where are we?"

"That's a long story. Right now, we're in a storage room on the estate of a man called Jopherus." Xari nodded at the shvri. "They're in league with him, though they haven't bothered to tell me why." She raised her voice in accusation at this last.

Ashe was positively seeping anger. If he felt fear at all, it was small enough that Xari wasn't picking up on it. "What—?"

Before Ashe could finish his question, the shvri with blue feathers flew over from the door and landed several feet from Ashe. A dozen other shvri peeled away from the walls and chair to stand behind their leader. Ashe tensed, his eyes narrowing. "Why have you brought us here?" he demanded, fury evident in his voice.

There was silence among the shvri for a moment, and then the lead shvri spoke. "We require certain things from you."

"What makes you think I will give you anything?" Ashe challenged.

"Because we have your speaker," the shvri said, his voice full of meaning. "If you believe you can protect her from all of us, then by all means, refuse. You didn't fare so well before."

Xari, still tuned into Ashe's emotions, felt that comment strike him more deeply than one of the shvri's darts—a sharp, intense sense of failure. She bit her lip to keep from telling him that he hadn't failed, as she knew that sentiment would not be appreciated, especially in the presence of the shvri.

"And what is it you think you need from me?" Ashe asked disbelievingly.

The blue-feathered shvri's eyes gleamed almost hungrily. "Knowledge."

23

Three days was an extraordinarily long time to spend almost nonstop in the back of a small wagon. Anathriel and Immen were allowed only brief respites to refresh themselves, but otherwise, Jopherus's men—who wouldn't even speak to them—kept them in the wagon. They stopped at night to give the horses time to rest, and then continued on, heading steadily north.

It would have been faster to use the river, but it seemed Jopherus didn't care how long it took. He simply wanted to assure they couldn't get back to his estate to try to do anything to foil his plan, whatever that was.

The time on the road gave Anathriel a lot of time to think—more than she wanted, perhaps, but that was something over which she had no control. Immen wasn't happy to be parted from the others, and Anathriel suspected the only reason he wasn't trying to escape was because Zeth had told him not to. Even so, he was restless and impatient, and a lot of the time his mind seemed elsewhere. Undoubtedly, he was thinking about the others back at Jopherus's estate. Zeth had always been important to him, and, well, Xari—

Anathriel looked swiftly over at Immen. There was a softness in his eyes as he looked at the other girl, or spoke of her, a tenderness that had become increasingly noticeable every day since they'd met her. Anathriel could not help but recognize it for what it was because it was what she had so vainly searched for in Immen's eyes since she had known him.

She had to wonder how cognizant the two were of their mutual attraction. With almost a lifetime's worth of experience in court life, Anathriel knew very well how to recognize these things, but in this case the talent left her with very little cause to rejoice. She was confused. Since their journey had begun, she'd come to realize more and more that Immen never had and never would admire her in such a respect—but Xari? Anathriel's respect for the other girl was fledgling at best, and she certainly couldn't understand her as a woman. What made Xari so much more preferable than Anathriel?

He'll never be interested in a girl like you.

Unbidden, Zeth's words of months ago surfaced in her mind. They had confused her at first, but having grown to know better the sort of man Immen Corper was, perhaps they now made a little more sense. Anathriel had thought she understood love, but now she was not so sure.

It was strange. She thought she had been in love with Immen, yet she realized now that she hadn't been before. She had admired his talent, his rising star in the court, and his good looks, without knowing a single thing about the man behind the handsome face. Now she knew that he was patient and forgiving. He was a gentleman in the true spirit of the word, not merely in standing. He was a good mediator, considering all the prickles he'd smoothed between Zeth and Anathriel. He was willing to believe in the best in people, as evidenced by his willingness to trust first Flute, and then Xari and Asheford. Anathriel was not so trusting. She wasn't sure if she ever would be.

Warm tears brimmed in Anathriel's eyes, and she slowly wiped them away. Now she knew who Immen Corper really was, and it hurt her to know that he really was someone worth loving, but she had been incapable of recognizing the fact. None of these realizations answered the question of why Xari was so wonderful, but maybe this was a mystery Anathriel would never solve. She realized, however, that for the first time in her life she was going to have to admit defeat.

As if sensing her thoughts, Immen chose that moment to turn toward her. A slight frown crossed his face. "Are you all right, Anathriel?"

Anathriel swallowed a lump in her throat, not sure if she would be able to speak. She was very proud of herself when she managed to say, without a quiver in her voice, "I'm fine, thank you." To take her mind off of Xari and Immen, she said, "How far do you suppose we are from Merenth?"

"I don't know. I've never traveled this way, except on Zephyr. I've been to Nanaene several times to deliver messages, and it always took a day and a half of flying—I would usually stop for the night in Ieryn. There's a Windrider waystation there."

Anathriel nodded mutely, wrapping her arms around herself and withdrawing into her thoughts again. What would happen once they reached Montressa, if they reached it at all? What would she tell Lord and Lady Kavela? What would anyone believe?

All thoughts abruptly ended when a long, loud screech sounded from somewhere above her. It was a sound that was very familiar, and she knew that the surprise on Immen's face must have mirrored her own. Both of them immediately stared upward, though of course they couldn't see anything through the roof.

They barely had time to look back at each other; the next instant, the wagon shuddered to a halt. Anathriel caught her balance, then stood as one of the men jumped out of the back of the wagon. "Stay here," he ordered them.

The second man glanced at them, then followed the first. Loud shouts—from the men, it seemed—met Anathriel's ears. Silence followed, so abruptly that Anathriel wondered what, exactly, had just happened. She and Immen waited for what seemed like an eternity, and then Immen cautiously moved to the end of the wagon.

"Immen—" Anathriel hissed.

"That was an eagle."

"I know, but—"

Ignoring her, Immen carefully pulled back the cloth covering and peered out. "I don't see anyone," he whispered. He leapt out of the wagon, coming to a sudden stop. "Anathriel! Come here!"

Curious at the mixture of joy and excitement in his voice, Anathriel slowly made her way to the edge of the wagon and peered out, immediately seeing the cause of Immen's happiness. Gasping, she carefully lowered herself to the ground and approached the giant silver eagle that Immen was gently stroking. "Zephyr?" she said with wonder. "How did she find us?"

"I'm not sure, but I think this must be what Zeth was trying to tell us."

"Where are the men?" Anathriel asked, glancing around. Even the man who had been driving the wagon had disappeared.

"They're gone. I guess that's all that matters." Immen took a step back and looked directly into Zephyr's eyes. "You know, don't you?" he said softly to the eagle. "You know so much more than I would have ever thought. I wish I could understand you."

Zephyr tilted her head to the side, seeming to study both Immen and Anathriel for a long moment. Then she lowered herself, a gesture even Anathriel could understand.

Immen glanced at Anathriel. Then he grinned. "How do you feel about heights?"

⌘⌘⌘

"Sprout. Wake up."

There was a pause, and then the voice came more insistently. It was not one that Flute recognized. "Sprout!"

Flute jerked awake, squinting in the white daylight that poured into the fairy prison cell. She could not see who was shaking her. The voice was feminine, but it was not Heron's. All that could be seen was a black silhouette between Flute and the doorway's opening. "I'm awake," she mumbled crankily.

Shifting up onto the heels of her hands, she looked around for Jesper, and found him where she had last seen him, glancing worriedly between her, the newcomer, and the other two shvri outside the doorway.

"Heron sent me to warn you," the female shvri said quietly. "Your speaker friends are in very great danger. It's—"

"Mortén," Jesper guessed, his brow furrowed in extreme concern.

The strange shvri nodded and straightened from where she'd been crouched beside Flute. Flute noted that instead of the bow she'd seen on so many other shvri, this one carried instead a long, colored staff almost as tall as she was. "He's just arrived. Heron wanted us to tell you—"

"Posey," called one of the shvri from outside in a low voice, cutting her off. The messenger Flute assumed to be Posey stopped talking and gave the other her complete attention, but he was still looking at something beyond their sight.

A moment later, Heron herself flew around the corner so urgently that all remaining traces of Flute's grogginess vanished. By this time, she'd gotten to her feet and went over to stand beside Jesper, wondering what was going to happen now.

Heron seemed on edge and somewhat winded. Her gaze took in

everyone, but settled on Flute. "Mortén is here," she said.

Flute's eyes widened fearfully, but before she could say anything, Heron continued in her urgent manner. "We must act quickly. Mortén did not present himself to Jopherus upon arriving. It is my belief that he wishes to move against the speakers without Jopherus's interference. You must understand, relations between Jopherus and Mortén have been disagreeable at best, and I do not believe that Jopherus wishes the speakers harmed. Mortén does. I fear for the humans' lives."

"Zeth," Flute whispered worriedly. Ashe might be able to protect Xari from Mortén, but who was going to protect Zeth? Without realizing it, she started forward, but Jesper took a handful of her tunic and held her back.

"Why are you telling us?" he asked Heron. "What do you care about Xari and Zeth?"

"Whatever else you think of my intentions—of *our* intentions—" she amended, taking in those around her—"you may rest assured that my purpose in keeping Mortén from acquiring the relics is the absolute truth."

"Yes, yes. You can believe that for certain, *fairy*," came a new voice.

Heron stiffened, as did all the other shvri. Her eyes narrowed and she pivoted back towards the doorway. Flute looked beyond with part curiosity and part trepidation. Where had the voice come from?

A moment later, her question was answered as the mean-looking, blue-feathered shvri who'd come to take away Magi Asheford hovered down from above. He brandished an arrow like a human spear in one clenched fist. He was followed by half a dozen other shvri, each looking as determined and murderous as he.

Heron turned. Flute could tell she was trying to look calm but wasn't fooling anybody. "Caw," she greeted, her voice light and neutral. "What are you doing here?"

"Exposing a traitor, Heron. And you?"

"Traitor?" she repeated.

"Did you really think you were fooling us?" Caw replied with a hard, grim set to his mouth. "You were warming up to the sprout, so we thought we'd see what she'd give you. And we were right. My thanks, Heron. You should have wrapped the leviathan relic in a ribbon, it was so easy." He smiled with fake sweetness at Flute. "Oh, yes. She told

Jopherus exactly what you told her. The leviathan relic will soon be ours. So, you see, Heron was telling the absolute truth. It's out of Mortén's grasp."

Flute was filling up with anger and shame like rain in a curled leaf during a storm. She should have known Heron wasn't really going to help them. She should have listened to the inner voice that sounded like her elders. Now Jopherus would have the relic, and Zeth was probably going to be killed. So much for her being a guardian. Flute's chin wobbled, and she bit her lip hard to keep from crying. Beside her, Jesper reached out with a gentle hand and squeezed her fingers between his own. She still felt helpless, and she wished she hadn't gotten Jesper mixed up in this, but she was glad he was here anyway.

"Caw," said Heron, turning to face him fully, but with great caution, "whatever you may believe—"

"I don't believe anything, Heron," he said, half-wearily. "I know. I've known for a while. But it's time to put an end to your duplicity. I don't need your weakness infecting our ranks before we strike."

"I am not weak," Heron snarled. "It is you who are blind, Caw. Your alliance with Jopherus will ultimately destroy what we're fighting for."

"Dallying with fairies even more so," he replied darkly.

Heron's wings snapped open violently and she sprung into the air with such speed that Flute gasped and stepped backwards. "I'm not going to just let you kill me, Caw," Heron said, voice hard.

"I wouldn't expect it of you." He gave a sort of mocking half-bow, in the manner Flute had sometimes seen Immen do, except Immen's bows were warm and polite. "But you know I'll defeat you."

"Maybe," Heron replied. Without another word, she darted forward.

Flute watched in horror for several sickening moments. She'd never before seen any of her race behave this way, so cold and vicious and cruel. It was wrong, her insides screamed. *Wrong, wrong, wrong!*

It didn't take very long—or very much perception—to realize that Caw had not been exaggerating his talent. He and Heron were engaged in some sort of ferocious duel, using their arrows the way Xari and Immen used their swords, yet it was different. How they hadn't managed to nick each other yet amazed Flute, but it wasn't going to be very long before Heron was overcome. The manic gleam in the blue-feathered shvri's eyes frightened her more than anything ever had.

Without thinking, she seized a handful of air magic from all around and within her, bound it into a thick cord, and thrust it firmly between the two combatants, shoving them apart. Then she tied Caw up so tightly he could barely even blink.

The shvri that Caw had brought with him stared in shock for a moment, then rushed forward to assist him. Praying to the Master for strength, Flute reached out to them too, knowing she wouldn't be able to hold so much precise magic for very long. "Jesper," she said tightly, looking sharply at a shvri wearing bright green, who was staring back with malice and confusion. "Help me, please." She was tempted to hold her breath, as though that would make it easier to hold so much magic as well.

"I'm here," Jesper assured her, and out of the corner of her eye, Flute saw the last two of Caw's shvri similarly immobilized, albeit somewhat more tenuously than Flute's own grasp.

It only took a moment for Heron to recover from goggling at this sight. Her features then set with grim, satisfied resolve, and she brandished her weapon high, aiming it directly at Caw's heart.

"No!" Flute cried.

Heron started, as did all the other shvri—those who could move, at least—and turned to stare at Flute in amazement.

Flute glared back. "You can't kill him," she said, glowering all the harder.

"It's actually not that difficult," Heron said stiffly, though Flute wondered if there wasn't some sort of strange, deep pain in her eyes as she spoke. "Especially when he's so still. You really must teach me this magic, someday."

"It's guardian magic," Flute said, glaring, "and it was never meant to be used to kill someone."

"If you allow him to live, you'll only be causing your people a great deal of future headache and trouble. And it will save the lives of most of my people if I kill him." She turned from Flute with a very superior air.

Flute recognized the gesture. She was being dismissed as too young. Someone who couldn't possibly understand the complete situation. Well, Flute was willing to admit that she didn't know as much as she used to think, but some things were very clear.

Heron lunged forward again, but Flute, drawing on a fresh burst of newfound strength, shoved the shvri back hard with another slam of air. "I said no!" she cried.

"Flute," said Jesper tensely from beside her, "I'm not sure how much longer I can hold this."

Flute wished she could risk a moment of concern for her friend, but if she broke a jot of concentration, she would also lose her control.

"You can't keep control of this situation forever, Flute," said Heron, as if reading Flute's very thoughts. She now seemed both shaken and angry. "And if you lose control, I assure you, he'll kill us all and your friends will die as well."

"I don't care," Flute said. "Killing is wrong, especially like this. The fairies were never taught to make enemies of one another."

"You don't know what you're talking about," Heron said through gritted teeth.

"Don't say that!" Flute shouted. She was surprised to find frustrated, near-hysterical tears in her eyes. "I don't know some things, but this much I know: it's the Master that says so, and he knows more than you'll *ever* know!"

There was a moment of disbelieving silence at this declaration. The shvri's expressions were a mixture of amazement and mild scorn, but nobody at first replied. As for Flute, the power of the words coming from her own lips gave her a heady feeling of confidence and, strange, wondrous joy. And in an instant, she knew what to do.

"You," she said, turning to one of Heron's shvri, "prick them with your weapon. Only enough to make them sleep, like you did with Magi Asheford."

The shvri hesitated, glancing uncertainly between Flute and Heron, who only stared straight ahead in anger, neither affirming nor negating Flute's command.

"Do it!" Flute snapped. She could see Jesper trembling out of the corner of her eye, and her own strength was waning faster than she liked. "Do it now, or I'll tie *you* up, too!" she repeated.

The shvri jumped a little, then gave a hasty nod and proceeded to do as she'd instructed.

Several moments later, the blue-feathered shvri and his friends were sleeping like nursery sprouts in a big heap in the small room that had recently been Flute and Jesper's prison. Being released, both from the prison itself and from the strain of magic, was a relief beyond words.

"How long will they sleep?" Flute asked Heron as they shut the door.

Heron still seemed mad at her, but she did not mention the matter as she replied. "Not long at all. The shvri have acquired a tolerance for the poison, particularly the warriors as practiced as Caw and his men. Building up the tolerance is part of their training."

Flute shuddered slightly at the idea of any fairy having "training" at all. "Well, maybe no one will know where to find them for a while. Is Zeth still in the next room?"

"He is."

Flute and Jesper immediately flew towards the door, but were halted before they had flown three feet.

"And just what do you think you plan on doing?" came Heron's voice, skeptical and amused.

Flute was a bit put off by this turnabout in temperament. She turned back proudly. "I don't know. But we'll do the best we can."

"You aren't going to ask for my help?"

"Why should I? You gave the leviathan relic to Jopherus."

"I never told you I would do otherwise. It was imperative that the relic first be retrieved from Mortén's possession. Had my plan succeeded, I would have eventually gained control of it."

"I still don't know if I should trust you."

"Well, like it or not," Heron said, looking around, "we still need your help, and especially that of your Magi Asheford. If we work together, we stand a much better chance of escaping Jopherus and Mortén than if not."

Flute knew there wasn't much time to decide. "If you're lying," she said finally, sticking her chin out with a challenge, "then we're *not* going to help you learn magic." Suddenly remembering something, she added, "and you need to give us the dragonfly relic, too, like you promised."

"I did promise," said Heron, looking somewhat annoyed. "But you waste time by arguing, sprout."

"Fine. Let's go, then."

"Two of my people are among those shvri guarding Magi Asheford and Speaker Xari. I must ensure they haven't been harmed by Caw's forces, if it's not too late already. I will do the best I can to free them, and your friends. You may devote your attention to the Eagle Speaker. There are a few shvri yet guarding him, but with your magic you should be able to subdue them easily. Free him and meet us outside by the well in the commons. There's a gear shed for the stables that usually isn't too busy this time of day. You can hide there."

"But—" Flute began.

"Posey," interjected Heron, "go with them, so that they know the way." Without another word, she gave a sharp turn and flew quickly out the open window, all but the staff-bearing Posey trailing hastily afterward.

Heron was right. It wasn't hard at all to deal with the three shvri who flew guard outside Zeth's door. Although Flute and Jesper were very tired and couldn't do as strong magic as before, it was still more magic than the guards knew. Also, Posey assisted them, flying behind and knocking two of the guards unconscious with a simple, well-placed blow to the head. The third one Flute and Jesper captured and froze into a water pitcher from the waist down. The pitcher was tall enough that it kept anyone from seeing him, and Jesper used a handy little air spell that kept him from being able to open his mouth so that he could not call for help. Flute had never been able to manage the spell, though she occasionally been the recipient of it.

Flute and Jesper flew eagerly into the room. Posey came more composedly behind them, looking all around her with caution. They saw Zeth almost immediately; he was already rising to his feet to meet them. "Zeth!" cried Flute happily, rushing forward. She wished she had time to tell him everything that had happened. "We're going to get you out of here!"

As quickly as they could, Flute and Jesper told Zeth the important parts of the plan as he hastily grabbed his pack and began throwing his belongings in it. "I hope you're sure you can trust these people," he said, glancing at Posey warily, who only stared back, stone-faced.

"I'm not sure at all," Flute admitted cheerfully. "But at least we're out of that cell and maybe I can help you."

"The plan is good. I need to get away from the estate as quickly as possible, once we're sure Xari's free."

"But why?"

Zeth took a deep breath and then gave Flute a very satisfied smile, eyes shining proudly. "Zephyr is coming. She's almost here." With a sharp intake of breath, his eyes darted to the door in alarm.

"Zephyr?" Flute repeated, confused, still trying to digest this piece of information. "You mean Immen's eagle?"

"Yes," said a new voice.

Flute froze. Across from her, Posey hissed slightly and hoisted her staff into an aggressive position. Flute swallowed and turned around.

"Zephyr has always had entirely too much troublesome cheek," Mortén continued. He was standing in the open doorway. "Maybe I'll finally get an opportunity to rid my hands of her interference."

"Mortén," Flute squeaked.

⌘ ⌘ ⌘

"Anathriel!" Immen's voice was difficult to hear, streaming away on the wind. Had Anathriel not been shielded beneath him, his mouth practically on top of her ear, she wouldn't have managed hearing him at all.

It had been awkward, getting onto Zephyr, especially as she wore no saddle. Immen wasn't bothered; he had ridden bareback before. Anathriel, who had never ridden on one of the giant eagles at all, was considerably more leery. Her skirts hadn't been as much a problem as she'd anticipated; they only had to be full enough for her to slightly straddle the eagle, essentially sandwiched between Zephyr and Immen. This ungainly circumstance left her torn between holding onto her dignity and accepting the ignominy of riding in such close quarters with a man. In the end, she had little choice if she didn't want to be left with the wagon. She braided her hair tightly to prevent it from flying into Immen's face and allowed him to assist her onto Zephyr with every ounce of poise she could muster.

The first few moments after Zephyr lifted off had been heart-stopping and terrifying, and all thoughts of impropriety fled her mind. Slowly, as the ride continued, as Zephyr's huge wings beat rhythmically and the cold wind streamed over Anathriel's skin, a strange sense of exhilaration had overcome the fear. Opening her eyes, she had dared to peek down at the countryside far below. She had expected to feel terrified, perhaps a dizzying sense of nausea, but to her surprise, it hadn't come. From this high up, the distance to the ground seemed almost unreal.

She had begun to understand why Immen, Regen, and all of the other Windriders cherished their jobs so much. There was a freedom up in the air, a sense of being alive unlike anything that Anathriel had ever experienced, and for an instant, it had seemed that all troubles and petty disputes were as far away as the ground below.

Reality was quick to set back in, however, and even as Anathriel had relaxed her grip, she had realized she had no idea where Zephyr was taking them. They were traveling south again, back in the direction that they had come, so Immen speculated that Zephyr was taking them back to Jopherus's estate, possibly having sensed or seen the predicament that Zeth and Xari faced.

Jopherus's estate was the last place Anathriel wanted to return to, and she still didn't know what she or Immen could do to help Zeth and Xari, but Zephyr seemed intent, obviously knowing something more than they did.

Anathriel was again amazed at the speed at which the eagle traveled. They had raced over the land, passing over towns and cities, farms and small lakes. Hours had passed, and she had begun to get hungry and thirsty, but still Zephyr did not stop. Before she knew it, the journey that had taken three days in the wagon was over. Zephyr began to drop and circle around a large cluster of woodland set some distance apart from the surrounding farms and meadows. It was several more minutes before Anathriel spotted the high fence and slate roofs among the treetops, which were strange to see from this perspective. They had, indeed, returned to Jopherus's estate.

"Anathriel!" Immen said again, as Zephyr flew more sharply downward, angling toward the ground. "Hold on! Zephyr's coming in steep!"

The sensation of Anathriel's stomach lurching into her throat was already telling her that. The ground was coming up fast, and then, abruptly, Zephyr landed. Immen immediately slid off, then took Anathriel by the arms and pulled her off too. As soon as they were out of the way, Zephyr rose into the air once more.

"Now what?" Anathriel hissed, watching the eagle disappear toward the other side of the main hall. "Those shvri could be anywhere!"

"Let's get out of the open," Immen said. "We have to get back into the house to help the others." He began walking briskly in that direction and Anathriel followed. She found the emptiness of the yard bothersome. Where were Jopherus's men?

They had made it about halfway when the stillness was broken by a familiar flash of light flaring before them. The hope that it was Ashe, Flute, or Jesper unveiling vanished. It was a shvri. She seemed to have appeared to them in midflight, and her body language was that of someone in a great hurry. Anathriel sucked in a sharp breath, hoping they hadn't come all this way back just to get waylaid once more by an army of tiny people, but to her utter surprise, the shvri only stared at them in amazement. "How did you get here?" the shvri asked with cautious suspicion.

Anathriel opened her mouth, but she never got the chance to decide whether or not it was prudent to answer this question.

"Never mind," the shvri continued. "There isn't much time. I need your help."

Immen and Anathriel exchanged glances that were part baffled, part wary. "You expect us to help you?" Anathriel demanded. "After everything—"

"I don't have time to explain," the shvri repeated.

"Who are you?" Immen asked, eyes narrowed.

"My name is Heron."

Belatedly, Anathriel realized the path of Immen's thoughts, as she too recalled Zeth's story about a shvri who had claimed to want to help him.

"Your friends are in danger," Heron continued. "The fairy sprouts are freeing your Eagle Speaker. I was on my way to try to free the second, as well as the Magi."

"What do you want us for?" Immen asked.

Anathriel shot him a sharp look, still not sure whether they should actually listen to Heron.

"Your weapons—I know where they are. If you think they will be of use—?"

Immen gave a grim, determined nod. "Lead on."

254

⌘ ⌘ ⌘

Xari's fear pervaded every nerve. Mortén and Zeth were together, and the emotions of both men assaulted her like the great waterfall of Réol. She was afraid, so afraid for Zeth that she couldn't even speak. Why, *why* was it Zeth who had to deal with Mortén? Xari had been his enemy longer. She had prepared herself to face him, to match him, to defend her life against him, and so had Ashe.

As for Ashe, he had very grudgingly and very patiently (certainly more patiently than they deserved) been teaching a handful of shvri the most rudimentary spells imaginable. The pride of the lost ones made them very slow learners, but Xari figured this was all for the better. It chafed hard that she and Ashe had not yet found a means to circumvent the hold the shvri held over them, but the fact of the matter was, they had simply never anticipated the sort of enemy the shvri had turned out to be.

When they had discovered the shvri's ignorance of magic, Xari had felt hope, thinking this would make all the potential escape plans she'd been pondering all the easier, but the guard was never lax, always watchful, and always in sufficient numbers to compensate for their underdeveloped power. It didn't help that they kept Ashe in a perpetually weakened condition with their poisons.

Focusing once more on the hatred and fear assaulting her from both Mortén and Zeth, however, she got the feeling that whatever happened today would put an end to the impasse, for good or ill.

She sent the most powerful wave of reassurance that she could muster to Zeth, squeezing her eyes shut and refusing to let any of the hesitation and fear she was feeling get through to him. She had no doubt in her mind that Mortén would kill Zeth if he had the chance...that he would kill *her* if he could.

Xari was startled out of her intense reverie when the door to her room slammed against the wall. Her eyes snapped open. The only times it had been opened before were at mealtimes, or when the shvri changed their guard, both inside the cell and without.

The human guard Jopherus had posted was slumped to the ground, and Immen and Anathriel were standing there, Immen with his sword in hand, Anathriel hovering right behind him. There was a shvri with him, one Xari had seen a couple of times, but whose name she did not know.

She had half a second to process this before all of the shvri had their weapons trained on the new arrival. "Heron," one of the shvri said, flying down to the other's level.

"Put your weapons down," Heron demanded of the other shvri, referring to the arrow he had cocked on his bowstring.

"Put down *your* weapon, traitor. Caw told us everything. He told us that—"

But they never found out what it was Caw had said. In that moment, with all the shvri weapons pointed away from Xari, a violent burst of wind slammed through the room, so powerful that it actually made Xari double over. She recovered her senses quickly and immediately found Ashe with her eyes. His expression was one of deathly determination.

Most of the shvri were knocked off balance or slammed full-force into the walls. Before they could react to the attack of air, there was a loud, grating sound, and chunks of rock began dropping off of the ceiling, a miniature avalanche that struck some of the shvri. Ashe was using earth magic to do that; it was more difficult than air and water, Xari knew.

She noticed that several shvri were recovering. One of them—a gray-feathered female—managed to get an arrow loosed, but did not fire at Xari or Ashe, or even at Heron. Instead, the arrow struck the shvri opposing Heron dead-on. For an instant, Xari thought she must have hit the wrong target, but then another shvri whirled around and shot the gray-feathered one. Sudden realization struck that perhaps Heron was not the only traitor.

Both shvri that were hit dropped like stones, and several arrows were fired toward Heron and Ashe. There was another sudden gust of wind, this one not as powerful as the first, but enough that the tiny little weapons were knocked askew. Xari saw that the room's small size was working to Ashe's advantage. With so many shvri packed into it, they were having a hard time not hitting each other.

"Xari—out the door," Ashe ordered tersely.

Unhesitating, Xari grabbed her pack and made a break for the entrance. She paused only to scoop from the floor the shvri that seemed to have helped them. Several arrows fired at her as she ducked through the doorway, but none hit their mark, probably Ashe's doing. This time, he was not caught off guard by so many shvri, and Xari suspected he had been planning for this eventuality ever since waking three days earlier.

Ashe was right with her, and as she stepped out the door, he turned back to cover their retreat. The next moment, Heron was yanked backwards—not, Xari noticed, as if she had flown, but as if someone had grabbed her with an invisible hand and tugged. As soon as Heron was through, Xari slammed the door and locked it.

"One of my people is still inside," Heron said tensely. "I do not think he was discovered, though, so he still stands a chance."

"Xari, are you all right?" Immen asked, deep relief in his eyes. He reached over and grasped her by her upper arms.

Xari still hadn't absorbed everything that had happened but knew she didn't have time to sort out details or loyalties at the moment. Her eyes landed on Anathriel, or more precisely, what Anathriel held in her arms: Xari's sword belt, with both blades still accounted for. "I'm fine," she said shortly, easing from Immen's grasp with a brief but sincere expression of gratitude. "Zeth's not." Knowing she was extremely short on time, she dropped her pack on the ground, then carefully transferred the unconscious shvri into Anathriel's hand, at the same time retrieving her weapons from the other woman's possession.

Anathriel jumped in surprise, staring down at her hand. Belatedly, Xari realized that the shvri was probably invisible. "It's one of Heron's people! Just be careful!" Xari called over her shoulder, already fleeing in the direction of Zeth and Mortén. She looped on her belt as she ran, praying that she would get there in time.

24

Anathriel could see that Immen wished to race off after Xari, but he also looked at Anathriel with a light of responsibility in his eyes. He was torn—the conflict was easy enough to read. As for Anathriel, she had no idea what she was supposed to do. Just stand there looking silly, holding a tiny person she couldn't see?

Heron flew down onto her hand, right beside the invisible weight that Xari had deposited in her palm. "Aster," she said in relief. She appeared to examine her friend for a moment. "She is very fortunate. The arrow hit only her shoulder, but it was still laced with poison. She will sleep for a while yet." Heron bent down, and a moment later, was holding a tiny shvri arrow in her hand. "I will tend her wound later."

Anathriel looked at the little creature in disbelief, still being careful to hold onto the shvri in her hand without squishing it. She wished she could see it. She could feel what she assumed were arms on her fingertips, and feathers tickled the palm of her hand.

Heron lifted off of Anathriel's hand once more. "Come," she said. Anathriel had the feeling that if she could have shaken them both, she would have. "If we all manage to get away from this, we will not have much time. There are things we must attend to. Things we must collect."

"We?"

"Yes, we! I cannot carry everything, you know!" Heron turned to Immen. "You, Windrider," she said.

Immen blinked at being addressed by his title. "Yes?"

"Believe me when I say the best thing we can do is not to fight but to flee. We will need your eagle's help. Go back outside and wait with her. I will take this human with me and find the relics. Be ready with your eagle to cover our escape."

"She's not my eagle, she's—" Immen began.

"Do you want to argue words with me, foolish human?" Heron snapped. "Go!"

Immen still seemed hesitant. He looked at Anathriel.

"Oh, for goodness' sake," she huffed. "I can take care of myself."

Watching him nod and retreat back the way they'd come, Anathriel didn't feel so certain, but she was willing to draw strength from Heron's confidence. This meant fighting back her lingering doubts about Heron's loyalties. But she had helped Xari and Ashe escape, and she'd also told them about Mortén being here, not to mention leading them to their weapons.

"Come on!" Heron urged. "We have the advantage of the moment. Most of the shvri are locked in that room or upstairs in a fairy prison!" She began flying down the corridor, opposite of the direction that Immen and Xari had gone.

Well, I'm in it this deep. I suppose I should see where the bottom is. Heaving a sigh, Anathriel quickly followed after Heron. "Where are we going?"

"Jopherus's office," Heron said shortly. "He has the relics there, and more."

"What about Jopherus?"

"He should be—" Heron stopped as she rounded a corner, so suddenly that Anathriel almost ran into her. When she saw what Heron was looking at, a knot of panic formed in her stomach.

Jopherus himself was striding down the corridor, and he paused, startled, when he saw them. "Heron," he began, his voice wary, "what is this?"

Anathriel's heart was pounding so hard she was positive that Jopherus could hear it. What in the name of Mount Pathon were they going to do now?

"Lord Jopherus, I'm so glad I found you," Heron said, hastening forward, her voice relieved. "This human just arrived back at the estate, right behind Mortén. I came to bring her to you and warn you of Mortén's intrusion."

Anathriel endured a sickening moment of betrayal. If Heron had been lying to them all this time, there wasn't much else to hope for…but why hadn't Heron mentioned Immen?

It seemed a lifetime of tension to Anathriel before Jopherus's eyes shifted to Heron, a flicker of alarm crossing his face. "Mortén is here?" he repeated angrily.

"Yes, yes!"

"Where is he?"

"He went to the human's room—the Eagle Speaker."

It was the first time Anathriel had ever seen Jopherus ruffled. Uttering a curse, he hurried past Anathriel, sprinting toward the center of the house. "Put her somewhere!" he said, waving a hand at Anathriel. "And find out if Corper is anywhere around! I'll determine how they returned later." He disappeared around the corner.

Anathriel and Heron stood there for several long, tense seconds before Anathriel allowed herself to breathe once more. Then Heron said, "We must hurry! Someone will warn him of my double-cross very soon."

Bewildered, Anathriel followed dumbly, pondering the encounter before she realized that by some miracle, Jopherus did not yet know Heron was a traitor. The little shvri's cool head had kept them from a nasty tangle.

It turned out that they had nearly been to Jopherus's office already. The door stood wide open. Heron flew in after a quick look inside, and Anathriel followed her straight to the large, opulent desk. "Open the side drawer," Heron told her. "There's a hidden compartment there."

Anathriel slid open the drawer. The items within looked perfectly normal. Quills, ink, some paper and other miscellaneous items rattled around inside.

Heron flew into the drawer and landed, disappearing into a dark shadow in the back. Moments later, there was a subtle click, and Heron emerged. "Push down on the bottom of the drawer," she instructed.

Feeling a strange sense of guilt—here she was prodding hidden compartments on Jopherus's desk while her companions were probably fighting for their lives—Anathriel quickly complied, being careful not to disturb the unseen shvri still resting in her hand.

The entire bottom of the drawer came up, knocking all of the odds and ends into the small compartment underneath. Anathriel took the bottom out completely, peering into the small space. Amidst the other items that had just fallen in, she immediately recognized Xari's otter ring and Zeth's eagle pendant. She picked both up and tucked them into her pocket. There was also an incredibly worn brown book. It looked ancient, and as Anathriel lifted it, she saw that it was locked. The metal of the lock was faded and chipped a bit, and in place of a keyhole was a large, oddly shaped impression. The edges of the paper within the book were yellowed with age.

"What is this?" she whispered.

"It is the journal that was written by Maehdron Vittes," Heron replied.

The name rang a bell in Anathriel's mind, but she couldn't place it. "Who?"

"The man who murdered the last twelve speakers! Would you please hide it quickly!? We need to take it with us." Heron sounded exasperated, which did not do much for Anathriel's already high-strung nerves.

"All right! You know, you're the one who asked me to help!" Anathriel tried to figure out where to put the journal; her pockets weren't big enough to hold it. She finally settled with tying the bottom of her skirt around it and letting it hang down by her feet. It looked strange, but it would do until she could get it out of Jopherus's estate. As it settled against her legs, another thought occurred to her. "Didn't Maehdron Vittes live hundreds of years ago?"

"Yes, but he went to great lengths to ensure the journal would stay preserved. My people likely helped with their magic. It was long ago. Come, we must leave."

"Where are we going?" Anathriel asked, once more following Heron out into the corridor.

"Away from the estate. My people know where to meet, and will bring your friends there if they can. The important thing is getting this journal away from Jopherus, and the relics away from Mortén."

Anathriel hesitated only a moment before hurrying after Heron. She knew she couldn't do anything to help the others; she had no weapons and no experience with any sort of fighting. And she wasn't stupid; she knew the importance of the relics she carried—she had listened to Flute and Xari, and even Zeth, prattle on about it often enough. If the only part she would be able to play in this battle was keeping these things away from Mortén, then she would do it.

As she made her way through Jopherus's home, she could only hope that if Xari's Master truly did exist, he would be able to get them all out of this mess.

"Stop right there, Mortén!" Flute cried. She was trying desperately to sound brave, but on the inside, she was trembling. Yes, she had bested Mortén once to allow Immen and Anathriel to escape, but right now she was exhausted from her fight with the shvri. While she still thought she could manage a spell or two, she wasn't sure it was best to try. Mortén was holding a type of weapon that Flute had never seen. It had a string and an arrow, just like Immen's bow, but it was small enough for Mortén to hold in one hand, his finger poised near a button on the contraption. Flute was afraid if she threw any sort of spell at Mortén, he would fire the weapon at Zeth, and she didn't want to risk that.

"You stay out of this," Mortén told Flute sharply, without turning his gaze away from Zeth. "Or believe me, I will shoot him."

"But you'll shoot me anyway, won't you?" Zeth asked, his voice deathly quiet. "I suppose there is something to be said about history repeating itself. It didn't work for Vittes. Why would you possibly think this would work for you?"

Flute glanced worriedly at Jesper and Posey, both of whom hovered in the air, otherwise immobile. Like Flute, they were probably trying to figure out what they could do. If Zeth could get Mortén talking, maybe it would buy enough time for Heron to release Xari and Asheford, or at least give Flute a minute to recover from her exhausting use of magic.

"You are a child," Mortén said coldly. "You know nothing of matters of nations. I saw your mind, lest you forget, Zelenthrius Rellwyn." It took a moment for Flute to realize that 'Zelenthrius' must be Zeth, just as she was really Fluttermouse. "You are a term-slave. A nothing orphan. Do you really think becoming a speaker makes you anything better? If you follow the original speaker teachings, then you will always be subjected to a Master."

Flute saw that this struck deeply, as Zeth's face tightened and his eyes narrowed. "Xari was an orphan," he replied, crossing his arms defiantly across his chest. "And she made something out of her life."

Mortén's eyes flashed. "Yes, Xari. Well, she isn't in a much better position at the moment. I will be seeing to her as soon as—" Then Mortén's eyes narrowed, and he spat out a curse. In the time it took Flute to blink, Mortén's finger depressed the trigger on his bow-weapon, and the arrow flew toward Zeth.

"No!" Flute shouted. Barely thinking, she felt her magic release from her. She had intended to blow the arrow out of the way. Her sudden, erratic burst ended up being just strong enough that the projectile twisted away from Zeth's heart with sudden force, but not far enough to keep it from splitting into his left shoulder with a sickening sound.

Zeth shouted with angry pain, and Flute turned about wildly, hoping to stop whatever Mortén would try next. She was met only with the sight of a slamming door. Then the lock clicked. Mortén was gone.

"What happened?" Jesper asked, looking baffled.

"Why did he leave?" Posey agreed, her eyes narrowed.

"Zeth, are you all right!?" Flute asked.

His shoulder was bleeding, and the arrow was still sticking out of it.

Zeth closed his eyes, breathing hard. "Xari's escaped," he replied, opening his eyes. "She's on her way here, and she's a bigger threat to Mortén." He was gritting his teeth even as he talked. "As it is, we're all locked in here now."

"Yes, except there are no shvri guarding the door anymore," Jesper pointed out. He turned to Flute, looking as grim as Flute could ever remember seeing him. "And the house may be stone, but the door is wood."

Flute's eyes widened. Could she burn through the door? She was already *so* tired. "But Zeth—" she began, eyeing his injury uncertainly.

"I'm not dead yet," he assured her tensely. "Let's get out of here. I'll do what I can while you work."

Nodding, Flute drew a deep breath, trying desperately to keep calm and focused. She didn't have a choice. She had to try, or Zeth *still* might be killed. "This might take awhile."

⌘ ⌘ ⌘

As Xari began sprinting toward Mortén and Zeth, she was very worried that she would fail to distract Mortén from his vendetta against the younger boy. Desperately, she sent a wave of roiling anger down her bond to Mortén, wishing, just once, that she could communicate directly, instead of with mere impressions. *I'm the one you want!* she thought desperately. *Fight me!*

To her surprise, he responded almost instantly. Perhaps it was his overconfidence, but Xari didn't waste time worrying why.

She reached the large common area at the same instant Mortén did. Back in the orphanage, there had been a room like this, stuffed with couches and tables and games, and there the children had often convened to play. Here, Jopherus had it sparsely furnished. Two couches lined the walls, and between them, in the center of the room, sprawled a low, wide, circular table. A couple of stuffed chairs were positioned around the room. Xari's practiced eyes immediately scanned it to see how much space she had to maneuver with her swords.

She only noticed that Mortén was holding a crossbow a second before he fired it at her. Ashe brought the arrow to a halt with a solid block of air, and then, his face a mask of concentration, cracked the wood of the crossbow in half—another earth spell.

Xari already had her swords out, which was a good thing, as Mortén quickly drew his own weapon and came at her full force—with the complete strength of the leviathan behind him. The shock of his first blow was even greater than Xari had ever imagined, and she'd spent a good deal of time trying to imagine this scenario and prepare.

It didn't take Xari long to realize that though she was better trained, Mortén needed little in the way of training to match her. He was larger and stronger, and was not going to tire as easily as any other opponent. She brought her second blade up to block his second swipe. Her bones and muscles cried in protest at the intense pain, and she staggered backwards.

Several shvri had entered the room and engaged Ashe in a battle of their own. Even in the midst of Xari's own fight, the sight of the shvri trying to best Ashe brought to mind the downfall of the last twelve speakers, and she prayed that the outcome of this conflict would be very different.

Knowing she needed time and space if she were to ever have a chance at coming out of this alive, she retreated further, and barely missed being cleaved in two by Mortén's third swinging blow, a brute, diagonal chop aimed directly at her head. Swiftly, she pirouetted neatly out of range, still at a half-crouch.

She barely had a moment to straighten once more into a proper defensive stance before Mortén came at her again. She jumped backwards to avoid him, but she could only go so far. He was backing her expertly against the wall.

Ashe bought her a moment when he sent a swift gust of air at Mortén, impeding him long enough for Xari to gain several feet of distance. To her left was one of the stuffed chairs she had noted earlier. The only way to escape was either over the chair, which didn't seem to offer much in the way of balance or stability should she attempt it, or to the right and back around him.

Mortén was far too smart to blithely allow Xari this out. Even as she tried to take him by surprise, sidestepping in that direction, he was ready, once again swinging at her with his weapon as though he were trying to hack a log in two. The next moment he hissed in pain and almost dropped his sword, but he quickly caught it with his left hand and regained his momentum. Xari caught a glimpse of his right hand and saw that it had been burned—Ashe's work, no doubt, and she wondered how long he could spare her aid and still keep the shvri at bay.

Seeking a new tactic, Xari brought both her weapons up, using the combined strength of both blades and both arms behind them to protect her head and try to ward him off. Then, quick as she could, she twisted her forearms to brace Mortén's blade between her own, hoping to jar the weapon out of his grasp.

She tried not to dwell too long on the ensuing disappointment. Though the technique seemed to take Mortén momentarily by surprise— she felt the vibration of the three blades scraping against one another— he was quick to recover, and gripped his sword tighter than ever. The maneuver resulted in a shift of position. Instead of moving toward the wall, they were now moving parallel to it, and Mortén was unyielding in his onslaught. Meanwhile, Xari's arms were raised above her head, leaving her midsection unprotected, and before she had time to think of a way to thwart him, Mortén struck with a well-aimed blow with his knee.

It was more than enough to shake Xari loose of the stalemate and fall backwards several steps, sharp pain blossoming in her ribs. She was almost positive at least one of them was cracked or broken. She desperately tried to recover her wits and her balance as Mortén advanced on her once more. Wondering if he fancied himself just toying with her,

Xari took off for the opposite end of the room as fast as she could manage, hoping Mortén would not be directly on her heels.

Ashe, meanwhile, was doing his best to fend off the growing shvri that had taken up battle all around him, and still diverting what attention he could to Xari. She could tell he was angry and frustrated, for he held it his first and most important duty to protect her, yet if the shvri hit him with their arrows, he would be able to do nothing at all. Xari could only hope they would run out of their arrows before Ashe got too tired to keep them at bay. He'd been rested for nearly five days, and the air spells he was so easily employing really did not do all that much to drain him. On the other hand, she didn't know exactly how all the poison in his system the past few days was going to play into the equation.

But Xari could not afford to waste much time worrying about Ashe, or she would get herself killed. Burin's voice was in her ear, warning her against any and all distraction, including pain.

As she'd hoped, Mortén did not immediately pursue her. When she finally darted around to face him, he was a good ten feet away, moving his feet and his body with coiled readiness. "You're going to get yourself killed, child."

Breathing hard, Xari wondered if trying to talk him down was really going to help anything. It was clear to her now that if she kept up an attempt to fight him, she was almost certain to lose, but with Heron's people helping, it was possible Zeth, Immen, and Anathriel could still escape. Xari only had to keep Mortén occupied long enough.

"Maybe," she said at last. "But Jopherus has the otter relic. What good would it do you then?"

She wondered if she could try making a run for it outside the far door. Mortén couldn't possibly guard both of them at once. Yet how long could she run and still elude him? Already her limited strength was waning. The effects of the fever still held some sway over her body. She did not have her full vitality, and would not likely have it for some days, according to Anathriel. In the here and now, however, the very idea of having days at all seemed dim and distant.

Vaguely, she noted that the number of shvri had grown since her last desperate count. How long could Ashe maintain such a fight? The shvri had the definite advantage of numbers. How many more were they likely to encounter in the surrounding corridors and tunnels of

Jopherus's mazelike home?

"Whether or not I take immediate possession of the otter relic matters little if you are alive, Xari," Mortén said coolly. "We both know that."

"You can't have the power of every relic, Mortén. They were never meant to be used that way."

"I intend to try. Where Vittes failed, I will succeed."

"Vittes was impeded by a greater power, Mortén, and I promise you, even if you kill me now, the same will befall you. The Master will not tolerate his gifts to humankind to be abused."

Mortén smiled and shook his head at her. "Those fairies really have filled you to the brim with their nonsense, haven't they?" He laughed. He seemed genuinely unconcerned by her stance or her words.

"You were chosen to be a speaker. How could you—"

"Don't be foolish, child. The fairies only believed I was chosen. I would have thought they would know that by now." Mortén must have seen her confusion, for he gave her a twisted smile. "No? You did not see it in my memories when you were awakened? Your loss, I suppose. I'm sure it would have saved your Magi Asheford a good deal of confusion."

Seeming to have finished with dialogue, Mortén closed his mouth and his eyes darkened once more with focus. Anticipating another attack, Xari did the best thing she could think of and leapt nimbly atop the low flat table in the center of the room. The only way she could protect herself from Mortén's aggressive, bludgeoning tactics was to get out from under him.

The strategy was a good one for a few moments. The table was sturdy and she was able to circle with him, warding off his bone-jarring attacks with slightly easier defense than she had before. She did her best to try to gain the upper hand as well as the upper stance, desperately attempting to assume the offensive, but with very little success. Xari couldn't remember the last time she had been so tired. Though she now had the advantage of height, she couldn't avoid the blades as easily as she had before, and it was more difficult to use her superior agility to her advantage.

She was about to abandon the tabletop in search of some better strategy when Mortén took the decision out of her hands. Unexpectedly, he reached out with his foot and kicked hard at one of the squat table legs, breaking it, and sending the whole thing both skidding and tilting at once. Xari, focused on not losing her balance entirely, was unprepared for the sharp slice Mortén landed on her forearm, splitting skin and muscle painfully. It was clear that only the erratic momentum of the crashing table and Xari's own fall had prevented Mortén from killing her.

Xari cried out and dropped her right blade. She had the presence of mind to bring her other weapon up to defend her weakened body, and then she rolled as quickly away as she could, making sure not to impale herself on her own sword as she did so.

Master, I can't keep this up much longer, she prayed, knowing her remaining time to be very brief indeed. *I need your help.* Her right arm was useless. She clutched it close to her side. Blood was already soaking her clothes.

She could hear the heavy footfall of someone new entering the now disheveled common room. She recognized Jopherus out of the corner of her eye, his distinctive red hair easily identifying him. He too was drawing his blade—a long dagger about half the length of Xari's own sword. Scrambling to her feet, wondering how in the world she was supposed to defend herself from *two* enemies in this condition, she steeled her courage to do whatever was left in her strength to do.

Mortén seemed unconcerned by Jopherus's arrival. He turned to note him briefly, taking in the man's drawn weapon before rounding his stance once more on Xari. "Do not meddle in this, Jopherus. It is necessary that I deal with her."

"Certainly not." It was Jopherus's only reply, and one which would puzzle Xari exceedingly in days to come, for what happened next surprised her more than anything had in a very long time.

With chilling calm, not even bothering to look at Mortén as he did so, Jopherus reached the place where Mortén was standing and plunged his dagger cleanly into the other man's back without breaking his stride, twisting hard with added venom. Mortén's eyes widened in a way not unlike Xari's, but he seemed incapable of speaking.

Within seconds, he slumped to the floor, silent and dead.

25

It hadn't been so difficult for Anathriel and Heron to get out of Jopherus's house. Heron relayed that her chosen route was not the shortest, but she assured Anathriel it was the safest. Its corridors were most commonly used by servants, and they were less likely to meet either guards or shvri. When they did meet someone, Heron assumed an authoritative air, training her bow and arrow on Anathriel as if she were escorting a prisoner. Anathriel couldn't tell if any of the servants seemed suspicious, but the one guard they encountered had certainly asked enough questions. Heron had been forced to spin a story for him, not unlike the one she had fed Jopherus. Most difficult to explain was what they were doing in this distant part of the house, but the guard at last bought her excuse and let them pass.

Once outside, Anathriel felt almost naked under the open sky. What would happen if she got caught? She would have only herself to trust, and Heron, about whom she still wasn't absolutely certain. She found herself wishing she'd gotten Immen to teach her how to do something useful with a sword, or a bow and arrow maybe. Even Zeth knew more about fighting than she did.

Deeming it now safer if she remained unseen, Heron went invisible and hid herself amongst Anathriel's thick curls in case they came across any other shvri. Anathriel had also swiped a stray scarf and shawl she'd found lying amongst some spare laundry, which she donned in the hopes that they would help keep her from being recognized from a distance. Though they were terribly hot, they helped lift her confidence a little. She also took a large handkerchief to conceal the unconscious shvri she still carried, fashioning it into a sort of small hammock. She tied her unwitting passenger to her belt, careful to make sure the shvri could still breathe.

Having one invisible shvri on her belt and another in her hair was a very odd way to travel. Also, the journal tied to her skirt flapped against her legs as she walked. She and Heron had agreed that the best way to get off Jopherus's lands was to walk away as steadily and calmly as possible without wasting time, and hope that Immen and Zephyr's support from the air would be enough to keep any pursuers away from them. However, they had heard nothing of either man or eagle since they'd arrived, and Anathriel was sure that every one of Jopherus's guards could hear the terrified pounding of her heart for dozens of yards around.

Heron told Anathriel that if she got shot with shvri weapons, one or two couldn't put her to sleep. It would take more to knock out a human, because it wasn't the weapons themselves that did it. They were far too small. It was the poison with which the weapons were laced. Anathriel wondered what sort of herb it was that caused such a strong reaction. It was certainly unlike anything she knew that grew in Merenth or the surrounding area.

Anathriel's fear escalated as a brassy warning bell broke the late afternoon silence. She didn't need Heron's frantic explanations to understand. The guards were going to be on alert now. Suddenly, it seemed as if they were everywhere, darting about in half-preparedness, but more and more attentive by the moment. Anathriel spied a stray milk pail and snatched it from the ground beside a nondescript shed of some kind, and did her best to look lost and frightened as any other hapless milkmaid who didn't know what was going on.

It was just too bad that some men had better memories than others did. She was a hundred feet away from the precious cover of the trees when two of them spotted her and the taller of the two called her to a halt.

"You! Wait!"

Anathriel slowed her steps and swallowed, turning warily to glance at him, wondering if there was some way to talk herself around his discovery. She recognized him. He had been with Jopherus the first time they'd met him and had guarded their door several times in the first few days.

"I know you," he said slowly, his manner suspicious and unlikely to be swayed. He reached out a commanding hand to seize her by the arm.

⌘ ⌘ ⌘

Xari heard footsteps behind her and knew that Zeth had arrived. Somehow he had been freed from his captivity, though he was in great pain. She received a flash of that pain from him before he gained control over their connection. A moment later, he came to halt beside her. He, too, was staring at Mortén's body and at the bloodied dagger in Jopherus's hand.

The place in her mind where Mortén had been for so long was a glaring, screaming void, but Xari didn't have the luxury to sort out this change. Her nemesis was dead, his murderer standing before her. Exhausted and breathing hard, she locked eyes with Jopherus, and the seconds seemed to stretch into hours within the nexus. She had no idea what to expect from him.

Finally, Jopherus looked down at the dagger with distaste. He pulled a handkerchief from one of his generous sleeves, wiped off his blade, and sheathed it, as calmly as an autumn evening. "And now what do we do, Xari Speaker?" he asked, clasping his hands behind his back and studying her.

"You tell me," she replied warily, still very much poised and alert. She'd never met anyone as utterly unfathomable as Jopherus in her life.

"And you, boy," Jopherus added, turning his attention to Zeth. Xari now pulled her eyes toward her companion and noticed with a rush of fear that his shoulder had an arrow protruding from it, and that blood had soaked his sleeve. "How is it you're out of your room? There seems to be a great deal of unsolicited free wandering going about in my house today. I don't suppose either of you know how your friends showed up back here? I'm certain I sent them with more than adequate an escort to see them all the way home."

Xari's eyes darted to the doorways on opposite ends of the room, wondering which was most likely to lead to a quick escape. She glanced at Zeth, wondering if he could pick up on her intentions.

Jopherus certainly did. "Oh, that won't be necessary, Xari," he said, finally releasing his deceptive stance of nonchalance. In three quick strides, he was pulling a long cord beside the doorway nearest him—the one he'd come through. "I keep my soldiers always on the alert when

Mortén is due for a visit. Including the shvri, who outnumber your Magi Asheford almost four score." He raised his voice on this last, looking around, probably for Ashe, who floated silent but watchful near Xari's ear. Xari noted that Ashe had somehow managed to dispatch the shvri he'd been battling before.

Jopherus didn't know that Flute, Jesper, and one of Heron's shvri were also in the room. Xari caught the eye of the stranger, a female who carried a fighting staff the length of Xari's hand. The female gave a tight nod. Jopherus wasn't exaggerating the shvri forces, then. Xari did a quick mental calculation. That meant she'd encountered less than half the shvri in her five days here. But how many were on Heron's side? There was no way to know.

"Lord Jopherus!"

A foot soldier hastened into the room, glaring fiercely in Xari's direction, though she wasn't sure what, if anything, she'd done to offend the man. Then he surveyed the area in frustration, searching the nearly empty air before speaking. Xari's stomach swooped apprehensively as she noted at least a dozen shvri that accompanied the soldier, led by the venomous blue-headed one.

"Caw," said Heron's shvri, a grim set in her eyes as she stared at him. She hoisted her weapon as Flute swallowed nervously, looking at Xari and Zeth with apologetic eyes. "You should have let us kill him," the female shvri concluded, though she did not look at Flute as she said it.

"The journal, Jopherus," Caw spat. "It's been taken."

"What?"

Xari was strangely relieved to see that this news, whatever it meant, had finally penetrated Jopherus's outer calm.

"How could Mortén possibly have managed—?"

"It was not Mortén," said Caw, sending a dark look towards the speakers. "It was Heron. She has double-crossed me. She helped these humans to get the journal away from the house."

Jopherus's eyes were suddenly livid with realization and calculation. "The Lelaine girl," he growled. "She can't have gotten far. Find her!" he ordered the soldier still hovering anxiously at his side.

"Yes, my lord." The man bobbed and dashed out the door.

"Xari, if you're going to make a move, now's the time," said Ashe.

Xari spared half a second to glance at him before nodding.

"No," said one of Caw's shvri, as most of them had turned to watch Ashe when he'd spoken up. "Look out, they're going to—"

"Briney, now!"

Startled, Xari didn't pause to wonder what her unnamed shvri ally was shouting about, but instinct propelled her into motion, using the momentary distraction it afforded to spring several steps backward. "Zeth, let's go!" she called over her shoulder, snatching her right sword off of the ground as she went, now holding both blades in her left hand. Her right arm was still cradled at her side, her hand slick with blood from her wound.

Zeth followed instantly as they ran out the door, which was the easy part. As Jopherus had warned, his forces were already prepared for action, and seemed to be lurking around every corner of the mazelike hallways. Privately cursing northern architecture, Xari disposed of what felt like the twentieth guard with a well-placed bludgeon to the head, clenching her teeth as each movement jolted her injured arm and ribs. Tears of pain leaked out of the corners of her eyes, and she blinked them swiftly away to maintain her eyesight.

She did not bother to watch the guard slump to the floor, unconscious, but focused on the next stretch of the house. She had the feeling they had taken the less direct route to escape, but there was nothing for it now but to plow forward.

Finding the next room mercifully empty—they seemed to be in the servants' part of the house now, and judging by the heat, not far from the kitchens—Xari slowed her step somewhat and rushed as softly as possible over to the far doorway to see what sort of surprises lay around the next bend.

"Once we get outside," said Zeth, coming up beside her, "Zephyr will be able to help us escape the grounds. But where will we go? Jopherus has resources. Men, dogs, knowledge. He'll surely be able to—"

"We have to get to the river," said Xari. "I'll take care of the rest."

At Zeth's confused expression, she merely smiled in secret satisfaction and turned to the fairies. She was surprised—and for a moment, alarmed—to see a fifth had joined them, a male, who hovered uncertainly beside the female shvri.

"This is Briney," the female said. "And I'm Posey. We fight with Heron."

"Do you know where Immen and Anathriel are?" Xari asked them.

Posey shook her head and looked at Briney, who also indicated a no. "Caw's first priority was alerting Jopherus of our betrayal," he said. "Last I was told, neither of your friends was accounted for."

"Immen is with Zephyr," said Zeth smugly. "He's safe."

Exactly half of Xari's worry became relief. "We have to track down Anathriel."

"And Heron," added Briney. "I believe they are together."

"If your friend has the journal of Vittes, she is in more danger than any of us," Posey added.

Xari started. "The journal of—" she began, staring at Ashe with shocked eyes. She could see he was equally startled, but she shook her head swiftly. "Never mind." It could wait. "Can you lead us out of here?" she asked the shvri.

Posey nodded. "Follow me."

⌘ ⌘ ⌘

Anathriel had always had something of an impulsive streak. In the years since she'd become a handmaiden, she had managed to tame it to some extent, but it still flared up often enough, particularly if she lost track of her temper. Now, however, she was not angry, but terrified. It seemed terror resulted in behavior even more rash.

"Thank Pathon!" she cried, and before he had time to think, flung herself hard into the arms of the first bewildered and unsuspecting soldier. "All those tiny people! And great terrible birds, and they did something to me, and, oh, I'm so happy to get away!"

If she didn't have to keep up the act, Anathriel would have giggled at the ensuing stunned silence. She could sense rather than see the two men look at each other in befuddlement, for her face was now buried in the first's shoulder and she had exchanged her senseless babbling for fake, heaving sobs of extremely exaggerated relief.

Finally, the man seemed to recover enough to pat her awkwardly once on the back of her shoulder. "Ah, miss, if you don't mind, could you please tell us what—" As he spoke, he put his hands on her arms and was gently but firmly trying to pry her away, but Anathriel's only response was to cling even harder.

"I was kidnapped!" she wailed. "Right from my home in Montressa, and Lord Jopherus was kind enough to send me home, and then that—that—*man* brought me back here."

Abruptly, she pulled away of her own accord and stared at the man with shocked hatred. "And there were little people," she whispered fiercely, a note of scandal in her voice. "All over the place. Fairies from stories. They did things to me, *unnatural* things. Sometimes I couldn't breathe, and—" She broke off, noting the knowing glances the two men exchanged.

"What?" she asked, suddenly sounding hurt. "You do believe me, don't you?" As if in desperation, she reached out for the closest guard's arm again, gazing at him with imploring, tear-stained eyes.

He finally seemed to soften. "Of course we do, miss," he said appreciatively.

Suppressing her inner triumph, Anathriel tightened her fingers on his arm in gratitude for half a heartbeat before delivering a swift and unsympathetic blow with her knee in such a way that the guard doubled over in pain, cursing loudly as he did so.

"Good," she said, smiling smugly. Hoping Heron would be able to deal with the second man—she felt her small companion dart from her hiding place, but still couldn't see her—Anathriel reached down for a large, sharp rock she'd noted out of the corner of her eye, picked it up with both hands, and slammed it against her victim's head with as much strength as she could muster. She felt a little sick as she did so, but barely had time to duck out of the second man's grasp as he sprang for her.

She ran as hard as she could, farther into the forest, only pausing when she heard the second man's cry of pain and anger and the crash of him stumbling to the dirt path beneath him. When she turned, he was on his knees on the ground, clutching his eye, which she could barely make out had been pierced by one of the dart-like shvri arrows. Heron hovered over beside her, now visible. "Hurry," she urged, waving her hands to prod Anathriel to keep moving.

Anathriel tried to calm herself, though she had the feeling she was going to be sick at some point in the next few minutes.

They had not gone far when they heard a sound most welcome: the scream of a great silver eagle, somewhere above and beyond them.

"Your eagle friend knows what she is doing," Heron said impatiently, as Anathriel turned to the sound. "We have to keep moving. We're safe for now. Your friends will follow. Hurry!"

⌘ ⌘ ⌘

Just outside the back kitchen door was a stretch of dusty yard, complete with pecking chickens, grunting pigs, and the lingering scent of wood smoke. Beyond that were large storage houses, outbuildings, and stables. Xari hurried after Posey and Briney, eyes constantly on the move, searching both for opponents and for allies. She offered a brief prayer that they would be able to find Anathriel.

By this time, the grounds were teeming with men and shvri at every turn, and stopping to confront those that stumbled across their path of escape gave those that were chasing them ample time to catch up, so that it wasn't long before Xari and Zeth were encompassed by obstacles. Xari lent Zeth her spare sword and he did his best to help her fight. He had much more trouble than she did, firstly because he only had a bit of sword training from Immen, and secondly because he was left-handed, and as that was his wounded arm, he was forced to use his right to battle.

Xari's greatest difficulty was in not killing the men she was fighting. Even with her right arm useless for the moment, they were really woefully unskilled as a whole, so defeating them was easy enough, but she had realized in the time spent here that most of them had no idea what was truly going on. They weren't bad men; they were simply doing their jobs.

Though their progress was slow, they did their best to keep moving. It was just at the moment that little Flute passed out from sheer exhaustion that they heard Zephyr's cry. As one, Xari, Zeth, Ashe, and the shvri turned their faces to the skies. Fierce relief swooped in Xari's chest at the sight of the great silver bird barreling down in a sharp decline toward them, scattering the small force of opposing shvri that had surrounded the runners and stirring the air with a mighty rush of wind. Zephyr was every bit as beautiful as Immen had claimed, but Xari was so grateful for her timely appearance that Zephyr could have been the ugliest creature in the world and Xari still would have thought her beautiful.

Jesper, meanwhile, had not turned his eyes on the eagle, but was frantically hovering over the unconscious Flute. Heeding his pleas for help, Zeth knelt down and gently lifted the sprout from the dust, grimacing as he used the fingers of his injured arm to hold her. "Ashe?" he asked, holding Flute up to him.

Ashe examined Flute and gave a relieved nod. "She's just overdrawn her strength. She'll be fine, but we have to get out of here first."

Zephyr had succeeded in warding off Jopherus's forces for a few moments and had alighted on the wooden-shingled rooftop of a nearby grain crib. Xari followed Zeth, who was already racing over.

A warm joy spread through her at the sight of Immen, sliding off the side of Zephyr's back to stand precariously on the roof.

"Don't get off!" Xari called up to him. "More men will be coming. We have to get to the river!"

"The large river is to the west," said Zephyr. "It is far for humans to run."

"It doesn't matter," Xari assured her. "We don't have to go that far. There's a tributary near here that will do."

Immen gave a slight start, then glanced down at Zephyr in wonderment. "Is she—? What did she say?"

"The river is to the west," Xari said, matter-of-fact. "Immen," she added, "have you seen Anathriel?"

"No," he said, his face taking on a grim set.

"Do you think she'd still be in the house?" asked Zeth.

"I don't know. I've been trying to watch for all of you at the same time. I may have missed her."

"Xari," said Ashe warningly, and Xari spun around to see two more shvri bearing down upon them, eyeing Zephyr nervously.

"It's all right," Posey said, flying forward. "Chitterby," she greeted the first. "Where is Heron?"

"Already on her way to the refuge," said the shvri named Chitterby. "Posey," he began, his face hardening, "Nettleblossom and Azure are dead."

Posey set her chin and shoulders. "Then we have no further cause to linger." She nodded at Xari. "We go. Now."

Already Xari could sense the approach of more of Jopherus's men.

"Agreed. Where is this refuge?"

"To the south."

With the great eagle holding their enemies persistently at bay, the small group made much better progress through the countryside. The shvri flew ahead, and soon they had picked up what could only be Anathriel's trail. Deeply encouraged, Xari took that moment to seek forward with her mind, searching for new allies, whom she'd taken the time to try to acquaint, as best she could, during her days in Jopherus's stone cell.

I need your help, my dear friends, she called, knowing that even if they couldn't understand her thoughts, they would feel the intent behind them.

The feeling of the otters reaching their minds joyfully back to hers was something Xari had greatly missed. She had not taken time to commune with her special brethren in a very, very long time. It did not take much for her to convey to them the gist of her request. As their excited agreement flooded over her, the travelers finally came upon Anathriel, ragged and winded, Heron at her side.

They renewed their flight with a fresh wave of strength and did not stop until they had reached Heron's refuge, under the branches of an ancient willow tree that slept on the bank of a dark, quiet creek several miles southwest of Nanaene in Threnphol.

26

"We can't stay here for long."

Flute heard voices. She knew she recognized them, but the grass she was sleeping in was wonderfully soft and smelled good, and she was very tired, so she wasn't ready to wake up.

"I know, but we're safe for the moment." The second voice was exhausted.

"How can you be sure Jopherus isn't going to find us?" came a third voice. "We didn't really come that far."

Anathriel, Flute troubled to remember.

"The otters obliterated our trail, especially the places where we followed the water. No dogs or trackers are going to be able to find it. They'll have to search more slowly. That gives us enough time to regroup."

Flute finally opened her eyes. The warm sunshine and the murmur of a gurgling stream enticed her senses, and she suddenly realized she was much more hungry than tired.

"Well, good morning, Fluttermouse."

Flute sat up slowly, rubbing her eyes with one hand, and turned to squint at Magi Asheford, who was sitting very close by, smiling at her kindly.

"You slept for almost a day," he informed her before she could manage to ask the question herself.

"What happened?"

"A good deal, which I'm sure Jesper will relay to you with much enthusiasm. I wanted to talk to you about something else first."

Puzzled, and wondering where they were and what there was to eat, Flute wasn't giving Magi Asheford her full attention when she asked, "What?" She looked around but couldn't see Jesper anywhere, though she did see Anathriel, Xari, and Zeth nearby, talking quietly amongst themselves.

"Here," said Asheford.

Flute turned back to him, and he handed her a small basket filled with blackberry seeds with a knowing smile.

"Thank you," she said, seizing it eagerly.

"We're still in Threnphol," Magi Asheford continued. "This is where Heron and her small group of shvri came when they wanted to meet separately from the others."

As she chewed her breakfast—or midday meal or whatever it was—Flute looked around. It was true that the big willow tree they were sitting under was very beautiful, as was the smooth flowing water beside it, but beyond the stream was an open meadow, and beyond that she could see human structures—a house, and what Zeth had called a barn.

"Fluttermouse," he said, becoming grave and mysterious once more, "Jesper told me what happened between yourselves, Heron, and the other shvri."

Flute put down the next seed she'd been about to devour, and hung her head shamefully, ready to bear the brunt of her elder's reproach. "I'm so sorry, Magi Asheford. I thought I was doing the right thing. I—" She looked up frightfully. "I'm still not sure if I did or not. I don't think the elders would have approved."

"Perhaps not," he said. Flute was surprised, because he did not seem angry, but rather very thoughtful. He was looking at her with a funny expression in his eyes. "But perhaps that is the reason it was you, and not one of your elders, who was given the choice."

"Magi?" she asked in confusion.

He sighed. "Flute, without Heron's help, I'm not sure we would have escaped Jopherus's clutches. Certainly, we would not have recovered the relics. And she wanted you to know that she—"

"She was supposed to give us the dragonfly relic!" Flute cried, her mind jumping excitedly ahead.

Magi Asheford laughed. "And so she did, Flute."

"She did!?"

"Yes, sprout."

Flute was so amazed she didn't know what to say. She relaxed her stance again and resumed eating, full of wonderment.

The dragonfly relic, she thought again, with a flutter of excitement. Then she looked at him worriedly. "But I promised we'd take her and her allies to Fairlight Forest," she informed him.

"I know. And something tells me it is actually a very good idea."

"Why?"

"Because I think it is time for our fear and ignorance of the shvri to come to an end."

"The elders aren't going to like it," Flute said knowingly, picking a small piece of leaf out of the basket and tossing it aside.

"I know," Magi Asheford chuckled. Then he added, "There's something else."

Flute looked back up at him, wondering what could possibly be better news than the dragonfly relic. "What is it?" she asked.

"Zeth has requested that you become his guardian."

Flute couldn't help it. Her mouth fell open in utter shock. "His—" she started to echo, but her words died. She began again. "But, Magi, I'm not ready to be a guardian. I realized that when we were captured. I don't know all the spells that you do, and—"

"I know that. And I'm not saying it will be easy on either of you, but I have agreed to let you if you're still willing."

"But why?" Flute demanded. She couldn't ever remember being more confused in her life.

"It is true that you lack experience," Magi Asheford affirmed, "but Jesper told me how bravely you defended Zeth against the shvri. Zeth was very impressed, as well. He likes you. And he trusts you. More importantly, though—" here Magi Asheford sounded very strange, and it took Flute a moment to realize the pride in his voice "—Jesper also told me how you stood up for the Master against all the shvri, and I am convinced that this is far more important than any magical skill. Flute, despite what the shvri believe, not as many of our people have this kind of faith anymore. And neither does Zeth. I believe he will need your help more than he knows."

Flute was quiet for a long time, staring at the sparkling water of the stream. She wondered how it was possible to feel so happy and so scared at the same time. Becoming a guardian was going to be a lot different from all of her daydreams; she knew that now. And yet, for some reason, Magi Asheford's words made her want to do it even more now than she had before, and for very different reasons.

At last, she looked uncertainly at her elder. "Will you help me?"

Magi Asheford tipped his head back, chuckling heartily. "Yes, sprout. I'd be remiss if I did not. I will help you as long as I am able."

"Well, then, let's get started!"

⌘ ⌘ ⌘

Evening time on the banks of Nettle Creek —as Heron said it was called—was sleepy and peaceful. Xari welcomed the contentment. Her arm, recently and industriously wrapped, salved, and splinted by a curt Anathriel, ached with quiet throbs, but to Xari's relief, it looked to be on the road to healing nicely. Her ribs had been bound as well. Two were cracked and a third bruised, from what she had been able to determine. Zeth's injury had been more difficult to handle. Fortunately, the arrow had gone completely through his shoulder, and with a little help of fairy magic, it hadn't been difficult to break cleanly and remove. Though very painful for Zeth, Anathriel had high hopes that it would heal over with no problems.

They had not lit a fire. Though Immen had brought back some small game, everyone agreed that a fire would not be the best course for a group of such recent escapees. Instead, Xari had convinced Ashe to cook the humans' supper with magic, something he had grumbled about, but did nevertheless. Now the four humans sat languidly against Heron's willow tree, watching the shadows grow dark with night. It was almost high summer now, and warm, but pleasantly so.

Xari closed her eyes lazily a moment, and smiled at the sounds of the sprouts' laughter coming from the bank of the stream several feet away. Through her bond, Xari could sense the unrestrained joy of her otter friends, with whom Flute and Jesper were playing some sort of game that involved a great deal of splashing and shrieking.

Also with them was another sprout, a young male less than half Flute and Jesper's age, who seemed in awe both at Flute and Jesper's presence and at their willingness to play games with him. The young sprout, named Snicks by his elders, comprised a nursery of one. He must have been very lonely, Xari decided, growing up here, his existence kept a secret from Caw and the other more militant shvri. It would do him good to play with otters.

And the otters did love to play. All of them, no matter where she went.

Mortén had always disdained Xari's share of the brethren, just as he had always disdained her gift. Xari had thought about it often. True, on the surface the otter might have been considered by some to be a lesser among the twelve, but those who thought so did not view the world through the Master's eyes. Childlike joy was one of the most precious gifts he had bestowed upon his children, and her sleek, slippery little friends had taught her as much. From them she had also learned the beauty of innocence, and of trust. Xari's gift, while not so seemingly flashy as Mortén's or Zeth's, had taught Xari things about her fellow men that otherwise might have taken a lifetime to learn.

Zeth, for instance, she thought, glancing at her fellow speaker. He was one who would do well to learn about life through an otter's eyes. While he had an extraordinary number of good traits—honesty, cleverness, a fierce loyalty to those he loved, and a deep thirst for justice—he was also far too hardened and disillusioned with the world for someone so young. It was a very difficult thing for Zeth to trust. This Xari could perceive without the help of a gift or a bond, but when she gauged him with the Master's bestowed power, there was a bitter, resentful scar seared into his spirit that pained her dearly.

Xari's heart reached out to him, in more ways than one. She recognized something of herself in Zeth. Someone she might have become had it not been for the timely intervention of Ashe and Burin into her life, as well as the otters. The nine-year-old orphan who had run away from the Nebraeth orphanage had been well on the road to mistrusting the world.

Anathriel was a more difficult puzzle, even for Xari. More than anything, she wanted to return to her former life. Right now she was happy. Very happy. Immen would be taking Anathriel home again— probably by means of Zephyr, as the older girl had seemed to have an odd affinity to eagle-riding that Xari certainly didn't understand—but she was also a little bit sad because she knew that things would never really be the same again. Anathriel, Xari reflected, was probably unaware of just how much she had changed since leaving Montressa. More than anything she was afraid to admit to her awakened curiosity about what life might be like outside the plans she had so carefully made for herself.

As for Immen—

The sound of Ashe's voice breaking the silence jarred Xari's thoughts from their course. "Heron." He hovered near the objects now half-forgotten in Xari's lap, though she had certainly spent her fair share of time marveling over them in the past day. "How is it that Jopherus came by this journal?"

Xari knew he'd been burning to ask this question since Heron had let them look over the book, which was locked tight with a strange sort of catch such as Xari had never seen before. The only reason the question had gone so long unasked was because Heron had shrewdly kept herself busy overseeing her shvri, half to avoid any such questions, Xari suspected.

Though it was difficult to make out Heron's face in the gathering dark, Xari could sense her hesitance and discomfort. The reaction was one that was long bred. Mistrust between the fairies and the shvri would not die easily. Then the sound of the young ones' laughter came again, and Xari saw Heron turn unconsciously toward them, and she seemed to take heart. "He stole it from Mortén," she said shortly. "Not very long ago, as a matter of fact."

Xari had a thousand questions of her own, but she had no idea where to begin. But Heron, it seemed, had now made the decision to be forthcoming, and kept talking. Xari closed her mouth and determined not to discourage the shvri as long as she was willing to talk.

"Their alliance," she said, "if it can be called that, was tenuous at best. Both men are very unwilling to delegate power to anyone else."

"Both men *were*," Zeth reminded her pointedly.

"True," Heron replied. She sounded neither pleased nor dismayed by the reference to Mortén's demise. Xari was still enjoying the freedom of Mortén being out of her mind, but on the other hand, reliving the scene of his death over and over was not exactly pleasant.

"They had reached a kind of impasse," Heron continued. "In order for their alliance to bear further fruit for either, one of them was going to have to give up something."

"In Mortén's case, this journal?" Anathriel asked, waving a dismissive hand toward Xari's lap.

"Yes. And the leviathan relic, which is the key to unlocking it. A long time ago, Mortén had promised Jopherus access to the journal, but never fulfilled his promise to Jopherus's satisfaction. Of course, Mortén would never willingly give up either. Some of us were dispatched to Montressa when we sensed the choosing of a new speaker. One of our tasks was to see if we could obtain the relic, but for once, Mortén did not have it on his person, perhaps because he was concerned that Jopherus would try to take it."

Anathriel straightened. "You were in Montressa?"

Heron nodded once. "At the very time you fled, as a matter of fact."

"Then perhaps you would know what happened to the envoy the fairies sent to find Immen," Ashe said. His voice was low and quiet, but he had a shrewd, calculating expression as he studied Heron.

She was a long moment in answering, then she said quietly, "He is dead." Her mouth was pressed into a thin line, and she looked back at Ashe with the same determined scrutiny in her eyes.

Ashe was silent, and Xari found that she was holding her breath; the tension between the two was so strong. She knew that Heron would not speak anymore, at least right now, about Thornbee's death. Ashe seemed to realize it as well, as he brought the subject back to Jopherus. "Why did Jopherus want the journal of Maehdron Vittes?" he asked.

Heron sighed. It was yet another long time before she replied. "Contained within its pages are Vittes's notes about the relics. Specific details of his conquest of the last circle of speakers and clues to where he hid the other relics—and with whom."

Xari had a hard time deciding whose excitement was greater, hers or Ashe's. Zeth however, seemed both annoyed and amused. "Well, that just figures," he said wryly. "Now we have it, but we can't get it open."

"What do you mean with whom?" Ashe asked Heron, brushing off Zeth's comment impatiently.

It was Heron's turn to be wry. "Had Jopherus been able to open the journal after we stole it from among Mortén's property, he may have discovered my secret—I cannot be sure until I myself can see the journal's contents. But this much we know: in order to protect the relics, and to ensure their survival, Vittes divided most of them among his most trusted shvri allies. None of the relic-keepers, as it were, knew the identity of any of the others, but Vittes was also a proud man, and enjoyed crowing over his victories and his own cleverness. I believe that is why he kept the journal to begin with. Very handy for our purposes, I should say."

"How is it you know so much about him?" Ashe asked. "He is a figure lost to the centuries."

"What I know is common legend among the shvri. The history of Vittes is very much entwined with the history of my people. As it happens, one of the shvri with whom he entrusted a relic—*this* relic—" she added, nodding to the dragonfly relic in Xari's lap—"was a sire of mine, several generations gone. I do not know what became of the other relics, but I know that the dragonfly relic is, essentially, exactly where Vittes left it all those years ago."

"Mortén was doing more than just seeking the allegiance of the brethren," Xari breathed, realization suddenly coming upon her. She was remembering with vivid clarity all the wide travels Mortén had made through the years. "Ashe, he was trying to follow the clues in the journal!"

"Without the assistance of the shvri," said Heron, "this would have proven very difficult, I imagine."

"Which is what Mortén needed from Jopherus," Anathriel observed.

Xari cocked her head, a little surprised. She hadn't yet thought far enough for this insight.

"Yes," Heron said.

"Maybe that's how he came upon the otter relic?" Xari wondered, turning the journal over in her hands. There were so many secrets contained in this book! If only they could get it open. Yet there were still questions this journal could not answer. "Heron, do you know how Mortén tricked the fairies into thinking he was chosen? He told me, just before he died, that he hadn't truly been chosen." This had been burning Xari since she had first learned of it, and Ashe had been equally, if not more, curious and confused.

Heron's eyes darkened slightly. "I do." She hesitated. "There was a servant in Mortén's household. It was he who was truly chosen. Because of the journal, Mortén was well-versed in speaker lore and knew the signs that came with one being chosen. When his servant approached and admitted that he felt a very strange sensation when he came in contact with the leviathan relic—which had happened by accident— Mortén realized at once what had happened. He also knew, from his knowledge of the past, that it was likely the fairies would be sending someone to assess the situation.

"With the fear most humans have of magic, it was not difficult to convince the servant that the fairies would cause terrible harm. Mortén gained the servant's assistance, in that when the fairies did arrive, the servant saw them and ran to inform Mortén. He then translated everything the fairies said to Mortén, and told Mortén where the fairies were. This gave the appearance that Mortén could actually see and hear the fairies."

"How is that possible?" Ashe asked. "There were servants, yes, yet none spoke but Mortén."

Heron gave him a very dry smile. "The servant spoke with his hands."

Xari's eyes widened. She knew some households had servants who knew how to use their hands to make signs to communicate, and she had even known that Mortén knew how to use his hands to speak, but the way Mortén had maneuvered himself into the position of speaker was astounding. The sheer audacity of it! He had taken some incredible chances; so many things could have gone wrong. But they hadn't, and look at the damage it had caused.

And yet, had it not been for Mortén's deception, the fairies would never have tried to keep the otter relic hidden. Ashe would not have had to steal it away from his own people, and Xari might not ever have become a speaker. In a way, it was because of Mortén that she was where she was today.

Master, even when things seem at their worst, even in the desperation and despair, you can bring good. You brought me hope and life, and I know you can bring restoration to this world, even if I don't always understand your plans. Xari closed her eyes briefly, a smile touching the corners of her mouth.

Heron was still speaking. "Not long after Mortén was awakened, he killed the servant, which, to my understanding, was witnessed by the fairies."

"That explains a lot," Xari said faintly.

"Indeed," Ashe said gravely. He turned narrowed eyes on Heron. "And how is it you learned this?"

"Jopherus knew of it," Heron replied.

"And what is Jopherus's connection to the shvri?" Xari asked, another mystery that had been plaguing her. "Most humans don't even know of the existence of fairy-kind anymore."

Heron seemed to recede into herself again at this question. "Another tenuous alliance. Forgive me, but that is far too painful a matter. I do not wish to discuss it now." As if sensing Ashe and Xari's disappointment, she added, "Perhaps with time."

"You've done more than enough already," Ashe assured her, though Xari could sense his reluctance. Taking a cue from him, she bottled her own remaining questions—the first of which was how Mortén had come by the journal in the first place, but she wasn't exactly sure that was something Heron would know, anyway. "You fulfilled your promise of the dragonfly relic," Ashe continued. "Perhaps we can do more to continue earning your trust."

"We will see," Heron replied.

Xari turned her attention from Vittes's journal to the new relic. It was hard to say which had consumed more of her attention since they'd been discovered. Like the otter and eagle relics, it was very beautiful. Xari had often wondered at the origin of the relics themselves. Whoever had fashioned them—and she had the feeling it had been twelve different people, for thus far the relics had been as unique from one another as the creatures they symbolized—had been mighty craftsmen indeed. This relic was a silver armband, twisting in almost two complete revolutions. Splayed across its coils was a dragonfly fashioned of not only silver, but copper as well, and further colored by small, precious gemstones. Xari couldn't wait to show it to Burin.

"May I?" asked Immen.

Smiling, Xari passed it to him. He studied it appreciatively for several long moments. Meanwhile, Ashe had returned the discussion once more to the journal.

"Didn't Jopherus ever think about opening the journal by force?" he asked.

"Of course," Heron said. "But it is very old. Jopherus feared that too much tampering might damage some of the contents within. I don't suppose there's a way to use magic to open it?" she asked thoughtfully, turning to peer at Ashe with interest.

"I'm not sure," Ashe confessed. "The first thing you ought to know about magic is that it only enhances those attributes of the Master's world that already exist."

Xari's eyes, with the help of a rising moon, had now become much better acquainted to the darkness, and she could plainly see the skepticism on Heron's face. Out of the corner of her eye, Xari noticed Immen passing the relic to Anathriel, whom Xari perceived thought it very beautiful also.

"In other words," Ashe continued, as though translating, "yes, I could probably get it open fairly quickly, but the same risk of damage that Jopherus was worried about is still there."

"Aha."

Before anybody had the chance to speculate further, there was a simultaneous gasp from Ashe and Heron, and a sound of surprise from Anathriel. "Ow!" she declared. She seemed almost affronted. Still holding the dragonfly relic in her hand, she shook her head slightly and looked over at Immen with puzzlement. "Well, that was strange," she said.

"Magi Asheford! Magi!" Flute's frantic cries distracted Xari from Anathriel's outburst, and she turned to see the small sprout rushing closer, Jesper right on her wings. Heron's shvri were all swiftly moving toward them as well, and both they and the fairies wore expressions of utmost shock and surprise on their faces. Flute and Jesper were looking at Ashe in a most expectant fashion. "Did you feel—" Flute began. "There was another—"

"I know," Ashe said. The stunned quality of his voice matched the astonishment of the others' faces.

"Ashe, what—?" Xari began, but her words died in her throat as she followed Ashe's line of sight back to Anathriel, who was still absentmindedly holding the dragonfly relic in her fingers, and looking at the fairies with the same puzzlement as everyone else. And suddenly all the pieces clicked into place.

Master, Xari thought, in equal parts amused and disbelieving, *you truly are a wonder.*

"What?" Anathriel finally asked, when she realized everyone was now staring at her.

"Fluttermouse," said Ashe slowly, an odd catch to his voice. "Would you be so kind as to go invisible?" Ashe's eyes were still fixed shrewdly on Anathriel.

"Yes, Magi," the sprout said obediently. There was a moment's pause. Xari, who had yet to learn any way for a speaker to distinguish whether or not a fairy was invisible, had no way of knowing whether Flute had yet complied.

"Well," said Anathriel impatiently a long moment later. She gestured with her hand. "Hurry up, what are you waiting for?" She turned to look at Ashe. "Magi Asheford, what is going on? You know, I really prefer it when Flute and Jesper stay visible all the time, because it's not fair to the rest of us that—"

"Anathriel." This time it was Immen who cut her off. Xari was grateful. She wasn't really sure she would be entirely capable of coherent speech for the next minute or two.

"What, Immen?" Anathriel said impatiently.

He took a deep breath and met Xari's eyes knowingly before turning back to Anathriel. "Flute is invisible," he informed her meaningfully. Glancing around, he added, "And so is Magi Asheford."

"What?" Anathriel laughed. "No, they're not, they're—" Speaking liberally with her hands, Anathriel happened to wave the dragonfly relic practically under her nose, and her words died as her eyes fell upon it. She blinked a couple of times, then glanced up at the myriad expressions staring back at her—Xari's and Ashe's of wonderment, Flute's, Jesper's, and the shvri's of shock, Immen's a calm sort of admiration, and Zeth's of almost horrified disbelief.

"No," Anathriel began, shaking her head, trying to be dismissive. "You can't possibly think—I mean, it isn't possible. Not me, I—"

Xari felt the pitch of Anathriel's panic and fear roiling off her in a great, overwhelming wave.

"Child," said Ashe with utter sobriety, "I'm afraid your journey home must be delayed yet awhile longer. It seems you have been chosen to become the Dragonfly Speaker."

Epilogue

I t was just over a day's walk to the river, even at the leisurely pace the companions set. Xari, Asheford, and Zeth had set their sights on Fairlight Forest with single-minded purpose. The younger fairies were going with them, as well as Heron and her party of shvri.

They wanted Anathriel to come, as well, and they were walking slowly in part to give her time. When they reached the river, she would have to choose. To the north was Montressa and the comfortable familiarity of her former life. It seemed the obvious choice. Though her time away had not even spanned the turning of a season, she had longed to return home with every step.

Despite his rather jarring initial declaration, Asheford assured her that she was in no way beholden to accept this speaker business.

"It may very well happen that we encounter someone else to whom the relic will respond," he said. "Some of my peers would argue, of course, but I don't believe the distinction between the choosing and the awakening is a mere inconvenience. Speakers who were forced into servitude would serve their purpose very ill indeed."

At this, Zeth had stiffened slightly, rubbing his wrist. Anathriel wished she had not noticed. She didn't like to think about Zeth's past.

"But I certainly hope you decide to accept," Asheford continued in an encouraging sort of way.

The morning that had followed Anathriel's unexpected encounter with the armband was hot, bright, and humid, another thing that contributed to their unhurried pace. As the sun had approached its zenith, Xari had called for a long lunch, during which Anathriel had spent a good deal of time studying the relic that had instigated her newfound mental stalemate, while the others talked or dozed about her. It was such a beautiful artifact—its beauty, in fact, had enchanted her from the moment she first saw it. It was clear that each relic was worth a small fortune in trade, yet neither Xari, nor Asheford, nor Zeth gave a second thought to their material value. It was something of an anomaly to a merchant's daughter.

"Why?" Anathriel had asked Asheford. She didn't consider herself cut out to be one of these speakers and certainly didn't understand how anyone else would.

"Because the Master wants you to," was his simple, unabashed reply.

"Magi Asheford, I don't know your Master or anything about him— oh, be quiet! Neither do you!—" Anathriel began, lashing out at Zeth, who had snorted quietly under his breath—"and frankly, if he exists, I don't understand why he would choose speakers outside of his followers." Anathriel had sounded almost accusatory as she spoke, nodding at Zeth to further emphasize her point. Zeth, she knew, didn't follow any gods, not even the paré of Montressa.

Choosing to become a speaker seemed a rather hazy business, in her opinion. For one thing, Asheford couldn't tell her much about a dragonfly speaker—what he or she did, not even what the gift was. "That, among many other things, has been lost over the years."

Would it mean traipsing about the countryside like Xari, chasing phantom rumors and wild animals? Would she truly have to put up with having Xari and Zeth in her head, and who could say who else in the future? On the surface, there was absolutely nothing appealing about it.

Yet when she really stopped to think about what returning home would mean, she was met with nothing but a large blank. For so many years, securing a marriage had been the sole object of her existence. For the past couple of years at least, securing *Immen* in marriage had been that object. This inner motivation being now removed, Anathriel couldn't imagine what else she had done with her time that had been truly worthwhile.

Strange as it was, there were fond memories she carried with her of these past weeks. Flute, for instance. Even with all her chattering, her accidents, her incessant questions, she really was sort of sweet, though Anathriel wasn't about to confess this to anyone. More than that, though, Flute had always liked Anathriel, in a way so genuine and unassuming that Anathriel couldn't help but wonder how many true friends she really had in Montressa.

Court life, at least for a lady-in-waiting, consisted mostly of superficial conversation and a social calendar. Anathriel had certainly gleaned plenty of praise and popularity, but she had never felt a pride or sense of accomplishment as strong as when she'd tended Xari, or a stimulation of her senses such as when she had used her own wits to escape Jopherus's guard. The fact of the matter was, Par Auspré was starting to seem a little dull in comparison.

I miss my father, and Regen, and Lady Rillandra. They will be worried about me.

But I will be the object of gossip and scandal if I return. Nobody will understand or believe the true reason I left.

But becoming a speaker? It's a lifetime, unbreakable commitment. Very unwise.

Zeth doesn't think I can do it, though. Ha! I could show him. Besides, there are unicorns...

Immen wants to stay with Xari.

Anathriel sighed. Odd as it was, this last argument was almost the most convincing. If she chose to return home, Immen would be coming with her, and she could see that he longed very much to stay. It was a mark of his honorable nature that he did not try to influence her decision. In fact, he had nearly avoided her completely the whole day. She also knew what he would face if he returned to Montressa. He would have to find a way to prove that he hadn't truly abandoned the Windriders, or face the consequences of desertion. If she knew him at all—and Anathriel liked to think that after everything that had happened, she knew Immen a touch better than she had before—then he was probably as torn as she was.

Frustrated, Anathriel kicked a pebble in the dirt path. Ahead, she could see the dark, verdant tree line that Immen was pointing out, marking the distant eastern bank of the great river. If she chose to do this, she would continue with the others—across the river, across Demuant and its hot, dry plains, and into a forest full of little people out of stories with power that frightened her.

All right, Master, she began, somewhat reluctantly, *if you're the one who expects me to do this, I'd really like to know why.*

"You know, I didn't know much about this either, when I decided to take it on."

Anathriel gave a start. She had not heard Xari softly fall into step beside her.

"Probably even less than you did," Xari said. "I was nine years old. The whole thing—the adventure, the magic—was like a dream come true for me."

"Nine?" Anathriel repeated. "Asheford let you become a speaker when you were nine?" When Asheford had mentioned his discovery and awakening of Xari, he'd certainly failed to mention that.

Xari shrugged. "Funny how things work sometimes, isn't it?" Her eyes gazed ahead to Anathriel's looming juncture. "I know this is your choice. We all want you to accept, but I won't lie to you. It's hard."

"You mean the magic and everything?"

Xari shook her head. "The responsibility. The existence—keeping your life open, ready to change your plans on a whim. More than anything, my hardship has been finding companionship in a world that has forgotten about the wonderment all around it. I've long prayed that someone more would come along to share it. Not just Ashe, not just my father." She smiled. "Lo and behold, I now have many more." She looked over her shoulder, and her smile widened before she returned it to Anathriel. "And maybe not one, but two fellow speakers."

"Why would you tell me you want me to do it if it's so hard?"

"Because," Xari said, her eyes lighting knowingly with a fervor Anathriel couldn't quite comprehend. "It's also wonderful. And I know you're strong enough."

Anathriel still didn't know what to say. If Xari's Master was using her as a mouthpiece, he'd been wise to try to appeal to Anathriel's vanity, but she was still not convinced.

Without warning, Xari paused in her steps, slowing to a stop. "May I share something with you?" she asked hesitatingly. Noting that the others had paused and were looking at them curiously, she waved them on. "Go on. We'll catch up in a minute. I just want to talk to Anathriel."

Anathriel watched the rest of them file away, except for Asheford, who flew to a polite distance and turned to watch the pair with silent comprehension. "What is it?" Anathriel asked. A light breeze ruffled her skirts, and she welcomed the waft of cool air.

"This is not something I often share with other people," Xari confessed. "Nor do I often employ this part of my gift, but—" She reached down and picked up Anathriel's hands, palm to palm, threading the fingers together. "As Otter Speaker, I am given the gift of empathy. I truly understand everything you're going through right now, Anathriel, because I can experience it for myself as if your turmoil were my own."

Anathriel sucked in a soft breath, not sure whether to feel comforted or intruded upon by this information. She didn't doubt the girl's words, which was the strangest part of all. Mutely, she allowed Xari to continue. "But I can also transfer what other people are feeling to you, Anathriel, so that you can experience it as well. And there's something I think you should feel."

Terrified, Anathriel stared back at her with widened eyes. At last, not sure where the words came from, she said, "Very well."

Xari closed her eyes and tightened her grip ever so slightly on Anathriel's fingers. A moment later, Anathriel sensed such a strange and wondrous mix of perceptions that she thought she might faint from the strangeness of it all. She recognized admiration, grudging respect, appreciation, amusement, contentment—the list went on and on, and merged and blended into a whole that could only possibly be described as—

Anathriel pulled her fingers swiftly away. "Who—?" she began. "Whose emotions are those? What—"

Xari smiled. "It's love, Anathriel. Mine, Immen's, Flute's. You're our friend. We all love you. We want you to come with us, even Zeth." She looked at Asheford with a smile. "We want to see what wonderful things the Master has in store for you."

Anathriel was amazed. "But—how could any of you possibly—? I mean, I haven't exactly been very kind every day, and I know for a fact that Zeth—"

Xari began laughing. "Oh, don't get me wrong," she assured Anathriel as they resumed a slow walk to begin catching up to the others. "I made sure I didn't throw any of the bad stuff in there. We all have our days." She laughed again when Anathriel threw her a scowl. "It just seemed to me you'd lost your sense of belonging," Xari added. "When you know someone is on your side, it makes up for all manner of other doubts. I wanted you to know that."

She walked on ahead, Ashe trailing behind. Anathriel stopped once more, still reeling from what she'd just experienced, staring at Xari's retreating figure. Then she pulled off the dragonfly relic and stared at it hard for a long time.

"Belonging?" she asked aloud. "Is that really what I need?"

Or purpose? Or usefulness?

She looked up at the sky and sighed. "All right then. So much for the handmaiden from Montressa." After one more glance between sky and relic, she added, "But did it have to be bugs?"

Anathriel hastened her steps to catch up with the rest of her friends. The prospect on the other side of the river didn't seem quite so daunting anymore.

About the Authors

FAITH KING lives in Canal Fulton, Ohio and works as an accountant, which comes as a surprise to a lot of people who don't know her professionally. She also has a second degree in Spanish. Faith began writing fiction in college as a stress-reliever, which didn't always work out as planned, but was nonetheless gratifying. She loves movie soundtracks, science fiction television shows, and traveling. She advises everyone to visit Mont Saint-Michel in France at least once in their lives, if they can.

LAURA JOSEPHSEN spent her early childhood in upstate New York before moving to Tennessee, and then eventually to Ohio. She is married and is a stay-at-home mother. She has worked as an editor. She enjoys music, reading, rainy days, and sci-fi and fantasy tales. She's been writing since she was old enough to form words on paper.

LAURA AND FAITH met in a writers' forum on the internet, where they discovered they had a mutual passion for many of the same books, mostly of the fantasy genre for younger readers. In very little time, they also discovered their shared Christian testimony. *Awakenings* was born of a desire to see more fantasy stories written for young readers with a deliberate inspirational bent.

http://community.livejournal.com/twelve_speakers
www.oaktara.com